SONS OF EARTH

Books by Richard Rhodes

Fiction

Sons of Earth
The Last Safari
Holy Secrets
The Ungodly

Nonfiction

Looking for America
The Ozarks
The Inland Ground

Sons of Earth

A NOVEL

Richard Rhodes

Coward, McCann & Geoghegan
New York

 Published on the same day in Canada by Academic Press Canada Limited, Toronto.

The author gratefully acknowledges permission to quote from the following material:
"Circumstances," lyrics by Neil Peart, © 1978 Core Music Publishing.
"A Farewell to King," lyrics by Lee Leifeson and Neil Peart, © 1977 Core Music Publishing. All rights reserved. Used by permission of Warner Bros. Music.
"Helpless," by Neil Young, © 1970 Cotillion Music, Inc., & Broken Arrow Music. All rights reserved. Used by permission of Warner Bros. Music.
The poem, "High Flight," by John Gillespie Magee, Jr., is gratefully taken from *Poems for Boys and Girls*, vol. 1, published by Copp Clark Ltd., Toronto, Canada.

Library of Congress Cataloging in Publication Data

Rhodes, Richard.
Sons of Earth.

I. Title.
PS3568.H64S6 1981 813'.54 80-25178
ISBN 0-698-11055-2

Printed in the United States of America

For Stan, astronaut brother, who saved my life

Oh sons of earth! attempt ye still to rise,
By mountains pil'd on mountains, to the skies?
Heav'n still with laughter the vain toil surveys,
And buries madmen in the heaps they raise.

—Alexander Pope, *Essay on Man*

One

The earth seemed heavier when I got back from the moon. Coming off the recovery helicopter onto the deck of the *Okinawa*, the rotors feathered and the wind freshening from starboard, I staggered. We weren't too steady anyway that trip. Even my flight suit felt heavy. Strapping on a rocket as hairy as the Saturn V and blasting away to the moon was like nothing I'd ever done before or may ever hope to do again. It was exhilaration, freedom, riding a rocket. It was fantastic. But it wasn't the best of those days. The best was zero gravity. Free fall.

You remember me—Reeve Wainwright, "Red" Wainwright. I was an astronaut. I walked on the moon. I wasn't the first or the last. I was mission commander on one of the earlier Apollo flights, with "Cowboy" J. G. Haines of Casper, Wyoming, as my sidekick in the LM and the Navy's and Omaha's Charlie McCray in the command module overhead. You remember our moonwalk, if you stayed up to watch it. Cowboy, who was almost an Olympic gymnast once upon a time, pulled a full somersault that nearly got him canned. We were the Prairie Crew according to the media—I'm from Kansas City, close enough—and our command module was *Buffalo*, our LM *Coyote*. We explored Copernicus on the Mare Insularum, landing inside the crater walls. Even if you didn't watch it, you heard about our return trip. We lost the CM's electrical and O_2 systems in a freak fire. Charlie was pretty badly burned. We almost didn't make it.

We came through, obviously. Charlie had first-rate treatment and he's okay. For the past couple of years Cowboy's been in charge of training the space-shuttle astronauts.

Free fall was light as air. I only had to shrug my shoulders to float up to the gray docking tunnel above my head. I could stop myself with a touch, pivoting on the tip of my finger as my feet came around to nudge the cabin wall. The CM wasn't all that big, however it looked on TV. With zero gravity there was room. It made everything easier. On earth my resting pulse is sixty. In space it was forty.

At first the lack of gravity puffed up our heads. We looked moon-faced and Oriental to each other and felt as if we had head colds. Blood wasn't pooling in our legs as it did on earth. Compensating for the swollen head, my mind was as sharp as it's ever been, bathed in an optimum supply of blood.

Floating to sleep with my eyes closed and the CM powered down, contained but not confined in the netting under the right-hand couch, I could turn my arms and legs on and off. The position sensors of my nerves, keyed to contact and gravity, sensed neither in free fall. My arms and legs drifted and disappeared. If I moved them, they appeared again as if they had solidified from thin air.

At the edge of sleep I dreamed of falling. I had nightmares of falling when I was a kid; before I adjusted on the way to the moon I would startle awake and clutch for support. A baby startles in the same way. It's the same reflex and it's old. We were arboreal once. We flew through the trees. We flew through the trees and then we left the free fall of life in the high forest canopy, life lived close to the sky and the light, for the gravity of walking on solid ground.

Bob Fizer, NASA Houston's director of long-range planning, told me once that the really hotshot astronauts courted him. He's a beefy, red-faced man with curly gray hair—the hair clipped high around the ears when I knew him but left long in fluffy sideburns that stuck out from his head—and the beer belly of a Chinese happiness god. He wears salmon or baby-blue polyester double-knits and white socks and white loafers. He doesn't have a dime beyond his salary and civil service benefits. He's sharp as hell, but he couldn't cut anybody in on any deals. Deals or not, the real desperadoes would take Bob out to dinner at one of the fish joints off 146 east of Clear Lake (the space center is south of Houston at Clear Lake, close to Galveston Bay). They'd buy his dozen beers and his grilled snapper and sooner or later they'd try to pump him for the inside skinny on what was coming next. Anything for an edge on a crew assignment. You weren't an astronaut until you flew, and the more missions you flew, the more astronaut you were.

Bob would check them out. He called it "man-rating" them. He wanted to see how hotshot they really were. He'd run through Apollo Applications and what have you—the sky was the limit in those days—and then he'd say, "How about going one way? If we could put together an early mission out to Mars but we could only make it one way, the first man on Mars but only one way, how about that?"

"Shit, Bob," Bob swears they'd say, "I'd do it. I'd do it in a minute." They all said they would. They even repeated it to him sober.

That was ten years ago, more or less. I'm ten years older now, forty-seven. I like to think I'm wiser than I was then. I wonder. I didn't tell Bob, but I'd have done it too. Have gone one way. Until very recently, to lift away the heaviness, I still would.

I have a farm south of Kansas City now. It's a toy farm, really—eighty acres. That's an eighth of a square mile, about twelve city blocks. If the land were downtown Manhattan, or downtown Kansas City for that matter, I'd be rich, but it's land people haven't decided to live on yet. I keep a couple of quarter horses, some whiteface steers for beef, a garden. No chickens, no pigs, but one buffalo. He's a young bull. When he's old enough for breeding I'm going to stake him to a harem of heifers. His run is the upper half of the creek valley below the house. It's planted in bluegrass and fescue and he lies up above the creek in a grove of black-walnut trees that so far have escaped the walnut-tree rustlers and down in the lower valley the steers crowd the fence to stare. I've heard coyotes around too. They howl at night, but they're too close to the city to howl at the moon. They howl at the sirens out on the highway.

I lived alone until the beginning of last summer. My son, Chris, moved in with me in June. It was five years since I'd left NASA, six years since the divorce. Chris had been living with his mother and younger sister across the state line in Johnson County, Kansas—his mother moved back here from Houston to be close to her family, and I suppose I followed her to be close to mine—and he decided he'd be better off living with me. He'd just turned sixteen, so he could drive, sort of, which got him to rock concerts and, after the summer, school, and marathon sessions of Star Trek at Bucky's Wristwatch, the one computer games center in Kansas City. He'd have liked it better if I lived in the city, but I started out a farm boy and after working hours I've gone back to being one. It suits me. Out in the country you can still see the stars.

And the moon. I run in the morning—for half the year, barely at dawn. When the moon's rising or setting at that hour it's huge and orange and plain-faced. I can see where I was. The Mare Insularum is dramatically rayed and it's prominent at one side of the Ocean of Storms. We didn't have the lunar rover yet, the electric moon car. That came later. But there was enough confidence in the spacecraft systems by the time we flew that we were able to work three separate periods of EVA—extravehicular activity, moonwalking—and we saw a lot and slept in between. The most important experiment we deployed was seismic and magnetic, to see if we could identify the buried central mass of the incoming body that formed Copernicus. That and setting up a structure of laser reflectors to measure the distance between the earth and the moon. It's been measured since, across 384,000 kilometers, to the nearest centimeter or two.

At one point I remember looking up and seeing the LM golden in the distance in that brilliant, razor-edged sunlight, Cowboy kangaroo-hopping toward me from the LM with the larger of the two experiment packages, the blue and white earth rising overhead three-quarters full, and for one second everything stopped and held for me, even the susurration of oxygen in my suit, and I felt some fantastic sense of connection. As if I'd been meant to come there. As if the moon had been waiting for me. And then a beat, breath's beat, and I was minding the timeline and back at work.

We left the descent-stage engine on the moon. I left my PLSS—the backpack that gave me life support—and my galoshes, my footprints, plastic bags of my trash. They'll be there a long time before the rain of micrometeorites wears them down. Inside the LM, when we'd powered up and got our helmets off, we could smell the dust of lunar soil that clung to us. It smelled like ashes.

No one goes to the moon anymore. We did it and it was done. Afterward, on the world tour, I heard that attitude was typically American. Even President Johnson thought so. He told Wally Schirra and Walt Cunningham once, "The way the American people are, now they've developed all this capability they'll prob'ly just piss it away." The intellectuals I met in Europe said so, and they didn't mean it for a compliment. *You know*, they'd imitate us in a clumsy drawl, *what's next?*

For Cowboy and Charlie and me, fame was next, the more inflated because of the CM malfunction and the fire. We got the full treatment, a year in the barrel. The "barrel" was a private joke among the crews. A horny old sourdough stomps into a Klondike mining camp looking for relief. The whores are busy. They figure the sourdough's too far gone to know the difference and send him off to the back room. He thinks he's being set up for a roll in the hay with the best reserve stock in the house. In the back room he finds a big barrel with a knothole in the side. He shrugs. "What the hell," he says.

Going out on PR duty during training was a week in the barrel, and we hated it. But it was only a warm-up for what happened after the flight.

I learned about fame. A guy came up to me at a drunken, sprawling, pot-hazed pool party in Bel Air. He was doing his bit, passing the word from an actress whose name you'd recognize that she wanted me to take her to bed then and there.

"She gives good taco," he said.

I said, "What's that mean?"

He said, "You don't know? You never saw the T-shirt?"

"What T-shirt?"

He shook his head. My ignorance amazed him. "The one that goes, 'God must have meant man to eat pussy, or he wouldn't have made it look like a taco.'"

I thought fame was the taste of cognac and silk women. I drank them both, and I fell into the barrel all the way, and eventually, when I finally got clear enough to see where I was, I climbed out. That was typically American too.

Claudia left me long before I reached the Bel Air stage, or I left her. She filed, at least, and that's how the record carries it. She was a fine, sharp woman, too sharp for life in the boonies with a test pilot. She married down when she married a pilot-engineer. Her maiden name was Desmond. If you know Kansas City, you know the name is old and respectable. Claudia thought the astronaut appointment would finally relieve her of the boredom. Instead it pushed her farther than ever into the boonies. She had to slug it out alone on the gumbo flatlands south of godforsaken Houston for weeks on end and months at a time because I was hopping all over the country checking out spacecraft systems and training. The training simulators were down at the Cape; that was where we trained; no wives allowed. I didn't make the rules.

I don't know if the marriage would have survived if I hadn't become an astronaut—there were gaps opening between us even before I applied—but it certainly wasn't strong enough to survive when I did. My assignment to an Apollo crew probably delayed the inevitable. Claudia did drama at Vassar. She liked the limelight. All the media attention around the flight flattered her, even though she should have known better than to take it personally. Wives were just as interchangeable as crew. But that—the attention and then the fame—tripped a switch too. Claudia's grandmother had taught her that one's name appears properly in the newspaper only three times in one's life: at birth, at marriage and at death. Deep in her bones, Claudia felt that fame was vulgar. And of course Claudia and her grandmother were right, fame is vulgar, especially in the United States. And no less to be coveted, if fame is what you covet, for that.

All sorts of people covet fame. You'd be surprised. Mobs of people scattered across the countryside, but also closer to home. Friends, acquaintances, people you haven't seen in years, people you'd least expect to care and people you'd think would manage a more realistic assessment of their abilities. They covet it in their own right or they figure they can piggyback off of you. Either way, it's not necessarily pleasant to watch.

One of my daughter's former boyfriends comes to mind. Diana was born while I was training for Apollo. We named her after the goddess of hunting and the moon. She called me at my office earlier this fall. She was almost fifteen at the time, her body full and womanly as her mother's—a source of power she hadn't hesitated to exploit—and because she's gifted with a logical, retentive mind, or because she loves so generously, I was closer to her then than to anyone else on earth.

"Hello," she said when I answered, "are you busy busy busy?" She felt awkward pretending to be an adult and disguised the awkwardness with comedy. She'd moved into a new body. It must have seemed as oversized and clumsy as a moon suit.

"Hi, love," I said. "What's up?"

And that abruptly, as if she had just enough of a lock on it to get past making the connection, she was crying. Crying all out, like her mother before her. I got some questions in through the gaps and eventually pieced it together.

The boy she'd met that summer on vacation with her mother on Martha's Vineyard, the boy she'd loved, the perfect boy who was going to move to Kansas City just to be near her, the boy who aged in the telling from eighteen to twenty-two as she saw that we would tolerate the discrepancy in years, the boy who, mysteriously, had no phone or mailing address, whose parents were millionaires, who slept on the beach, who supported himself teaching masterful *tae kwon do*, the boy who intended to be the next Mick Jagger and who hadn't communicated with Diana in any way, shape or form in the two months since she'd returned home and whom she had cried for and cursed and then realistically forgotten—this would-be superstar had called abruptly to apologize, claiming he'd passed two months in silence because a car wreck had put him in the hospital, for what fraction of the two months he apparently didn't say.

"I wish he'd just leave me *alone*," Diana told me when she finished crying. "Why'd he have to *call* me? It was all over with and I'd worked it out and now I don't know *what* to feel."

"What do you feel?" I asked her.

"I *loved* him, Daddy. I didn't even *want* to. I told him we didn't have to. I told him it was okay. *He* was the one who wanted it serious. So I thought, okay, it can be a serious vacation. After that, who knows?" She stopped for breath. "*Jes*us, even if he was in the hospital he could have *called* me. Hospitals have *phones*, don't they? The *least* he could have done was called. He just let me *sit* here—"

I interrupted. "Did you tell him that?"

"Sure I told him. That's not all I told him."

"What else did you tell him?"

"I told him to *fuck off.*"

So, logically: "Then you told him it was over."

"Sure," she said, starting to cry again, "but what do I do with these *feelings?*"

I might have explained that they'd take care of themselves, that she'd forget his face and eventually even forget how it felt to be held warm in his golden summer arms. I might have, but who wants to hear that time will blur her life away?

I said, "Peace, sweetheart. Be glad you've got them."

Diana was missing her brother. She was thinking of joining us at the farm. Brother and sister were born a few months less than two years apart. They were almost twins. They felt like twins, Diana told me. She wasn't sure she wanted to live in the country. She didn't want to hurt her mother's feelings either, but moving in with me wouldn't be a rejection of her mother, only a shift closer to Chris. When they were together they talked for hours, she said, Chris guiding her and she guiding him. They wanted to have that again. She was too tactful to explain why they'd had it to such an unusual degree in the first place: because they'd raised each other while Claudia collapsed from boredom and I trained for the moon and then went into a parking orbit around a bottle of Black Jack.

I was surprised that she and Chris talked. I hadn't known he did. He and I hardly ever talked at any length, though I wasn't particularly worried about it. We didn't know each other that well yet. I had stayed closer to Diana than to Chris through the years of only seeing each other for a few hours at a time on weekends. I didn't understand how his mind worked and I didn't think he understood mine. Talk or not, we got along.

Like Diana's Vineyard boy, Chris wanted to be a rock star. Meant to be one as much as I had meant to go to the moon. He played the drums, eighteen hundred dollars' worth of beechwood Sonors that we stole for eight. When Chris played the drums, up in the attic of that high, narrow, brick-Gothic farmhouse where we lived, the buffalo sauntered over from his walnut grove to listen. Scout's honor. I swear it. Just on the basis of talent, Chris had as good a shot at fame as anyone. He also had my name, such as it was, and whatever I'd done to muddy that name before, by last fall it was something to trade on again.

Six months earlier I'd published a book, *The Coming Solar Age*. It hit the best-seller list within weeks and stayed there. I didn't think it up. An editor suggested it to me. My two partners and I had started an energy-consulting outfit in Kansas City, Energy Alternatives, Inc., EAI. The Department of Energy awarded us a development contract. Since the award went to a former astronaut, *Time* picked up the story. The editor read my comments on the energy situation in *Time* and called me. He introduced himself as Jeremy Utter, explained why he was calling and invited me to New York. It was his nickel, so I went.

We had lunch at the Four Seasons—in the dining room, not the grill. Jeremy, who was thin and owlish and High Church, turned out to be a closet solar freak. Solar was the answer, he told me—I think so too—but it was getting short shrift from the politicians because it's a dispersed technology, no pork-barreling, with a dispersed constituency. What solar needed, Jeremy argued, looking at me intently over his Perrier and lime, was a respectable, credible national spokesman. And who better than a celebrated former astronaut?

I didn't quibble with the "respectable." I said I couldn't write my way out of a paper bag. Jeremy, sounding like my mother, said if I could learn all I had to learn to get to the moon and back then I could learn to write, and in any case he'd be there to tie my shoes. He briefed me on how books work—advances, contracts, royalties, first serial, reprints, options, the whole antique system. It was new to me and fascinating. From my astronaut days I assumed books were all written by staff people at Time-Life. He mentioned dollars. I'd sunk everything I had into EAI, the little that I'd managed to accumulate since the divorce. We shook on it.

For whatever reason—because energy's topical and beginning to look desperate, because the astronaut label will sell anything, even books, because we published in early spring when people really appreciate the sun—*The Coming Solar Age* took off. I did the whole dog-and-pony show: Cavett, Cavett somehow remembering working with Claudia at Vassar in his Yale Drama School days; Carson; *Today* and *Tomorrow* and *Good Morning;* the national tour. I drew the line only at the *PTL Club,* praise the Lord. Touring sells books. *Solar* was a book, by the time I'd finished writing it, that I wanted very much to sell, not merely for the royalties but for the conviction I'd come to, and passionately wanted the nation to come to, that anything less than a full-scale, all-out switchover to every form of solar energy would be an unmitigated disaster—the DOE's bloated vision of vast refineries boiling up synthetic fuels the most disastrous of all.

So the fame was back. *Variety* started listing my visits to New York and L.A. and *People* called me for quotes. It was good for business. It got us off the ground. The second time around I was handling it. Book people don't call you at four in the morning in any case, or camp at your hotel-room door, not unless you're Alex Haley. Energy freaks do, but for all their earnestness and, I think, their submerged and even vengeful anger at having been locked outside the halls of power, by and large they're gentle souls. Sometimes those gentle souls came packaged in dynamite bodies and that was okay; it was a big farmhouse and I was unattached.

I liked my work, far more than I had expected to like any work after the work of the moon. That was half the battle. The other half, gentle souls notwithstanding, wasn't going so well. I was alone, and alone at forty-seven wasn't freedom and it wasn't fun. I was alone and I'd rather not have been. Having Chris there helped. But why is it that our lives never seem to come into sync through every level at once? There's something like gimbal lock in lives as in spacecraft, isn't there, when the inertial guidance platform gets tipped too far to one side and has to be refigured and realigned.

Children. Let me tell you something about children. In Rome, on our world tour, Charlie and I were moved one evening to ask our hosts if we could go back and see the Pantheon again by night. We'd learned enough diplomacy not to say: without the gimcrack altars and the hidden pipe organ playing "Ave Maria" for the tourists. It rains into the Pantheon through the perfect circular opening at the height of the dome and the rain falls unimpeded all the way to the intricately worked marble floor. A yellow egg of sunlight enters through that opening and visibly moves around the magnifying interior wall. We wanted to look up in the darkness into the great pagan dome and out to the stars. The Italians were delighted that we liked their temple. Fingers snapped; aides darted off and reappeared; after the ices and the espresso a mean black limousine raced us through Rome with motorcycle *polizia* whupping their sirens fore and aft.

The silence of the Pantheon silenced us. It felt more alien to me than the moon. The moon took our impression. We were the first life to visit it; we left our footprints behind and our trash. Space was alien, not the moon, alien as the Pantheon in its paganness was alien that night—alien but riveting too.

Afterward, coming out from the temple to all the gods, I noticed a young girl crossing the old, built-up piazza and . . . and what? I shivered, though the evening was warm. Remembered Diana, because the girl looked about the same age as Diana was then, nine or ten, Diana whom I hadn't seen to spend time with in months. Felt compelled by the innocence and the delicate beauty I saw in the shape of the girl's head—the hair long and dark, combed straight from the crown, schoolgirl's hair—and in the slightness of her thin shoulders and straight back and thin, sturdy legs. And wanted, urgently, to speak to her. To catch up with her and ask her name. And even started toward her, away from the loose line of security police. Who would have stopped me, for security's sake, but before that could happen I stopped, because the girl had slipped into the darkness of one of the narrow Roman streets that led off the piazza and was gone.

I saw her again in other cities on the tour—Paris, Teheran, Delhi, Tokyo, the capital cities of the world. I thought at first I was only seeing similar children. Then I thought my eyes were playing tricks; I was worn out from partying; déjà vu.

It wasn't a similar child. It was the same child. She always disappeared before I could speak to her. I chased her once. I was drunk. Her small flat shoes clicked on the sidewalk ahead of me. Her pace didn't change but I couldn't catch up. She turned the corner. When I rounded it she wasn't there. So much in those days was fog: booze fog, fame fog, fog of groupies who spoke a dozen different languages and the same soft language of flesh. The child I saw first in Rome and then saw everywhere wasn't fog. She may not have been real. I don't know about that. She was far more real than the rest of my life at the time.

One of my partners, a sharp young architect, is visited by something he calls elves whenever he mixes booze and grass. They stand on the back of the toilet seat when he's relieving himself and talk to him. He tells them they're not real and they laugh and nudge each other. They're good company, he says.

I read a fine biography of George Ellery Hale when I was looking into the history of sun studies for my book. Hale pioneered the study of the sun. He's better known for masterminding the big 200-inch Hale Telescope at Palomar. He was a man driven to achieve. He drove himself to the point of ruining his health. He knew he was overdoing it but he drove on anyway.

Traveling in Europe, late in his career, pushing too hard, Hale went up to his hotel room one night and found a little man standing beside his bed. The little man proceeded to lecture him on the importance of taking care of himself. The apparition didn't scare Hale—he was too much the scientist for that—but the thought that he might be going crazy did. When he got home he discussed the incident confidentially with his doctor. His doctor wisely told him not to worry about it. Hale's little man visited him after that, off and on, for years, always discreet, always concerned, Hale's conscience, Jiminy Cricket, and Hale came to trust his judgment and discussed his projects with him and took his advice.

I like to think the child I saw was sent to wish me well. She may have been. I can't be sure. She never spoke to me. She was simply there, again and again, there in the midst of the pomp, the fawning, the veiled display of national power of which Charlie and Cowboy and I were merely counters, in the midst of the vulgarity and sometimes the obscenity. She was always fresh, sturdy in delicacy, alive.

My children are my treasure. This child of streets and courtyards too. I value them more than gold, more than fame—more, God knows, than any mark in the record book so temporary and also-ran as walking on the moon. But walking on the moon had its consequences. My children weren't spared.

Two

A man named Karl Loring Grabka was the instrument of those consequences. He was an entirely modern man, orders of magnitude more modern than the old-fashioned hotshot barnstormers and professional pilots who signed on for Apollo. Now and twenty years from now, for what he did to me and mine, if I could get close enough to Karl Grabka I would kill him without any remorse of conscience whatever.

I know a lot about Karl Grabka. A friend of mine has thoroughly tracked him down.

He won't sound modern: big and fleshy, pallidly white, with a curving thick nose and lips the color of liver. Balding in front, his hair growing out in back dirty and black, long enough to pull into a ponytail. Bad teeth. Bitten fingernails. Cheap clothes—white permanent press wash shirts and khakis and black bluchers. He worked as an orderly at Crown Hospital. He had a one-room apartment in midtown Kansas City with a galley kitchen, a frayed armchair, a lamp from Goodwill, a sour bed covered with gray, matted sheets. Hard-core magazines scattered on the bed and under the bed. He dreamed on that bed: that's how modern he was. Believe me when I tell you that dreamers who dream on beds like that one dream dreams of enormity.

He was twenty-eight, a little more than half my age, a little less than twice Chris's. He loved machines—technology—cloyingly, the way some people love cats and small dogs. He bought and read *Popular Science* and he usually kept a copy of *Scientific American* around his apartment, although I don't see how it can have made much sense to him. He collected *Omni* and underlined whole paragraphs at a time of its flakier speculations. *Omni* was about his speed, really, technology leavened with science fiction with a little of the UFO–Bermuda Triangle–Pyramid Power bullshit mixed in. In his more unraveled moments I suspect Grabka thought he was an alien himself, sent to this small blue planet to accomplish an important mission for Intergalactic Command before returning to his rightful place in the hereditary line of emperors on Antares IV or Deneb II.

What gives these people their terrible power is their absolute purity of motive. If they could turn it around, aim it in a different direction, they'd be saints.

So Grabka was walking on the Country Club Plaza, Kansas City's pseudo-Spanish shopping area, one Saturday afternoon last August, and he came to Bennett Schneider Bookstore. Bennett Schneider doesn't have window displays, but there's a display area not far inside its east doors in full view of the sidewalk. Outside was hot, the store was air-conditioned, *The Coming Solar Age* was stacked up on display, and in Grabka went. One of the salesladies noticed his blotchy red cheeks. He took so much time looking over my book, cooling out, that the blotchiness faded away. Finally he carried the book to the checkout counter, the ladies there stepping back involuntarily from the advancing wall of his rankness. It was why they remembered him. Referring to the dust-jacket bio, he asked about me. They assured him I was local and on hand. With that he bought the book. Carried it home and read it, filling the margins with notes in the form of exclamation marks like inverted teardrops levitated on little hollow spheres. It was just that easy for him to make my acquaintance. It cost him all of twelve ninety-five.

Grabka's rankness was pungent as recently as last summer. A few years before, when he was in the Air Force, it overwhelmed with such knockdown strength that an entire barracks of airmen still remember it.

As all Air Force enlistees do, Grabka went through basic training at Lackland Air Force Base outside San Antonio, Texas. They shaved his head and threw him a duffel-bag load of uniforms and assigned him to a flight, which is the Air Force's equivalent of what the Army calls a platoon. He got in because he was bright, because none of the services screens recruits psychologically, figuring basic will weed out the misfits soon enough, and because he didn't have a juvenile record.

They taught him to trim his bed so well that a quarter would bounce off his blanket. They ran him through classes from 0600 hours in the morning to 1600 hours in the afternoon, getting him ready for cargomaster school, for God's sake, and around the edge of his classroom work they marched him up and down the drill field or made him police the squadron area for butts. It was more discipline than Grabka had ever been subjected to before.

He lived with about forty other airmen in a peeling wooden barracks left over from the Second World War. It was laid out in one long open bay with steel double-decker bunks lined up on two sides of a central aisle. The floors were deep-purple linoleum tile polished for weekly inspections to a high gloss with black Shinola shoe polish, which took a much higher polish than ordinary floor wax. Each airman had a footlocker at the foot or the head of his bunk and a rack on the outside wall, between the windows, where he could hang his uniforms. The bunks were so close together that good health practice required the airmen to sleep alternately head to foot. That was supposed to prevent them from breathing each other's viruses. Even with precautions, a few airmen every year managed to pick up deadly cases of meningitis, and one flight or another would have to be dosed with gamma globulin and quarantined.

Grabka wouldn't shower. Wouldn't wash his body. He pretended he did and at first no one noticed. The shower was a big, doorless room off the throne room, separated by a wooden partition. Grabka would find a time when no one else was showering and go in and run the water. It never occurred to anyone to check him out. The guys who noticed the hours he kept just figured he was modest.

But of course he started to smell, that sickly sweet smell the body oozes when it ferments beyond honest sweat. Counting cadence, Grabka's flight marched its dirty fatigues to the laundry and the laundry boiled them clean and starched them stiff enough to stand at attention unoccupied: Grabka reached a state of funkiness that even clean fatigues couldn't contain. As the starch softened he outgassed through the weave.

Eventually the boys put it together. They set a watch in the latrine to make sure they weren't mistaken. Then they assembled out of Grabka's hearing and laid their plans.

They chose a night when their drill sergeant was off at the NCO club washing away the south Texas dust with a keg of Coors. Grabka was sitting on his bunk reading *Hustler*, thinking pink and rendering the immediate area unfit for human habitation.

They'd picked four of their number by lot. The four advanced on Grabka from four different directions. They jumped him. He was surprised, annoyed, bewildered. He protested. They didn't explain. They hauled him toward the latrine. Where they were taking him began to seep in. He started to struggle. They kept him moving. He was big and fairly strong and he fought back. Two more joined in. He was lashed with arms and a crowd of feet moved him on. It must have looked like a squad of Secret Service men working an assassin away from the scene of his crime.

Then someone screamed, a single hoarse scream. Not Grabka but the guy Grabka bit—bit the guy's thumb all the way to the bone, so that later that night the medic on emergency duty not only stitched the thumb but also protected it from the delayed effects of Grabka's mad-dog mouth with a tetanus booster. Shocked by such a surprise escalation, the Secret Service squad came unglued and Grabka bolted for the far corner of the barracks and attached himself hands and feet to a support post.

The boys took caution from the ravaged thumb and decided to move on to more professional measures. They stripped blankets off the nearest beds as they advanced. Grabka snarled and swatted from his post like King Kong on the Empire State Building.

They meant to handle him then the way orderlies handle violent psychotics, but violence begets violence. They threw the blankets over him like nets to confine his flailing, but some of them started pounding him at about where they figured his head would be, watching for teeth. They peeled him off the post and more got into it with more blankets and more beat on him as they dragged him to the latrine.

They had enough hands now. A big Arkansas kid threw a full nelson on Grabka to immobilize those deadly teeth. He was under control. They got the showers going, warm and inviting, and then they stripped him down and shoved him in. Whatever his problem was, when he hit the water he screamed. It was a high, shrill scream. The Arkansas kid said it sounded like a shoat being cut.

Years later, Grabka's barracks mates remembered that night as the high, or low, point of basic training. Grabka never spoke to any of them again, ever, but afterward, for as long at least as he was in the Air Force, he bathed.

Notes on Grabka's childhood

Fine, sharp ice crystals in the ice cream they sold at the Velvet Freeze.

His father was a cutter on the killing floor at Swift. His mother was a bacon packer. They were both big people. They both drank beer.

Orange crates with ends like pictures. Slats of splintery wood.

He got beat up at first. His brothers beat him up. He ran and hid.

The dump where he played was full of wheels. Rubber tires, baby carriage wheels, wheels of wagons, spoked bicycle rims. When the wheels got bent and couldn't carry their weight anymore people threw them on the dump with broken cardboard litter and all the trash and iceboxes.

The west bottoms flooded in the flood of '51 and his dad and mom were laid off. Swift put a brass marker eight feet up on the wall at the plant to show how high the water got. There were people killed and steers and hogs washed away from the flooded stockyards, bodies floating in the river. That was the year he was born.

Guinea hens screaming at his grandmother's house. "You know what they're saying, Karl?" "Huh-uh." "They're saying, '*Gui-nea hen, gui-nea hen.*'" That was what their screaming sounded like.

He learned "off-ten" for *often*, "warsh" for *wash*, "boughten" for *bought*.

If he didn't have a penny he put a metal junction-box slug on the railroad tracks. The engine and the cars mashed it out oval. Even after a hundred cars went by it stuck to the track, farther down. All the wheels rolling over it made it warm.

Summers they went barefoot. The pavement was burning hot and there were green chunks of Coke bottles in the gutters.

They ate apple butter on day-old bread.

He learned a song:

At the boardinghouse where I lived,
Everything was growing old.
Old cat hairs were in the butter—
Silver threads among the gold.
When the dog died, we had sausage.
When the cat died, catnip tea.

When the landlord died, I left there—
Spareribs were too much for me.

In school he drew rockets in his Big Chief tablet, one to a page. If he could get the drawing just right then the rocket would be perfect and he could build it and get away. When he ruined it again he turned over a page and started over and drew it again.

He showed his brother his finger with the nail the pop fly had torn off right through his glove. His brother brought up his hand to pretend to look, but when his hand was close he flicked the hurt raw and Karl screamed.

Out in the country at his grandma's house, in the cemetery down the lane, riding the horses of gravestones that were smooth granite cylinders on pedestals. Listening for noise. Noise then and running away and getting his pants caught on the barbed-wire fence and the noise coming and he wasn't there, he was somewhere else riding a rocket.

When he had his tonsils out he dreamed a colored whirlpool with his head down at the bottom in the center of the pool and his body up at the top on the outside. They told him he could breathe with the mask but they lied to him. He smothered and they held him down. His brother had his tonsils out too and when he woke up his brother was vomiting blood.

One of the kids at school had some carbide. He made him give him some. He dropped it in a puddle and it made bubbles that smelled like farts and he lit the bubbles and they burned.

At night in the pine cabin at the Lake of the Ozarks, when his dad pumped up the Coleman lantern and it put out white light and hissed, hundreds and hundreds of walking sticks of all different sizes came and hung on the screen door. His oldest brother said they were poisonous. They all sat there and the walking sticks watched them through the screen.

He chose the ailanthus tree for his project in the fourth grade because nobody else wanted it. Everybody hated it for a weed tree and because it stunk, but in times of scarcity its remarkable sap could be an important feedstock in the production of natural rubber. People called it the tree of heaven. Its real name was *Ailanthus altissima.*

He learned a song.

Lulu had two boy friends,
They both were very rich.
One was the son of a banker,

The other was a son of a—
  Bang, bang Lulu,
Bang her good and strong,
Who's gonna bang my Lulu
When I am dead and gone?

  Lulu had a boy friend
Who used to drive a truck.
He took her up the alley
And taught her how to—
  Bang, bang Lulu, etc.

  Rich girls take it on the bed,
Poor girls on the floor.
Lulu takes it standing up
And gets six inches more.
  Bang, bang Lulu, etc.

  Rich girls get diamond rings,
Poor girls get brass.
Lulu has a little brown
Ring around her—
  Bang, bang Lulu,
Bang her good and strong.
Who's gonna bang my Lulu
When I am dead and gone?

He was good in shop.

The best knives for butchering came from a chilibelly up on the hill on the West Side. The chilibelly made them in his garage from the leaf springs of old cars and they took a wicked edge.

None of that really explains what turned Grabka into a sociopath, does it. Who knows?

We had our share of hygiene problems going to the moon. Given our close confinement, they were inevitable. The Gemini orbital missions, if you can remember back that far, locked two adult males into a space the size of the front-seat area of a Volkswagen for up to fourteen days. The Apollo command module was larger—about the volume of the passenger area of a limousine. Because of weight limitations, the LM flight deck was even smaller, too small for couches. We flew it standing up. Neither the CM nor the LM had any provisions for showering, as Skylab did, or anything like a standard toilet.

Ten years ago I found it difficult to discuss bodily matters outside the NASA engineering world and the private world of my immediate family. That was my upbringing, and I've changed enough in the years since to wonder now what all the fuss was about. We're of the earth, earthy, as the Bible puts it; we manufacture fertile new earth within our bodies as certainly as the worms do that enrich and aerate the soil. NBD: no big deal, not anymore.

I'm surprised it ever bothered me. By and large, pilots are a raunchy bunch. Living conditions in the high-performance aircraft they fly don't give them much choice. Most fighter aircraft have funnels attached to rubber evacuation tubes for bladder relief. There was no place anywhere on the T-38's we flew, training for Apollo, to store even a suit bag. We stuffed our traveling clothes under the seat cushion and went rumpled. Training involved lying on our backs all day in the spacecraft simulator or in the CM on the launch pad. The urine collection device sometimes came off. We had no choice then but to urinate in our space suits. First you'd feel warmth spreading over your pelvic region, the warmth flowing slowly up your back; then you'd cool out to clammy. We had a name for guys who pissed their suits. We called them wetbacks. Most of us were wetbacks at one time or another.

On the farther shores of raunch, I once saw two distinguished astronauts going two on one with a certain notorious Cocoa Beach deb. And raunch or not, how we answered the calls of nature in weightless space was almost always the second or third question people asked us when we traveled those weeks in the barrel in the name of holy PR. You've seen some version of *that* checklist before. It counted twenty-four different steps involving plastic waste-management bags with sticky circular lips . . . but I won't go on. It was a joke in the earth-to-moon segment of *2001*.

No joke, for us, was the odor problem. We could sponge-bathe with wet wipes and keep ourselves minimally clean. But all our drinking water came from our fuel cells, which combined oxygen with hydrogen to produce electricity and delivered water as a waste product. Unfortunately, not all the hydrogen combined with oxygen. Some of it went into solution in the water, and when we drank it we started passing the foulest kind of gas. The spacecraft air supply was filtered through activated charcoal, which helped, but all the way to the moon and back we lived with each other's stink.

I understood then why Americans devote a fair proportion of the GNP to deodorants. Human odors are markers. They're unique to each individual, they're challenging and they rule off territory and warn against trespass as certainly as the scent posts of dogs and wild game do. To work together as strangers, in close quarters, something our prehistoric ancestors would never have thought of trying, we devise ways to blank out our smells. Apollo flights demanded an extra degree of tolerance. Otherwise we'd have been at each other's throats.

So I don't feel sorry for Grabka for his humiliation in the barracks at Lackland. I think his stink was deliberately aggressive, another way he'd come up with to dominate people. He was tenacious and he was adaptive, and lacking any more traditional access to power, he revived an old and useful mechanism. It took overwhelming force to convince him of his folly. Even then he slipped partway back into it after the Air Force spit him out.

Purity again, purity of purpose and implacable method. Skunk Grabka homing on my life.

On November 12, 1976, Karl Loring Grabka was convicted at court-martial of attempting to smuggle a kilo of cocaine from Bogotá, Colombia, into the United States. He was sentenced to dishonorable discharge from the U.S. Air Force and to three years' imprisonment at hard labor at Leavenworth Federal Penitentiary in Leavenworth, Kansas, thirty miles up the road from the two Kansas Cities.

Grabka was an airman first class at the time, working under a staff sergeant cargomaster on a C-5A that flew supply junkets out of Kirtland Air Force Base in Albuquerque. He put on a stupid show of making a big buy in Bogotá, connecting through some of the Colombian personnel at the air base there. The dealer sold him tourist coke stepped on with quinine, a kilo packed in a plastic bag and hidden inside a hollowed-out wooden statue of the Virgin Mary. The dealer collected from Grabka and then proceeded to alert U.S. Customs to the sale and eventually also collected a nice reward from them.

The customs agents met the aircraft expecting to have an easy time turning up the statue. But although Grabka had stupidly overreached himself with the buy, his natural instincts for concealment, for squirreling things away, had served him well. The C-5A is the largest aircraft in the world. It took the agents and the Air Police who joined them a full week to find the coke. They had to bring in a dog to sniff it out, and when one dog couldn't cover that vast aircraft they had to bring in another. They located the stuff eventually. Grabka had removed it from the statue and hidden it under a fuselage panel on the C-5A's upper deck. He went to prison. The joint, as he liked to call it. When he got out, eighteen months later, he swore he'd make someone pay.

What did Grabka dream on his matted bed? I'm not a shrink. I know Grabka had a script, as all of us do. I don't know the dynamics of that script. I know some of Grabka's dreamings because he told them to some of the people around him, professional and otherwise.

He dreamed, after prison, that "they" owed him one. A big one, the biggest, in return for all he'd suffered. One big enough to use to turn the world to his secret vision.

His secret vision made everything all right. His secret vision was a perfect world of universal love. Hate was banished. Everyone in the world held hands. Everyone in the world had enough to eat and a roof over his head and warm clothes to wear. Everyone in the world put on a happy face because Coke adds life. Everyone in the world loved everyone else in the world. Sometimes even bodily: everyone in the world in one vast daisy chain with K. L. Grabka somewhere near the middle celebrating love. And anyone who dared to raise so much as a little finger against the universal love of the Grabka-ordained millennium would have his heart cut out.

Sounds a little like the Moonies, doesn't it. Or maybe Jim Jones. No. Karl thought it up all by himself.

He knew how much he had to do to make his vision a reality. Reality was the blanket party at Lackland. Reality was the Colombian dealer's double cross and a dishonorable discharge and eighteen months in the joint dodging the less discriminating of the chicken hawks. The world was a cold, heartless place and you had to be outwardly cold and heartless too if you wanted to be the one who did the pushing instead of the one who got pushed. You could build a world of perfect, universal love, but you had to start cold and tough. Grabka figured that was where Jesus of Nazareth went wrong. He wasn't cold enough or tough enough. Which was strange, because he was definitely a time-traveler come back to biblical times from the future, which explained his miracles.

You had to be cold and tough enough to put together a dealie big enough to give you the necessary venture capital. And it could be done, it could be done, but what was it? It had to be original. It had to be a fucking work of art so that afterward they'd recognize it as the work of a real genius.

The one thing was, you didn't want to cause any pain. To hurt anyone. You wanted to raise a real big stake but without harming so much as a hair on someone's head. Then they couldn't accuse you of any more than a political crime. You could appeal to the masses and they'd stand behind you, but you couldn't proclaim universal love to the masses if you yourself were guilty of causing bodily harm. So that ruled out any kind of robbery that involved threatening people, like a bank.

There was embezzling, but you'd have to work your way into a position of trust at a bank or an important American corporation and he couldn't do that with a felony conviction on his record.

It had to be like a sting. Like the sting Bob Redford and Paul Newman pulled on Robert Shaw. So that whoever was the mark wouldn't dare call in the pigs or the FBI.

How much? Ten million? That was too much. People didn't keep that kind of capital in cash or liquid. They invested it in capital investment that took time to liquefy.

How much then? One million? Even that was too much if you wanted to get in and get out fast. Maybe half a million. Anyone who had money ought to be able to raise that overnight just by asking their banker to get it together. Their banker would do it. He'd do it no questions asked if they were the right kind of customer.

So what would a half-million-dollar sting be? What could you pretend to have or what could you arrange to get that a millionaire would pay half a million dollars for?

Grabka knew the answer then. That abruptly. He asked the right question and it triggered the answer. He knew what. He just didn't yet know who.

He was studying who when he bought my book.

Three

Paige Elder called me from New York at about the time Grabka began working me into his impossible dream, something like early September, renewing an old connection. Paige is a writer. She'd say journalist. We were together for a while after Claudia flew home on me in the middle of the world tour.

"Reeve?" She called me at my office and my secretary announced her and put her through. I was a blissful innocent; I didn't know Karl Grabka from Adam, yet.

"Paige. How the hell are you?"

"Fine. Jealous. You beat me to the best-seller list."

"Shucks, now, did I? How about that."

"Our corn-pone authors."

She was forty. Petite and very feminine. Brown hair beginning to gray, brown eyes. Sun wrinkles at the eyes. Delicate wisps of hair at her temples where she brushed it loose, delicate wrists, fine hands, small breasts, small bones. She weighed maybe one-ten. Petite women who look vulnerable usually aren't. Paige was blooded in Mississippi with SNCC. She followed Robert Kennedy for her first book and she was in the hallway, helpless, when he was murdered. Mayor Daley's storm troopers kicked her around in Chicago in 1968. She free-lanced to a string of small periodicals from Vietnam. She kept up with Cowboy and Charlie and me on the world tour. She covered Jonestown and Three-Mile Island.

"It's a first-rate book, Reeve," she went on, dropping the banter. She could kid, but she had to warm to it.

There was more between us than business and I wasn't necessarily ready to be serious. "Just first-rate?" I asked her. "No better than that?"

"I've done enough on energy to know how it connects," she said, straight. "You've changed the terms."

"Yes ma'am."

She ignored it. "Have you had any response?"

"Sales. Talk shows. What kind of response?"

"From Washington."

"Who wants to know?"

"No one official."

"Not a peep from Washington."

"There will be. Joe's going to call you." Joe was her ex. Joe worked for Ted Kennedy.

"The senator's going solar?" I asked then.

"The senator's going presidential. Joe thinks. Don't pass it on. He needs his own energy program."

"Joe asked you to call?"

"No."

"You called on your own?"

"No."

"I didn't think so."

"I wanted to," Paige told me. "I wasn't sure we were friends."

"Hell, lady, we were lovers."

"Lovers aren't necessarily friends."

Paige had joined the festivities in Rome. We had journalists coming out our ears, and I'd say I hardly even noticed her at first, but my actions prove otherwise. I wasn't aware I noticed her.

The young girl I saw in the Piazza della Rotonda, outside the Pantheon, released something in me—remorse, joy, bitterness, new resolutions all at once. Back at the villa where the Italian government had billeted us I confronted Claudia with the silent battle we'd been fighting since we started the tour. Maybe since we started the marriage. It seemed to be a battle about propriety, about how each of us expected the other to behave when we faced the world. It was really a battle for dominance, pushing rigidity and sabotaging change. We fought half the night. Not very hard, because there wasn't much love left. The next day she flew home. The State Department pissed its pants. Neither one of us cared. I was through being leaned on and Claudia was through playing the dutiful wife.

I wanted to talk to someone. Get away from the tour and talk. I'd held it all in for years, the program and the marriage, and I'd just about had it.

Paige popped into my head. She wasn't an obvious choice. She was following us on assignment from *Esquire*. We figured *Esquire* specialized in snotty ridicule and we'd all agreed to watch out for her. I don't know that I thought she was sympathetic—she probably wasn't at the outset—but I felt from the little I'd seen of her, snap judgment, we all make them and sometimes they change our lives, that she was sensible, and sensible is a kit of tools considerably superior to tough that serves where tough can't cut it. I needed someone sensible.

I found out where she was staying—the Hassler, where else?—and called her. I told her I wanted to get away somewhere for a day and she could have an interview if she cared to arrange it. She did and she did.

I canceled the next day's official business. I was scheduled to visit a factory somewhere. She picked me up at nine in the morning in a hired Rolls. She was nervous. When I got in she shied over to her side of the backseat. She was wearing a white silk dress and white sandals. She had a notebook, not the stenographer's or the half-stenographer's but a small black leather notebook that she wrote in with a big black ink pen.

"It's Paige, isn't it?" I started out.

"Paige, yes."

"Hell of a name for a journalist."

She blinked. "Do you prefer to be called Red or Reeve?"

I shrugged. "Whatever." I sat back in the seat and the driver closed my door. The car smelled of leather. I remembered the smell of the CM before we trashed it: paint, hot plastic, ozone. Leather was better. This woman's perfume. Later I learned its name: Joy. "Where're we headed, Paige?" I asked her.

"I feel silly calling you Red," she told me. The driver was waiting in position, checking through the rear-view mirror. She looked at him. "We can start, Mario," she said quickly. Back to me: "It's a standard day-tour out of Rome. To Ostia and then down the coast to Anzio."

"The beach?"

"That too if you like."

I shook my head. "I mean Anzio Beach. Where the troops landed in the Second World War."

"Oh." She smiled. The driver, Mario, was nodding. "Yes. I thought you meant you wanted to go to the beach."

"Not today." I sorted behind the confusion. "What's Ostia?"

"Ostia Antica. It was Rome's port. It's been partly excavated. It's not Pompeii, but it's pleasant."

Mario was easing the Rolls through the Roman traffic. People watched us going by. Mario had a head like a suntanned cannonball, set solidly on his shoulders. His close-cropped black hair thinned on top to a tonsure. The sun was shining. It was going to be hot.

Paige asked me questions as we drove. I was self-conscious at first. I was trying to answer honestly without NASA's all-purpose toothful clichés. She defeated her nervousness with questions. She didn't ask the obvious. She didn't ask what I thought or how I felt at this or that Historic Moment. She asked how something worked, what I did next, what something looked like, what it sounded like, why. I said because of this and that. She asked why this and that. I said because of that and that over there. She asked why that and that over there. She understood that technology is a nest of Chinese boxes. As often as not I ended up reviewing basic physics with her. She listened. She was quick. When she understood something she filed it and afterward she knew where else it fit.

From time to time Mario shone his astute olive face on us. He meant to appear a *padrone* revealing to us the essential Italy beyond the ruins, not merely a chauffeur. So he gestured right and left as we passed out of Rome southwestward on the Via Cristoforo Colombo toward Ostia, indicating the business suburb that was started, he said, "in da Mussoline times." He ended every sentence with a question: "y'know?" We drove into E.U.R., y'know?, the exposition-*cum*-suburb, y'know?, past the monumental, sterile Fascist palaces and office buildings, past the modern palazzo the Romans call "the square Colosseum" and the concrete flying-saucer restaurant high on its pylon to the north of the road and then we were beyond E.U.R. of da Mussoline times and out in the country. Paige went on with her questioning. I felt I was connecting with a mind as intense as my own. I hadn't had that experience much around women, not astronauts' wives and sure as hell not the kind of women who collect astronauts.

We walked in Ostia. I was more taken with the trees than with the excavations; they were umbrella pines, the trees of classical painting.

I'd thought the painters had made them up. Here they were, broad-spread and real. The brickwork at Ostia impressed me, though. The Romans did incredible things with brick and cement. The Pantheon, that fantastic dome.

We went on to the coast road and turned south. The coast south of Ostia was beach. Yellow sand. Mario had plans for our lunch. He passed up three or four restaurants. The one where he stopped didn't look much different from the others except for the cluster of Mercedeses and Citroëns parked in front, grave chauffeurs observing from the shade trees beside the road.

Mario went inside and returned with a trim, handsome, middle-aged Italian in elegant shirt-sleeves, his cuffs turned back, his collar unbuttoned and his silk tie loosened. Mario introduced him as the owner, y'know? He welcomed us and led us through the bar and the inside dining room out onto the roofed terrazzo, which overlooked the sparse beach and was open to the air. The iodine smell of the sea breezed in as it had breezed into the CM at splashdown, sharp, a pleasure. The smiling owner gave us his second-best table. At his best table, to our left, a tanned businessman fed his two gorgeous teenage daughters bites of fish. Giggling, they let him. It wasn't something you'd see in America, where we confine our intimacies at home—they reminded me of birds feeding and fed.

We ordered the *fritto misto* and a carafe of white wine. The wine was cool enough to bedew the full-bellied carafe. The owner poured it with a flourish. He left us and we sipped and talked, not business now but each other. Paige's divorce, Claudia, my increasing disillusionment with NASA (now that I'd gotten what I wanted from it), what you do when you've walked on the moon, what you do when you've seen a Kennedy murdered. The owner mixed us a light salad. I noticed that the teenage girls on the beach beyond the terrace went topless. The *fritto misto* arrived. The batter was delicately golden: rings of squid, tiny octopuses, shrimp with the coral of their antennae showing through and set with seed-pearl black eyes, crisp flakes of fish. No talking: we ate. We watched the bare-breasted girls and their boys. We watched the owner passing graciously among the tables, the businessman doting on his daughters. We watched the sea.

After lunch we drove on down to Anzio. Mario let it be known that he'd been in the tank corps in North Africa. I remembered the brutal motto I'd heard of at least the British tank corps in North Africa: If you can't eat it or fuck it, shit on it. Mario had survived. He was sensible to how many British and Americans had not. He pointed out the military cemeteries on the drive back to Rome. He explained that the German artillery had battered the coastal plain from the hills inland toward Rome while the Allied naval artillery had battered the plain from the sea. The invasion forces advanced across the plain. Now it was called the *capo di carne*, Mario said somberly. The plain of meat, y'know? I heard Paige's intake of breath at the translation. There was death even in Arcadia. Especially in Arcadia there was death.

Nothing more than talk happened that day. We talked, Paige and I. That was what happened. More happened later.

Paige's call. "If you didn't call on your own," I asked her, "who did you call for?"

"*Playboy* wants you for an *Interview*," she said.

I thought about that.

"You can make the points you made in your book."

"My book and what else?"

"The space program. What it was like to go to the moon. The accident on the way home."

"And groupies, booze and divorce, right?"

"Not much. I told them I wouldn't do much. They said they wanted you to put the case for solar."

"When did *Playboy* get into the energy field?"

"That's the kind of question some devastating New York intellectual would ask, Reeve. The answer is, they deal with politics and controversy and they're as concerned about energy as the rest of us."

"Why you?"

"I've worked in the field. They know I know you."

"Was it your idea?"

"They decided on the subject and asked me who. Amory Lovins isn't exactly a household name. You are."

"Tell me there's not more to it than that."

Paige was honest. Ruthlessly honest, I'd sometimes thought. "I read your book," she said. "I liked it. It sounds as if you're back from wherever you went. I remember us. I'd like to see you again."

"That's nice," I said. "Kind of a long intermission, babe. You missed the gory parts."

"If you feel I let you down, I'm sorry."

"Hey, don't be sorry."

She pressed: "Do you want to try the interview?"

"When?"

"Not for a few weeks. I've just finished doing my homework for an *Atlantic* piece and I've got to write it first."

"What's it about?"

"Strip-mining in Montana."

"Amazing." I thought: what's to lose? "Okay," I said. "Give me a few days' notice before you come out so I can clear my schedule. You want to stay at the farm? Chris's with me. Diana may be too by the time you get here."

"Do you have room?"

"Lots of room."

"Good. I'd like to see the kids again too. Okay, the farm. This will be tape, Reeve. I need days of it."

"We were good at talking."

"We were."

We were. We were good at a lot of things.

With *The Coming Solar Age* well thumbed, Karl Grabka drove downtown to the public library. He parked in the lot behind the building, a modern building just west of Kansas City's Depression-era, Gothic-skyscraper county courthouse, and walked around to the front and went in. He was carrying a three-ring Star Trek notebook and a brace of yellow pencils. On the cover of the notebook Captain Kirk leaned into the foreground flanked by Mr. Spock and Bones. Grabka asked at the checkout table for reference help and the librarian there directed him.

The librarian at the reference desk was a tall, extremely thin woman in her fifties who looked older because her white hair was blued. She didn't mind helping people work in the library, but deep down, like many librarians, she didn't believe books should circulate. Someone could damage them. So she wasn't keen on dirty paws. So Karl wasn't exactly her kind of guy.

He stood above her. "Good morning," he said. She glanced up at him and barely nodded. "I have been assigned a research paper for my graduate seminar in clinical psychology," he announced. "The topic is etiologic responses to stress."

That didn't sound quite right, but the librarian let it go.

"I have chosen the American astronaut Reeve C. Wainwright as the subject of my study," Grabka went on. He really talked like that sometimes. He thought all us educated people did. "Since Commander Wainwright is a resident of the Greater Kansas City area, I have arranged to interview him. Before I do so, however, I wish to assemble as much document material concerning his life history and career activities as possible. I would appreciate any help you might be able to offer."

The librarian looked Grabka over then, taking in the notebook. "Are you a student?" she asked.

"As I said," Grabka answered, a little tighter, "I am studying for my doctoral degree in clinical psychology."

"I should think you'd want to use your university library, then," the lady goaded. "It's a far sight more complete than ours."

The blotches bloomed on Grabka's cheeks. "I'm actually a student at Columbia," he lied, meaning Columbia, Missouri, the location of the main campus of the University of Missouri, 125 miles away in the center of the state. "I'm embarked on a program of independent study."

"I thought you said this was for a graduate seminar."

By now, in his running private fantasy script, Karl had probably already hog-tied the lady and beaten her to a pulp, but he asked her soothingly, "Is there some problem? It was my understanding that the library's facilities were open to the public."

Oh well, the librarian told herself, what's the difference? She sniffed. "What was the name again?"

"Commander Reeve C. Wainwright, the astronaut. He's a Kansas City resident."

The librarian nodded. She wasn't quite through. "And how do you spell that?"

The graduate clinical psychologist spelled out my name. She showed him the basic reference sources he needed and sat him at a table and left him to his work.

He started with *Who's Who in America* for 1978–1979, the fortieth edition. He found me on page 3,353 of volume 2, between WAINWRIGHT, NICHOLAS BIDDLE, Princeton A.B., historian, director emeritus of the His. Soc. Pa.—the Historical Society of Pennsylvania—and WAINWRIGHT, STUYVESANT, II, Yale LL.B., lawyer, former OSS officer and Congressman. Neither one was near kin, so far as I know—my father was a farmer and later, when the farm wasn't big enough to support us, a carpenter. But we'd all come a long way from our beginnings. A wainwright was a man who repaired farm wagons. I don't know if Grabka knew that or not.

Here's what he found—quite a bit, really.

> WAINWRIGHT, REEVE COLLIER, conslt, engr., former astronaut; b. Kansas City, Mo., Aug. 28, 1932; s. Arthur R. and Anne (Collier) Wainwright; B.S., Mass. Inst. Tech., 1952; M.S. in Aero. Engring., U. So. Calif.; m. Claudia Coates, Aug. 21, 1959 (div. Apr. 27, 1973);

children—Christopher Coates, Diana Anne. With Lewis Flight Propulsion Lab, NACA, 1956; then aero. research pilot for NACA, later NASA, High Speed Flight Sta., Edwards, Calif.; astronaut Manned Spacecraft Center, NASA, Houston, 1963–1974; pilot Gemini 13, Dec. 1966; comdr. Apollo 12B, Feb. 1970; established record 7 hours and 53 minutes outside spacecraft in extravehicular activity on surface of moon; pres., Energy Alternatives Inc., Kansas City, Mo., 1976–. Commd. in USAF, 1953; fighter pilot, U.S., Europe, 1953–1956. Recipient Presdl. Medal of Freedom, NASA Distinguished Service and Exceptional Service medals, numerous others. Fellow Am. Inst. Aeos. and Astronautics, Am. Astronaut. Soc., Soc. Exptl. Test Pilots; mem. Intnl. Passive Solar Soc. Office: EAI, 2440 Pershing Road, Kansas City MO 64111.

He copied the entire entry into his notebook. He underlined my birth date, my Apollo flight, my business connection and address, the names of my children.

He read Paige's piece on the world tour in *Esquire*, an account in *Harper's* of my troubles with booze and my divorce (part of a postmortem on the Apollo program when NASA's budgets went into a tailspin in the early seventies), a *Newsweek* update in its "Where Are They Now?" section in 1977 and the *Time* story on the development contract from the DOE. In *Star*, the Kansas City *Star*'s Sunday magazine supplement, he studied pictures of me in the farmhouse living room and out in the pasture with the buffalo, not to mention walking on the moon.

He took notes, filling in the facts. From one source or another he established that I'm five feet nine and three-quarters inches tall; weigh one-sixty; have red hair and hazel eyes and freckles; vote a middle-of-the-road independent ticket; hunt quail and pheasant in season and favor a .410, which I keep on hand, along with other sport weapons, at the farm; have good eyesight; sleep well; and haven't had a drink in years.

He learned that Jason N. L. Hawthorne of *The New Yorker*, a direct descendant of Nathaniel Hawthorne, had written a book about the accident, *Fire in Space*, and after he finished with the in-library references he located the book and checked it out.

Grabka was orderly about his research. Did I make him seem too disturbed before? He was disturbed, but it showed up least in his planning. Planning is a lot like daydreaming anyway. The commitment's mental; no one gets burned. Christ, can you imagine all the plans at the Pentagon alone that people have thought up, all the plans they've got on file? Fifty ways to leave your lover and a hundred ways to demolish every major city in the world. Grabka loved to plan. This one of his dozens of plans—schemes—he happens to have carried out. He was working through a passage. He was ready to settle down.

In the Kansas City phone book Grabka found my address listed unhelpfully as Lee's Summit, which was the town and post office nearest my farm. He copied down my home phone number. When he was ready he drove around to Crown Center, to my office on Pershing Road at EAI, and checked the place out and waited for me and in his nondescript clunker Datsun boldly followed me home.

After that he knew where I lived. He watched the farm before and after work, mine and his. He learned who came and who went. He learned that I left for work at eight and usually got home by six. He learned that Chris lived with me and drove a yellow VW convertible and attended private school, the Angelus School at 120th and Holmes in south Kansas City. As Grabka sometimes followed me back and forth, so he also sometimes followed Chris, noting that Chris picked up Diana at their mother's house on the way to school and dropped her off again after their seventh-block classes, at 2:35 every schoolday.

You'd be amazed how much you can learn about people from the public record, especially so-called public figures. We're buck-ass naked, by law. In that sense, fame is what it seems to be anyway to serious people: the emperor's new clothes.

Grabka wrote all these facts and habits and details into his notebook as earnestly as if he were keeping a Starlog.

Events don't foreshadow events—people who think they do are already drifting off course toward one fanaticism or another—but this comes to mind for its coincidence. Chris worked for me around the farm last summer and the biggest job he took on was cleaning out the old well. It was necessarily a two-man job. We did it when I was home, evenings and weekends. It gave us a chance to begin to get to know each other again. There aren't many jobs odder, this late in the twentieth century, than cleaning out a well.

The farm has two wells, the original well we cleaned out and the new well I paid to have drilled when I bought the place. The new well is nothing more than a pipe drilled like an oil-well pipe down below the water table. Inside the pipe, at the bottom, underwater, there's a sealed, electrically powered pump that pumps water directly into the house. It's just as if we were hooked to a city water line except that the water is biting cold, winter and summer, and sweet, without chlorine.

The original well was dug by hand almost a century ago. It's forty feet deep and four feet in diameter, cased in mortared limestone. The bottom was silted in almost to the level of the water table. We could have plugged the well and left it, but I liked the idea of having a working well in the front yard where I could drop a bucket and crank up a dipperful of cold water and I figured it was a project Chris could learn from.

There was an old-fashioned cast-iron pump at the well head that we pulled—its pipe was rusted out, so much so that it crumpled in our hands like autumn leaves. With a sledge I broke up the concrete slab that had served as a base for the pump and a well cover, exposing the old casing. We rigged a wooden stand over the casing with a spare-tire wheel mounted dead center, free to spin. I had a winch on my pickup that I used to haul logs out of the timber for firewood. We built a wooden box with a sling on it that we could hook to the winch cable. We ran the cable from the winch on the truck, over the wheel on the stand and down into the well. That way Chris could ride the box down and then fill it with the mud he dug. I fitted him out with a hard hat and a battery-powered miner's lamp so he'd have light.

I ran the winch. There wasn't room inside the well for me. Chris was almost my height—he'd be taller when he finished growing—but he was rail-thin. One-thirty or thirty-five. His build was about the same as mine and he looked a lot like me. All male Wainwrights inherit the same basic set of features, back through at least my grandfather: high forehead, narrow mid-length nose, square jaw with a dimple in the chin. Chris's hair grew to his shoulders. He pulled it back into a ponytail when he worked. Brown hair. Neither of my children inherited my red hair. I was wiry and thin when I was Chris's age too. The drums toughened him. He didn't have an adult's strength yet, but he certainly wasn't soft.

So I sat on the ground, on the old limestone casing, and dangled my feet into the well, holding the winch cable to steady it, and Chris stood in mud up to his thighs, wearing my waders, shoveling muck into the box, forty feet below me in the bottom of the well. The acoustics were fantastic. We could talk normally and hear each other as clearly as if we were in the same room.

One of Chris's first comments: "This is really weird."

I spoke downward into the dark, cool well shaft. "Not too many guys your age clean out wells." I could see Chris's small headlight moving below.

"Huh. Tell me about it."

"Make it last. At least it's air-conditioned."

"Yeah. It's cool down here but it's really humid." His head turned as he inspected, aiming the light. "There's a lot of moss on the wall."

"I'm not surprised. If that's all that's growing down there, we'll be lucky."

"Yeah. There's rock missing from the wall too." He looked up, his light flaring. "How deep you think I'll have to dig, Dad?"

"I don't know. I've never dug out a well before. Maybe ten feet."

"That's a real burn."

Burn to me was a rocket firing. "What's a burn?"

"You know." He was starting to shovel. I could hear splashing and feel vibrations along the cable. "A burnout."

"You don't have to do it all today. Take your time."

He dug for a while in silence. His boots made sucking sounds when he changed position. Up on the surface it was hot, glaring bright, but a good breeze worked the leaves of the oak that shaded me and the well. Down along the creek the white-patched sycamores rustled. I like sycamores. I watched their broad leaves blow.

"Dad?" Chris called up.

"Yes?"

"You know when you went to the moon?"

"Yes?"

"Did you ever feel really closed in?"

I hadn't thought it would bother him. "Are you feeling that way right now?"

He was surprised. "No. I was just thinking about it."

"It's okay if you are. We don't have to do this little project."

"No sweat. Some people freak out, right?"

"Right. It's called claustrophobia."

"Yeah, right. Did you?"

"No."

"In your suit? Wasn't it weird in there?" Before I could answer he added: "I think I've got a load."

"Okay." I walked back to the pickup, started the engine and ran the winch. When the box of mud swayed just above the ground I cut the winch and dumped the box; then I ran the winch again to lower the box to Chris. "Not really," I said, picking up the conversation. "I'd worn the damned thing so much by then it was just like home."

"Even with moon gravity?"

"That made it easier."

"Didn't you think about the vacuum outside? About maybe cracking your helmet or a meteorite puncturing your suit?" He grunted, I suppose lifting a rock—I heard dripping and then a thump in the box.

"We had so much to do I didn't have time to think about it. I thought about it before we left."

"A vacuum's got to be strange. You know? Even underwater at least you can hold your breath." He paused, thinking. "What about on the way back? When you had the fire?"

"That was pretty hairy. I guess I came pretty close to panic then. We were damned lucky we had our suits on. All we had to do was grab for our helmets and slap them on and pop the hatch. That took care of the fire."

"Yeah. I was scared. They didn't tell us about it at school. Mom told us when we got home. I listened on the speaker." The speaker was the direct line we all had into our homes from Mission Control. "I wanted to stay up but Mom made me go to bed. I couldn't sleep."

"How old were you then? Seven?"

"Let's see. Yeah. I was just a little kid."

"I'm surprised you remember it."

"I remember lots of stuff. It was pretty freaky."

What that meant he didn't explain. He worked in silence again. Then: "Did they really dig these things by hand?"

"Sure. They didn't have any other way to do the job."

"How'd they keep them from caving in?"

"They lined them with timber until they could build the casing."

"I'd sure hate to get stuck down here. That's when I'd hulk out."

"I read about a man in Indiana a hundred years ago who fell into a well. He was crossing a prairie, miles from the nearest house, and there was a well someone hadn't covered. The bluestem had overgrown it and he stepped into it and fell in."

"That's wild."

"It was something like eighty feet deep, twice as deep as where you are. He was down there for a week. He figured someone would notice his horse wandering loose—he'd been leading his horse when he fell in—and the horse would lead them to the well. No such luck. He had a broken arm. You know what he did?"

"What?"

"He climbed out."

"Weird."

"Took him two days."

"To climb out? How could he keep climbing for two days with a broken arm?"

"It was climb or die, Chris, so he climbed."

"Glad it wasn't me," Chris said. He looked up then, his headlight flaring, and I heard him snort with surprise and then he shut off the light.

"What?" I called down.

"It's cool, Dad."

"What?"

"I can see the stars."

"Really?"

"Yeah. I can see the stars. It's cool."

I thought: so are you, Chris. I thought how lucky I was.

Down there in the well, sixteen years old and going with the flow, my fine young son started singing.

In late September Karl Grabka, facts at his fingertips, drove to a lumberyard. He bought two 4×8 sheets of three-quarter-inch plywood at $19.95 each; one half-sheet, 2×6, of three-quarter plywood at $8.25; two pairs of five-inch zinc plated strap hinges at $1.80 the pair; three packages of flat-head steel wood screws 1½×8 at 39¢/package; one aluminum soffit vent at 66¢; twenty-five feet of bell wire at 96¢; a large roll of silver duct tape at $6.98; and four steel latches at 89¢ each, for a total of $65.08. The lumberyard agreed to deliver the large sheets of plywood to an old detached garage he'd rented off a residential-street alley near his apartment. He paid with cash. He'd need other supplies later. He already owned a power saw.

Grabka was ready to roll. He was going to build himself a box.

Four

PLAYBOY: We suspect that Tom Wolfe's version of Life Among the Astronauts, in his best-selling book *The Right Stuff*, is closer to the truth than the version given out to the media. Are we right?

WAINWRIGHT: Partly. The truth's somewhere in between. Wolfe never acknowledges it, which I find questionable, but the version he offers of the program and the guys, what they did, what happened to them privately, is pretty much the Walt Cunningham version. Walt flew with Wally Schirra and Donn Eisele on Apollo 7, the first mission off the mark after the Apollo 1 fire, and a few years ago he wrote a book called *The All-American Boys* that's similar in many ways to Wolfe's book.

PLAYBOY: Are you charging that Wolfe plagiarized Cunningham's book?

WAINWRIGHT: Not at all, only that Walt was obviously Wolfe's most important source, not necessarily for information, although many of the stories match up between the two books, but for a point of view about how to interpret what went on. Or maybe they cross-fertilized each other. Walt mentions Wolfe's ideas about "the right stuff" and single-combat warriors two years before Wolfe's book appeared.

PLAYBOY: What do *you* think of those ideas?

WAINWRIGHT: I think they're about eighty percent bullshit.

PLAYBOY: Why?

WAINWRIGHT: It just didn't feel that way. Not to me. It may have to Walt. To me it felt like honest work. The publicity complicated it—Wolfe's right enough about that—but with a few exceptions, most of us just didn't go around thinking we were all that special. What Wolfe describes as some kind of personal code of crazy self-testing, the Drinking & Driving and so on, was more the naive exuberance you get in pilots. Most pilots haven't been around much. They've been in training. In school. They're really a fairly innocent, fairly unsophisticated bunch of people.

PLAYBOY: Are you?

WAINWRIGHT: I was. I don't think I am anymore.

The next thing on the tape after my generous vote of self-confidence was spontaneous laughter, the sound of Paige Elder cracking up.

She flew in to Kansas City to do the interview on October 4, which was a Thursday. We were going to try a long weekend. We'd tape whatever felt good and she'd run the tapes up to Chicago for transcription and then see if we needed another session later.

She was coming in from New York on TWA and she landed at Kansas City International at 1:03 in the afternoon. I saw her before she saw me. She was wearing a sheepskin vest, a beige blouse, boots and designer jeans and she stuck her hands into her hip pockets and looked around, blinking, all eyes. She wore contacts that didn't always sit well with her eyes. I'd forgotten how tiny she was. If it makes sense to say it this way, she remembered bigger.

I crossed to her at the gate. She saw me then and shifted back her weight and cocked her head at me, squinting one eye. "Han Solo?" she said.

"Princess Leia?" I countered.

We laughed and hugged—nothing more than a hug then, friendly and wary. She'd walked out on me when I was up to my eyeballs in the wine and roses, and knowing she had a right to, and was *right* to, hadn't left me any less aggrieved. I'd thought, as people always think when they're behaving badly, that the people I was behaving badly toward ought to make allowances to keep the faith. We'd talked since, written letters since, seen each other once or twice since. Nothing serious, though, and it had been serious before.

She traveled light. She'd deboarded with a worn brown leather flight bag plus a leather purse and her tape recorder. That was it. We didn't have to wait for luggage. Off we went.

"What's new?" I asked her as we drove.

She tossed it back. "What's new with you?" She was sitting half turned, checking me out.

"Insolation rights."

"The sun shines in."

"Right."

"You look great."

"Thanks," I said, glancing at her. "So do you."

"The flesh loosens on the bone," she said seriously.

"We've hit forty. After that the DNA stops repairing itself."

She was striking rather than conventionally pretty, not at all the kind of woman I'd have expected to choose or be chosen by. Sex with Paige had been deep and good but not wildly passionate. Something else had connected us. I could talk to her. She could talk to me. We were two intensely competitive people who didn't feel competitive with each other. Something like that. Something besides trust.

> PLAYBOY: We landed men on the moon. Was it worth the cost in money and lives?
>
> WAINWRIGHT: I can't speak to lives. We all knew the risks and we took them and some of us lost. It was worth the money. I thought so then and I think so now.
>
> PLAYBOY: What if those billions had been spent to attack problems here on earth? Wouldn't that have been a more humane investment? Wasn't the space program *show* more than substance?
>
> WAINWRIGHT: The space program was the moral equivalent of war.
>
> PLAYBOY: That's what President Jimmy Carter called the energy crisis.
>
> WAINWRIGHT: It was William James' phrase before it was the President's, and it meant a humane program of goals as large as society. Look, we committed a small fraction of our GNP to a distant, chancy goal. It was more a love affair than a practical investment, although an awful lot of people took

> home paychecks along the way. The money wouldn't have been forthcoming for anything else. I don't say anything *less*. Just anything else. What we did had important military significance in terms of the development of rocketry and accurate navigation and so on. It had significance in terms of that vague business known as national prestige. Hell, I don't know. I thought it was worth it at the time. So did a lot of other people, from John Kennedy on down. I could say it saved some lives, and someone at NASA would be glad to show you all the spin-off technology in medicine and what have you. You're right, we could have spent the money differently. Maybe more practically, in the short run. A love affair's a love affair. When was a love affair ever practical?

"Somehow we fell in with these people for dinner," Paige was telling me as we drove. Kansas City's a sprawl. We had a drive of almost sixty miles from KCI down to the city and then east and south to the farm. There was plenty of time to talk. Paige was recalling a big convention for writers at *Playboy* a few years back. I don't remember why she was telling me the story. At the time I listened and watched the road. "Don Tucker was with us," she said. "With me, I guess. He'd started in on me the minute I came into the room. Do you know who I mean? The poet? The South's latest gift to a grateful nation?"

"'To do no more than watch the moon and see the slow silver / Casting of its face shifted westward.' That the guy?"

She smiled. "Those would be the lines you'd come up with. It always amazes me that you read."

"I don't read. Mike Collins reads."

"Anyway," she went on, "Tucker's huge. He must be six eight. One of the stranger sights of the convention was the cocktail party the first evening. Michael Crichton, the film director, was there. Crichton's as tall as Tucker. They homed on each other. They got together in the very center of the crowd, head and shoulders above the rest of us. Maybe because they could *see* each other, maybe because it improved the packing. But really, I think, because they felt literally superior."

I nodded. We were approaching Municipal Airport, the old commercial airport directly across the Missouri River from downtown Kansas City, where I'd learned to fly.

"Tucker decided to pursue me." Paige looked over and blinked. "I'm not bragging. It wasn't flattering. He was a mess in those days. He's long since remarried and he's better now. He was standing-up drunk and I was the only thing available at hand. It was hard work, too, because I was a good foot and a half below him, almost far enough down to shout.

"So we went to dinner," Paige continued. "Joe was entertaining a *Playboy* editor and an extra couple we'd picked up somewhere, and down at the other end of the table I was listening to this amazing line of Tucker's. Poems, tags, brags, grins, flattery. He was getting drunker and drunker. Something must have clicked, because abruptly he asked me point-blank—whispered to me—if I'd like to leave that instant and go back to his room and fornicate. He said 'fornicate.' I told him no thanks. He grinned that big cannibalistic grin of his and repeated the question as if I hadn't heard and I turned him down again and then he got mean. He called me something like a fucking Jew-bitch cunt, whispering, grinning. I decided to ignore him, turned to Mike and the conversation at that end of the table, and after a while he growled and stumbled off alone. I can't say I felt sorry for him."

I paid the twenty-cent toll on the Broadway Bridge, which was spring green in sunny October, and turned onto I-70, swinging east around downtown toward Lee's Summit.

"That's background," Paige said. "What I was thinking of was what happened the next day. *Playboy* had set up a twenty-four-hour bar in a lounge on the twelfth floor of the hotel. They understand writers' needs. Joe went in there about midafternoon to get a drink. David Halberstam was there, Michael Arlen, Studs Terkel and so on. Tucker sitting on a couch, still drunk, staring out, back to the wall. Joe started kidding Halberstam about all the time he'd invested in Vietnam, what had it got him and so on—understand, it was stupid of Joe in any case, but this was just before David published *The Best and the Brightest*—and it piqued Tucker's curiosity. Joe saw him watching and turned to him mock-politely and said, 'Good afternoon, Mr. Tucker.' Tucker looked him over as if he were something he'd turned up in the kudzu. 'Who *ah* you?' he asked him. 'Where d'you *come* from? What d'you *do?*' Joe said, 'Don't you remember me, Mr. Tucker? You propositioned my wife last night.' Tucker: 'She a-cept?' Joe: 'No.' Tucker, very heartfelt and with a sigh: 'She's *lucky*.'"

> PLAYBOY: So Kennedy was looking for a gimmick and a man on the moon was the gimmick.
> WAINWRIGHT: No more than was the discovery of the New World.
> PLAYBOY: We knew the moon was there.

WAINWRIGHT: We knew the moon was there. We didn't know we could get to it. No one who wasn't part of the whole incredible business has any idea how delicate the connection was, getting there. Arthur Clarke put it as well as anybody. He said space travel was twenty-first century. It should never have happened when it did. It was pure crazy bravado that we did it when we did. We should have started with earth-orbital systems like the space shuttle and proceeded step by step. Landing on the moon from lunar orbit was like Columbus anchoring his ships in mid-Atlantic and pushing on to America in a rowboat. Look, the moon program wasn't necessarily pretty. We wanted to beat out the Soviets. We thought we'd be annihilated if we didn't. Sputnik put us on the moon. It was a pissing contest. The difference is, what it came to be came back to us as vastly more than what it started out to be. Someone handed us an apple. It went around the earth and it beeped. We bit. Newton had good luck with apples too.

PLAYBOY: What's the bottom line?

WAINWRIGHT: The bottom line for Newton was gravity. The bottom line for the moon program was antigravity.

PLAYBOY: Meaning?

WAINWRIGHT: Meaning the human race learned with the assurance of absolute fact that it isn't mired to the earth anymore. Earth's not our burial ground, it's our staging area.

PLAYBOY: Who said astronauts couldn't talk?

WAINWRIGHT: What else would you like to talk about?

PLAYBOY: You fly to the moon. What then?

WAINWRIGHT: They let you stay a little while.

PLAYBOY: You're playing our song. But seriously—what then?

WAINWRIGHT: You come back and go about your business.

PLAYBOY: Did you?

WAINWRIGHT: After an appropriate period of readjustment, yes.

PLAYBOY: You had some problems.

WAINWRIGHT: Don't we all?

PLAYBOY: Specifically, you dropped out of the space program, you were involved in some questionable business dealings, you were divorced from your wife of fourteen years, you struggled with and overcame a serious drinking problem. Care to talk about any of those things?

WAINWRIGHT: The divorce is private. The drinking problem was a bore, and it's in hand. The business dealings are still in litigation and not presently open to discussion. Want to talk about energy?

PLAYBOY: Why do we get the feeling you're avoiding something?

We spent the afternoon taping at the farm, sun streaming into the white living room. Chris came home after school and disappeared upstairs. At five, when he started practicing, we stopped taping. I used the hour to check the livestock and show Paige the farm. She'd heard about it but hadn't seen it. The buffalo delighted her. She was Main Line Philadelphia—not wealth, just birthplace—and a buffalo was as exotic a beast to her as a rhino. The buffalo came up to the fence for the drum practice and Paige could study its massive, shaggy head. I noticed its coat was thickening for winter.

Back at the house we cleaned up and drove over to Snead's Bar-B-Q and bought dinner to carry home—sliced beef and ham, a slab of ribs, French fries, slaw. Chris collected his portion and carried it off to his room. Later he went out. Paige and I settled into more taping.

We ran down at about nine that night. We'd been over most of the areas Paige wanted to cover at least once and she had a nice stack of tapes. She shut off her little metallic-gray Sony and laid it on its side. Outside was dark. The music-stand spots aimed at the wall of bookshelves and memorabilia brightened the room. I was sitting in my leather armchair, Paige on the carpet at the side of the coffee table leaning against the couch.

She took a silver cigarette case from her purse, a joint from the cigarette case. I slid an ashtray her way along the glass-topped coffee table and she lit up, looking at me to ask if I wanted a hit. I shook my head. She smoked and we were silent, making a space. We'd talked all day about everything but each other.

"I'm glad this happened," I said finally.

She answered by leaning forward and brushing my hand with her fingertips. The armchair was an Eames, a shell of walnut and leather cushions, shaped something like a spacecraft couch. The quality of light in the room, the darkness outside and the quiet felt like a big spacecraft, felt as if we were that far away and enclosed.

"I'm being extremely selfish," Paige said then. "I needed you."

"Feels okay to me."

She nodded. "Me too." She grinned, maybe a touch of giddiness from the dope. She looked at me and blinked. "But that was the idea."

I turned on my side to face her. "Maybe you'd better tell me about it."

She shrugged. "I was with someone. He didn't want to be with me anymore. I thought it was my arrangement. It turned out to be his." She shrugged again. Not her normal behavior at all. "It's an old, old, sad story," she said.

"Hey. Paige. Where'd you go?"

She nodded. There were tears in her eyes, on her face, but she wasn't crying. The tears ran off unacknowledged. "It's age, Reeve. Midlife crisis. Passages. That vulgar."

"Vulgar's a taste."

"Not of mine."

"How about me?"

She looked at me.

"Barbecue? Kansas City? Well-known astronaut? That's not vulgar?" She wasn't listening. When you try to cheer people you expect them to listen. What the hell. I wondered why I was being charitable anyway. To make conversation? I asked: "Anyone I know?"

"I can't say."

Which is about how close we are, I thought.

She lit the joint again, hit, held, exhaled, hit, held, exhaled. Sent it back to the ashtray. Stared off. "You know I'm not usually stupid," she said. Then she was silent for minutes, staring off, I suppose saying what she wanted to say three or four different ways to find the right way. And then, still staring: "He's in government. At the very top and vulnerable. That's all. You don't care if you know."

I thought: the hell. "No."

"It was strange. Almost accidental. I think I convinced myself I could use him in some way. I needed an explanation and that's all I came up with. I thought I'd finished with people in government when I finished with Joe. And I assumed he was using *me*. Amusement, my name such as it is, that I'm a journalist. Let him co-opt the journalist and I'd co-opt the insider. It wasn't any of that. He felt empty. I felt empty. What we had in common was that neither of us had children or ever would. It worked." She lowered her head slightly, looking, I guessed, at the plants below the windows rather than into the darkness beyond. "Except that I'm not stupid. I watched what was going on. I watched us brutally. I wasn't about to be caught out."

She went silent again, for minutes again. I'd long since turned faceup in my chair. I had my hands folded behind my head and while I waited there was time to drift. I was sleepy from the heavy food. The sleepiness and the soft leather and the position of the chair, canted back, brought me close to free fall. If I'd unfolded my hands they'd have floated over my head. I was light, lifting off the chair. Light was easier. I could wish I was light.

Paige came back. So did I, necessarily. "I wasn't about to be caught out," she repeated, picking up where she'd left off. "And he sensed that. That I was watching. And he took it for the treason it was, given what he needed, what he was offering, what he was risking. And he let me go. I wasn't enough. It hurt me terribly, Reeve." Her voice had changed. "I'm unhurtable that way, fools and foolishness, and it hurt me terribly. That I wasn't enough. Wasn't enough for someone, not to be nice about it, for someone like him, a Washington man." Then she looked at me: daring me.

I didn't have to think. It was obvious. It's always obvious to everyone but the poor suckers involved. "Tell him to kiss your ass," I said.

She closed her eyes, slowly, and held them closed, and opened them. "I know," she said.

"Not really. Unless you already did."

"I haven't."

"You should."

"I will. Lay off."

"Roger, Elder, I copy."

She let the dust settle. Then she was standing. "Let's go up," she said, elaborately neutral. "I'd like to fuck. Would you like to fuck?"

I stood too. "Sure." Gallons of poisons to flush out, both of us.

Because she was small, because she liked to control and probably wanted to feel *in* control too, she rode. I looked up in the lamplight to her face, drawn with the poisons and not beautiful. No more mine when she looked down. She was pale in the light and in the cool room her small breasts were contracted hard above her tight ribs as if she wore a G suit. Below the waist we were juicy enough. Anger juices a fuck. I don't call it that and I hadn't. She had. She was right. After so long it was just the best we could do.

So she controlled and she rode. Until she came, noise down her throat, her head bending back in seizure and her face contorted. Miles away. And then came I.

I got in from running, checking the cattle, and Paige in the morning living room wearing my big terry bathrobe was laughing. She held out the newspaper, the Kansas City *Times*, and I went over to look.

"The cartoon," she said. "*Guindon*. I've never seen it before. It's wonderful."

It showed a man standing at a cluttered business desk, another man opposite holding his hand over the mouthpiece of a telephone. The man with the telephone announced: "It's some terrorist group claiming credit for the leisure suit."

I snorted. "He's that good almost every day," I told Paige. No—the desk was an editor's desk. Jar of pencils, typewriter, typing chair. Pencil behind the editor's ear. The odd things you don't notice. I went upstairs to shower and dress.

When I came back down Paige had a tray with buttered toast, two jars of my mother's jams, coffee in my big earthenware mugs. I got my coffee and took to the Eames.

"The Senate approved the energy board," Paige said, handing me the front section of the paper.

"It figures. When the heat's on, the politicians always hide behind the heavies. So much for the democratic process, right?"

"The real battle's in the House," Paige said, leaning back against the couch. She was one of those people—most of them women, because women fold better than men—who prefer the floor.

"You think?"

"Don't you?" She looked at me.

"I think if Congress and the Department of Energy turned into pumpkins tomorrow and rolled away it'd be years before we missed them. Energywise. It's a local problem, not a national. It just happens to be local almost everywhere at once."

"Let me get this on tape," Paige said, reaching for her recorder.

I held up my hand. "Let's not. Let's have a little morning first, okay? I'll get into it later."

Chris came in then, ready for school. School cost two thousand a year and he dressed for it in jeans frayed at the bottoms to a sort of denim filigree and cotton flannel shirts shrunken halfway up his forearms and unbuttoned down to the navel to expose his narrow, wiry chest. And boots worn to wood at the heels. He did his own laundry, so I couldn't speak to socks or undershorts. Maybe. But good enough. He wore what he wanted to wear and it was something like a uniform to his gang. "Hey, how's it going?" he asked us.

Paige smiled at him. I said, "It's pretty cool out there. You might want a sweater."

"It'll warm up. Can I have a ten for gas?"

"Sure." I dug for my wallet and gave him the money. Thought of

Diana and gave him five more for each of them, petty cash. "What's up this afternoon?"

"I thought I'd go play Star Trek. I've got a drum lesson at Jack's at five. After that I'll be home."

"What's your Star Trek level?" The levels were progressively harder.

He shrugged. "Five."

"Way t'go."

"You ought to try their moon-landing sequence," he said, speaking to me but looking to Paige and smiling at her.

"I did that, thanks. About ten thousand times."

"Yeah." His hands into his back pockets. "Guess I'd better get going."

He went.

"I like him," Paige said as the VW chittered away.

"So do I. I haven't figured him out yet."

"He's exactly what he is, isn't he?"

"More, I hope."

I got a glance. "Were you?"

"I was an Eagle Scout with clusters."

"My point," the lady said.

We read the paper. The pope had been in Iowa and now he was in Chicago. It would be sunny and cool today with southwesterly winds ten to fifteen miles an hour, high upper sixties, low, low forties. For the second time in two months, Nixon had to give up on an apartment he was trying to buy in Manhattan. He got on the horn to us when we were limping back from the moon and told us he was rooting for us. He said he'd had crises too. It wasn't the most historic phone call since the Creation.

Paige chuckled. "Okay, Wainwright," she said into the paper. "Confess. It'll go easier on you." Lowering the paper: "Where are they?"

"What?"

"The moon rocks. It says here NASA's missing scads of moon rocks. Proxmire released an auditor's report."

"Who's supposed to have them?" I was watching her face. I liked her better than I had the night before.

"It doesn't say. NASA claims they're missing ten to twenty ounces at most."

"That's a fortune."

"Did you keep any?" Serious question.

I shook my head. "I didn't need to. I was there."

"I know," she said quietly. "It's just as extraordinary as it seems, isn't it."

"Yup."

"Yup? *Yup?* Jesus, you clown. You clowns didn't *deserve* to go to the moon."

"Who would you have sent? Tucker?"

"Tucker. Mailer. What's wrong with me?"

"Send a *girl?*"

"You joke, but that's what they really thought. The bastards really thought that, didn't they."

"The moon board did. It was like the energy board. 'Wa, how would them little honeys *pee* out there? No sir, cain't allow no *fe*males along.'" I nodded. "Sure. That's not news."

Ordinary morning. We kept on. We made love there in the sun-flooded living room, kneeling, another way Paige liked. So did I: guiding those taut hips, acutely curved, against me and away: probing: and then docked.

At 5:30 that afternoon Jack Pupp called. Chris's drum teacher. Chris hadn't shown up for his lesson.

Chris never missed a drum lesson. It was worth checking into. Maybe he'd pranged his car. I called Diana. He wasn't at his mother's. He'd dropped Diana off on his way to Bucky's. I called Bucky's. The attendants had changed shifts at five, so the evening attendant I talked to hadn't been there at four, when Chris would have come in. I got the day attendant's name—he was the owner, a kid of twenty-two—and called him at home. His roommate answered. The owner was in the shower. He'd call me back. No big deal. I waited ten minutes, going over the possibilities with Paige, who tended to discount the thing as teenage unreliability—I did too, but I didn't, because it was a drum lesson and Chris had said he'd be there—and then the owner called, Bill somebody. He knew who I was.

"He was there, Mr. Wainwright," he told me after I'd explained. "A man came in at four-thirty and talked to him. Your son went out with him."

"That's it?"

"That's it."

"Did you know the man? Was he someone you'd seen in there before?"

"No."

"What did he look like?"

"Big. Dark. Hair in a ponytail. He smelled."

"He smelled? What's that mean?"

"He needed a bath."

"And you never saw him before?"

"No."

"Thanks, Bill."

"Okay."

You see already: big, dark, hair in a ponytail. Who stank. The rest came swooping down. I couldn't figure it out. While I was trying to we got a call and I jumped for it. A man's voice, muffled, directing me to go to my mailbox out on the highway. I did. I found the note.

It was typed, all capital letters. It was Xeroxed. It read:

> COMMANDER WAINWRIGHT:
> (1) DO NOT INVOLVE THE POLICE AS ANY CONTACT WITH THEM WILL CAUSE US TO ABANDON YOUR SON TO HIS FATE. YOU CANNOT HAVE F.B.I. AGENTS RUNNING AROUND YOUR RANCH OR PLACE OF BUSINESS WITHOUT US DETECTING THEM. (2) YOUR SON IS BURIED IN AN ESCAPE-PROOF CAPSULE. THE CAPSULE IS A COMPLETE, SELF-CONTAINED LIFE SUPPORT SYSTEM WITH ENOUGH FOOD, WATER AND VENTILATION POWER TO KEEP HIM ALIVE FOR SEVEN DAYS. CONSIDER WHAT THIS MEANS IN TERMS OF YOUR DILEMMA: (A) IF YOU CAPTURE US, ALL WE NEED TO DO IS REMAIN SILENT AND YOU HAVE NO EVIDENCE TO CONVICT US; WORSE YET, YOUR SON WILL SUFFOCATE AS YOU WILL NEVER FIND HIM; (B) IF WE ARE SCARED OFF BY THE DETECTABLE PRESENCE OF THE POLICE, YOUR SON WILL BE ABANDONED TO DIE; (C) IF YOU FAIL TO PAY THE RANSOM YOUR SON DIES AS WE WILL NOT RISK LETTING HIM GO FREE TO TESTIFY. WITHOUT A BODY, NO COURT WILL BE ABLE TO CONVICT US; (D) AS YOU CAN SEE, OUR CAPTURE, WHICH YOU COULD CONCEIVABLY ENGINEER, IS THE LAST THING YOU WANT. THEREFORE, YOU HAVE NO NEED OF OR USE FOR THE POLICE. YOU HAVE NO CHOICE BUT TO PAY AND FOLLOW OUR INSTRUCTIONS TO THE LETTER; WE LEFT YOU NO ALTERNATIVES. (3) YOU WILL RECEIVE PROOF THAT WE HAVE YOUR SON. (4) YOU WILL ARRANGE THROUGH YOUR BANK

TO WITHDRAW THREE STANDARD GOLD BARS, THE EQUIVALENT OF APPROXIMATELY $500,000.00 IN GOLD AT CURRENT RATES; YOU WILL PLACE THE BARS IN A STANDARD SUITCASE OF STRONG NEW CONSTRUCTION (THEY WILL WEIGH 81 TROY POUNDS); YOU WILL TAKE THE BARS HOME, LOCKED IN THIS SUITCASE. (5) YOU WILL BE CALLED AT IRREGULAR INTERVALS. THE CALLS WILL BE BRIEF AND UNTRACEABLE. WHEN YOU ARE READY TO DELIVER THE GOLD, YOU WILL RECEIVE INSTRUCTIONS, REEVE, TO DRIVE YOUR SAAB AND THE GOLD TO A RENDEZVOUS WITH OUR MESSENGER. YOU MUST BE <u>ALONE</u> IN THE CAR, <u>REEVE.</u> (6) FOLLOW YOUR INSTRUCTIONS TO THE LETTER—THEN LEAVE. DO NOTHING MORE OR LESS, AS YOU WILL BE OBSERVED BY AN ARMED MAN. (7) YOU <u>MUST</u> ARRIVE AT THE RENDEZVOUS WITHIN THE TIME LIMIT SET DURING THE PHONE CALL. IF YOU ARE LATE, WE WILL NOT CONTACT YOU; ERGO, CHRISTOPHER DIES. YOU WILL BE ALLOWED ONLY A SHORT TIME MORE THAN IS REQUIRED TO DRIVE FROM YOUR RANCH TO THE RENDEZVOUS—SO BE PREPARED, BUT DRIVE WITHIN THE SPEED LIMIT, AS THIS TIME HAS BEEN REASONABLY CALCULATED. (8) CHRISTOPHER IS SAFE AND COMFORTABLE. NO HARM WILL COME TO HIM UNLESS YOU FAIL TO FOLLOW THESE INSTRUCTIONS. IF YOU ACT IN GOOD FAITH, HE WILL BE RELEASED UNHARMED AFTER YOU DELIVER THE GOLD. YOU WENT TO THE MOON, REEVE. THIS IS MUCH EASIER TO ACCOMPLISH. DO NOT FAIL YOUR ONLY SON.

KANSAS CITY CELL
THE RED COMMUNE

It might still have been a hoax. I knew it wasn't. Chris hadn't made his drum lesson, and Chris always made his drum lesson. Chris hadn't come home, and Chris always came home. If he hadn't, he couldn't. Some terrorist group was claiming credit for Karl Grabka. Chris was out there somewhere in the darkness, buried alive.

Five

The garage where Karl Grabka built the box for Chris's burial smelled of dry rot. It hadn't been used in years. It faced a graveled, weedy alley behind a retired schoolteacher's house. Its white board siding was peeling, its wood shingles split and hung on rusty nails and weathered gray. There were small, dusty, four-paned windows on three sides. Rafters inside woven with cobwebs. A single bare light bulb on a cloth-sheathed cord, a round black and white toggle switch on the upright just inside the doors, which swung outward from the center. It was a one-car garage, prewar. The floor was dusty. Leaves piled in the corners and filled the cracks. A discoloration of oil on the floor had long ago soaked deep into the concrete. It was the sort of place where great inventions take their cue from bicycle parts and great discoveries start from molds drifting in the window.

Grabka got busy as soon as the lumber arrived. Now that he had laid plans to make his fortune, his life was satisfyingly full. It acquired direction and purpose, like any other entrepreneur's. He had his job at the hospital. He had his surveillance of me and mine. He had his planning. He had his carpentry. It almost needed scheduling. It almost needed a secretary and an answering service, maybe an agent. Grabka spent less time with his magazines in that sweaty bed. He woke up raring to go, the son of a bitch.

He had money. He'd never spent much of his paychecks. Now he traded his Datsun for a Toyota pickup, used. He bought the rest of his carpentry supplies, including two-by-fours for sawhorses and a jigsaw and an electric drill. He built the sawhorses first for a work surface and then began on the box.

He marked the four-by-eight sheets of plywood down the middle and divided them one at a time with his power saw—the cord dangling from the extension socket he'd installed overhead, the sawdust flying like blizzard snow in the glare of the light—making four pieces, each two feet by eight. He marked one piece for the bottom of the box, narrowing it by one and a half inches with his saw so the sides could overlap it, and shortened the bottom and sides to allow for the ends, so that the outside dimensions overall would match the two-by-eight lid. He worked the edges a little with coarse sandpaper to take off the worst of the fray from the saw. He'd bought one-side-good plywood so that the inside of the box would be smooth. The manufacturer had plugged the knotholes on the bad side with wooden ovals of pine veneer pointed at the end of the long axis like eyes and the knothole eyes looked out. The effect was cabalistic, as if a Mason had gone wild with a stencil.

The two-by-six piece of plywood Grabka cut into thirds, two pieces for the ends and one piece, which he trimmed, as a partition inside the box.

That much was one evening's work.

Another evening he marked and drilled holes for the screws, fifty-three in all, that would hold the box together, and another evening he started and tightened the fifty-three screws to assemble the basic box. The screwdriver raised a pillow of blister on the palm of his right hand.

I don't know what he thought. I doubt if he thought. Most of us don't think when we're working. That's one of the reasons we work.

Before he installed the inside partition Grabka cut a rectangular hole into it with the jigsaw for the aluminum soffit grill and mounted the grill. Screwed into place at the six-foot mark, the partition divided the long housing section of the box, where Chris would be confined, from the short equipment section.

The equipment consisted basically of a battery, a light and a fan. The battery was a twelve-volt car battery. The fan was one of those egg-shaped rubber fans people used to mount on the dashes of their cars to defog the windshield—if you're over forty, you'll remember them. You can still buy them at auto supply stores. Grabka mounted the fan inside the near end of a ten-foot length of clothes-dryer exhaust ducting so that it would pull down outside air into the box. Chris would be able to turn it on and off with a little toggle switch plugged into the housing side of the partition. The light was an automobile interior light, operated by a second toggle switch. Grabka wired the fan and light in parallel to the battery. He ran them, did some calculating and figured the battery would last at least seven days if Chris spent most of his time in the dark.

Even though the box was screwed together, all its seams got a triple covering of duct tape to make them waterproof. Then the lid went on, four strong strap hinges on one side and four latches on the other, with turnkey restraints. A hole drilled and jigsawed through the lid over the equipment section to pass the exhaust ducting and the ugly coffin was done. It was a torture chamber, a chamber of horrors. Grabka was proud of it.

I think of Pad 34 and that criminal, charred Block I command module where Grissom and Chaffee and White burned to death. They couldn't get out. Neither could Chris.

Once he had his "capsule," Grabka had to find a secluded spot to dig a hole. The hole had to be more than eight feet long, more than two feet wide and at least four feet deep. That's a lot of digging, some nine cubic yards of dirt to move. He needed privacy and time.

He drove half an hour south of Kansas City into farm and ranch country and hunted through a weekend, taking oiled side-roads and dirt roads off of those and grown-over section lanes off of those. The land wasn't all fenced as it once would have been because farming is specialized now and not everyone raises livestock. Grabka was looking for woods and he found them, back-lane stands of scrubby, cutover blackjack oak and cedar. He would have found forest once, shaded and cool: tall, straight, high-leaved white oak on the hills and gigantic sycamore in the creek valleys or tall-grass prairie grown up to the waist of a man riding through on horseback. Now the woods were scrub oak and cedar laced with tough creepers and poison ivy. But within the snarl there were clearings and late Sunday afternoon Grabka selected one of the three he'd found that suited him, a well-drained site on a rise, and drew himself a map and the next weekend went back and started digging.

The small clearing stank of dying weeds. Grabka had driven out early on a Saturday morning from Kansas City and it was cool. At first he kept on his gray sweatshirt. He'd brought a spade, a long-handled shovel and a grub hoe. He outlined the hole he intended to dig with the spade, cutting through the weedy sod and driving the spade to its full length into the soil, standing up on the blade. Missouri south of the river isn't glacial, but because its bedrock is limestone, because of the action of carbolized water on limestone, its soil is rocky in places with a kind of yellow-orange flint called chert, and this was one of those places, and Grabka's spade often struck chert and turned jarringly aside or ground and stopped.

With the hole outlined he used the broader shovel to skin off the sod, two inches of weeds and trash on top of a thin loose layer of forest mulch. After he'd skinned the hole he dug in earnest, throwing up dirt and gravel onto a pile along the length of the hole; a gravedigger. He didn't think he was digging a grave. He thought he was digging a brilliant stash for his collateral, a safe-house. He imagined himself buried in his "capsule," which gleamed in his vision now like a spacecraft turning in the sunlight, and warped as he was, institutional basket case that he was, he convinced himself it wouldn't be bad at all.

A foot down, the chert thickened, worked by freezing and thawing into a layer just above the frost line. Grabka hacked and scraped it away and stopped to rest. Then and later he hiked out to the road to see if he could be seen, but he was far away behind the back fields of a man who farmed eight hundred acres, the working part east across two lines of hills. Grabka drank Seven-Eleven coffee from the thermos he'd left on the seat of his pickup and studied the country, maybe pretending he was a cowboy, and grinned and capped the thermos and went back to digging.

He had to grub through thick, tangled roots, oak and cedar. He hacked with his grub hoe. It was sharp when he bought it but he'd sharpened it finer with a file and he put the edge to good use.

Below chert and roots was yellow sandy subsoil packed with slabs and small boulders of yellowish limestone and lumpy irregular balls of yellow-brown clay. The clay stuck to shovel and hoe and had to be scraped off. It stuck to Grabka's shoes and smeared the legs of his pants.

Toward dusk he noticed the crows. They were big black common crows, hundreds of them flapping and cawing in a broad line into the trees around the clearing. They bothered him. He wondered why they'd come. Some of them inspected the clearing, landing at the edge and walking in toward him a few steps at a time, cocking their shiny black heads. He felt watched. He clapped them away, lobbed chert at them. They flew off cawing and flapping, but others came to replace them. He didn't realize he'd chosen a site within a rookery.

As the sky darkened the crows flew in to nest. Grabka was shaking with exhaustion. He covered over the hole with a used army tarp he'd picked up at a surplus store and left for the night.

He came back Sunday morning with the "capsule" in the back of the pickup. He was sore, but the work limbered him again and he finished digging by early afternoon.

For reasons I don't know and he doesn't either, he masturbated then, standing up in the hole. Maybe the smell of the earth in that vicious grave excited him. There's nothing pretty about any of this.

He hiked back to his pickup and hauled the "capsule" off the floorbed and dragged it into the woods to the hole. He'd stored two lengths of new hemp rope inside and he used them to lower it in. The foot end caught. He had to haul out again and shave away the sides of the hole. That started a small avalanche of subsoil. He left it. The level suffered accordingly, the foot end of the box resting eventually several inches higher than the head.

He looked over his work, the trim, straight-sided hole, the raw box down inside with shining silver-gray duct tape framing its corners, the monumental long barrow of earth piled above. It felt good. It felt serious. In imagination his plan had fogged his head like so much else of resentment and want, ambition, demented megalomania and greed. Now it was real, with all the hard-edged assurance and innocent-seeming inevitability of the real. Who could blame a plywood box or a hole in the earth in a clearing in a rookery? Grabka knew now he'd go through with the rest of it. The real hole convinced him. The "capsule" convinced him. That's what objects do. That's why surgeons cut and soldiers go to war. That's why depressives don't keep guns at home and why Sputnik with its intolerable beeping put us on the moon.

He was almost ready. He needed a little more time and a little more equipment. He needed handcuffs and a gun. At a gun store in downtown Kansas City that smelled of machine oil, where the customers were ruddy, weathered, close-cropped men in baseball caps, he bought nickel-plated handcuffs and an Iver Johnson six-shot .22 Magnum revolver, ugly and plain, that cost only sixty bucks and that he didn't intend to fire. He needed injectable Thorazine and crystal Thorazine he could dissolve in the drinking water he meant to store in the "capsule." He stole both from the hospital the day before he quit. He needed a fake detective's badge. He bought a real patrolman's, old, at a downtown pawnshop and polished it to a fine chrome glow. He needed the ransom note. He spent two days on it, working in little details—the kind of car I drove, Chris's name, my astronaut affiliation—to let me know he was well informed. He typed the note on a rented office Royal and Xeroxed it so that the typing couldn't be matched and then burned the original. He cleaned up the garage—threw away the scrap, swept out the sawdust, loaded his tools in the pickup, set the sawhorses out for trash. He withdrew all his remaining savings, $1,248.74, in cash and closed his savings account.

He followed Chris minutely then until he—Chris—my son, my only son—went alone to Bucky's.

Bucky's Wristwatch is one of a kind, at least in Kansas City. It takes its name from a demonstration program in a legendary introduction to computers, a big *Whole Earth Catalog* of a book called *Computer Lib*, which was one of Chris's several bibles. A couple of computer addicts not much older than Chris started Bucky's on a shoestring, a storefront in a row of storefronts. Coincidentally, the tables are plywood sheets supported by sawhorses. M. C. Escher posters and computer graphics hang on the plain gray walls.

Much as I had used them, computers to me were only tools. To the kids at Bucky's they were more like alter intelligences woven into and through all the causes of adolescence—in Chris's case, the cause of rock music. Programming was power. Computers were power. The kids sensed that the future lay in that direction and they felt like pioneers. That's what they told themselves, but underneath there was something more urgent: they could talk to the machines. They usually couldn't talk to their parents. The machines didn't judge them. The machines didn't ask them their age.

Bucky's has a wall of standard electronic games, the kind you find in airports and bus terminals, for the hoi polloi, but the serious equipment is three bright Apple II 16K computers with color CRTs and double floppy disks. They cost $1.10 for ten minutes of playing time, $6.60 an hour, and Chris played them for an hour at a time whenever he could assemble the change from allowance and chores and, probably, a judicious turn of dealing a little dope on the side. I didn't inquire too closely into that. Once in a while we talked about it and he assured me he didn't do much more than lay off his own expenses and that only among friends. Some questions you avoid asking your children. Some questions your children avoid asking you.

Chris was playing Star Trek. I don't know a lot about the game except that it was made up over the years by programmers who didn't have enough to do on night shifts around the country and that it could be fairly simple or fiercely complex. It was a sort of progressive labyrinth and Chris was slowly working his way inward. Basically it involved controlling the starship *Enterprise* as it negotiated various navigational and equipment-related problems while fighting off anticipated and surprise attacks from hostile Klingons. The game simulated all kinds of real-world situations—inventory control, resource allocation, war-gaming and so on—and it could be consuming, feeding back (on paper) potent punishments and rewards.

So Chris wasn't exactly all there when Grabka came in. He was off in the galaxy somewhere, making hard decisions about his options maneuvering the *Enterprise* with low fuel. Grabka, Grabka with his ponytail, in a dirty green windbreaker and white open-collared shirt and khakis, the revolver stuck hidden in his belt, stood behind him and watched and Chris didn't even smell him. Breathing over Chris's shoulder. Getting up the nerve.

Then he struck. He reached into his hip pocket for his wallet, for the badge pinned inside. "Chris?" he said. Chris heard him, far away, but the voice seemed less urgent than the problem on the display and he didn't respond. "Chris Wainwright?" Grabka questioned.

"Not now, man," Chris said distractedly, making a gesture. He still hadn't looked around.

Grabka hardened his voice but still kept it low. "*Now*, boy," he said. "This is police business. Turn around."

Chris turned, confused: started to speak: and just then Grabka flipped open his wallet to the badge.

"Narcotics division," Grabka said. "Let's go."

Chris flushed. His age group calls police "pigs" without understanding the malice of the tag; he thought Grabka was one weird-looking pig and for once the tag was right. He was shaken but he had enough presence of mind to ask, "Go where?" Then he registered that Grabka had called his name and added, "How'd you know me?"

"We picked up a friend of yours," Grabka said, putting away his wallet. "We want to talk to you." Grabka figured schoolchildren will do more or less whatever an adult tells them to. He jutted his thumb back over his shoulder, indicating the door.

And dutifully, wondering which of the several dealers he knew had been busted, Chris went. Grabka followed behind. At the door Chris turned back abruptly and it was Grabka's turn to be surprised. "I'll catch my tab later," Chris called to the day manager. Then they were on the sidewalk.

"I'm parked in back," Grabka said, coming up beside him.

"What about my car?" Chris looked at Grabka. What he saw didn't exactly inspire confidence. "Are you arresting me, man?"

They were walking up the alley between the storefronts. The wind blew through the tunnel of the alley, blowing Chris's hair. "This isn't an arrest," Grabka said, imitating that tone of patient superiority the police cultivate. "We've got some questions for you. After you answer them I'll have someone bring you back to your car." He guided Chris by the elbow, picking up the pace. "Let's go."

By then Chris had worked out a scenario. Grabka was an undercover cop. He'd been investigating dealing in Kansas City and he'd pulled in one or more of the dealers Chris knew. They'd fingered Chris. Now it was his turn to finger them. The pig was giving up his cover. His cover explained the way he was dressed and why he was driving—as Chris now saw—a pickup.

Chris believed Grabka because he thought most adults were basically truthful and benevolent. He thought so because he'd grown up around NASA and the space program and I'd been derelict enough not to teach him otherwise. He called policemen pigs, but he trusted them. They were the guys who kept the weird tourists off the lawn during the Apollo mission and cleared a lane through the camper traffic so that he could get to school. If he had any prejudices, they were prejudices against reporters. He hadn't even trusted Paige at first. Reporters were people who broke into his room at night from the patio or who stuck mikes in his face or who tried to bribe his friends to talk about him. Reporters were the enemy, not cops. So he got into the pickup.

Grabka waited until Chris was up on the seat with the door closed. He went around to the driver's side and got in and closed his door in turn. Then he pulled the revolver.

Chris went white. "*Hey,*" he said. His voice cracked.

"Cool it," Grabka said. He fished in the pocket of his windbreaker for the handcuffs, found them, shook them free. "Stick out your left hand," he told Chris. Chris did and Grabka snapped a handcuff over the thin raw-boned wrist. He pulled with the handcuff to move Chris's hand to the right until he could slip the free cuff through the hole in the door arm. "Now your other hand," he ordered. Chris gave him his right hand and he snapped the cuff around that wrist. Then he straightened.

Tears of frustration and fear started in Chris's eyes. "Jesus," he asked, "what's going *on?*"

"I'll fill you in soon, Chris," Grabka said, saying "Chris" intimately as if he'd known my son for years, as he wrote "Reeve" in the ransom letter to gloat over his forced intimacy with me. "For now all you need to know is that everything's going to be all right. No one's going to hurt you in any way. You just sit quiet while we get rolling and then I'll tell you what this is all about. Okay?" And he glanced at Chris while he started the pickup and poor bewildered Chris nodded.

Grabka drove. It was rush hour, people pouring home from work in downtown and midtown Kansas City, everyone going south toward the suburbs. White-collar Kansas City runs straight as an arrow from the river south, dividing off after 47th Street toward Kansas, west. With his wrists handcuffed Chris couldn't have done anything even if he'd wanted to, but if he'd made faces or mouthed "Help!" at passing drivers they'd have noticed his shoulder-length hair and assumed he was just another hairy hippie trying to insult them. They're still fighting that battle in Kansas City, I'm sorry to say. Anyway, Grabka had a gun.

"I represent a political group, Chris," Grabka said after he'd driven awhile.

"I thought—" Chris began.

"That was to make sure you'd come quiet. No, I'm not a cop. I represent a political group. The people need to hear us and for that we need the media." He looked over at Chris and ahead again. "Your dad's a big wheel. We're going to hold you for a little while. You'll be perfectly safe. We're not going to hurt you in any way, okay?" And he looked at Chris once more, radiating what passes with Grabkas for confidence.

Chris swallowed, Adam's apple bobbing, and nodded.

Grabka smiled.

South of town Grabka began threading the network of country roads that led to the burial site. On one stretch of road he was stuck behind a farm truck and they both ate dust. Methodically Grabka worked his way back into the country. Before long they were alone. Still some distance from the site he pulled onto the shoulder and cut the engine. He fished under the seat for a shoebox and hauled it into his lap, then turned to Chris. "I'm going to have to give you a shot," he said soothingly. "It won't hurt. It's just a tranquilizer to make sure you stay calm."

Chris was trying to keep it together, but the muscles of his face weren't cooperating. "Do I have to?" he asked, pleading. "I won't do anything. I swear I won't." Grabka had worked up Chris's sleeve by then. He took out the syringe and unsheathed the needle. "Don't give me a shot, okay?"

"It's just a tranquilizer," Grabka repeated. He wasn't listening. He filled the needle, a jet of clear liquid fountaining above the point, and then with his left hand he shook free a cotton ball he'd soaked in alcohol and wrapped in Saran and leaned across again and wiped the back of Chris's left arm and Chris tried to pull away, straining against the door, but Grabka took hold of his arm and held him still and clumsily jammed the needle and injected the Thorazine.

Chris made a noise. Grabka withdrew the needle, his hand shaking a little, dropped the syringe back into the shoebox, covered the box again and slid it under the seat.

"Now we wait," he said.

Chris was trying to think how to negotiate. "Man," he said, "my dad's a cool guy. If you'll just get in touch with him I know he'd be glad to help you out any way he could, you know? Just call him up, you know, and talk to him." He was looking from Grabka's mouth to his eyes, back and forth, trying to project that deep, hopeful sincerity we all try to project when we're in a bind and need help from total strangers, trying to appeal to the altruism we hope they've got hidden away inside. And getting nowhere—dead Grabka eyes, cruel Grabka mouth with its Lee Harvey Oswald secret smile, the universal secret smile of sociopaths everywhere. Never wanted, much less needed, himself, Grabka felt fantastic when someone needed him and he was in a position to fail them as he'd been failed. Under the secret smile was indignation worthy of Napoleon at Elba that anyone expected help from *him* when he'd wanted help when he was a suffering child and so on and no one had helped *him* and so on and now they could all go fuck themselves, *et cetera, et cetera.* Chris bargained on but he might as well have been bargaining with a wall and then the Thorazine hit and he went rubbery and there began to be gaps in his scanning. It felt like dope without the buzz.

Grabka saw it hit and started the pickup then and drove on.

Chris heard Rush come in somewhere in his head blasting "A Farewell to Kings":

Cities full of hatred
Fear and lies
Withered hearts
And cruel tormenting eyes.

* * *

He heard the lyrics and sang them in his head, but with his body and louder than lyrics he felt the drums, felt himself playing them.

> Scheming demons
> Dressed in kingly guise
> Beating down the multitude
> And scoffing at the wise.

Rush's drummer, Neil Peart, led the group. He wrote the lyrics: *And scoffing at the wise.* They all three wrote lyrics, Geddy Lee and Alex Lifeson too, but Peart wrote most of them and the best.

"Listen up, Chris," Grabka was saying. "You aren't listening." Chris concentrated. They were parked again. "It's got a life-support system," Grabka said. "There's a fan you can use to circulate air down from outside."

"What does?" Chris asked, rattled. "I missed it. I didn't hear. Why don't you just call my dad, man? Why won't you call my dad?"

Grabka stared him silent. "*Listen*, Chris. I'm only going to tell you once. There's a capsule. It's underground. It's got a life-support system. There's a fan. There's a light. If you just use the light once in a while, the fan's good for at least two hundred hours of operation."

"Oh, man, underground. What's that mean, underground?" Chris started to cry, shook his head, shook off tears. He was trying to listen.

"The fan switch and the light switch will be above your head, over your left shoulder. When you get in you should check them. There's food. There's a pad and blankets if you get cold. There's a jug of water down at the foot of the capsule and a tube up to the head. When you get thirsty all you have to do is suck on the tube and you'll have water."

"Shit, man," Chris said, shaking his head, "shit, man, you're going to bury me. I won't do anything. Don't bury me. I'll do whatever you say. Shit, call my dad, man. Call my *dad*."

"Chris," Grabka said, catching Chris's chin and raising his head, looking into his eyes. "You're perfectly safe. You won't get hurt. Soon as your dad agrees to cooperate with my group we'll get you out of there and get you home. It's all up to your father, *comprandee?* You know he'll come through for you so you know you'll be okay. We'll be nearby. But listen, Chris. Don't try to break out of there. There's water. You get it? The capsule's sealed, but if you break through anywhere then water will leak in and you'll drown. You understand?"

Chris nodded against Grabka's grip and Grabka let him go. He was weak, dazed from the Thorazine, and he kept hearing Rush winding up "A Farewell to Kings" like a jet engine winding up, screaming the rhymes in falsetto: *lies*, *eyes*, *guise*, *wise*.

Grabka released the handcuffs from the door arm and locked them in place again on Chris's wrists. He reached across and opened the door and then drew the revolver so Chris could see it and pushed on him, indicating that he should get out. Chris did and Grabka retrieved an olive-drab pack from behind the seat.

They came down off the shoulder, Chris stumbling, stepped across the roadside drainage ditch, scuffed through the autumn leaves in the brushy wood up the rise to the clearing. Chris saw the tarp. Grabka pulled it off. The box was open. "Get in," Grabka ordered, gesturing with the revolver.

Chris was crying. His shoulders shook. He was afraid but he also was sure he was dreaming. It all might have been a song: handcuffs, a clearing in a woods, a grave, a man with a gun, a young rocker going to his death in the autumn of the year . . .

In the autumn of that year
When the man took me away
When I first knew fear
In the autumn of that year

He stumbled down into the box, the man holding his arm. There were groceries at the foot of the box and a white jug. A pillow, a blue foam blanket and on the floor of the box a yellow vinyl mat. The man pushed on his shoulder and he squatted but couldn't keep his balance and fell forward onto his knees. He started crying again and shook his head to stop. Crybaby crybaby. Crying wouldn't do any good. He looked up at the man and held out his handcuffed wrists. The man unlocked the handcuffs and took them off.

"Lie down," Grabka said. "On your back."

"I don't *want* this," Chris said, his voice rising. But he lay down. There was nothing else he could do.

The man covered him with the blanket, reaching down to tuck it around him.

"I'm going to take your picture now, Chris," Grabka said. He found the Polaroid in the pack, set the distance, framed Chris's face and the upper end of the capsule. "Let's have a smile, Chris," he said. "We want your dad to know you're okay."

Chris smiled. The camera flashed and whirred. Grotesque.

"Okay, Chris," Grabka said, stowing the camera and slipping the developing print into his jacket. "Let's see you operate the switches. The top switch is the light." Chris turned it on and off. He flipped the other switch. "Yeah, that's the fan," Grabka said. "Remember not to use the light unless you have to. If you run the battery down you won't be able to get enough air and you'll smother. Keep the light off unless you need it and just use the fan."

Chris was dazed, staring. It wasn't happening. What was happening wasn't happening.

The lid banged shut. He heard the latches turned. Blackness. He started calling. He heard dirt hitting the lid. Clods. Shovelfuls. At his feet. At his waist. Above his head. When it hit above his face he flinched. Covering him up. The sound changed. Dirt was hitting dirt instead of wood. Muffled. It went on. He feigned calm. In a calm voice he called to let him out. He called to get out, get his dad. He called and called and then in the midst of the calling he didn't hear the dirt anymore.

Six

At first I was beyond anger. I reread the note. We had returned to the house by then. Paige reread the note with me. I didn't really store what I was reading except for the bare fact of the kidnapping itself. I had to go back later to see what the note said. All that logic to convince me to keep it private. Grabka's logic, the giddy pedantry of a nasty twelve-year-old. Grabka's idea of a *sting*. I was incredulous the same way someone is incredulous when a tornado takes the roof off right over his head. He looks up where the ceiling was and sees the black driving night and blinks: no way: somewhere else. Even though I knew it wasn't.

"Call the FBI," Paige said. We were standing in the front hall. We'd forgotten where we were.

I looked at her.

"I know," she said, answering my look.

"The dirty goddamned sons of bitches."

She nodded.

"Who the *fuck* do they think they are?" My little leaks of raving. "The Red Commune. The Red Com*mune*. What kind of name is that?"

Paige shrugged.

I guess I took her arm. She told me later I started shaking her. I wasn't shaking her—I wasn't shaking Paige. I was just absently shaking the person who happened to be standing next to me because at that moment she represented the human race and the human race included whatever bloody-minded bastard sons of bitches had kidnapped my son. She pulled free and told me to cut it out. I looked at her again and then I pushed past her into the living room. There wasn't any love lost in the look. I think I wondered what the hell she was doing there. I remembered that she was a journalist and believe me, they piss me off barrels more than they pissed off Chris. That passed too. I sat down on the Eames footstool and Paige knelt in front of me.

"Call the FBI," she said again.

It was seeping in. I was tingling. I heard roaring in my ears. "Why?"

"They help. They're professionals."

Snap judgment: "Fuck that." When the shit hits the fan you do what you always did. My deal was the one-man band. Pride cometh after a fall. I quit drinking on my own because I didn't want to be one of those poor bastards who have to stand up at AA meetings and confess their helplessness. We looked like team players on Apollo. We weren't. We were Lone Ranger nut-cutters except when we had to team something to get the job done. We were about as much of a team as a bunch of world-class milers are when they run off an exhibition relay, all smiles.

"Fine," Paige said. Then a beat. Then: "Are you okay? Can you think it through?"

I was already thinking it through. The adrenalin pumps you up and you make *fantastic* connections. "You bet your ass," I told Paige.

"Fine." Her face was expressionless except that her eyes were wide and there was comprehension in them, offered without comment. Her crisis face, probably. Her Nam face and Jonestown: the look she gave to casualties. She said: "Then the next question is, do you want me to help? I can stay or go, I can help or shut up. You say."

"Stay." Paige wasn't help the way the FBI would be help. More like family. And someone to man the phones.

I read the note again and this time I concentrated.

"It's a straight kidnapping," I said. "Nothing about anything political."

"Yet."

"Yet. Get the gold, wait for their call, make the delivery, wait for them to call in the coordinates on Chris." It still hadn't hit me: that Chris might already be dead. Then it did.

"Reeve? What is it?"

I was seeing the fire, Charlie's hair burning, yellow smoke filling the spacecraft. We ran simulations on everything, even fire. Especially fire. The real thing was different. But Chris was alive. No sons-of-bitching kidnappers would go to all the trouble of inventing that life-support story or comping up that giddy logic. They were too proud of it. Chris was buried somewhere in a box. He'd fallen into a well, only it wasn't one he could climb out of. I was going to have to climb in and get him.

I shook my head. "Listen," I said. "Critique me as I go along."

Paige nodded.

"We need to keep the house phone open for their calls. We need a second phone for our own calls. Let's use Chris's phone for the second phone."

"Fine."

I was looking at the note. "Why the hell is this note *Xeroxed*?" Paige didn't answer. It wasn't a question. I laid the note down on the floor beside me. Paige was facing me, sitting on her heels. I reached out to her. I held her or she held me—whoever needed holding. I guess we were both pros. At disasters and disaster control we were pros. Dry-eyed. Then we let go.

She raised her eyebrows, meaning: next sequence?

"We say nothing to anyone," I said. "If people call on the house phone, I'm out. Whatever."

"Fine."

"I'm supposed to pick up Diana for the weekend tomorrow morning. We won't change that. She can hold off Chris's friends."

"Is that a risk?"

"No."

"Fine."

I couldn't sit still. I got up and went around the couch to the bookshelves and straightened books, working them forward to line them up with the forward edges of the shelves. Then I sat on the arm of the couch. "The money's a problem."

"I have a little."

"If I need it." I counted, starting with my thumb. "This farm's worth fifteen hundred an acre. Less at a forced sale. There's isn't time to sell it. The bank might buy it. There's maybe fifty thousand left on the mortgage. That's seventy thousand max." That was my thumb. Then my first finger: "We've got twenty-five thousand due in accounts receivable at EAI. My share's a third. I could borrow against it. I could probably borrow a hundred thousand around town."

"Your book," Paige said. She'd turned around to face me, tucking her feet under her and leaning her elbow on the footstool.

"That's the serious money."

"How many copies?"

"One-sixty-three last week."

"Thousand?"

"Right."

"At what?"

"Twelve ninety-five."

"Call it thirteen," Paige figured. "At fifteen percent of retail?"

"About two bucks a copy."

"Then one sixty-three times two. Three hundred twenty thousand dollars more or less."

"Less," I said. "I had a forty-thousand-dollar advance."

"Two hundred eighty thousand."

"Not enough." I cleared my throat. "Shit."

"What about the paperback?" Paige asked.

"What about it?"

"Haven't you sold the reprint rights?"

"Should we have?"

"Six months after publication? Yes. Of course."

I turned up my hands. "We ain't."

"That's extraordinary," Paige said. "I wonder why they waited?"

"How much?"

She was staring. Like a lot of bright people I've known, she shut off her face when she was thinking. She came back with: "At least half a million, Reeve. If you signed a standard contract, you get half."

My stomach unknotted. "That makes it." I had to go see Jeremy in New York. I had to get there and back fast. I had to call Cowboy at Houston and pick up Diana in the morning and then I had to take off with Cowboy in one of NASA's beautiful T-38 two-man jet trainers. Every minute belonged to Chris and the T-38's good for seven hundred knots, which is eight hundred miles per hour—Kansas City to New York, halfway across the short end of the continent, in an hour and a half.

A two-by-two box six feet long can seem surprisingly roomy, nearly a walk-in closet, but not if it's pitch-black and escapeproof and buried in a grave. The Thorazine dulled it, but Chris panicked. Wouldn't you? He couldn't see his hands in front of his face. Underground the earth is dark. I've done some spelunking and I know. This dark: the things that live there are blind.

He panicked, beat on the flat hard lid. Remembered what the man, the weirdo, had said about water leaking in—Grabka was lying, the ground was fairly dry, but Chris didn't know that—and stopped his fists, pressed them to his face to comfort himself, pressed his arms together against his chest, made himself compact. And then panic came in a wave and he arched back his head away from his comforting fists and screamed.

He fumbled for the light, found the fan switch and switched it on, switched it off, switched on the light. It shone harsh and white through the grill. He could see the lid above his face in ghastly shadow that confined him, a coffin seen from inside. Vampire shows: Rocky Horror: troll time. Every second of light shortened his life. Without the battery he'd smother. He flicked off the light and felt goose bumps rising on his arms.

He wanted out. He was possessed with wanting out. He couldn't see, but in the darkness that prevented him from seeing he saw the weight of dark earth above his burial. He chanted his panic and cried: *I want out I want out I want out. Let me out let me out let me out.* His nose ran from crying and his sniffing punctuated the chant. Without realizing what he was doing he was making his panic rhythmic and as it became rhythmic it solaced. We improvise tools from whatever materials we find at hand, always. Even time.

He thought he'd never stop. He thought there was nothing else he could do but panic, chant, beg as he knew he was begging. *I want out I want out I want out. Let me out let me out let me out. I want out let me out let me out I want out. Please let me out.* Please *let me out. Let me OUT! I want OUT! LET ME OUT!*

It made him mindless for a time. It made him hoarse and it warmed him. He didn't will the panic away but it went away, helped along by the tranquilizer. Nothing happened abruptly. The terror faded. The chanting came in diminishing bursts. Finally he was clear. He reached down beside him for the blanket and found it and spread it over him and the familiarity of a blanket over him made him calm.

In space, once we realized what was disturbing our sleep—weightlessness—we slept better with a cover, something to hold us down.

By the time his tears dried Chris was ready to check the place out. He spread his elbows until they touched the sides of the box. He raised his knees and found there was room for them. He turned on his side and flexed and found room that way too.

The pad was thin, the floor of the box hard and cold. The blanket felt big enough to wrap completely around and by squirming on the pad, raising his body in sections, he worked it under him.

He propped himself on one elbow, flicked on the light and quickly surveyed the supplies at the bottom of the box: the jug of water and the tube running up beside him with a clamp on the near end; a packet of Hershey bars; a box of breakfast bars; a bag of red Spanish peanuts; Doritos in a yellow sack; a plastic grocery bag of apples; a package of little red boxes of raisins; a roll of toilet paper; a pan with a top shaped like a toilet seat (a bedpan, but Chris didn't know its name; he'd never seen a bedpan before). He switched off the light.

He caught up the water tube and worked the clamp, took the tube in his mouth and sucked. When the water came it was bitter and he almost spit it out, but he forced himself to hold it in his mouth and blow it back into the tube, into the jug. With the water's bitterness he felt panic pushing in.

It was stuffy in the box. Chris switched on the fan. At least he could run the fan. It whirred into life on the other side of the grill and he breathed fresh outside air and his edge of panic eased.

He wished he had a radio. He wished the weirdo had left him a radio.

He wondered: how long before I could get him out? What did the weirdo want me to do? The weirdo'd have to connect with me. I'd have to set something up. Maybe get the weirdo's people on the tube. After that they'd tell me where Chris was and I could get there and dig him out.

That was at least a day. That night and the next day. Chris had gone to Bucky's at four. It was getting dark when they got to where he was in the pickup, maybe six-thirty or seven. It was later now but Chris didn't know how much later. He thought not much. He needed a radio. He needed a way to tell time. He wished he'd worn the wristwatch he'd gotten for Christmas the year before. He didn't wear it because it looked jocky. Jocks wore watches, freaks didn't.

He could figure the time. He could go through the whole scene in real time, the way it was happening. Figure how long each part of it was taking and fill in the time with songs. He knew how much time most of the cuts took that he listened to and played. Like, Rush's "A

Farewell to Kings" ran 5:53, five minutes and fifty-three seconds. "Circumstances" ran 3:42, "a boy alone, and so far from home." What was the last verse?

> These walls that still surround me
> Still contain the same old me
> Just one more who's searching for
> The world that ought to be.

He realized the fan was still running and turned it off. In the sudden silence he could hear himself breathing.

Why was the water bitter?

So the weirdo had shoveled in the dirt and then he'd covered the mound, walked back to the pickup and driven off. It was maybe forty-five minutes into town. The weirdo had the Polaroid. He'd run it by. He'd call. He'd have to call.

Chris figured Grabka was somewhere on the way between Kansas City and the farm. He gave him thirty more minutes to deliver the photograph to my mailbox. He thought that was step one after the kidnapping itself. With anyone normal it would have been, but Grabka was playing games, toying with us, drawing out his debut. First the note. The photograph he sent by mail.

To keep track of time, Chris could sing or play, one or both. He turned on his side and stiffened the first two fingers of each hand into drumsticks and laid down a roll on the side wall of the box and started singing "A Farewell to Kings." The box made an echo chamber. Even in extremity, even at the ends of the earth, the small fine fitnesses of the physical world comfort us. Chris never sounded better.

I parked outside Claudia's house before eight, a little early, pulled on the emergency brake, honked the horn. I'd tried to sleep against the days and nights that were coming and caught at least a few hours, hours broken waking startled to the low light of the music-stand lamp shining on the bookshelves in the living room where Paige and I waited. In the years when the habit of nightly boozing took over my life, after I came back from the moon, I couldn't have handled the emergency I was facing now. I would have stopped the boozing for the duration, you understand—it was a nasty game, not a fatal insanity—but I wouldn't have had the energy reserves. That may have been part of what the drinking was for, sedation. Sedation and deceleration—a way to return through the atmosphere without ablating completely away.

Diana was dawdling and I was impatient. I honked again and saw the shutters open in the bathroom window upstairs and saw her hand waving compliance. Two minutes and she was out the door in jeans and a white sweater, her brown hair that she lightened to a reddish cast with Luminize flaring, her long navy-blue coat open and blowing as she crossed the yard. She was carrying her overnight case.

I rolled down my window. The air was crisp and clean, bright sunlight, the temperature in the thirties but above freezing. "Did you bring your sterilizer?" I called. Diana wore soft contact lenses that had to be sterilized nightly when she took them out, if she took them out—they were comfortable enough that sometimes, unauthorized, she slept in them.

"Sure," she said, opening the Saab's passenger door and slipping in, her case at her feet under the dash. "Why? Are we going somewhere?"

"Hang on," I said, shifting and starting off. Diana was bright, so bright that she topped the intelligence tests at school across the board, and with the brightness came compulsive curiosity. She squirmed now for this mystery, seemingly routine.

"Well?" she said. "Daddy? Why'd you ask?"

"Sit back, sweetheart. Listen carefully."

She sat back. "I can't stand it."

"Chris didn't come home last night."

She glanced at me quizzically. "Maybe he stayed with a friend."

I was wearing a windbreaker over a turtleneck and slacks. I dug in the pocket of the windbreaker and pulled out the ransom note and handed it to her. "He's been kidnapped," I said. Her eyes widened. She almost looked angry—at the word, not the fact. She hadn't had time to register the fact. "I think he's okay. We got this note last night. I'm going to need your help."

"*Any*thing, Daddy." She snatched the note from my hand. "I can't believe it." Unfolding the paper, rapidly scanning. "*Bur*ied? My God, *buried?*" She looked up. "Why *Chris?* We're not rich." She snapped back to the note. "Five hundred thousand dollars in *gold?* Are they crazy?" And she looked up again and I saw in the expressions that flashed across her face her struggle to comprehend what had happened, her struggle against childish terror, her struggle to handle the strangeness of it as she thought an adult would—and, involuntarily and blamelessly, her fascination. "Jesus," she said then, "why *Chris?*"

"It could have been you."

And vehemently: "I wish it *had* been."

"No you don't. Neither do I."

Suddenly there were tears in her eyes. "Poor Chris," she said, shaking her head. "Poor Chris."

"Listen carefully." I'd reached the interstate. I turned up the ramp, heading east. "I think I can raise the money in New York. Cowboy's on his way from Houston in a T-38. I'm going out as soon as I get you to the farm. Paige Elder is there. I want you to help her. She's going to be manning the phones night and day, keeping away callers and waiting to hear from the kidnappers. You can keep an eye on Chris's phone and deal with his friends. We want this kept absolutely secret for now. Don't tell anyone, not even Annie." Annie was Chris's girl friend.

"What *do* I tell her?"

"I don't know. Tell her Grandpa got sick down in Florida and I went to him and took Chris with me."

"He'd have called her."

"I don't know, Diana. I can't worry about it now."

She was looking at the note. If it had been radioactive and glowing cobalt blue it couldn't have seemed more sinister and more compelling. "Why not tell anyone?" she asked me. "Shouldn't you tell the FBI?"

"Use your head. What if the kidnappers found out?"

"What about Mommy?"

"What about her?" I'd honestly forgotten about Claudia. That's how finally separated we were.

"Shouldn't she know?"

"Should she?"

"She's got a right to."

"I don't give a damn about rights at the moment, Diana. The only operative question until this is over is what's good for Chris. It's good for Chris that as few people as possible know. It's good for Chris that only one person at a time make the decisions that have to be made. Do you think your mother and I can work together on this thing?"

Diana couldn't have been clearer. "With Paige here?" she said. "Nope."

"Then we shouldn't tell her."

"I agree, but she's going to be really *pissed* when she finds out."

"There's no reason why she should have to go through all this."

"Why'd you tell *me?*"

"I wanted some family around and I figured you could handle it."

Diana was quiet, thinking, looking away out the window, and then she said, "Yeah, I guess I can."

After I dropped Diana and spoke with Paige I drove back west to Richards-Gebaur Air Force Base south of Kansas City, my old olive-drab nylon flight suit rolled on the seat beside me. The air base was a ghost town since the Air Force had moved its regular personnel to St. Louis, but the local Air Force Reserve unit still maintained the field for training. Cowboy had called Paige to announce his arrival while I was picking up Diana. I saw the T-38 on the field, her sleek, arched fuselage striped NASA blue, as I wound my way onto the base. She was parked elegantly with her canopies up and her speed brake down.

A circle of admiring reservists, pilots and flight engineers, surrounded Cowboy inside the Flight Ops office in the hangar where he was smoking one of his foul cigars and tanking up on coffee. They knew me from past visits to the field, but Cowboy was a fresh face and still NASA and that much more a celebrity. He nodded when I came in the door—it might as well have been a wink of conspiracy—and then lapsed into Wyoming. "Red," he drawled, this Ph.D. astrophysicist, "now ain't you a sight fer sore eyes."

I joined the circle, collecting hands on both shoulders that lifted helpfully as I shook out my flight suit and began pulling it up. "You look just as mean as ever, Cowboy," I said. "You think New York can stand to take on two of us at a time?" He didn't look as mean as ever. He looked older. He was tanned as always, rail-thin as always in his gymnast's compactness, but he was almost completely bald now and his face was far more weathered—wrinkled, aged—than it had been when I saw him last, not that many years ago.

"Shit, Red," said Cowboy, "those suckers will just have to try." He knew I was in a hurry. I'd called him the night before from Chris's room, Rush and Led Zeppelin posters psyching me from the walls, told him what had happened, told him about the money and how I proposed to get it. He looked around his circle of admirers. "You boys want to excuse us?" he asked them. "We'd best be on our way."

Good wishes, hands to shake, from the flight engineers a few autographs for Cowboy to sign and then we were walking around our aircraft on the runway apron making our exterior inspection while the fuel truck topped off the tanks and pulled away.

"Christ in hell I'm sorry to hear about Chris," Cowboy said to me as soon as we were alone. "Anything new?"

We hadn't received the photograph yet. "Nothing. Thanks for coming. I'm sorry to mess up your schedule."

"There's nothing going around Houston anyway with the goddamned shuttle cut back to nothing." We were ready to strap on that aircraft. Cowboy sized me up. "You want to fly this thing?"

Chris or not, I grinned. It was what I needed. If I'd had to fly copilot, sit on my hands, for an hour and a half that morning, I'd have gone bananas. I winked at Cowboy and went up first. There was a spare helmet already on the seat for me. Cowboy went up behind me in the number-two position. The T-38 seats two crew, one behind the other, the pilot in front. They communicate by radio, the mike built into their oxygen masks, the headphones into their flight helmets. On the ground we let our masks hang open to one side to keep our mikes within range.

With our canopies secured we ran through the checklist, Cowboy calling out the items and I confirming them.

"Nosegear pin?" That was Cowboy on the intercom.

I looked into the box below me at my left and identified the pin. "Removed and stowed."

"Seat and rudder pedals?"

"Adjusted." Both of us had to check that item, so Cowboy called back in turn, "Adjusted."

"Circuit breakers?"

"In."

"In." Cowboy. "Gear handle?"

"Down."

"Speed-brake switch?"

"Out." The speed brake is a flap under the fuselage you can hydraulically lower into the airstream to slow down in a hurry.

"Landing-taxi light switch?"

"Off."

"External power?"

"Connected and on."

It all went quickly. We were old hands at flying together. We'd zipped back and forth between Houston and the Cape for years.

"Oxygen system?" Cowboy itemized. "Just figure you've got this baby for the duration," he went on. We could talk in between while one or the other of us was checking an item. "New York, wherever, I'm at your service, pal."

"Thanks, Cowboy. How much do they know in Houston?" I was checking oxygen-regulator levers, pressure gauges and so on.

"I told them I had a personal emergency and left it at that. No sweat. Things are slow. With all the whiskey runs they've made over the years, they don't scream too loud."

"Oxygen system checked."

"Gyrocompass mode?"

When we'd run through the preflight I started the engines, one and then the other—lovely whine—and radioed for clearance. I got it as we were taxiing and rolled into lineup and ran her up and then I cut in the afterburners and we were wheeling on the long runway under a clean blue sky. At sixty knots I disengaged the nosewheel steering and flew the aircraft on the ground, working the rudder pedals and the stick. Twelve knots below takeoff speed I rotated the aircraft ten degrees up, clearing the nosewheel, and we flew off the runway at military power. I raised the gear and adjusted the throttles, two mated handles to my left that I worked with my left hand while I flew the stick with my right, and with fuel to spare for the New York flight and the violence of Chris's kidnapping thick in my throat I kicked us back into our seats in a steep climb all the way up to flight level at 410, forty-one thousand feet. There, high above the earth, riding the thin air eastward, I leveled out, eased the throttles, trimmed the aircraft and settled back to fly. For years it had been my joy. It was bitter joy now, the long way around to bring my son the short way home.

Seven

Air hissed on the fuselage. Less than a hiss: a *shhhhhhhh.* The quiet rub of atmosphere on the skin of the aircraft, as distinctively the sound of high flight as the racket of servos and attitude-control jets was distinctively the sound of space travel. (The LM was worst of all with its walls made of plastic film and foil—the sound like someone beating on a washtub.)

There's a poem called "High Flight," the only poem most pilots know. It was written by a young hero named John Gillespie Magee, Jr., whose father was rector of Washington's St. John's Church, across from the White House. Young Magee joined the Royal Canadian Air Force at the beginning of the Second World War. He flew a Spitfire in the Battle of Britain. It killed him, at nineteen. "High Flight" became his epitaph, not a bad one as epitaphs go:

Oh, I have slipped the surly bonds of earth
And danced the skies on laughter-silvered wings;
Sunward I've climbed, and joined the tumbling mirth
Of sun-split clouds—and done a hundred things
You have not dreamed of—wheeled and soared and swung
High in the sunlit silence. Hov'ring there,
I've chased the shouting wind along, and flung

My eager craft through footless halls of air.
Up, up the long, delirious, burning blue
I've topped the windswept heights with easy grace
Where never lark, or even eagle flew
And, while with silent, lifting mind I've trod
The high untrespassed sanctity of space,
Put out my hand, and touched the face of God.

The final piety's a disguise. Penetrating that, notice how arrogant the poem is. Arrogant and slapdash. Truly a poem for jet jockeys. "And done a hundred things / You have not dreamed of" catches the spirit. It's what I was thinking about as I flew toward New York, away from Kansas City and Chris: arrogance: rebellion: the long reach of consequence that put Chris in jeopardy.

I wanted to be an astronaut for the same reason I'd wanted to be a fighter pilot and then a test pilot, because it was a way to rebel. I didn't know that at the time. I didn't know much of anything except my trade. I learned later, the hard way. I was still learning. Chris's kidnapping began to look a lot like final exams.

Flying fighters and test-piloting had been rebellion, taking risks, doing what other people didn't do and didn't, I thought, dare to do. I figured riding a rocket into space would be even more so. For as long as I could remember, I'd wanted to show people. Every astronaut I knew wanted to show people, except that some were more ferocious about it than others. That's the real explanation for the jet-jockeying and the hot-rodding, and that's why NASA just barely kept us under control on duty and off and especially while we were actually flying a mission.

Truth to tell, none of us was much to look at. None of us was really prepossessing. We dressed badly. We were anything but polished. We were generally narrowly educated. (Obviously there were exceptions. Al Shepard knew all the forks and spoons; Mike Collins was well read; John Glenn was handsome, I guess; Pete Conrad went to Princeton and so on.) The only important top forty we'd made up to that point in our lives was the top forty in risk-taking. We'd grown up misfits and we'd compensated by taking risks. As an artifact of the selection process, we all happened to take the same kind of risks—risks to life and limb in high-performance flying machines—which means we all had the same screws loose.

We weren't really that different from the guy who lets them shoot him out of a cannon. That's the level we were operating on and that's about how much staying power we had with the public at large. Ask any old barnstormer and he'll tell you that when people flock to an exhibition of aerobatics they bring along their spoons to pick up the blood: once we shot out of that Jules Verne cannon and landed on our feet the show was over. The stunt piloting was over. We were supposed to prove it could be done. We did, and what else was there to see?

I'd thought this through before. I thought it through again up there in the brilliant, *shhhh*-ing jet stream on my way to New York. Sometimes past experience confuses the present instead of clarifying it. I was flying to New York to raise money to ransom my son. But I was flying a T-38, not a 727, and that necessarily reminded me of the many times I'd risked my life in experimental aircraft to look down my nose at the crowd—risking leaving Claudia a widow and Chris and Diana fatherless. There's nothing particularly risky about a T-38. I only was confused for a moment deciding if this particular flight was legitimate or another game, another getaway.

I felt guilty, with reason. If, looking for an ever flashier style of rebellion—*flying high*—I hadn't progressed like an addict from fighters to experimentals and then into the space program and then to the moon, I wouldn't have acquired the visibility necessary to be a target for extortion, and Grabka wouldn't have kidnapped Chris.

That sounds farfetched, I suppose, past being past. But I felt that way and morally I was right to. We were rolling for high stakes, most of us—maybe Glenn was rolling for Mother and Country, but then why'd he go into politics? Karl Grabka was rolling for high stakes too. The U.S. put me in a compact, fragile life-support system and sent me off to a hostile environment to measure its genital heft against the Russkies'; Grabka, by a nice economy of coincidence, put Chris in a compact, fragile life-support system and buried him in a hostile environment to quantify in gold bars the nth degree of my vulnerability. The difference is, I volunteered.

"She's pretty out there, isn't she, Red." Cowboy came in quietly on the intercom. He'd sensed that I was preoccupied and so far he'd given me room.

"She really is."

"I wasn't sure you'd remember how to fly this baby. It's been a long time."

"No sweat."

"Roger on that." I hadn't answered his question, so he decided to go direct. "You all right up there?"

"Just thinking it through, Cowboy," I said.

"Be my guest."

"Thanks." I meant it.

Risk-taking served a double purpose. It was a way of rebelling, of showing off, of scaring people who cared for us and of revenging ourselves on those low, stolid souls who—we imagined—looked down on us and took us for granted. At the same time, it served in fact to remove us from the ranks of the ordinary. Laying your bones on the line for a rocket ride certainly removes you from the ranks of the ordinary. It's probably even important to the future of the species, as I told Paige/*Playboy*. But it's not exactly serious, is it. So long as there is poverty, so long as the murder of man by man continues to be sanctioned by human institutions, so long as human beings starve anywhere on earth, you can't honestly claim the space program is serious. And if it isn't serious, then neither were we who served as its eyes and hands and specimens.

We'd taken the ultimate risk in our special corner of the risk business—high-performance flying machines—the ultimate *available* risk, which was going to the moon (you see where the one-way-to-Mars business comes in). Then the measure of what an older generation would have called our spiritual development was: what next? At great expense, for the first time in history, the human race picked us as its representatives and sent us out from the planet, out to where the earth was a disk no bigger than a half-dollar, to look around, on the first leg of a diaspora that inevitably must achieve the stars. What did we do when we got back?

Nothing very imaginative. Certainly none of us was transformed, like St. Paul. But some few of us did well, conventionally speaking. Moved on from obsessive risk-taking into adult responsibilities. Glenn comes to mind again, Mike Collins in a way (Mike took off for Washington and planned the Air and Space Museum and is moving up at the Smithsonian), but most of all Neil Armstrong, who was the definitive astronaut, the type specimen, the first man to set foot on another world and for that reason the only one of us who will truly be remembered down through the ages.

After he got back, Neil could have had—the moon. He'd seen that seductive piece of real estate close up and he didn't want it. He came from Ohio. Wapakoneta. He went back to Ohio, to the University of Cincinnati, and taught engineering. No books, no commercials (until recently—inflation got to him, I guess), no posters or T-shirts, no crackups or religious conversions or politics. He was cool, he was calm, he had a steel-trap mind and vast reserves of what country people call grit, and apparently he understood the historic value of the moon program and was willing to do the work. He also seems to have had a personal interest which was rare in those days of glitter-mongering: to Neil the moon program may have been the ultimate engineering problem. He was that single-minded.

We got two senators, Glenn from Ohio and Jack Schmitt from New Mexico. Glenn was Glenn—I never thought of him as an astronaut, exactly, and of course he didn't go to the moon—and Jack, the one scientist among us who did go to the moon, is excluded by that very qualification from the ranks of the rebels. He learned to fly because he had to, not because he was dying to hang out his tail on the turns.

That's about the extent of it. The rest was potluck: businessmen, some of them competent and some of them just a hair shady; an evangelist or two born again to Jesus (Jim Irwin calls his operation "High Flight"); enough consultants to paper a rec room with business cards; a little bit of aquanatics, a little bit of psychic investigation, some enhanced military careerism; and—my category—some 3-D, meaning drunk, disorderly and depressed. The drunkenness and the disorder came first. The depression came later.

I'm trying to think of an analogy for what it was that got to us—got to me, at least—and what occurs to me is the Spanish fighting bull. Pardon the pretension, but the shoe fits. He's raised in splendid isolation. He's good stock to start with, he's cared for, he runs in his youth in green pastures, he perfects his horn work with his young brother bulls. But he never sees a cape, never sees a matador, never sees the flash of that short, lethal sword until the very hour of his glory.

We weren't quite that isolated. Cocoa Beach was wall-to-wall groupies, full-bodied and reckless, and we had some notion of what fame would hold in store for us from our weeks in the barrel. But month in and month out for years we worked our butts off training and putting the program together. We not only flew the equipment: we helped design and manufacture and then man-rate most of it. We were *busy*. I remember one morning overhearing Chris and Diana playing Office. Chris said, "I'm going to the office." Diana said, "When will you be home?" Chris said, "Two weeks," and Diana never batted an eye.

We were good at flying. We were good at getting ready to fly. It didn't prepare us for afterward. They kill the bulls. Afterward there was very little left for us to do, people thought we were Magic Slates to write their wishes on, and some of us, myself included at the head of the class, found shabbier ways to rebel than high-performance aircraft.

I've made a good job of forgetting those days. Faces converge and one night of drunkenness remembers much like another. Cowboy was with me through some of it, as I've said. He shook himself free sooner than I did.

Women sought us out. Not the Florida children at the Cape, the girls superficially so like California girls but with the swamp of redneck Florida behind them driving them on to the beaches, driving them to wild, fearless, futureless scoring. Not these but women: divorcées and wives, mothers and widows in every city in the land. You got so you could spot them across the room. They stared. They had hungry eyes. They looked as if they could eat you for breakfast and if you let them they did. They marked us for their saviors. We weren't. Outside our specialty, as narrow a specialty as point-kicking in pro ball, we probably weren't as much as their husbands. Some significant minority of the entire U.S. population of women who were thirty or older in 1970 didn't believe that. They were urgent for smart-ass jet-jockey heroes.

Years ago I asked Paige why. Her answer made sense. "They think some of it might rub off on them," she said.

I met a women in Atlanta, at a party. She was thirty-four. She was married. The party was a garden party in the penthouse of an MIT classmate of mine, a rich consultant. He automated assembly lines—cotton mills, bottling plants, you name it. Saved them from the labor unions. In his spare time he was working with an ambitious Atlanta cutter designing an artificial heart.

I don't remember the woman's name. It was spring, the magnolias were blooming and she was invited along as company for me. The arrangement was obvious, so when I'd had a few nice double Black Jacks and gotten loud I swept her up. She sat next to me at dinner, sharing her smooth, stockinged foot, and after dinner I took her with me back to my high-life room at the Hyatt, where everything was clean and expensive. I brought out my bottle; she brought out her poppers; we had us a nice wallow and then she told me her story, no more bizarre than a couple dozen other stories I heard.

She'd met a fine, dark Italian-American. They'd dated. They'd gone all the way. He was passionate. He satisfied her. They saw a life together. They got engaged. They got married. On their wedding night he was impotent. The next time she was able to coax him into bed—weeks later, apparently—he was impotent again, but this time he beat her up for enticing him. It wasn't nice, he said. That had been three years ago. They hadn't had intercourse since. He respected her totally. He treated her the way he treated his mother. It was the old mother-versus-slut syndrome at work. She'd been seeing a shrink. He'd advised her to get a divorce. She was working on it, but her husband had threatened to kill her if she so much as looked at another man.

Maybe that was a true story. I had no way of knowing. I never did know. It was just as likely, so far as I could tell, that she'd made it up. I didn't much care to find out. We all ride Einstein's elevator; who knows what's going on outside? I sent her home to her presumptively homicidal husband well before dawn, set the dead bolt and took the bottle to bed.

I met a woman in Salt Lake City. She was thirty-eight, my age then. Her husband was a judge. She was part of the welcoming committee. She drove me around the sainted city. She drove me out to the Great Salt Lake in the middle of winter when the marina was closed and the beaches bare and the islands hunched in mist and the water dark in its bitterness and we got together in the front seat of her Cadillac, tasting the salt our bodies drew from the air. Her husband had been a fine lawyer and she had loved him very much, but for more than two years now he'd had trouble getting out of bed in the morning. He'd been upwardly mobile, promising, a possible governor or senator someday, and then he stalled. She'd wake him and turn over and go back to sleep and then she'd startle awake to the phone; the court clerk would be calling, ready to open court, and she'd turn over and there was His Honor hiding out, the covers over his head.

Maybe that was a true story too. She wanted to run away with me. She was a beautiful, aristocratic woman of some wealth. I thought about running off with the wife of a judge in Mormon country and ran away from her instead, out to the airport, moving on.

Understand: these weren't lost souls. These were good women—clean, hard-working women whose men should have been proud of them and probably were. But something had gone wrong. They'd followed the rules and the rules had failed them. They were preparing to blow the hatch and bail out. Granted my sample was skewed; granted the ones I met had their parachutes on; but my God, how many of them are there? We'd fan out from Houston in every direction, a crowd of guys, the NASA first string, and faithful and unfaithful alike would come back with tales of incredible offers they'd had and terrible stories they'd heard.

I got the impression relations between men and women aren't in very good shape across the land. When boys in space suits collect the honors ordinarily reserved for a cancer cure they aren't.

It didn't dawn on me until later that I was bailing out too.

Eight miles below me, eight hundred or so behind me, Karl Grabka called the farm. Paige caught the phone on the first ring, answered "Wainwright residence," heard the silence of Grabka's suspicious pause and thought fast. "Mr. Wainwright isn't available," she improvised. "May I take a private message?"

Grabka breathed. Paige heard traffic in the background. He was calling from a pay phone, outdoors. He knew how these things are done. We all do. Television teaches us.

Paige was afraid he'd spook. She kept on. "I'm a friend of his. He hasn't notified anyone. I'm merely answering his telephone. May I take a message?" She could have been FBI. We'd considered that reaction. The note claimed the kidnappers were watching the farm.

Grabka decided to talk. "Where is he?"

She still had to be sure. "May I say who's calling?"

"Don't fuck with me, honey," Grabka spat back. "What's your name?"

"Paige Elder."

He'd read the *Esquire* piece but like most people he hadn't bothered to notice who wrote it. "How'd you get there, Paige?" he asked, warming.

"From the airport. I came in for the weekend."

"When?"

"Thursday afternoon."

"Some weekend, huh Paige?" That was rhetorical; he didn't wait for an answer. "Where's our boy Reeve?"

"He's on his way to New York. He had to go there to raise the money."

"The hell he is."

"Please. I have every reason not to lie to you."

"He must think there's all the time in the world. I doubt Christopher sees it that way."

"He's flying a NASA jet. It's very fast. He should be back with the money tonight. How can he get in touch with you?"

"You keep saying 'money,' Paige. Now, Reeve understands about the gold bars, doesn't he?"

"Yes. Excuse me. I mean gold."

Grabka let up. "Hey, Paige, you sound like a foxy lady. You stay by the phone now and see that Reeve keeps to the rules, okay?" Paige heard the change in his voice as he grinned. "Don't you call me. I'll call you." He clicked off.

She set down the phone nauseous with his greasy familiarity. *Paige. Reeve. Christopher.* She didn't know that the man on the phone was Karl Grabka, she didn't know that he stank, but she imagined Chris confined in a cold, lightless place underground, she sensed that the man on the phone was sick and it seemed to her that she could smell the sickness coming off him in sour waves. She went then to find Diana, for comfort and to give the living room a chance to air.

Grabka, driving again—he'd been aimlessly driving since early that morning—was shaking his head, the objective observer. By his twisted version of things, he was Chris's protector now. He thought it was pretty damned heartless of me to go all the way to New York to raise a paltry half-million dollars in gold while my son was enduring the trauma of living burial. If I screwed up to the point where old Karl had to cut and run, theoretically leaving Chris to his fate, then old Karl would just have to conclude I was a rotten parent.

That's what he thought. This is what he felt: that with his brilliant mind and his powerful body and his two talented hands, using nothing but the simplest tools, he had personally caused a decorated astronaut of international reputation to order up from an agency of the United States government a powerful jet aircraft—probably supersonic, probably costing *mucho* millions of bucks—and fly it across the length and breadth of the land. You can't hardly buy that good a feeling anymore.

Chris had sung. He'd drummed on the side of the box—with his stiffened fingers first, then with his knuckles, then more softly with his open hands, bongo-style. He wouldn't drink the bitter water but when he got thirsty, sometime in the night, he ate an apple. Panic would advance on him in the silence and darkness and he would push it back with singing, with drumming, with sound. Except for sleep he had never in memory known so consistent a silence.

When he had counted enough time, when he knew it was at least late at night, then he knew I knew. I'd seen the photograph. The weirdo had called. I was wheeling around Kansas City waking up television people in the middle of the night. I had to argue with them, convince them. They weren't sure. They wanted to call in the pigs. I said no. I said that was risky. I was an Apollo astronaut, so they agreed.

He could sleep on that. Unwittingly he did, going off so quickly there wasn't time to catch himself. He dreamed he was crowded into a corner. He dreamed he was deaf, entranced in a coffin with hands coming down with a stake and a hammer, and he woke panicked, crying, and tried to sit up and banged his head on the lid of Grabka's box.

And lay crying, his body shaking as he cried, tears lining his cheeks, nose running. After a while he wiped his nose on his turned-back sleeve and bare hard wrist.

The box was stuffy. He'd taken a hell of a chance falling asleep. He flicked on the fan. Its whir was already a sound as friendly to him as the purring of a family cat. He listened to it, feeling then the cold outside air circulating through the grill.

"Fan really kicks ass," he said aloud. It hadn't occurred to him before to talk.

Or to answer. "Hey, talking to yourself, real crazy man."

A different voice: "I don't want this. I don't *want* this."

He switched off the fan. He was lying on his back and to reach the fan switch he twisted to his left. With the switch thrown he continued the motion so that he turned onto his side. He lay on his side momentarily and then continued the turn onto his belly, jerking his arms and legs, and then turned again fully around to his right, twisting the blanket as he went and wadding the pad under him; turned again faceup, letting it out, raging, drumming his feet on the bottom of the box, beating his fists on the lid and his elbows on the sides and his head on the bottom through the wadded pad. "Goddamn dirty son of a bitch! Asshole! Fucking peckerwood! Shitface! Shitty baby, shitty baby! Fuck you, you cocksucker! Oh fuck you, just *fuck you!*" The tears that came this time were tears of anger.

"Ah do believe you ah fucked, Mistah Chrissie," he told himself when he'd calmed. Talking helped. The box reverberated; he sounded like a DJ blasting through a wall of kick-ass speakers.

He squirmed, straightening out the pad and the blanket. When the pad wouldn't come free under his shoulder he flurried once more briefly in tantrum.

Wondering what time it was he lay still, monitoring himself the way we do. He wasn't aware of it, but he was beginning to use his body for a clock. He sensed that he hadn't slept long; underneath the hyperactivity of panic he was bone-tired.

"Go to sleep and you'll smother, dimbulb," he said.

"What the fuck do you know about it?"

"Co_2's heavier than air. It collects down here."

"Hot air rises."

"That's why it gets stuffy, right? What an asshole."

"Am not."

"Are too."

"*Am not.*"

"*Are too.*"

"Takes one to call one."

When he stopped talking the darkness closed in. When he talked there was something in the box like light. Sound like light. He heard music sometimes like light when he was high.

He wished he had a joint. If there was ever a time for the warm, drifting mellow of a j it was then.

"Ain't no j."

"Man dint leave us none."

"Beat all."

He dropped the clowning and wondered seriously if he could sleep. As soon as he asked himself the question he knew he didn't dare take the chance. He was afraid he'd run the battery down if he ran the fan while he slept.

So to stay awake he sang, improvising:

> Ain't no j.
> Man dint leave us none.
> Beat all.
> Ain't no j.
> Man dint leave us none.
> Beat all.
> Ain't no j.
> Man dint leave us none.
> Beat all, beat all, beat all beat all beat all.

Screwing around on public-appearance tours was a grim way to rebel. I didn't realize how grim it would be until I got into it, I was that primitive. The Florida girls hadn't been grim. They were all very much alike, featureless reincarnations of spring vacations on the beach at Fort Lauderdale. They had warm, tanned skin and they came soft on soft blankets in the sand under a sky bright with the stars of Apollo navigation. The Florida girls were mostly too young to have problems worse than acne and cramps. They weren't even interested in romance. They wanted to score; we wanted to score; bubble-gum card collecting met high-tech decompression and the feeling was neutral.

So, being stupid (but I learn fast), I didn't expect to be hauled all unwittingly into the gladiatorial cockpit of other people's marriages. That began to look like work. After seven years of slugging away single-mindedly to get to the moon, work was the last thing I wanted more of. I *do* learn fast. I hung up my uniform on married women and narrowed the field down to singles.

I narrowed the field when I was sober enough to know the difference. For a time there after I got back, not very often. Alcohol was the other lean mean rebellion machine. I'd always been an occasional drinker, taking my social three or four highballs most happy hours but once in a while—every few weeks—hitting the bottle hard. Cowboy sat up with me sometimes. He'd follow me for a while, interested in the sparks I was generating, and then as my tongue thickened he'd get bored. It turned Charlie off. He didn't approve, especially when we were training for our own mission, so he'd go on to bed. The Florida girls politely passed out, to be wakened later by this moaning madman burrowing his nose into their muffs.

Every few weeks became every other day after I went to the moon. I learned to pick up the first drink of the evening with both hands. Then I'd soar: magic thoughts, magic plans, the sky was only the beginning. I went to Mars a lot. I saw exactly how to get there. I invented new navigation systems. I completely disassembled and reassembled NASA, increasing its productivity a thousand percent.

One line of complaint came through the bingeing often enough to convince me it was the central theme. "Goddamn it," I'd bitch, "people expect me to be *adult* all the time." I swore I couldn't be. It hurt too much. It was too lonely. It was everyone else leaning on my shoulder and no shoulder for me. And I still don't know—maybe it was. Or maybe I was too afraid of losing control to lean. With the whiskey I had an excuse to lean: I was too drunk to stand up. I could black out and blame the loss of control on alcohol. Dr. Jekyll, meet Mr. Hyde.

I figured Paige would be my shoulder. She was, but not the way I'd expected. She was strong for me, but her strength consisted in part in not putting up with Mr. Hyde. When Mr. Hyde put in an appearance she sent me home or went to bed. When Mr. Hyde called her long-distance from wherever in the world he was appearing nightly—Bangkok, Nairobi, Moscow, Copenhagen—she hung up. We split because I wasn't ready to be treated that way. Paige obviously expected me to be *adult* all the time.

Otherwise our time together was fairly fantastic.

To say it simply: when I got back from the moon I went a little crazy. I called it decompression. It was. We were a freakish combination of corporate executive, professional athlete, engineering troubleshooter and media event. The pressure was god-awful. I'm surprised more of us didn't snap or crack. Eagle Scouting doesn't prepare you for that kind of dogfight, even on laughter-silvered wings.

The space program, through no fault of its own, took what we wanted most—the number-one high performance of high performances, which happened to measure a deep rebellious flaw in our personalities—and split it along the seam and turned it inside out. We stung for a long time and we required a long time to heal.

I used poultices of whiskey and jellyroll. I came through, not without hurting other people. With hindsight I can see I might have spared them. In fact I didn't. I used to think that was a psychological matter. Now I think it's a moral matter. I've earmarked a certain amount of the rest of my life to making it up.

If you understand that the look on Chris's nine-year-old face the night I walked out on his mother was an acid test of fatherhood, an acid test I failed, then you understand why I sorted through everything again on my way to New York.

Cowboy and I talked, casually. Not much. We had catching up to do but we figured it could wait. We approached La Guardia. I checked in with flight control. It was Saturday and traffic was comparatively light for LGA. We opted for a low approach, throttled to seventy-five percent and dumped the speed brake, descended fast and straight cutting back to two-five-oh knots below ten thousand, leveled at minimum and slowed to one-seven-five, made our final approach, dropped flaps and then gear, flared and touched down nicely, rolling. A sunny Saturday in October. Twelve thirty-four eastern daylight time. I'd called ahead. Jeremy was waiting for us outside the terminal in a limousine.

Eight

When Karl Grabka woke that morning in his gray bed I'd guess he felt fear first, fear that he'd done something irrevocable. He'd been a loser everywhere else—why shouldn't he be a loser in this? It must have taken a second or two for his protective mechanism to snap into place. That first numbing sense of fear—like the first cold breath of space—would have actuated it. He got up uncertain, not yet elated, still unsatisfied with his plans.

So he drove around. Any number of people do that when they're nervous. It was eight o'clock Saturday morning and the streets were almost empty and then it was nine o'clock and the traffic of clerks to Saturday-morning stores made incoming lines at stoplights. Grabka bought a bag of glazed doughnuts and a thermosful of coffee at a Winchell's and ate the doughnuts in the pickup, wiping his fingers on the front edge of the seat.

He didn't know yet what I'd do. Con that he was, basket case that he was, he sentimentalized the happy childhoods of people like Chris (when he wasn't dismissing them contemptuously as weak, sissy, productive of fags and chickenshits), so it never occurred to him that I might refuse to pay—it never occurred to me either—but he wasn't sure if I'd keep everything private or call in the FBI.

Grabka was selling me Chris. That's what it came down to. It was really almost an experiment: ascertain by destructive testing the monetary value of a father's love for his son. Obviously Chris was the son in question, but by the transformations of the experiment Grabka was also the son. Chris's value to me translated into his ransom—in a sense, his inheritance. And Grabka would receive that inheritance in Chris's place. It was tainted, because force was involved, but Grabka was too thick-skinned to lose any sleep over that. As far as he was concerned, all the gold in Fort Knox wouldn't compensate him for his sufferings anyway. Plus, it had to feel good to coerce a man—I mean me—he perceived to be powerful enough to stand in for the father he dreamed of who was so much more than the father he'd had.

Lord deliver us from the dreams of young men. Robert Goddard, the rocket pioneer, dreamed at nineteen of rockets that would deliver the human race to a happier home at the dying of the sun. Maybe they will; in the meantime we have the ICBM. Karl Grabka, the Kansas City cowbird, dreamed of realizing on earth his vision of perfect love and Chris was buried, cut off. I'd gladly have helped the bastard apply for a grant, you know?

Driving, Grabka was thinking that Chris had seen him. The people in the computer place had seen him. If the lumber for the capsule was ever traced, the people at the lumberyard had seen him. One of the things he had to do was figure out a disguise.

He rubbed his chin. Believe it or not, he shaved. He'd shaved that morning. He could let his beard grow. Better yet, he could shave his head. The Kojak look. He liked it. A lot of niggers at the joint had shaved their heads. They looked real macho. If he let his beard grow and shaved his head no one would ever recognize him.

Later on, he thought—unwinding it—when he had the gold, he'd do more. He'd hire the best plastic surgeon in the country to reshape his nose, change his prints. They got you on prints. They had voice prints now too but no one had him on record yet. He'd need to be careful with the phone.

He ought to buy himself an electric razor.

There was a Skagg's drugstore ahead of him on Main. He could see its yellow tower with the broken clock. When he got there he turned off the street into the parking lot and went in. The place was almost empty, just the clerks in their red coats and a couple of bluehairs blocking the cosmetics aisle. He crossed to the magazine rack in the front of the store to browse. Plenty of time. Skagg's had a lot of magazines, odd ones like *Fusion* and *Mercenary* plus all the car and bike and boat and ski and gun and muscle mags plus the girlie mags. Grabka thought the girlie mags were a joke. Once you'd seen the real thing, all the way, they were just a joke. Catty-corner across from the Skagg's, a block down, was an adult bookstore that had the real skin mags. Something else he'd do would be to set up a deal to make skin flicks. He'd pick the girls and check them out himself to make sure they were hot enough and knew what to do. He'd probably have to direct. Even with the big flicks like *Deep Throat*, except for a few like *Behind the Green Door* they were lousy. They almost never showed the women getting off, just the men.

The new *Omni* was out. Grabka took it with him to the small-appliance counter and looked over the electric razors inside the glass case. He liked the Norelco. No one showed up to help him. He stood waiting, turning through the *Omni*. Then he noticed the bell on the counter and tapped it and a woman at the lunch counter with black hair and a hard face slipped off her stool and hooked her thumbs into the pockets of her red jacket and came over.

The woman showed him the Norelco. He told her he'd take it and then he realized he'd need a pair of scissors too. She pointed him to the notions aisle and he found a pair of sewing shears and came back. She punched the prices into the cash register. Grabka undressed her mentally while he waited and decided she'd be okay. Her hands were okay and she had nice long fingernails even if her face was hard.

He paid her. She put the bills on the ledge of the register and made change. When she closed the change drawer she tore off the register receipt and after she'd loaded the razor in its box and the scissors into a brown paper sack she folded down the end of the sack and stapled the receipt onto it. Grabka noticed a multiple-sclerosis box on the counter with a picture of a crippled child. A crippled child was a sad thing. He dropped the coins the woman had given him into the box for multiple sclerosis.

He went out the back door, the way he'd come in, into the parking lot. There was an outdoor phone against the wall of the building near the street. After he'd tossed his sack into the pickup he crossed to the phone and fished two dimes from his pants pocket and dialed.

That was his call to the farm, the call Paige took. It elated him. He walked back to his pickup with a bounce.

He was curious about Paige. He'd meant to return to his apartment and shave his head. He put that on hold, turned south out of the Skagg's parking lot and drove the half-hour drive to the farm. Past the front gate on the road up the next hill—the far slope of the creek valley—he pulled onto the shoulder and parked. He'd added a pair of cheap binoculars to the pack with the camera and now he glassed the house. He was looking for the FBI. He hoped he'd see Paige, but she was inside and out of view. The mail carrier came inching up the hill, driving from the right front seat of his car. Grabka started up and took off.

As long as he was out south he decided he might as well check on Chris. Chris wasn't all that far away. It took less time to go from the farm to Chris's location than to come from Grabka's apartment to the farm.

No FBI: he was happy now. The gold bricks were the smartest part of it. Half a million green in small bills had to be too bulky and almost too heavy to carry, not to mention the serial numbers. The gold was perfect as far as getting away was concerned. The trouble was going to be selling it. Somehow he'd have to melt it down into smaller pieces like little bricks or coins. Once the word was out everyone'd be looking for the full-size bricks.

He didn't know yet what he'd do about that. With different looks he'd be able to slip out of Kansas City easy. He had enough cash to go all the way to Mexico. He could decide about the gold there. The chilibellies worked with silver. They could melt gold. He'd have to be careful. They were real animals and they'd cut him into little pieces if they knew all the gold he was carrying.

When he thought of the double cross they'd pulled on him in Bogotá with the cocaine he could do a little cutting himself.

Coming in from the east he had trouble finding the road that led to Chris. He passed it twice, turning back and hunting, before he recognized it.

He stopped at the edge of the clearing. The tarp was still in place. He thought about listening at the end of the duct pipe but something kept him where he was. He didn't really see Chris in that grisly burial anymore. He knew he was there but he blocked thinking about him. He excluded him from the fairy tale. Why talk ye of graves? Yea, space commander Reeve Wainwright roared even now in a fast jet to New York to return to the young genius Karl Grabka three glowing gold bars.

Driving back to his apartment he let the pretty pictures out. He needed the plastic surgery and tailored clothes. He'd convert the gold to pesos and open an account in a Mexican bank. Then he could cross back over into the States and draw on the Mexican account. He wouldn't come near Kansas City. Kansas City was the asshole of the universe anyway. He'd go someplace like San Diego or L.A. Set himself up as a kind of futurist. Buy some commercials on TV so people would hear about him. Get seen in the right places.

He'd meet beautiful women that way. They'd catch on that he had money and go for him.

He'd get some of the gold made into rings and chains. Maybe a big bracelet for his wrist and a watchband.

Change his name to Gold. Karl Gold would sound Jewish, so just Gold.

He'd find a woman worthy of him. She'd be beautiful, hot, a little crazy, ready for anything, on his side all the way. She wouldn't care how many other women he brought in with them and she'd do whatever he asked.

He wouldn't have a church exactly. Just an organization. He'd tell people how perfect the world could be and they'd see he was right and they'd want to work with him to make it happen. He'd start with one or two and keep growing until he had thousands. They'd have to pay in twenty-five percent of everything they made.

It might have to be a church for the tax angle.

The Gold Way. That's what he could call it. That was just about a million-dollar name. The Gold Way.

Dreaming along, Grabka arrived back at his apartment building. He parked, took his sack of barber gear, locked the pickup and strolled along the sidewalk to the front door. He felt great. He was alive to the day. He went in to the continuation of his destiny like a novice going in to the sanctuary to take his final vows.

After Grabka's call Paige climbed the stairs to Chris's room. She found Diana lying on Chris's bed—it was carefully made: Chris was almost compulsively neat—staring at his drum set silhouetted against the front windows. Paige didn't speak. She was hearing Grabka's voice, replaying the repellent call. She sat on the bed and took Diana's hand.

Diana studied her. "What's wrong?"

"He just called."

"The *kidnappers* just called?"

"Kidnapper, I think," Paige said. "I think there's only one."

Diana turned onto her back to look up at Paige, scooting with her feet on the bedspread. It was something a child would do and a woman wouldn't; Diana was both, the two intermingled and the transition not yet made. "How come?"

"The way he talked. At least I don't think he's part of a terrorist group."

"I *hate* him," Diana said.

Paige squeezed her hand. "He didn't say anything even remotely political."

"What did he say?"

"He said he'd be in touch. He was surprised your father went to New York."

"What'd he expect? He didn't think Daddy could come up with half a million dollars in Kansas City, did he?"

"So it appears. He was relieved to hear Reeve was trying to raise the money." Paige shook her head, correcting herself. "The gold. He wanted to be sure it would be gold."

"What a *reep*."

"What's odd—I've seen it before and it constantly surprised me—is the intimacy a crisis forces on everyone. I wonder why. I wonder if it doesn't facilitate communication. I sensed his relief that we were actually doing what he set out to force us to do. As if he were a servant who decided to rob the family and couldn't stop saying 'Yes sir' and 'No ma'am.' Before it's done we'll know his strengths and weaknesses and he'll know ours."

"Like what?"

"For one, his pretensions. The note was incredibly, grotesquely pretentious. For another, his emotional damage that lets him do this ugly thing to another human being without guilt. On our side, how much we value Chris. How much your father is worth."

Tears welled in Diana's eyes.

"You're close to Chris," Paige said quietly.

Diana nodded and the tears broke and traced. "I feel like I'm with him," she said thickly. "I feel like I'm buried with him." She blinked at Paige. "Do you think I could be picking up his ESP?"

"At least empathy."

"We're *so* close. I always know what he's feeling. He's used to having his way. You know? He's pretty selfish." She shook her head. "I'm not putting him down. It's just the way he is." She sniffed hard, sniffing back the tears. "He's got to be madder than *hell* part of the time because someone is controlling him and *scared* as hell part of the time because of where he is. Part of the time just crazy. *I'd* be. I'd be crazy *all* the time."

"Is he up to it?" Paige asked quietly. She sensed Diana's intelligence. She didn't ask her by way of making conversation. She trusted her judgment.

Diana started to wipe her nose on her hand, looked at Paige, thought better of it, sat up, swung her feet off the bed beside Paige and crossed the room, her feet padding on the bare oak floor, to the bathroom. Paige heard her blow her nose. She came back into the room touching below one eye and then the other with a Kleenex. She smiled in apology. "I smeared my mascara," she said. And taking up the question as if there had been no interruption: "I was thinking about that before. He dug out the well for Daddy last summer. He told me it was really a kick." Diana flopped onto the daybed-couch Chris had arranged at a right angle to the bed. "He could see out. He said he could see the stars in broad daylight. I go, 'Uh-*huhh*,' and he goes, 'Come on down and I'll show you.' No *way* I was going down there. So yeah, he can probably handle the burial thing. He's got to be scared, but he's got to know that Daddy's going to get him out." She looked at Paige. "If the guy wanted to hurt him he wouldn't have gone to all the trouble to make up a story about a capsule, right?"

"Yes," Paige said. "I assume so."

"So it's just up to Chris to keep his head together, and it's up to us to handle the phones, and it's up to Daddy to get the gold. Right now what matters is being really *for* Chris. *Hoping* for him. I just think he'll *know* if we are."

"I do too," Paige said. She didn't, but she was a long way farther down the road than Diana, and she knew at least that Diana would know.

Diana smiled at her. Paige was someone she admired. She felt especially close now. "How come you were here?" she asked.

Paige smiled back. "*Playboy* sent me to do an interview."

"With *Dad*dy?"

"Yes."

"Is he *that* big?" Diana came up onto her elbow, supporting her head with her hand.

"His book," Paige explained. "Energy and the moon both."

"Yeah. I forget."

"Didn't Chris tell you I came in? Thursday afternoon?"

"Just that you were here. He didn't tell me why."

"Maybe he didn't know. I don't recall discussing it."

Diana nodded, her forearm moving with her head. "He knew. He just didn't bother *tell*ing me. That's what I mean about him. That's why I think the hardest thing for him is going to be getting mad. I guess if he's buried in some kind of capsule he can't hurt himself, but he *really* gets mad. It even scares *me* sometimes and I'm used to it. Like, when he's driving us to school he cusses all the other drivers. He drives too fast. He's a *ter*rible driver because he gets so mad all the time. Is there any way he can hurt himself?"

Paige turned up her hands.

They were silent together, wondering, and that faded and there was awkwardness.

Diana moved it on. I'd tried to train both my children to trust their feelings. It was something I learned late. "I love your eyes," she said to Paige. "How do you do them?"

Paige thought it was the wrong time for makeup lessons and frowned and then she thought: why not? "I use a lightener underneath. That's probably what you're noticing. That plus the outlining. Would you like me to show you?"

Diana hadn't missed the frown. "It's okay, isn't it? I'm not forgetting Chris. If I keep busy maybe I won't get so *crazy.*"

Paige stood, holding out her hand. "I know you're not. Come on."

Walking to the other end of the upstairs hall, to my bedroom where Paige had her bag and her small makeup case, Diana asked, "What happens with the *Playboy* interview?"

"I suppose when this is over we pick up where we left off."

"It'll be a lot bigger story now, won't it."

"I hadn't thought." Paige remembers blushing then. "Yes," she told Diana, "it will be."

Chris was fighting that morning to stay awake. Through the night he'd thought his worst problem would be waiting. Staying awake was worse. He ached. He felt drugged, not with the injection now—that had worn off hours ago—but with his body's natural urge to sleep, the healthy urge of a healthy teenaged boy. He could hardly fight it anymore. Shaking his head, pinching himself, sucking bitter water from the jug at his feet to wet his mouth and his face worked less and less well. He sensed the shortening intervals between the points when he fought sleep the hardest and he could project the coming time when he wouldn't be able to fight it anymore, when the intervals would merge.

It made him think.

He didn't know how long the battery would last. The weirdo had said the fan was good for a week. He hadn't said it was good for a week if it ran all the time.

Then he didn't dare go to sleep with the fan on.

Unless. If there was any other way to move the air, he could risk the fan now.

He turned onto his belly so that he was looking directly at the grill in the partition. Then he switched on the light.

He flinched, seeing white and then seeing red pain as he shut his eyes tight against the brightness. He let his eyes adjust and slowly he opened them.

The grill was aluminum. A sheet of thin aluminum cut into three small panels of strips, the horizontal strips bent out at their lower edges to make vanes that directed the air flow downward. Behind the aluminum some kind of screening.

He worked one strip. It was thin and soft and it easily tore away. He switched off the light and in the darkness he tore away all the strips from the central panel, making a hole large enough for his hand.

The screening was aluminum too. Chris pushed it up and out of the way with two fingers.

He switched on the light again, this time anticipating the glare, squinting. Through the hole he could see the light, the battery, the fan and the air pipe. The pipe ran in through the top of the box. It was nailed to the bottom of the box and the fan was nailed inside it, blades facing out.

If the battery ran down, he could pull the pipe through the vent and breath directly into it. He ought to be able to move enough air that way to breathe.

Then he could run the fan and sleep.

These things happened at more or less the same time—about twelve-thirty Kansas City time, one-thirty New York—that Saturday: Paige and Diana, subdued, sat down to lunch at the farm, lunch of chunks of orange and avocado tossed with yogurt; Chris, having first twisted the six vent strips he'd torn from the grill into two reasonably stiff five-inch drumming instruments and drummed on the side of his imprisoning box to relax after having managed to do something to control his situation, fell gratefully asleep to the hum of the fan; Karl Grabka emerged into the sun of the grassy yard behind his apartment building whitely, grotesquely bald, imagining himself disguised; and Jeremy Utter, Cowboy and I arrived at the littered curb before the expensive modern offices of my publisher—as mean a place for prospecting as any I can think of, but there we were.

Nine

In the elevator, incredibly, Jeremy dropped a bomb. "Red? One caution," he announced. "I haven't told Chuck yet."

"Jesus H. Christ, why not?" Obviously Jeremy knew about the kidnapping. I'd alerted him the night before. But Chuck was his boss and my publisher, Charles A. Hyerding, the man who was supposed to be in charge of the money, whom Jeremy had called in on a Saturday from God knows where. And Hyerding didn't know.

Jeremy was surprised I was surprised. "You wanted to keep it quiet."

The elevator stopped abruptly at the seventy-sixth floor and we lifted low-G on our toes and then settled.

"Not *that* quiet. Not quiet from the guy who's got to hand over the money." The doors opened onto a darkened reception area—thick beige carpeting and shadow-box book displays shadowy on the walls.

"Not to worry." Instinctively Jeremy had quieted, or maybe it was the carpeting. "Chuck's an independent cuss. No telling what he'd have done if I'd tried to handle it by phone. He might have called the FBI. This is better. This way you can interface with him *mano a mano*."

I looked past my editor to Cowboy as we left the elevator. Cowboy rolled up his eyes.

"The point is," I told Jeremy, "we've lost a morning. He could have alerted the bank. But okay, we can start where we are. We've got to *move*, you know?"

Jeremy took the lead, his hands going to his pockets, and I'd swear I saw him flinch on "*move*," and over his shoulder he said, "Actually, Chuck insisted on giving you a lunch."

Cowboy grabbed my arm. I don't know what I was ready to say, but it shut me up. Jeremy looked back to gauge the effect of his announcement and saw my face and scuttled ahead, his legs working out in front of his body.

"It won't take any longer," he said, his voice off.

"It can't," Cowboy said evenly, riding shotgun. "Red's got no time."

Jeremy turned left down a long hall. Double doors at the end. They were opened to a sitting room. "The dining room's here," he said. "It won't take any longer to talk to Chuck over lunch. You have to eat."

The room, the company's private dining room up high in a blank modern office building, looked to have been imported in one piece from a British club: threadbare Orientals on the floor, floor-to-ceiling bookcases with a fair number of leather-bound sets, paintings of noble folk, reproduction antique love seats and chairs. Hyerding was standing with a glass of something, waiting for us. And, shit, some guy with him, a stranger. I'd hoped he'd be alone.

Hyerding's height reminded me that Cowboy and I were smaller men and that taller men usually command in the United States. He was six three or so, broad-shouldered, tanned, handsome, with silver-gray hair, dressed in what even I could recognize were handmade duds—shirt and tie and suit and shoes, probably shorts and socks as well. He could afford to grin and as we came in he gave us a big one. We'd never met. We'd talked on the phone and I'd had a letter or two.

Jeremy introduced us. The sidekick's name was Marc Lowe. He was Hyerding's special assistant. Sallow. Mid-thirties. Sunken chest and dead-fish handshake. Thick glasses in black frames. Oiled hair. I could guess and I did: the financial man, the guardian of the treasury. Lowe was all that and more, as it turned out.

Hyerding essentially ignored Jeremy. After the intros and the small talk he steered Cowboy and me to chairs and sat us down. A black man appeared in a white waiter's jacket and took drink orders—what the hell, might as well splurge, I had what Cowboy in more relaxed circumstances liked to call Pierre water, Cowboy had a CC

Pres: a Canadian Club Presbyterian, that is, half water, half Seven-Up.

It was Hyerding's style, or Hyerding's con, to act as if he'd known you all his life: to meet you as if you both knew how superior you were to the poor bastard hangers-on you had to put up with. No hellos or how-are-yous. A wink, a manly grip on the upper arm—the sort of thing you'd get from your best friend if you moved in the brushed-jeans set and had best friends. I'd seen the style before. It was a favorite power style. Lyndon Johnson used it on people he didn't own. A lot of politicians used it, but Hyerding was better at it because he had more background. Not many politicians know enough to buy their suits hand-cut on Saville Row. Not all that many politicians can read without moving their lips. I swear they liked the Apollo program most of all because they could follow it not in thick GPO reports but right there on the color TV.

He wasn't that much older than Cowboy and me, Hyerding wasn't—maybe mid-fifties. He looked as if he played a lot of tennis. I guess it's a rule in New York that publishers have to play a lot of tennis. Anything that takes up expensive surface area is desirable in New York. Hence tennis, handball, interior courtyards, sculpture gardens, Central Park.

"We're damned proud of that book of yours," the man said to me for openers. "Not everyone around here saw its potential."

I wanted to get down to cases, but Jeremy spoke first. "The Executive Committee had its doubts. The attitude was, 'solar doesn't sell.' Chuck dialogued with them and brought them around."

"I'm glad," I said to Hyerding. "Thanks, Chuck."

He grinned: no problem. "They're a good bunch. It's part of the process. Jikokuno's just damned open about everything, only they have to be clued to the stateside potential."

"Jikokuno?" Cowboy said. "The Japanese outfit?"

Jeremy said, "They're actually multinational."

"It's a marvelous book," Hyerding said, coming in at an angle. "You've shaken Washington. I understand Ted might be calling you."

How the hell did he hear about Kennedy? "Chuck—" I started.

Knowing I wondered, he winked at me. "We keep our spies peeled."

Jeremy laughed at that. Nearsighted Marc Lowe watched us like a bank security system.

Cowboy nodded encouragement and I tried again. "Chuck, when

Jeremy called you he couldn't explain why I needed to see you on such short notice."

"It was time we got together," Hyerding said.

I kept going. "We need to talk about money. My son was kidnapped last night. I came here to raise the ransom. I don't have much time."

Not a blink from either of them—Hyerding or Lowe. Maybe Lowe's eyes got wider.

Either Hyerding was the coolest guy in town or it went right past him. "With a book like *The Coming Solar Time*," he said, "money's just not going to be a problem."

"Great," I said. I told him about the note. I told him about the so-called capsule with its homemade life-support system. "Cowboy flew up this morning from Houston in a T-38," I finished. "If you can help us we can be back in Kansas City tonight."

"I'm behind you one hundred percent," Hyerding said decisively. "What kind of money are we talking about?"

Jeremy came in. "Half a million, Chuck."

Lowe had whipped a miniature notebook out of his inside jacket pocket and was taking notes. There was a little credit-card-sized calculator strapped onto the cover of the notebook.

"In gold," I added.

"Hmm," Hyerding hummed. He looked to Jeremy. "How many copies of *Solar* have we sold?"

"Better than one hundred fifty thousand," Jeremy said.

Hyerding nodded in my direction, acknowledging. He was about to wink but he remembered we were talking about a kidnapping and aborted it. Back to Jeremy. "How did we do on the reprint?"

Jeremy's eyes bulged. Truth. The color drained from his face. "Oh my God," he said to himself. He raised his hand as if his head were coming off, fingers spread to catch it. "Oh my God," he said again, shaking his head now and making a fist—he looked like someone getting ready to give blood. His color returned. "I don't know how, Chuck, I honestly don't know how, but we forgot to auction it."

That at least penetrated Hyerding's plating. For a fraction of a second he was out in the open, glaring at Jeremy with total contempt; then he snapped the cover back into place and beamed benevolence at me. "True to the modern tradition," he said, ruefully tossing his handsome head. "And they say we're a commercial house." He paused. Lowe's fingers flew on the little calculator now as if he were reading braille, and Hyerding looked at his notebook and his numbers before he went on. "What other sources have you tapped?" he asked me.

I should have known right then.

"None," I said. "I figured this would be the best shot. I came straight here."

"Well advised. I think you know how we feel about you. Now, have you contacted the Bureau yet?"

"You mean the FBI?"

He nodded.

I explained why not.

"I have friends in the Bureau" was his response. "I'd be glad to give them a call."

He hadn't listened. "Chuck? Listen. Right now what's important is the money. I'm due maybe two hundred eighty thousand dollars on *Solar* for the hardcover sales—"

"Less retained allowance for returns," Lowe said automatically. He didn't even look up from his notebook.

"Whatever. That's a good chunk of what I need. The question is, can you come up with the rest of the half million on the strength of the paperback, reprint, rights? They've got to be worth half a million. I'd be glad to sign a personal note or whatever you'd like me to sign."

Hyerding beamed around—at Jeremy, at Cowboy. The look said: you see what decent, honest people our authors are? "I wanted to puke," Cowboy told me later.

But before Hyerding could say anything, this couple appeared at the door to the dining room—a husband and wife rubbing their hands and looking deferential. They were obviously French. Obviously lunch was served.

Hyerding took my arm on the way in. "We'll work this out, Red," he told me quietly. "Be sure of that."

It wasn't time to be rude. I sat where I was supposed to sit. The table was a long oval, large enough to accommodate twenty people. We were seated clustered at one end. Vichyssoise was waiting at our places; my place was the end of the table, with Hyerding on one side and Cowboy on the other. The Frenchwoman—in a white apron, *n'est-ce pas?*—brought around a bottle of wine. I inverted my glass.

"You're passing up a 1975 Chablis," Hyerding said to encourage me. The woman stopped to see. "'Les Vaillons.' I've been a guest at the estate. Outstanding year."

I was working at being civil. "Sounds great," I said, "but I don't drink."

"Ah. Pity." Hyerding must have heard that often enough from friends—for sure from authors—to know what it meant and to leave it alone. He spoke to the woman in French and she went on to the other glasses.

And no one said a word, and we ate our soup.

As the couple began clearing away the bowls, Hyerding dribbled the ball. "You know how reprint money is paid, don't you, Red?"

"Not really."

Hyerding: "Jeremy?"

"Usually in three parts," Jeremy explained. "One-third on signing, one-third on publication of the reprint edition, and one-third six months later."

Cowboy had been wiping his mouth. He threw down his napkin. "How's it paid when your author's kid's been kidnapped and buried alive?"

"*Yes*," Hyerding said approvingly, as if he thought Cowboy was being witty. "Exactly. But you see, what we want to talk about is looking beyond *Solar*. That's where we can move much more quickly for you."

"Such as what?" I asked.

"Such as—" he began. Then the door from the kitchen swung open—"Ah, here we are." The Frenchman carried in a great silver salver with two monster lobsters raised on it as if ready to do battle. Between them was a sort of Trajan's Column of lettuce, tomato, lemon, one whole truffle and a silver hood ornament surmounting all. "*Homard à la parisienne*," Hyerding said grandly.

The man served me first. Medallions of lobster lay overlapped along the beasts' tails and backs, each medallion glazed with aspic and dotted with a truffle eye. Underneath the medallions the shells had been stuffed with a vegetable salad and around the tray there were deviled eggs and small tomatoes balanced on artichoke bottoms. I helped myself and the tray moved on to Hyerding.

After he'd taken a portion he picked up where he left off. "All manner of possibilities," he said. "You have a readership now, Red. You have a record of success on the promotional circuit. Bookstore people know you. Our salespeople know you and know you're commercial. That's good. But now we need to think very carefully about what we want to give them next. We've set up some very high expectations. That's as it should be. That's a clear challenge. I was thinking about it this morning on the tennis court. I think we can see a way to meet it."

"I don't understand," I said.

"Chuck's talking about a new book project for you," Jeremy said.

"This isn't the time to talk about *books*," I said. "Why are we talking about *books?*" I couldn't believe these people.

"Chuck sees his responsibility as innovation. He likes to stay at least two years out in front."

I'd turned to Jeremy; I turned back to Hyerding. "It's definitely something to think about, Chuck, but right now we need to think about how to raise half a million dollars in gold." They were all managing to eat. Even Cowboy was eating. He wasn't enjoying it but he was putting it away against whatever was to come.

"To be sure," Hyerding said. "But stay with me for just a few minutes, my friend. There was the Time-Life contribution. There was the Mailer book—what was it called?"

"Of a Fire on the Moon," Jeremy said.

"Right. Not his best. He ought to tackle the big novel. One of the Apollo Eleven astronauts wrote a book, didn't he?"

"Two," I said.

"That's right. What were they called?"

"Mike Collins's book was *Carrying the Fire*," I said. "Buzz Aldrin's was *Return to Earth.*"

"I remember. Aldrin's was rather a confession, wasn't it? It didn't sell. And Von Braun and so on. And now this new book of Tom Wolfe's that's picking up sales. But pieces, right? Fragmentary perspectives. *No one has told it all.* Do you see what an achievement that would be? *The* big book on the space program. Von Braun and his team coming over here after the war, Sputnik, Kennedy pulling the moon landing out of his hat, Mercury and Gemini and Apollo. The fire on pad thirty-four. The private lives of the astronauts. What it was really like to go to the moon and what happened to everyone when they got back. By *God* what a book!" He caught my eye, the loony bastard. I knew what he was going to say next. He did: "And Red, you're just the man to write it."

There were half a dozen things I could have done then, most of them felonious. What I did, for a few seconds, in self-defense, was to tune everyone out. Staring at Chuck Hyerding in his fatuous livery in his fatuous dining room eating his fatuous lobster salad I remembered Chris the year before he moved in with me, Chris not quite so tall, not shaving yet, his face thin and the bone structure changing but not yet shaped to the cragginess of manhood. Chris was visiting me over a weekend—I think it was March, April—early spring. Bud casings thick on the yard, warm days, cool nights, the pastures just greening. He wanted to work his way into rock music. He'd been studying the classifieds and he wanted to buy a set of drums.

Not just any set. A set of beechwood Sonors from Germany that someone was advertising at eighteen hundred dollars—snare, ride toms, floor toms, a row of Roto-toms, a bass, with Ziljan cymbals and solid chrome-steel stands for all. That was too rich for my blood, but I was feeling indulgent and Chris said the guy was willing to take less, maybe twelve hundred, and I thought of a way to bring that down to a level I could afford. We called the guy—he lived in the northeastern section of the city—and arranged to see the set the next morning. We went to the bank and I withdrew eight hundred dollars in new hundred-dollar bills. I told Chris not to wet his pants, to check out the set without giving anything away. He nodded, solemn as an altar boy.

The guy who was selling the drums was a kid of nineteen or twenty living in a bare little bungalow on a street of bare little bungalows. He was almost an albino—white eyebrows, white-blond hair, pale skin, pale eyes. There was nothing in the little living room but an upright piano and the Sonors. A musician's house, everything for making music and no place to sit.

Beautiful drums. Chris managed to keep a straight face checking them out. We retired to the Saab. He said they were perfect.

Up the street we'd passed an old fieldstone church. The morning was warm and the church's windows were open and as we went back into the drummer's house we heard the congregation start up singing, fantastic black gospel. It was gloomy in the bungalow, but the Sonors glowed. I explained to the drummer that we couldn't afford twelve hundred for drums. I pulled out my wallet and extracted the eight hundred-dollar bills and fanned them under his nose. He was working as hard as Chris to keep a straight face—awe was his problem, not elation, he'd probably never seen eight hundred dollars in cash in his life. He stuffed his hands into the back pockets of his jeans and pretended to think. I'd swear I smelled the bills. They gave off a crisp freshness like chilled romaine.

He took the money. He needed it or he wouldn't have offered that fantastic set of drums for sale in the first place. I didn't feel we'd cheated him. There was a time factor in his need and he adjusted his minimum accordingly. He got what he wanted. We got what we could afford. But we were only bargaining with drums.

The drummer helped Chris break down the set and we started carrying it to the car. Heading back for another load, I passed Chris coming out. Widest grin you ever saw.

It was dawning on me—slowly, because I'm a fool—that Hyerding wasn't the somewhat dense, warm, well-meant guy I'd taken him for. It was dawning on me that he was a tough-minded businessman who hadn't climbed to the top of one of New York's largest publishing houses on fatuity. I was beginning to understand that he was doing what Chris and I did to the near-albino drummer in Kansas City: with nothing to lose, he was gambling with my urgent necessity. He was trying to see how much he could get in return for helping me ransom my son. And he didn't really care if the bargaining didn't produce any return. For all the protestations of friendship, for all the human urgency of my need, I was nothing more to Charles A. Hyerding than another grubby author with his hand out.

"I like it," I said then about the big space book. "It's a great idea. Don't you think it's a great idea, Cowboy?"

Cowboy was chewing. He stopped chewing and looked at me. He started chewing again and swallowed. Time enough to think. "First-rate," he said.

"You're right, Chuck," I told Hyerding. "It's not a book anyone else could do. Oh, someone could do the historical parts, I guess, what they could piece together from what's already been published. But the guys who flew aren't going to talk to anyone from the outside, you know? They told Wolfe a little of it, but not very damned much, you know?"

"Certainly," Hyerding said, pleased. He looked to my editor. "Jeremy? You see?" And Jeremy nodded. Which meant he'd been in on it all along.

"Not to mention actually flying, Chuck," I went on. "No one who hasn't been in space can even *guess* what that's like. Right, Cowboy?"

"Damned straight," Cowboy said. "No one."

"Then there's the fire we went through coming home. Hawthorne's little report in *The New Yorker* was nice, but it didn't give the *feel* of the thing. He told it from the point of view of the guys at Mission Control. Believe you me, it looked different from where we sat." And slapping my hand on the expensive linen, I summed up: "Damn, Chuck, I think you've got yourself a book."

"Well," Hyerding said, looking pleased, "that's splendid."

I nodded. "Now let's talk about money."

"Certainly." Hyerding turned then to his special assistant. "Marc?"

Lowe pushed aside his plate—the Frenchwoman came running over to fetch it—and sat straight, his notebook flipped open in front of him. He licked his thumb—honest Injun, he licked his thumb—and turned through the pages of his notes. And then he looked at Hyerding, and then he looked at me. "Chuck's had a real good idea here, guys," he said, addressing us all, sounding like a basketball coach at strategy time. "We build on Red's solar book to publish the definitive space book. Swell. In the meantime, Red needs an early payout on his earnings over advances for *Solar*. Plus he'd like to borrow against a possible reprint sale of *Solar*. What he needs is a quick half million."

He did a little bounce in his chair, a sort of physical punctuation mark to indicate he was moving to the next Roman numeral in his mental outline. "Now, Chuck," he said then, "it's whatever you want, of course, but I'd say we can't get at all the *Solar* money yet. It's been a neat sale, but we just don't know yet what the returns are going to look like. We could be up to our ears in returns and already have paid out the royalty to Red here and then we'd be in trouble." He looked at me questioningly. "I don't guess you figure you'll get the ransom money back, do you?"

I stared at him.

"No, I guess not," he said. "So that means we can't really tap all that money yet. The Executive Committee's not going to go for the idea of loaning out a truckload of money when we don't have a reprint commitment, either."

"But you *forgot* to sell those rights," I said.

Deadpan: "We don't admit to that, Red. There's no time limit in your contract as to when we sell the reprint rights. I'll check with our rights people, but I expect they were deliberately holding out to maximize the bid." He turned to Chuck again. "Now, that leaves the new book, the big space book. And it makes real good sense to go ahead and come to an agreement about that."

"How much would you guess if you were guessing, Marc," Hyerding asked him, "just for a ball-park figure?"

He tapped his pen on the table. He leaned over his calculator and played braille songs again. He looked up brightly, if that's the right word. "I'd sure think one hundred thousand, Chuck," he said. He blinked. "I'd say more, but you know, even if that Wolfe book goes, astronaut books just generally don't sell."

Hyerding took thought. "In anyone else's hands," he said after a moment, "I'd agree with you one hundred percent. Given any other author, I'd be hesitant, because the space story isn't automatic by any means. But I think Red can make the book mature and original. I think he can bring it off. We ought to offer more."

"How much more?" Lowe asked him. Be sure I appreciated this bargaining on my behalf.

"I'd say three hundred thousand."

"Chuck, you know the Executive Committee would never agree."

"Still, we must offer more. Would you say they'd agree to two hundred thousand?"

Lowe calculated. "If we could tell them Red was willing to general-account the two books, I think they would."

"Red?" Chuck. "Could you accept that?"

"What's general-account?"

The French couple brought in some kind of strawberry concoction with whipped cream and purple candy flowers. I waved mine away. I was tired of screwing around.

"We account the two books together," Jeremy came out of his complicitous silence to say. "Both books stand responsible for the advances. That way, if one of them doesn't earn back its advance, the other one pays it off."

"So I take all the risk," I said.

"It lets us work from strength," Chuck said mysteriously.

"And you're offering two hundred thousand? What about the half million I need today? What can we do about that?" I looked to Lowe then. He was obviously the trainer. He walked the dog.

"One hundred thousand for *Solar,*" he said, fingers flying on the calculator. "One hundred thousand for the space book as an advance on signing against a total advance of two hundred thousand for the finished manuscript, no more to be paid after the initial advance until the manuscript is delivered complete and accepted, and a loan of one hundred thousand against the reprint sale of *Solar* or the final advance payment for the space book, whichever is first." He looked at me then. "The loan at an interest rate of fourteen percent," he finished.

"That's only three hundred thousand," I said. Stupidly, because they could add. Damn straight they could add.

Hyerding took over. "It's possible we could come up with something better, but we'd have to justify it to the Executive Committee. We couldn't move as quickly as I gather you'd like. There'd be some selling involved. *I* can certainly make a case with *myself* for better numbers than that." He smiled, one of those generous grouper smiles that swallow. "The most important thing, the overriding thing, is that we're proud to be your publisher and we want to go on being your publisher."

"Three hundred thousand won't do it," I said, looking at them one at a time, Hyerding and Jeremy and Lowe.

Jeremy spread his hands—he only took orders. Hyerding smiled a brave smile. Lowe said, ever so generously, "I feel like Chuck, Red, we're real proud of being your publisher, but you're sure welcome to look elsewhere. The important thing is that *you're* happy."

Cowboy wasn't saying. Obviously I had to take the deal. The sharks chewed on the tuna. If you were hungry you ate what was left. "When can you have it?" I asked Lowe.

"Not before Monday," he said.

"Bullshit. Tomorrow."

"But the banks are closed."

"That's your problem." I stood, dropped my napkin on the table. "Have the bank get half a million in gold ready," I said. Cowboy was pushing in his chair. "I'll be back here tomorrow with the other two hundred thousand. Okay, Cowboy?" He nodded. "I'll be back here tomorrow with the other two hundred thousand and you'll deliver the full half million in gold and we'll have us a book contract."

"A two-book contract," Lowe said.

"Yeah. A two-book contract." I was moving.

Hyerding came up and got his hand out. We sort of shook. "I knew something splendid would come of this," he said.

"Sure," I said. "Tomorrow."

Jeremy followed us to the elevator. We arranged where to meet. The elevator arrived and Jeremy went back to the shark tank and we went down.

When we came out onto the street the limousine was gone. I almost looked for a pumpkin and some mice. I wouldn't have been able to spot them anyway for the trash.

We caught a cab.

"Where the hell can I raise the other two hundred thousand?" I asked Cowboy once we were rolling. He'd lit a cigar.

"I was thinking about that. You know what's-his-face? Got a religious foundation down in Washington?"

"Who?"

"Ernie Defleurs. Apollo Eighteen command module pilot. What's it called? Yeah, Prodigal Sons. He does a TV show five mornings a week. He's raking it in."

"You think he'd make a donation?"

"He always was one buddy-buddy asshole. Worth a try."

"Then let's get to Washington."

Cowboy looked at me. There was anger in his eyes for what we'd just been through. He was ashamed for them and ashamed for us and he wanted to say something to make it up. He tried. He tried for comedy. Comedy and continuity. "You think Washington can stand to take on two of us at a time?" he asked me.

I didn't answer. I looked out the window. It was a good shot, but we both knew it wasn't funny anymore.

Ten

Children mature not steadily but in spurts. I wasn't always there to see my own. What I saw was awesome. The whole business of children is awesome. To get so much out of one sperm and one egg, out of one mated strand of DNA only a few angstroms wide. It's two meters long, but still. It's the information-carrying equivalent of a complete encyclopedia, but still. One encyclopedia doesn't seem enough to make a Diana or a Chris. Yet they elaborated from that bare chemical template in their own custom fluid chambers, their own individual life-support systems where they floated neutrally buoyant at zero G. (I'm not immune to symbolism. We were aware of the symbolism of what we were doing in the space program even if we never paid it much attention. We left the symbolism to the shrinks and the poets. They probably had a field day. I wonder if the rocket has permanently displaced the cigar in the world's dreams?) After Chris and Diana were born they progressed in spurts. Claudia used to say when one kid was serene, the other was impossible and vice versa. Apparently they alternated years, one good year, one bad year. We had an agreement not to take any drastic action to salvage either of them from a phase until the phase had gone on for at least three months. "Give it three months" was a family joke.

Chris in his box was maturing overnight. He was learning at the fierce, terrible rate that disaster forces on you if you are lucky enough to be prepared to survive—if the particular disaster that you're hit with doesn't demand some other set of skills than the skills you happen to have. I'm no stranger to disaster and I'm here to tell you that you learn. Chris was learning.

He woke during the afternoon, Saturday afternoon, knowing where he was. This time he didn't fight his way back through panic. He didn't bump his head. It depressed him to wake to the ugly reality of darkness and burial but he accepted it. He thought of the fan first. He came awake thinking of the fan and immediately shut it off.

He needed to pee. He'd managed the bedpan once before—"last night" as he thought of it even though there was only "night" underground as there had only been "day" on the way to the moon until the body of the moon blocked out the sun—and now he worked it with his foot carefully up within reach of his hand. He positioned it at his side, turned on his side to face it, unzipped his jeans, found his penis, aimed over the opening shrinking from the cold edge and deliberately made an effort to relax. When he felt the hot flow he realized how cold he was.

After he finished he moved the bedpan back to the bottom of the box and retrieved an apple from the store of supplies. Then he wrapped himself more tightly in the blanket, leaving one hand out to hold the apple, which he ate. The tension still told on him: he was a boy who routinely drank half a gallon of milk a day and now he wasn't hungry, hadn't been hungry since the dirt rattled its tattoo on the lid. He ate the apple because he was thirsty and didn't want to drink the bitter water. When he'd scraped all the meat off the apple he sucked on the core. He was beginning to realize that neither I nor his mother nor his sister could do anything for him so long as he was buried, that he would have to take care of himself, husband himself, marshal his resources.

I looked into disasters after I got back from the moon, after the disaster of our return with an essentially dead command module. I was curious how other people had handled that kind of emergency—an emergency of confinement, so to speak. One study I found that fascinated me concerned a group of Canadian coal miners trapped underground for a week by a mine collapse. A team of sociologists interviewed the survivors and cleverly identified the leaders by counting up when and how often the survivors mentioned each other as leaders in their stories. At first, when the situation was new to them and all they could think of was getting out, the trapped miners identified as leaders the take-charge guys who worked themselves silly trying to find or clear a passageway. In a couple of days, when the take-charge guys had failed to dig them out, when they knew they were stuck until help came down after them, the miners identified another group of leaders, men skilled at counseling patience, at keeping up hope. Neither kind of leader, active or "passive," was superior to the other. Each made sense at his appropriate time. The group determined appropriateness by talking through an implicit group estimate of the probable return in security for a given expenditure of energy. The limiting resource in the Canadian disaster was water, and the miners were reduced to drinking urine before they were done.

Chris was working that afternoon on making a similar changeover within himself. Since he had fruit juice, he didn't have to drink the suspect water yet, much less urine. But he saw that he needed to stay calm and he managed it by convincing himself that I'd contrive somehow to rescue him (so one of his skills going in, I'm glad to say, was a healthy trust in the power of love). And he found absorbing distraction. Pulling together the fragments he'd improvised before, he began working on a song. It would be a rock ballad, the story of what was happening to him. "Kidnapped," maybe, or "Buried Alive." He was having an experience. He figured he might as well use it.

Grabka was packing. He'd dug his olive-drab Air Force duffel from the dirty little closet in his room and loaded it with his shirts, T-shirts, pants, socks, his sweatshirts, his gray stained briefs. The porn magazines, covers of women with their heads thrown back riding bored, hairy men, got stuffed into the duffel under the wadded clothes. His old Trac II razor and aerosol Gillette shaving cream and his new electric Norelco earned a brown paper sack. No toothbrush. Grabka didn't own a toothbrush.

He'd had to snap into position and throw the right switch. Move Chris and thereby move me. Now he could relax and follow. In a sense, I was doing the moving now by being where I was and doing what I was doing and taking the time I necessarily took. I was his gofer. He liked it that way, following out the timeline on automatic sequence. He felt it was really going to happen—"it" meaning here that within another night and day and night he, Karl Grabka, would receive three gold bars worth five hundred thousand dollars extorted in a kidnapping for the forgiveness of sins. So happily he packed, preparing to cool out those thirty-six hours by waiting in his pickup, making ready to get the hell out of town, out of state, out of the country after the drop.

The more solidly events fell into place, the more Grabka felt them. He'd long ago sealed himself off from ordinary reality as if he were some alien life form that had to be isolated from the lethal oxygen atmosphere of the earth, a methane breather from a swamp planet by the smell of him. So, normally, he felt very little. It took a lot of reality to make him feel—a barracks blanket party, say, or a cocaine bust, or the pure power surge of bending a famous astronaut to his will. It took that much violence to get through the isolation garment, so to speak, that he wore. He was drawn to violence—stumbling, blinded, weighted down—because he was just as interested as any of us in feeling, wanted just as much to be touched, needed just as much something warmer than the dim half-light that filtered through his helmet.

That's not sympathy for Grabka. The son of a bitch chose what he chose. He was exactly what the prosecuting attorneys accuse kidnappers of being when they're not accusing the bastards merely of greed: a thrill seeker. He didn't have to be.

I said early on that Grabka just "happened" to carry out his plan to kidnap Chris. That's not strictly true. For one thing, nothing human beings do, as far as I'm concerned, just "happens." Grabka was responsible. We are all responsible. But Grabka's wasn't a standard, rational, factor-weighing decision. Oh, he planned the kidnapping. Planning neat crimes was his hobby. Some people plan gardens, some people plan vacations: Grabka planned crimes. But following through on his plans took some snapping. Grabka wasn't a self-starter. He was a snapper. He walked around in a perpetual fog inside his swamp suit until something painful, violent, *felt*, got through to him and snapped him into another mode, and then he followed that mode until something snapped him again, on down the ways. In this instance the snap happened at Crown Hospital, where he worked. It happened between the time he built the box he would bury Chris in and the time he actually dug the grave in the little rookery-surrounded glade south of town. What happened was a nurse, a bright, attractive young black woman named Daylena Madison.

Daylena was assigned to the Emergency Room, which means she wore surgical greens, nice color with her almost milk-chocolate skin. Her shift sometimes coincided with Grabka's. She was slim, with the high, narrow hips so many young black women have. Her lips were full, her nose short and turned up and slightly splayed. She trimmed her hair fairly close to her head in a smooth black cap. Large, friendly brown eyes. She had beautiful hands.

She was very good at what she did—ER nurses usually are—and she remembered Grabka afterward. She remembered that he was weird, but before he gave her reason to think him weird she'd felt friendly toward him, felt some curiosity about him—felt sorry for him too.

She'd first noticed him one night when a bad accident case came in. Two men and two women, a carload. Hardly men and women: nineteen-year-olds. The two kids in the back seat sustained concussions and multiple fractures. The girl in the right front seat got her knees crushed and a face full of glass. But the boy who was driving had a crushed chest and a torn aorta. The chest filled with blood, the blood ran to the floor. They were loading the boy with fluids. Trying to keep his pressure up. Four criticals at one time taxed the ER staff and Daylena drafted Grabka, the nearest available orderly, to help out. She sent him after blood. Usually he shuffled off to Buffalo but for once he moved. Back with the blood he helped hold the boy, who was screaming, writhing, who hurt so much he preferred dying to being touched. The aorta sits at the back of the chest, up against the spine. The resident had to work his way through the chest to suture it.

It made Grabka sweat. I'd guess part of him felt the boy's agony right through the swamp suit. The other part, one of the other parts, would have watched, distant and judgmental, thinking it served the guy right. Thinking he should have had his seat belt on. He should have made the others buckle up too. He didn't because he wanted the girl to work him over while he drove, Grabka figured. So this was the payoff for that.

But our Judgment Angel drifted from condemning the broken, blood-drenched boy to watching Daylena Madison working quickly, efficiently, beautifully, with the others around the table, to save the boy's life: plugging in the blood Grabka had brought, calling up the surgical instrument packs that he left the table long enough to fetch, filling syringes, stripping open an IV drip, whatever had to be done—and those beautiful, long-fingered hands. Beautiful even in pale-yellow surgical gloves. And the slim shoulders, the nice breasts alive under the surgical blouse, the muscles of the hips and legs that flexed as Daylena worked.

She and her crew got the boy stabilized enough to move him to Surgery—they ran fifteen pints of blood through him first—the other three victims were already on their way, then everyone helped clean up the pool of blinding red blood so vividly the complement of their surgical greens, and in the swell of comradeship that follows an emergency Daylena invited Grabka to the cafeteria to join her, join them—one of the two other nurses, the one paramedic, the resident—for coffee.

No big deal. You know, everyone happy, a little giddy from the adrenaline, sauntering along to a break, lounging together at one of the long Formica tables. Kidding each other. Letting down. But Grabka was like some vast pelagic fish Daylena had reeled in, barely hooked, rolling a fishy eye, ready to spit the hook and run. And I don't know how they stood the proximity. Maybe the strong hospital disinfectants masked the stink.

Daylena to the paramedic, Sam: "Say, brother, who taught you to move like that? Your mama teach you to move like that?"

Daylena to the nurse, Ersey, her disco buddy: "Thought we'd lost that boy for sure."

Then Daylena to Grabka, her voice gentler than with her friends, serious—she knew his name: "Karl, you were good help. Thanks a lot." Smiling at him, perfectly normal.

Which was all it took to set Grabka off. After that he watched her. Whenever they shared a shift and he found excuse to hang around the ER he watched her, on the sly. Around corners. Through windows. In mirrors. She was black. Her mouth would be strange, the big lips. She'd have the same kinky hair down on her belly. He was a white guy. They liked white guys. White guys had all the power so the black guys looked like nothing.

Grabka began buying a different kind of magazine. You could buy black men with white women or white men with black women. Grabka bought the black women. He studied them as he masturbated. It was almost like being in love.

Daylena was aware he was watching her. The sneakiness felt a little creepy but she was used to being looked at. She guessed Grabka was shy. He was, to be sure, for which we may all be thankful.

She'd sit down across from him in the cafeteria if she happened to come in alone (he was always alone). Innocent talk. She'd tell him about a case she'd had in the ER. She wasn't flirting. She thought he was one of the ugliest men she'd ever seen. But she was a good nurse and even with staff, unconsciously, she nursed—especially the walking wounded.

Those things happened through the time Grabka found *The Coming Solar Age* and then found me, studied me, began charting my routines, Chris's routines, even bought the lumber and built the box. I'd guess he was orchestrating both lifelines—both *event trees*—together, setting up one as a shunt for the other. People do that every day. A guy's in a bad marriage, "coincidentally" he falls in love and the marriage breaks up and surprise, he's got someone else on the line, no down time, no risk. We had redundancy piled on redundancy in our spacecraft. Three reentry control systems backed up one behind the other, three fuel cells side by side and so on. Grabka was running two redundant systems side by side. Odd sort of redundancy—one was one hundred eighty degrees the opposite of the other. That was Grabka for you, ever the original. But he paralleled them for their magic, not their reality: one would produce the dark, secret love of his life, wild nights of taboo passion; the other would compensate for lost life, lost love, prison, the hurts of unrecognized genius, with gleaming bars of purest gold. They were almost equal. Except, of course, that both were poisoned by his hate.

Balanced on that crucial point—the box built, the burial place not yet scouted—and as if throwing dice, taking a reading on entrails, Grabka wrote his presumptive playmate a letter:

> Dear Daylena,
>
> I know what is happening. I never thought it would or could but here we are. Never the twain shall meet. Well they do!
>
> I will be real good to you. You won't be sorry you decided. I got it for you good, little colored gal. You saw to that.
>
> Black *is* Beautiful, like they say.
>
> Lots of love, baby,
> Karl L. Grabka

I was interested to compare the love letter with the kidnap note. The letter's far less literate. Most of us turn our brains off when we're in love. Why shouldn't Grabka? But I thought of something else when I first made the comparison: that all sorts of people, astronauts especially included, function at far higher levels when they're doing their technical thing than they do when they go about the ordinary business of living. They learn their technical skills in school and repeat them and practice them and correct them (if only in simulation—Grabka with his hobby and astronauts with their simulators). Whereas personal skills get picked up haphazardly at best. Grabka probably hadn't written five love letters in his life. So the one he wrote to Daylena was undisguised: pure Grabka drool.

He sealed it in an envelope, wrote Daylena's name on the envelope and left it at her desk in the ER.

He was out of the room when she found it. She opened it, read the signature first. She was surprised. Embarrassed when she read the body of the letter—embarrassed to have been so grossly misunderstood. Then she reread it and picked up the racial slurs, the implication that she'd led him on, the confidence that he was a catch and she had to want him and who'd have thought he'd condescend to fall for a nigger gal? Which made her mad.

He came along with a cartload of instrument packs from Central Supply. Began putting them away in the ER storage cabinets. Glanced at her.

When she found time she went over to him. "Karl?" she said. He wouldn't face her. She stood arms akimbo with the open letter in one hand. "Hey. Stop. Look at me." He did, sort of—his hands going slack at his sides and his eyes not resting on her, not resting anywhere—and she wished he hadn't.

She held out the letter. "There's nothing to this," she said. "You understand? I go along to get along and that's all. You just made up the rest, man. So forget it."

She offered him the letter. He wouldn't take it. He smiled his secret smile, the Mona Lisa–Lee Harvey Oswald smile. She pursed her mouth in exasperation, released the letter to flutter through the air down to Grabka's big feet, turned on her heel and crossed the room to work.

It wasn't Daylena Madison's fault, but that quick final turn armed the switches that fired Chris's kidnapping.

So Grabka was packed. He slung the duffel over his shoulder and carried it down the back stairs. Two more trips loaded the odds and ends. He didn't even give his room a final look. He got into his pickup and drove away.

Diana was restless. She brushed her hair at the mirror in the hall bathroom, went downstairs, spoke to Paige, went out. In the tack room in the barn she lifted the quarter-horse mare's bridle from its peg and headed for the pasture fence. The little mare, called Sola for the book money I bought her with in the dialect of the city the money came from, was waiting at the fence in a patch of sun and willingly took the bridle. Diana led Sola along the fence to the gate and on to the breezy barn aisle, hitched her to an upright while she saddled her. Then she mounted impatiently and rode out. She meant to check the livestock as she'd seen me do. It was cool in the October late afternoon. There was a breeze. Things moved. Nothing was only waiting.

Riding through the upper pasture, riding back a little in the saddle descending the slope, Diana kept one eye on the buffalo. It rested under a walnut tree chewing its cud. It didn't bother to watch her pass.

She let her mind go. It zoomed in on Chris. It always did since she'd heard. She could see his long, narrow face, his strong nose, his brown eyes, his shoulder-length brown hair that was frizzy at the ends because he refused to spray it with conditioner before he blew it dry, his mouth made a little strange by the bulge of his braces. As if in cutaway she saw his familiar face, his head, his lean body wedged into a plain, narrow coffin, and each time she had the vision—nearly the hallucination—her stomach contracted into a knot. She couldn't have stood it. She'd have screamed the whole time. How could he? How could he?

The pasture was dry but still touched with green, the grasses that had gone to grain matted over. The trees had turned: the elms yellow-brown, the walnuts yellow, the sumac along the creek bank magenta and brilliant scarlet. The sky was clear and cobalt blue, but she could see into the ground and down below ground it was black.

She let Sola walk at the edge of the pasture, following the curve of the creek. The saddle that had been cool was warming and the warm horse moved under her thighs.

"It's just *hor*rible," Diana said aloud. Sola rotated back one ear, rotated it forward again.

Diana was a small child when I went to the moon—six years old—but precocious enough to know I was gone and to have some vague idea how far away. She'd felt the distance. She'd looked up at the moon and it had seemed worlds gone, lifetimes gone, as hard to catch hold of as the unconsciousness of childhood from which she was already emerging. The distance chilled her. She was afraid I'd never come back. When our accident talk picked up on the squawk box at the house Claudia hadn't worried about Diana hearing it because she'd assumed Diana was too young to understand. She wasn't. She could hear the danger in our voices. She understood that our ship was broken and Charlie was hurt and the trouble was serious. She understood by identifying: felt fear within herself physically as a hollow emptiness, a draining like the draining of water from the bathtub that once she had feared would drain her down into the black, sucking darkness of the earth.

She felt that hollowing now again in fear for Chris, but with a difference: it sucked less powerfully, as if it passed through thicknesses of air and earth to draw her. She thought she might be receiving Chris's signals because she sensed that distance. He was down in the earth that scared her. If *she* were buried alive, she knew she'd transmit her cries for help by ESP if anyone ever could. They could. Science was beautiful but it wasn't all and there were too many documented cases. She and Chris might as well have been connected by a cable. He was one end and she was the other. She read him five by five.

She was receiving something else too, something spread out, something vague and low-frequency and strange, like the light of half-day during an eclipse of the sun, the light that had darkness in it. She knew what that other reception was: the mind of the kidnapper somewhere out beyond the farm. It seemed nearer at some times than at others and she suspected that at those times he was watching them. She thought she could sense where he was by a feeling of pressure in the air. It was like the pressure of air that build discomfort before a storm.

She wasn't crazy. Sometimes she thought she was crazy. She felt crazy about half the time. Half the time she felt like a little kid. Half the time she felt old, older than anyone, older than me, than her mother, than Paige; aeons older than Chris; as old as the world: as old as the moon she was named after. When she and Chris had done acid together one weekend with Jamie, her ex-boyfriend now unlamentably outgrown, she'd seen an aura glowing around Chris's head and she'd seen herself change to flowing moonlight silver. Diana huntress. Diana of the moon.

She dismounted to let herself through the gate between the upper and lower pastures. As she mounted again, the steers in the lower pasture looked up from grazing to watch her. She walked Sola over to check them.

What was the worst thing she could think of?

The instant she asked herself she knew. She'd heard the story from Blair Haldane, one of her classmates at Angelus, whose father was a gyn. He worked out of Crown Hospital (like Grabka: coincidence? Yes, but Kansas City, though it counts going on a million souls, manages to be a small town—"small world") and he'd picked up the story there and told Blair's stepmother when Blair was in the next room.

One of the staff doctor's favorite patients was having a baby. For some reason it had to be delivered by caesarean section—which meant cutting through the abdomen, cutting into the womb, bringing the baby out that way—instead of natural childbirth. And whenever doctors operated on the abdomen, besides putting the patient to sleep, they had to make the muscles relax enough to work with. The anesthesiologist did that by injecting a kind of curare that paralyzed everything, shut everything down. The patient couldn't move *anything*, not even an eyelid or a little finger. The anesthesiologist even had to pump a bag to make the patient breathe.

But this time he screwed up royally: he didn't give enough gas to go with the paralyzer. And *the paralyzer didn't take away pain*. So the woman had a caesarean section without any relief for the pain of cutting through to the baby and sewing everything back up. She heard it all. She felt it all. And she couldn't even scream.

Blair said his father said that when the woman came out of the paralysis she started screaming and screamed for two days, wouldn't stop, wouldn't look at her baby, and the asshole anesthesiologist knew what had happened and stayed with her the whole time, big deal.

Chris was the baby. She was the woman. The kidnapper was the doctor.

Diana shook herself then, there on horseback in the pasture—shook away the horror. She thought of me. She told me later she saw me in the T-38 flying somewhere to raise the money to ransom Chris, leaving a double contrail, and felt better. At the same time she thought of the three gold bars like three wishes. She realized they'd be beautiful. She thought of the word *gold* and remembered King Midas, Rumpelstiltskin.

Her horse was real. Sola was real. She turned the animal to circle back and nicked softly, nudged with her heels, and Sola paced up to a run and brought Diana home.

The ride to La Guardia was longer than the flight to Washington. Fairly heavy overcast in the Baltimore-Washington area. We elected to come down on TACAN at Andrews AFB. No presidents in transit that day. If retired astronauts had friends, Washington ought to be the place to find them. I was beginning to wonder. I called Ernie from Andrews, told him Cowboy and I were in town. He said, "God loves you, come on over."

Eleven

"Praise Jesus, how are you men?" Ernie Defleurs welcomed Cowboy and me into his office. It was all paneling and built-in bookshelves, the bookshelves given over to gaudy memorabilia—cups, plaques, medals and certificates, a harvest of electroplate. A model Saturn V rose from one corner of a huge oak desk. The desk featured a flag stand with Old Glory and a Christian banner set staunchly side by side. Ernie favored one of those high-backed leather chairs congressmen command that look as if they're designed to protect against whiplash. God's office couldn't be snazzier.

I told Ernie we were okay. He'd shaken hands. He was still holding mine and I let him swing me into a short, leather-padded chair facing the desk. Cowboy flopped down in another one next to me.

Ernie was one of your compact astronauts—five six or so—and the desk dwarfed him. When he sat down he got taller. I'd seen the trick in the military: you crank up the chair. His feet probably didn't touch the floor. He used to have a cowlick, Ernie did, used to be a cowlick kind of guy with pudgy cheeks, a drawer-pull nose, a little splash of freckle across the nose. Now the hair was blow-dried into a fluffy light-brown helmet, with sideburns. Touched with gray. A Sun Belt tan out almost to the ends of his fingers. Manicured nails.

"Great to see you guys," Ernie said, meaning it just about that much. He took time to study us. We hadn't played in his backyard before, when we were training at the Cape and raising hell, so why were we showing up now?

"Nice place," Cowboy said, studying it.

"Why, that's right kind of you, Cowboy." Ernie's gold sword letter opener was stuck into a Lucite rock, like Excalibur. To play with it he pulled it out. "It's not my doing, though, you know? It's the Holy Spirit working *through* me." He grinned. Is there a school they all go to?

Cowboy cleared his throat, *uhg-unng*. "Yeah."

Ernie wouldn't leave it alone. "We can do *all things* through Christ Jesus." He said *Jeez*-us. There has to be a school.

I already saw I couldn't stop Ernie but I thought I might be able to slow him down. "Ernie," I said, "we've got a real emergency on our hands. We figured you could help."

"Praise God," said Ernie, leaning forward and looking serious—he said *Gauw*ud, just like Billy Graham—"that's why we're here. People come to us from every corner of America, Red. Fly here, drive here, call in, take a Greyhound. *Yes*. They know we'll help. They know we'll pass the word on to Jesus."

"Ernie?"

"Let me just tell you, Cowboy, Red"—he glanced to Cowboy and back to me—"let me just tell you—"

"Ernie?" I interrupted again. "Wait. It's my son. Chris. He's been kidnapped."

Ernie missed a beat, raised his eyebrows—I thought I saw a flicker of life in there somewhere before the eyes glazed over again—and whistled. "The Lord *Gauw*ud works in mysterious ways, doesn't he? Kidnapped." He shook his head, looked up toward the ceiling. "Here's a man, Lord, who's walked on Your moon, who's been closer to You than all but a handful of Your people, and Lord, Lord, his son's been kidnapped." Ernie hadn't walked on the moon, he'd only orbited overhead and that on one of the last and least-noticed Apollo mission. That may have been the problem to which all this holiness was the solution.

"I'm trying to raise the ransom money," I said. "We've got three hundred thousand. We need two hundred thousand more."

Ernie went on addressing the ceiling. "He needs two hundred thousand more, Lord. Two hundred thousand more." Then back to me. "God's going to provide that, Red. I *know* he is. I *feel* it. Praise Jesus."

"Can you help? We've got to move. Chris is buried somewhere in a box with a limited life-support system."

"*Bur*ied," Ernie repeated, eyes aloft. "His son's been *bur*ied." Eyes to me, rolling: "Is Chris anointed? Has he walked with Jesus?" How the hell was I supposed to respond to that? I shrugged. Ernie frowned at my shrug and started to say something but thought better of it.

"Can you help?" I asked again.

"I hope so, Red," he said a little archly. "Truly I hope so. You know our story here? Prodigal Sons?"

I shook my head. Some other time I might have been curious.

Back to sincerity: story time. "I felt an emptiness when I was training. I felt it even more when I was alone up there orbiting the moon in the command module. You remember around behind the moon, when the sun was occluded, how you couldn't see the moon at all but just a big black hole—I don't mean it was a black hole, just a big black stretch of darkness—without any stars?"

"Sure," Cowboy said. He wasn't embarrassed anymore, not for himself.

"I felt an emptiness then. That was the beginning of it. We shouldn't allow our minds to dwell on negative things. God's already made *his* decisions. All we have to do is take the Holy Spirit into our hearts. 'A merry heart doeth good like a medicine.'" Ernie shifted, holding on to the arms of his high chair. "A great emptiness. You remember my wife, JoeEllen? We'd drifted pretty far apart by the time of the mission. I felt pretty lousy about it and the feeling stayed with me after I got back. I didn't know what to do with myself. I guess I was angry. JoeEllen sensed it. She's always walked with Christ Jesus, you know? She's always 'kept and pondered these things in her heart.' She wasn't going to leave me angry and down like that. She wanted me to come to Christ, renew my faith, but I was resisting.

"Well, sir, it got down to where I lay abed one entire week. I hardly could get up to answer nature's call. Oh, it was darkness, just darkness. I couldn't even watch the TV. What I saw was that black stretch of moon. I was just about as far from God as you can get."

Ernie had tough, knobby, farm-boy hands. I noticed he was sawing at a thumbnail with his index finger. It was the only sign left of tension and he'd been a tense man. As my daddy used to say of all the hordes of people who lower their expectations to let themselves off the hook, *Must be nice.*

"So JoeEllen came in and sat down beside the bed, turned on the lamp, and she had her Bible. Honestly, I didn't think there was anything in the Bible strong enough to help me. Can you feature that? I'd been raised in the Holy Spirit, but I'd lost my way years before.

"JoeEllen knows her Scriptures. She started to read. She read me the One Hundred Twenty-first Psalm. 'I will lift up mine eyes unto the hills.' But that wasn't the verse that started me out of there, out of the darkness. It was the sixth verse that got to me. As if the Father God was looking right at me, looking me in the eye. You know what that verse was?" Dutifully Cowboy and I shook our heads. "That verse was 'The sun shall not smite thee by day, nor the moon by night.'" Big grin. "Hey. Does He number the hairs of our heads?"

Ernie's intercom buzzed. His secretary. Time to tape tomorrow morning's show. I hadn't realized it was taped. Ernie invited us along to watch. What else could we do? We went. He finished up the story of his miraculous healing. "And all the rest was added unto us" was his punch line. By then we'd walked a hall and descended in an elevator and were standing off the set in the studio. Ernie's own studio, with a satellite feed. Very nice. Religious groups don't pay taxes, which means, in effect, that they're government-subsidized. It's amazing what you can do when you're government-subsidized. We went to the moon. Ernie was building a new career selling promises and hot air.

I asked Ernie not to say anything about Chris, on the program or afterward, explaining that it could endanger Chris's life. He agreed.

Cowboy and I sat with the studio audience then, up near the back. I recognized that audience: white, southern, poor but proud. Not too different from Missouri country people except deeper South. Ernie was one of those people once, before the layers of college and pilot training and test-piloting and then NASA were added on. He'd turned around to minister to them. I don't know if he was sincere or not. I guess he was, as much so as evangelists can be. Obviously there's a lot of deliberate not-knowing.

The *Prodigal Sons Show* was like the other shows of its kind except that the backdrop to the set, déjà vu, was a huge blowup of the moon. Clicking through the channels at odd hours of the day and night back when I used to binge, I'd watched those shows. Whether broadcast early in the morning or later in the day, they were usually imitations of the *Tonight Show*. A host, the evangelist—in this case, Ernie. A sidekick announcer, a big bear of a guy like Ed McMahon. Guests called on at regular intervals to talk, although here instead of talking about their latest book or movie of the week or series they usually gave their witness. Testified. A band, even at six in the morning, but with a harp added and a chorus, and always one black or one Oriental in the chorus, no more. Commercials disguised as appeals for memberships or offers of the host's latest book or tapes. Then an important difference from the talk shows, borrowed I suppose from charity talkathons: a tiered bank of people manning telephones, taking calls, helping sinners in the here and now right on camera and incidentally soliciting contributions. The telephones had special noise suppressors screwed onto their mouthpieces so the counselor-solicitors could talk through the noise of the Praise Jesuses and the band, and beside every counselor-solicitor, like a Merck Manual, a Bible lay open for quick reference.

I ought to be kinder, but I didn't glimpse God out beyond the moon, I don't believe prayer cures cancer and I dislike people who sell hot air.

Ernie opened the show with a monologue, just like Johnny. Not humor, though: uplift. I heard isolated phrases: "Thank *God* for *God* . . . . Our minds are so powerful . . . . We have to make those *quality* decisions . . . . You get connected to the Father God, you don't *wait* for an emotion . . . . My life—my Christian walk . . . . We want to lead that spirit-filled life. . . ." The clothesline Ernie was hanging all the jargon on seemed to be a combination of old-fashioned evangelism plus modern-day pop psychology plus motivation training. "Benefits of knowing the Lord" was another phrase that caught my attention and I wondered if I'd hear about stock options and God's group medical plan.

Ernie introduced his first guest. Her name was Sondra Zook. Former drug addict, Ernie said proudly, former drug dealer. Sondra came out in a purple velour jump suit, looking a little lumpy, a little the worse for wear. A lot of miles on her eyes. The Ed McMahon clone gave her a handshake and a hearty smile and settled her in the love seat across from Ernie's table. The furniture on the set was traditional, another difference from the secular talk shows.

All Zook's sentences sounded like questions, with a lift at the end. "Aspen?" she eventually said. "That's where ah did ma big dealin'? Them rich folks out there'll buy anything? Ah was sellin' marijuana, LSD, cocaine, angel dust, you name it? Sellin' like wholesale? Makes you wonder what they thought they was missin' that they had to get out of their heads so much? They was just like little spoiled kids? Same way little kids is with candy, grab, grab, grab? Never seen nothin' like it before or since?"

"Wasn't there law enforcement out there, Sondra?" Ernie asked.

"Well, there was? But the police and the dealers was in cahoots? An', Ernie, that led me even deeper into sin? 'Cause ah figured they was worse than ah was? 'Cause they was sworn to uphold the law?" I could see Zook on the studio monitors, right and left. She took over the camera, looking directly into the lens. She was good—fluffy blond hair, tarnished beauty, hard years. Setting an example. Speaking from experience. "Course they wasn't worse? Ah sinned just as bad as they did? 'Judge not that ye be not judged'?"

On the celebrity circuit after the moon I'd missed Aspen. From what I heard it wasn't much different from the other scenes. The actress in Bel Air did give good taco, and that's what the whole business came down to, junk food. Ways that people who buy people and who submit to other people buying them fill time. I guess Cowboy and I were bought too. We didn't feel we were, not as much as the Hollywood people seem to. Bureaucrats aren't that brutal, though politicians are. The actress had a remarkable body, smooth, uniformly tanned without patch or line, beautifully muscled, flexible as a dancer's, which among other things she was. I'd seen her on the screen, and even though I was a big boy I'd daydreamed about her once or twice. So at first it was fantasy land. But the fantasy faded fast. She was dumb and she whined. Her perfume was awful and she had a vicious mouth.

Look who's talking.

I concentrated on bodies and it worked out well enough.

Zook had 'fessed up, she concluded, and cleaned up her act. She was trying to start a ministry to the drug culture, naturally, another tax shelter. Have her Aspen and eat it too. Ernie mentioned that we'd carried morphine on our Apollo missions—Charlie McCray had reason to know we did—and on that note of irrelevancy he handed the little lady down and introduced a singer. The singer was a round-faced man in a green western-cut double knit with saddle stitching. Ernie said he wrote his own songs, words and music, and the title song on his new album, *Praise Him*, was number one on the gospel charts and in real life the singer was a federal poultry inspector.

The poultry inspector sang the title song first. He'd worked in every biblical reference to praise that you could imagine, actually rhyming them. It was amazing. More amazing was the end, when the poultry inspector started something that sounded for a minute like scat. I couldn't figure it out. Cowboy and I looked at each other. Then it came to me: the guy was speaking in tongues. Something like *ely-lely-lalo-whyee-dono-zono-habe-do*. It blew everybody away. The poultry inspector watched the ceiling all through the song, just as

Ernie had done in his office. Later, when he was singing a song he'd written from God's point of view, I noticed he sang looking down toward the floor and they dollied the camera in low and he seemed to be looking down from on high. If you think of God as a round-faced federal poultry inspector who speaks in tongues you'll feel a lot less like sinning.

After the song the Ed McMahon clone called Ernie to the bank of phones and held up a thick stack of baby-blue messages that the counselor-solicitors had assembled for him to pray over. He let the announcer read through them. "Depressed, discouraged, down-hearted, financial reverses," the man read, skipping through. He named towns all over America: Tucumcari, New Mexico; Pocomoke City, Maryland; Richland, Washington; Athol, Massachusetts; Vine Grove, Kentucky. "Family difficulties, losing faith, drinking problems, serious illness of a grandchild." The country was in terrible shape.

Ernie picked up on "serious illness." He turned to the camera, taking command. "We've seen healing here, friends," he said. "Cancer, heart disease, stroke, arthritis, lupus . . . Legs have been lengthened, backbones straightened, joints loosened. Cataracts have been cleared. Yes. Cancer of the stomach, cancer of the colon, cancer of the lungs. Remissions that the doctors can't explain. We've seen healing directly in answer to prayer. Praise Jesus. We'll pray over these prayer requests right here and now. Pray with us. Then call Prodigal Sons and see a miracle happen in your life. We're here to help you because we care about you. The only thing you need to do is pick up your phone and call, so why don't you do it now?" As Ernie began praying I saw Cowboy shaking his head. I agreed: that was a load of promises to a load of sick people just to paper over a hole in the sky where the moon should have been.

I wondered how Chris was doing. I had to believe he was all right. And yes, Ernie could preach a sermon on that theme about the substance of things hoped for and the evidence of things not seen.

He wasn't done. He welcomed another guest, someone Cowboy and I recognized vaguely from NASA Washington, J. Calvin Lockamy. Dr. Lockamy. Nominally a physicist. He was ninety-nine percent bureaucrat and I guess he'd found religion or never lost it. Ernie said he was going to tell us about the latest developments in astronomy.

"You know, Ernie," Lockamy began, "it's a lot more miraculous out there than anyone ever suspected a few years ago. Our Heavenly Father had a good time creating all those different kinds of stars." He was bald, thin-faced, with darting eyes. He wore a short-sleeved white shirt closed at the collar with a black string tie and a silver Thunderbird slide. He looked like a lot of the technical staff at NASA except crazier.

"Take your neutron star," he went on. "That's a star about twice the size of our sun that burns out and collapses in on itself. It collapses until it's only about fifteen miles across. Now, that's a lot of star stuff to squeeze into such a small space. A teaspoon, just a *teaspoon*, of neutron star stuff would weigh—on earth, of course—would weigh a *billion tons.*" Nodding. "That's right. A billion tons. If you dropped that teaspoonful on the ground it would fall right through the earth just like a rock falling through the air."

Ernie looked out at the audience, at the camera. "Isn't that wonderful, friends? Psalm Eight, three: 'When I consider thy heaven, the work of thy fingers, the moon and the stars which thou hast ordained.'" He winked. "I know something about it, friends, because I've been there." He looked across to Lockamy. "What's this business with the Big Bang, Cal? How do you see that as fitting in with Scripture? I've thought and prayed a lot over that question."

"Now certainly we have to be very careful here," Lockamy said. "It's a nice theory and it explains a lot of facts." He stopped to scratch his bald head. "But for one thing, the explosion of the singularity that made what we call the Big Bang seems like the biblical account of the Creation. 'And God said, Let there be light: and there was light.' Genesis one: three. 'And God saw the light, that it was good: and God divided the light from the darkness.' Genesis one: four." Lockamy frowned and his face darkened. "But to propose, as the astrophysicists do, that all this foofaraw took several billion years to happen, that there wasn't any light until billions of years later when the gasses blown out from the singularity had clumped together into stars, that the earth wasn't formed until ten billion years *after* the Big Bang—well, that's your Devil talking, Ernie, as far as I'm concerned."

And Lockamy peered into the camera lens as if he expected to find the astrophysicists there, as the delegation from Rome had expected to find a phony plaster moon inside Galileo's telescope. "Beelzebub's on the march, you know," Lockamy ranted. "He wants the atheists to triumph. He sees to it they get preferment over the few of us who still believe. Oh yes indeed. I've suffered for my faith, Ernie. I've known ridicule and abuse. I've been held back and I've been set aside. And that just when these new views of the heavens are *confirming* the

Bible's old, old story. *Confirming.* Why, you take black holes—"

"What a witness this man is, friends!" Ernie interrupted Lockamy to shout. "What a witness!" And then more quietly: "For those of you who haven't heard, let me just say that a black hole is a star, a big God-created star, that collapses when it burns out until it's so packed together and its gravity is so strong that not even light can escape from its surface. Right, Cal?"

"That's *right,*" Lockamy grabbed, blowing the words like a diver coming up for air, "and we think the universe is full of black holes, big ones twelve to two hundred miles across and little ones as small as atoms but powerful as hydrogen bombs. And this much I'm personally certain of, Ernie"—Lockamy's eyes were dancing now—"black holes are *entrances to heaven.*" He looked around proudly. "Praise God, *entrances to heaven.*"

"Well, well," Ernie said. It might have been too much even for him, I couldn't tell. I wondered if they screened them and how they decided, given the general atmosphere of casual hallucination, which ones were the loonies.

If I hadn't been worried about Chris I might have found sympathy for them. Below the crassness it was a way they huddled together. For thousands of years one guess had been as good as another; nothing checked out; any system that cohered would do; and they had worked divination with their big black book as a way of holding together what there was of civilized life, swallowing the mythology along with the good sense. It was just a cataloging system, binary, clean/unclean, and they weren't any different from the tribesmen who worshiped the moon or a chunk of meteorite, although they thought they were.

And then science had come along and slowly, systematically, over three or four centuries it had displaced their big black book with its own enlarging text and authentic miracles: feeding the hungry, healing the sick, lifting the yoke of labor from the shoulders of men. Science might have seemed some earthly manifestation of the power of God, and I guess to the confused, to the liberal churchmen, it did. But along with its miracles came its terrible truths: that the universe was old and vast and automatic, that the earth was no more than a speck of a speck in that vastness, that men were animals evolved to exceptional intelligence with no more claim to souls than chimpanzees or juniper trees.

Which was at least clear, with the elegance of clarity and with the sense of perspective on human problems it gave. But an awful lot of people felt afraid, unprotected, lonely and alone. They missed the warm parental glow, however imaginary, of their personal Father God and Mother Mary and Son Jesus Christ.

So they performed the casual daily miracles science had found for them but chose not to believe. All sorts of people didn't even believe we had actually gone to the moon. Didn't want to. Thought the moon was vaguely heavenly and didn't want to picture us violating it. Like Galileo's contemporaries, who feared the craters Galileo found might be smallpox scars. Galileo was a cheerful man. He tried to disabuse them. Through telescope lenses rainbow-blurred by chromatic aberration, the moon looked to him like a peacock's tail, the craters its iridescent eyes.

We followed Ernie back to his office after the taping. It was six-thirty, five-thirty in Kansas City. He was glowing. He was high on audience reaction. When I'd known him before he'd been shy except when he had a few drinks. He'd changed. It was the kind of change that comes to men when they finally grow up. If you've been around them much, you know they grow up at different ages. Some at twenty-five; some not until their forties, like Ernie; some, the pitiful ones, never. And for some the growing up is wonderful to see and for others it's terrible, a new death-grip of rigidity. Ernie seemed to me then to have combined both states into one. Outwardly he was warm, confident, authoritative, but behind the eyes I saw a desperation I'd seen only flashes of before. Which made sense: evangelism at bottom is really, finally, a desperate effort to please.

Cowboy led the conversation. He'd known Ernie better than I. They'd been backup crew for one of the Gemini flights. He told Ernie in more detail about the kidnapping and about raising three hundred thousand in New York.

"You haven't let the grass grow under your feet," Ernie said noncommittally.

"We're talking about my son," I said.

"That's when I thought of you," Cowboy told Ernie, no Wyoming icing now, playing it absolutely straight. "I figured your organization had that kind of money and I figured this deal is what you'd think that money ought to be used for."

"Course there's a responsibility that goes with the gifts we receive, Cowboy," Ernie cautioned.

"Sure there is," Cowboy came back. "There's probably a dozen different deals that money's been earmarked for. But the thing is, you'll see it again. There's just no way this kidnap outfit's going to get off with three gold bars. If they'd ordered cash, small bills, then maybe. But not gold bars. People who trade gold to that extent know each other. They're going to know when someone slips in that much extra, even if it's been melted down." Cowboy changed position in his chair. You tended to slide off the front of those chairs. Ernie probably had them doctored, the front legs cut down. Cowboy: "So there's nothing to lose and there's Chris Wainwright's life to save. That looks to me like something real fine for the Prodigal Sons." You could doctor the legs of chairs to make people uncomfortable and still be a Christian. You just told yourself there was evil in the world and you were fighting fire with fire.

Ernie brought his palms together at his mouth: praying hands. I checked out the memorabilia. We each had a collection somewhere. I displayed mine on the bookshelves at the farmhouse. You couldn't buy much in the way of models anymore. The only company that still made them was British. Americans wanted World War II aircraft or they wanted *Star Wars.* The Saturn V, the LM were primitive. Chemical fuel. No warp drive, no Death Stars. If there were people who didn't believe we'd ever gone to the moon in the first place, there were thousands and thousands of other people who would never forgive us for going no farther than the moon and for doing nothing more when we got no farther than the moon than picking up a few hundred pounds of rocks.

"Thank you Jesus," Ernie said quietly as he opened his eyes. He leaned forward and laid his hands flat on his desk. "The Lord's shown me a way to help," he said.

"He has?" Cowboy.

I didn't say anything. I figured the Lord had cooked up a deal.

"He sure has," Ernie said. "Let me just ask you first of all, has either of you taken Jesus Christ as your lord and savior?" We stared. "No? No, I didn't think you did. I guess I knew a little about the way you two lived when we were in the program." He held up his hand. "I'm not judging you now. But if either of you felt called at this difficult time to give yourselves in trust to Christ Jesus, you'd find a powerful source of strength working for you. Paul says 'In everything I know how to be content.' When you belong to Jesus, when you're a bond slave unto Jesus, then Jesus is there in everything you do. Even in this terrible tragedy of your son's kidnapping, Red"—he caught my eye, total conviction, I come for help and I get a fucking sales pitch—"but you've got to make the decision yourself, got to go through the valley of the shadow yourself, until your eyes are opened and you see. 'Having eyes, see ye not?' Jesus said. 'And having ears, hear ye not?'"

"It's something to talk about," I told him. "After Chris is safe. That's all I can deal with right now." I meant it—I meant I'd spend the time with him, listen to his pitch, in exchange for his help if that was the price. That wasn't the price.

"Sure," Ernie said. I thought I'd sounded convincing but I'd disappointed him. He'd have liked a conversion right on the spot. "Well, Red, I won't say I can help you with the money—how much did you need again?"

Cowboy answered, through his teeth. "Two hundred thousand."

Ernie whistled. "Two hundred thousand. You know how much our average contribution is here? You don't? Well, it's eight dollars. That's right. Eight dollars. Which means, what, twenty-five thousand people would have to have contributed for us to have two hundred thousand dollars lying around. Anyway, I won't say I can help you with the money, but just supposing I could, what would you say to appearing on the show after you've got your son back and telling the whole story, Red? You think you could agree to that?"

"Sure. Absolutely."

"You wouldn't mind doing that? You wouldn't mind if I told the people that Prodigal Sons was able to help, and you'd bring along the boy and maybe the gold to show?"

"I'd be glad to, Ernie."

He nodded. "And just if we could raise some of the ransom money for you, you wouldn't object to signing a note for it, would you? You've got some sort of collateral? Own some buildings somewhere? Own some land?"

"I've got a farm. It's eighty acres, a house, barns, fences. It's worth something. Fifteen hundred an acre. One hundred twenty thousand."

"Praise Jesus. Don't the Lord remove obstacles, though? And just this last little thing, Red. You think you could bring yourself to give the Good Lord some of the credit if this deal works out? I don't mean I'd want you to say anything against your beliefs, but if you think there's any likelihood that some power beyond yourself and Cowboy here has had anything to do with all this, would you be willing to say so on the show?"

I thought: just like Hyerding. Maybe friendlier because we'd been through the program together. But otherwise just like Hyerding.

Make sure it's all covered and then make it pay twice. Fine. Why not. Me too. "Sure," I said.

"So what we're talking about is an exclusive on the publicity after your son's found. Is that agreed?"

"For how much?" Cowboy asked, no warmth at all in his voice.

"Well, how much." Ernie spread his hands. "A good chunk. Not all. Pretty high on the hog, but not all."

"Just work up the script, good buddy," I said. "I'll be back here as soon as this is over." Like hell I would.

"Praise the Lord," Ernie said, jumping up—down, really, out of that high chair—"praise Jesus. Come on with me." He beckoned. We followed him to a section of bookshelves on one side of the office with cabinets built in up to the waist level. He snapped open the cabinet doors and there was a safe: brown crinkled enamel and a serious-looking combination lock. He knelt to the lock, spun it left and right with a pleasant clicking. Stopping on sixty-nine—he'd probably never even noticed—and worked the handle and swung open the door.

Shelves of bills, banded. Nothing but hundreds showing.

This time Cowboy whistled.

I couldn't guess how much. Not to prolong the suspense, I asked.

"A hundred thousand," Ernie said proudly. "Did you bring along something to carry it in?"

Cowboy and I looked at each other. We hadn't thought.

"Never mind. I'll dump out my briefcase and let you take it in that." He was grinning, Ernie was, like the cons on the midway who work their flying fingers over the vegetable machine and suddenly you're standing there with your mouth open and a tray of radish roses in your hands.

He got his case, emptied it on his desk, brought it over, set it on the floor with the lid open and began packing it with bundles of bills. It wasn't new money or old. Just money. Green as a meadow.

"Don't you believe in banks?" Cowboy asked Ernie, more pleasantly now.

"This isn't Prodigal Sons money," Ernie said, squeezing out the last few drops of mystery. "At least, it's not from contributions." He chuckled. "At least, it's not from *regular* contributions."

"Irregular contributions?" Cowboy asked.

"You know," Ernie sidled into it, "Chuck Colson's a great worker for the Lord. Some people—"

"This is *Colson* money?" I butted in. I couldn't help it.

"—don't think he's sincere—no, not Colson money. Chuck sincerely came to Jesus, but he wasn't the only one. There were others. Some you never even heard about. Some who never were named."

"Watergate money," Cowboy said. We stared at it.

Ernie finished loading, fifty bundles of twenty bills each, snapped shut the case. He stood nodding. "The real thing. The *actual bills* themselves from the secret fund. Given to me to use for a good cause. Well, I think I've found it. Praise Jesus. Praise the Lord." And good old Ernie, he handed me the case.

Which was fantastic, praise the money laundry, praise Ehrlichman and Nixon and Deep Throat and the eighteen-minute gap, but Ernie had his secretary type up papers. When I walked out of there into the clearing Washington evening, I'd signed away my only collateral. And we were still one hundred thousand dollars short.

Twelve

What to do next? The collateral I'd pledged to Ernie I might have used in Kansas City. I wasn't above pledging it twice over if I had to. Talking in the street as we fought the good Washington fight for a taxi, Cowboy and I agreed we'd better establish a local base of operations first and make a few calls. He had some ideas—Al Shepard, the only authentic millionaire among the astronaut corps (self-made, in real estate), was one—and I wanted to check in with Paige. We flagged a taxi finally, ordered the Capitol Hill Hyatt. They recognized me at the desk. They only knew Cowboy by name. If we'd had time for foolishness he'd have made me earn that one. Despite the usual wall-to-wall conventioneers we got a room. Cowboy had room service working on a six-pack before we even finished checking in. The bellhop hauled the briefcase, our one piece of luggage—not knowing what a hell of a bundle he was carrying—and the minute he left I called Paige.

Chris's number, of course, so of course I got Diana. "Oh, *Dad*dy," she said, sending all her love along, which helped. She shouted downstairs for Paige. I heard them talking, heard Diana saying what if he *called*, she didn't see how she *could*—I supposed Paige was asking her to answer the other phone if it rang while we were talking on Chris's—and then Paige came on and told me about the contact earlier with the creep we didn't yet know was Karl Grabka.

"Whatever," I said impatiently, meaning it didn't matter if we were dealing with an individual or a political group. It didn't, not at that stage. The only thing that mattered was raising the gold. I told Paige about New York, about Hyerding and company, the bastards, and then about Washington and Ernie Defleurs. "So we're still short. We've checked in at the Hyatt. Copy the number, will you?" I gave it to her. "We're going to try calling around. Think about all your contacts. Maybe you know someone you've forgotten who owes you a favor who's rich. Maybe one of your magazines could come up with a hundred thousand in exchange for a piece of EAI and an exclusive on the story. How about *Playboy*? Would Hefner do that?"

"He might," Paige said, but it sounded reflex: she was distracted. Then she focused. "I have a better idea. Stay there. Let me call you back. Washington might be the answer."

"Who in Washington?"

She wasn't telling. "It's a good chance. Let me call you. Can you keep the line clear?"

"We'll try around. If the line's busy, ask the operator to cut in."

"Fine." She clicked off.

The beers came. I let Cowboy call Al Shepard. They'd been neighbors. I flopped onto the bed. Disasters overlap. Your body and your brain learn the work. Suddenly and vividly, as if I'd videotaped it, I remembered the disaster of our spacecraft fire and the long ride home.

In hindsight I'd say we had warning. Houston couldn't find us on the moon. *Macht nichts*, we were too busy to worry about it. *We* knew where we were. Halfway down the EVA timeline Cowboy said, "Red? Here goes the big one, buddy." And did that famous somersault, in moon-slow motion, at one-sixth G. It was fantastic, except the powers that be threw a conniption later when the world went to bed. It didn't help that they couldn't get a fix on our base.

Descending in the LM the computer flashed a 1202 program alarm—"executive overflow," too much data—and I went manual and flew that baby down and we landed inside Copernicus off the Ocean of Storms, the dark walls of the crater rising up around us. Then EVA, Cowboy's contraband acrobatics, work. Despite our built-in cooling systems we sweated like long-distance runners. I poured out puddles later when I took off my gloves. But walking on the moon was like walking on a trampoline. Even falling down was no big deal (now at least there *was* a down). I weighed all of twenty-six pounds, my suit and PLSS about fifty-nine, compared to a combined five hundred twenty on earth. Light or not, the inflated neoprene bladder lining our suits that kept our blood from boiling was stiff as hell. We kangaroo-hopped because we could flex our boots more easily than we could bend at the knees.

Then, during ascent, we heard an ungodly *woo-woo*ing on the VHF. Charlie in the command module said it sounded like wind whipping around the trees. There aren't any trees on the backside of the moon. The whipping wind was only interference between the two spacecraft radios and we'd had the same noise briefly the day before on descent. But we were warned. It crept up on us.

Do you remember the layout of those fantastic machines? They were all handmade. They were beautiful. The command module was a smoothly rounded cone, a pressure vessel twelve feet across the base and about ten feet up to the apex. The tunnel and hatches that accessed the LM when the two spacecraft docked exited from the apex. Inside the command module we had our three couches; a closet-sized area, the lower equipment bay, where there was space to stand; instrument panels overhead and around; everything painted battleship gray; hundreds and hundreds of circuit breakers. Relatively roomy—zero G helped. With the service module attached she flew like a bomber, meaning not sluggishly, exactly, but judiciously.

The service module fitted onto the base of the command module. It was a big tin can with a single flaring rocket bell stuck on its end. It held our consumables and our power—three fuel cells for the command module's water and electricity, the big course-correction engine, cryogenic O_2, all except the batteries and tanks we needed for reentry.

The LM was a weird-looking contraption but I loved it tenderly. Like the command and service modules, it came in two parts. The descent stage, the lower part, was an octagonal box with one big engine and fuel tanks and four springy legs that led to feet like foil-wrapped saucers. Five different shapes were welded together to make the ascent stage. The part we lived in was a section of stubby cylinder eight feet high across the diameter and only three and a half feet thick, with two downward-looking triangular windows. Everything in the LM was engineered to save weight. They built up the walls of sixteen layers of plastic and foil and you could just as easily have run your fist through them. No couches or seats: we stood to fly, braced with guy wires. Terrible racket when the thrusters fired outside those thin walls. But the lightness paid off. The LM flew like a chopper. I trained in choppers to fly it.

We left the descent stage on the moon. The ascent stage took us up to meet Charlie. It climbed like a dingbat.

Cowboy and I merged our orbit with the command module's in two separate catch-up burns and set up station keeping behind. Charlie translated the command module to face us. We flew formation that way until we'd all come back around in front of the moon. Then he flew in the probe, firing a nitrogen bottle to lock on. We opened the hatches and took down the probe and drogue and floated through the tunnel. Charlie got his first smell of the moon then, the dust on our suits. We were still in our suits with gloves and helmets off. Charlie too, standard precaution.

Then all hell broke loose.

This is what they taped on the downlink:

> CAPCOM: Buffalo, Houston. Over.
> SC: Go ahead, Houston.
> CAPCOM: Roger, Charlie. We're curious about your crew status. Have Red and Cowboy transferred over yet?
> SC: Rog, that's an affirm. We're all three back inside. We're running a pressure check. Leak check. Everything's—Jesus Christ. Jesus Christ.
> SC: What the hell. Look out. Fire. Fire in the cockpit.
> SC: (Garbled) that hatch. Charlie. My God. Get your (garbled).
> CAPCOM: Buffalo, Houston. What's going on?
> SC: Christ, hurry. Help Charlie. I'll get the hatch.
> SC: Hang on (garbled) better. Don't let go. For (deleted).
> CAPCOM: Buffalo, Houston. Do you read? Apollo 12B, if you read please respond. If you read please respond. This is Houston, over.
> SC: Houston, we read. We had a fire. We popped the hatch. Fire's out now. Charlie got burned. Hang on and we'll get back to you.
> CAPCOM: Rog, Red. We're standing by. We're here, buddy.

We didn't know what hit us. One minute we were going about our business and the next minute the spacecraft was full of acrid yellow smoke billowing from behind a panel and Charlie's hair was burning. There wasn't time to think. We'd had fire drill and we reacted. Cowboy pushed back through the tunnel to the LM and grabbed our helmets and gloves. I worked over Charlie—God, there was skin coming off his head—to put his hair out and get his helmet and gloves on so we could pop the hatch. Took a thousand years. We got the hatch open, we were safe in our suits, the spacecraft was airless but the panel still burned. Cowboy figured it out: an O_2 line had burst. He found the valve and shut it off and the fire sputtered out.

That was just the beginning of it.

The fire had charred an entire panel of circuit breakers. The O_2 had fed the flame. The O_2 made the fire a lot worse than it would have been at cabin pressure, which was only five psi.

Plus, the spacecraft had jolted. I'd noticed it even in the confusion. So had Cowboy. When we got the hatch open I could see a cloud of gas coming off the service module behind us. It was thinning out in sheets, dissipating into space. We'd had an explosion. Something had burst and vented and thrown us around.

We were showing an undervolt on our Main Bus A. That was our prime electricity supply from the service module. Main A was reading zip.

Charlie was close to shock. His head was a mess.

I called Houston while Cowboy ran a quick check to see if anything else was burning. Nothing. He closed the hatch. You could hear the disbelief in Houston. After the Apollo 1 fire that killed Gus and Ed and Rog we'd redesigned the spacecraft. The second one up, Apollo 8, they sent all the way around the moon before they'd even checked out the LM, they were that confident. These Block II jobs were supposed to be fireproof, but listen to me: nothing's fireproof when there's a busted O_2 line around.

Cowboy brought up cabin pressure. It held—at least the seals were holding. We got out gloves and helmets off. Charlie was coming alert and starting to feel the pain. I talked to the flight surgeon direct—unheard-of any other time, usually everything goes through the Capcom—and the flight surgeon proposed we break out the medicine stores and give Charlie a morphine injection. I wrestled him free of his suit, free of the arms and torso of his suit. I couldn't inject him through the suit. God knows he might still need it. The O_2 cryo number two, one of the service module's two cryogenic oxygen tanks, was reading empty. We'd lost power and we'd lost half our O_2. Babe, we were a long way from home.

Houston woke up and shook itself. It could monitor our systems. We were less than ten minutes from LOS, loss of signal as we passed around behind the moon, out of contact with the earth on our line-of-sight radios. Houston had telemetry. It knew what we knew about our spacecraft systems and a little more. What it knew as soon as it started believing the telemetry was that the service module and the command module were badly damaged, short on oxygen and short on electricity. One fuel cell and what oxygen was left in the one O_2 cryo was all that was up. So they made some quick decisions down below and we got the fateful word.

> CAPCOM: Red, we advise powering down the command module and making your way over to the LM. That'll have to be your lifeboat for a while.
> SC: Roger, Houston, we copy. Cowboy and Charlie are in the LM.

We'd already started the move on our own. I stayed in the command module to power down, everything but the lights, the radio, the cryo heaters and fans and the inertial guidance platform. We needed the guidance for TEI, trans-earth injection. We needed the big service-module engine to kick us out of moon orbit where we were stuck. The LM ascent engine didn't have enough juice.

What I was doing would have been Charlie's job as command module pilot. Obviously he wasn't in any shape for it.

Then we had LOS and we were alone with our cripples—one ship, one man. Our earth connections. Our moon connections worked flawlessly.

I wish I could tell you I thought about the significance of what was happening to us. There were various morals to be drawn, reaching as far down as Bobby Baker's part-ownership of the vending-machine franchise at North American Rockwell, and the press eventually drew them ad nauseam. I thought about some of it later, while we were limping home, and I'll get to that. Immediately it was all technical. Spaceflights were, which is why the media perceived us—I mean the whole astronaut corps—to be heroic nerds. The truth is, most of the time we had our hands full. NASA had lost three guys on the pad. They were sending teams of three—maybe as many as twenty teams, they thought, something less than sixty guys—far beyond the help of rescue systems. So they overengineered everything, doubled and tripled and quadrupled everything, which kept us damned busy during ordinary flights and which made horrendous complications in emergencies. We had to wade through all that engineering to take control.

I'll cut it short: behind the moon we did as many of the several hundred things we had to do to get ready for a rocket burn as we could do without talking to Houston. In forty-five minutes the earth surged over the jagged horizon, a burst of lovely blue and rust and swirling white, we acquired signal, we came around in front of the moon again. Houston called up our burn pad—the numbers we needed to program our computer, set our times and point ourselves in the right direction. They won't make much sense, and I can't say I remembered them verbatim lying on my bed at the Hyatt, but I've looked them up since and I'll give them here so that you can see why we weren't drawing any morals:

> CAPCOM: Apollo 12B, Houston. If you're ready to copy, I've got your coming-home information for you.
> SC: Stand by.
> SC: All right, ready to copy.
> CAPCOM: Rog, 12B. Get a TEI 30 pad. TEI 30 SPS G & N 36 691 minus 061 plus 066 135 23 41 56 NOUN 81 32 correction plus 32 0 11 plus 06 818 minus 02 650 181 054 014. Apogee is NA. Perigee plus two balls 230 32 86 correction 32 836. Burn time 2 28 32 628 24 151 1 35 7. Next three lines are NA. NOUN 61 plus 11 03 minus 17 237 11 806 36 275 195 04 52. Set stars are Deneb and Vega 242 172 012. We'd like ullage of two jets per 16 seconds and the horizon is on the 10 degree line at TIG minus two minutes and your sextant star is visible after 134 plus 50.

Emergency or not, I read all that back, because a wrong number could send us out on a one-way tour of the planets.

Cowboy and I worked our butts off getting ready. Then LOS again. Behind the moon in the command module I set up the burn. We were passing through the moon's shadow, Ernie Defleurs's bad moment on a later flight. There wasn't any earth, there wasn't any sun. Around in front the moon was bright, enormous, visibly a sphere, but here it was a presence only as an absolute blackness that blotted out a vast disk of stars. We could see tens of thousands of stars thick through the rest of space but we couldn't see the moon or the earth or the sun.

We counted down to the burn—the computer was controlling it—and the SPS gently kicked in. The service propulsion system doesn't have a mule kick. It's a twenty-thousand-pound thrust engine and it was pushing one hundred thousand pounds, which means the boost was only one-fifth G. So we didn't feel it much. But we saw it: as we came around the moon it looked to us as if we were going straight up. Like Superman. Up, up and away. I was never so glad of anything in my life.

Getting home was mainly going to be a matter of hibernating. We had to keep everything we could spare, including ourselves, powered down. We could draw power intermittently to charge the LM batteries from the one fuel cell in the service module that was still working, but the fuel cell used oxygen and we didn't have much oxygen and we could limp home only if we kept breathing. So Cowboy and I operated from the LM. Most of the time we fiddled with the attitude controls to maintain some semblance of a thermal roll, to keep the two joined spacecraft rotating in relation to the sun so they wouldn't bake on one side. The system was computer-aided in the command module. Not in the LM. We worked it by hand for two and a half days and it was a bitch. Usually, instead of a roll, we got a wobble. As the wobble increased we'd start approaching gimbal lock, which we especially didn't need with no more navigation aids than we had in the LM. So we'd have to hand-correct for the wobble, firing the LM thrusters, and that would start up another wobble and after a few hours we'd have to go to work again.

Charlie found a home floating in the tunnel between the spacecraft, trying to stay out of the way and warm. He was floating in more ways then one. He had pain. After we used two of the three morphine injectors in the medical kit, the flight surgeon directing us, we switched to pain pills. Charlie's head was horrible, crust and discolor and ooze, frizzed hair on the sides. He tried not to move his scalp, what was left of it. He held his face expressionless and floated in the tunnel, his body flexed semifetally. It flexes that way automatically in zero G. We did what we could for him. With the painkillers and the strange environment he really went down the rabbit hole. Wouldn't you know the flight surgeons were having a field day. Burn management in space was a big deal.

Not even Cowboy and I, old friends and fellow hell-raisers that we were, found much to say. The command module was dark and cold, getting colder. The LM was chilling. Our space suits were too bulky to wear, too stiff. Without power they couldn't be ventilated—they'd be clammy in no time. We gave Charlie the skimpy Mylar blankets in the emergency pack. There was nothing to do but shiver in our inadequate nylon jump suits and look out the windows. We seemed to hang motionless in space; the moon shrank; the earth slowly, much too slowly, enlarged. To a shipwrecked sailor the sea is wide and empty and space is wide and empty to an astronaut in a crippled spacecraft. No one was ever endangered so far from home before. Not Earth but only the earth itself could rescue us. Once Chris had asked Cowboy and me who would be driving. Cowboy had winked at me and said Isaac Newton would be driving. Now he was.

Frost built up on the inside of the command module windows. The temperature got down to thirty-five degrees. The LM was warmer, but not by much—five or ten degrees. You could feel the cold of deep space on the windows and you could feel it through the hull. It transferred from outside through your flesh down into the marrow of your bones. Space hadn't seemed hostile before. When I'd floated out to EVA on Gemini 13, attached in silence by a tether, racing around the earth, I'd felt at home. Now the cold was implacable, drawing out heat into a region of immense, inhuman emptiness that could swallow up you and a billion billion of your kind.

I'm only human. On the way back from the moon and again lying on the bed that evening at the Hyatt, part of me wished I were anyplace else. I tuned in Cowboy's conversation with Al Shepard on the phone. "If God had meant Texans to ski," I heard him say—it wasn't an odd thing to say to Al—"He would have made bullshit white." I remembered that the moon had been solid under our feet and we had walked there. Nothing hostile even though it was airless: rocks, soil, horizon, morning sun. It looked like the high desert country. Briefly it had been a place to live. The Apollo 12B fiasco and Chris's kidnapping connected this way: the same hostile medium positioned itself between me and those I loved: cold: the cold of space and the cold of a hardened human heart. I think the heart more culpable.

We had to hang on for two and a half days and hanging on was hard. Cold was the worst of it, worst of all for Charlie. Once he shivered uncontrollably for four hours. Cowboy and I took turns rubbing him. We weren't hands-on men, not in those days, but it helped us all. The LM and even more the command module were dank caves: icy water dripped from the walls. We called the command module "the refrigerator." The cold made sleep almost impossible. I averaged something like three hours a night.

Cowboy and I put in a lot of hours worrying. We worried about Charlie, but after the first twenty-four hours his condition stabilized and then we relaxed to the point of watching him to make sure it stayed that way. He was wearing a biomedical harness, as we all were, and the medics back in Houston continuously monitored his vital signs. We kept him doped; we tried to keep him warm; we fed him the little he'd eat of cold food, mostly orange drink and grape drink but also the chicken stew and chicken and rice in spoon-bowl packages that didn't have to be rehydrated. Water was critical. We gave him as much as he'd drink. Cowboy and I stinted and got dehydrated, which made us stupid toward the end.

The rest of the time we worried about reentry. Was the command module hatch really tight? That was one question. Could we successfully jettison the LM? That was another. Normally it would have been left behind to crash into the moon, and we didn't want it following us down the reentry corridor and possibly rear-ending us as we slowed. Had whatever happened back in the service module damaged the command module heat shield? If it had, we'd burn up when we frictioned our way into the atmosphere at a starting velocity of twenty-four thousand mph.

Plenty to worry about. Cowboy stared out the window a lot. So did I.

Take a look at us coasting in a powered-down spacecraft somewhere between the earth and the moon. Charlie floats in the cylindrical tunnel—it's six feet long, three and a half feet across—that connects the refrigerator upstairs with the LM ascent stage. He's vague, quiet, wrapped loosely in crinkled aluminized Mylar with his booted, Velcro-soled feet showing and his burned, crusted head.

Cowboy lounges back behind me in the LM. Behind the stand-up compartment, with its space for two suited pilots at waist-level controls facing the two downward-looking windows, is a compartment that starts a little below waist level that's dominated by the big cylindrical popcorn can of the ascent engine cover. Cowboy "sits" on the ascent engine cover—actually, of course, he's floating. Maybe, rarely, he squirts himself a drink of water through the polished aluminum LM water pistol, clicking metered swallows into his mouth a shot at a time. If a drop gets away, it immediately forms a wobbly sphere and looks and acts much like a glob of Jell-o. All kinds of things float around the spacecraft, eventually ending up on the intake screen of the recirculation system where we sort recoverables from junk.

Cowboy's eyes are red-rimmed and his lips bluish with cold. He's made a good start on a beard. The chest area of his jump suit looks like a much-used baby's bib because even with the best of intentions we lose some of our food to our fronts. Newton's driving that too. Everything the Saturn V brought up—the spacecraft, the three of us, the missing pliers that drift onto the intake screen, down to the drops of water and crumbs of cinnamon-toast cubes we lose—is individually and separately a satellite of the earth on this homeward journey, and whenever it isn't nudged or restrained it coasts inertially on its own personal trajectory. Outside the windows the scraps of metal from the explosion that fixed us in dangerous emergency lope along beside us like voiceless coursing dogs.

And where am I in this snapshot? Maybe I'm working on the

reentry checklist—basically, taking inventory and letting Houston know where we've stored equipment and what's left of the consumables. If so, I'm up in the refrigerator moving around, and the dialogue with Houston sounds like this:

> SC: I think the quickest thing is to go through page by page the first part of the checklist where it has a map. Starting on the page with compartments L2 and L3. Are you with me?
> CAPCOM: Roger. With you.
> SC: Okay. L2 is as shown. L3 is as shown. There's about half the food remaining in L3.
> CAPCOM: Roger.
> SC: Where it says "and note" the CMP PGAs are located in the L-shaped bag with the other two PGAs. The CMP's helmet and gloves instead of being in the sleep restraint are in the hatch bags.
> CAPCOM: Copy.
> SC: In compartment A, one 16-millimeter magazine will be located in window number 04 instead of 05. Tissue dispensers, there's only one of them left and compartment U3 the 16-millimeter bracket is on window 04 and add 10 pounds of LM miscellaneous equipment. We told you 5 the other day. We think 10 is probably closer, over.
> CAPCOM: Copy.

Exciting stuff. In the meantime, I'm trying to stay warm, rubbing myself, moving around, but moving takes almost no effort. It's impossible *not* to move. Suppose you sit in a chair. First you're still. Any slight movement will start a chain reaction. If you even relax your shoulders back into the chair, you'll begin to float away. If you grab a chair arm to stop yourself, the torque of pulling on one side will start you turning toward that pull. If you grab the other chair arm to stop the turn, you slam back into the chair with more force than you intended, which, given the elasticity of flesh and chair, bounces you out of it even faster than the first time. You can work yourself up to a real struggle. What you learn to do instead is something like what you learn to do when you're braking a car to a stop without jerking the passengers: you let up a little at the end of each motion, damp it out. You're still at the mercy of all the interconnected elastic systems of your body, of materials—at the mercy of action and reaction, equal and opposite, of Newton's law and the law of the universe.

So we passed the time. Through it all, outside one window was the moon, outside the opposite window was the earth, and slowly, without motion, the earth waxed, the moon waned. We were making it: we were going home.

I left out: we stink. We've got a burn case, we've got charred plastic, we've worked hard and we haven't had a bath for a week.

Closer in we got busy. We didn't want to jettison the LM until the last possible moment—that was one of the schemes Houston had worked out to make sure it didn't come crashing down around our heads on reentry—but we had to get rid of the service module on schedule, not least because it covered up the command module heat shield we needed to come home. No one had ever made that jettison with the LM attached before. Our buddies down at the Cape stayed up two nights running working it out on a simulator, and when the time came it was easy (except that only two of us were in shape to handle what three should have done).

We loosely strapped Charlie into one command module couch so he wouldn't go flying. Cowboy worked the command module; I worked the LM. First I fired the LM thrusters to move us all forward (the service module technically backward, rocket bell foremost) at half a foot per second. Then Cowboy fired the pyros—the shaped-charge explosives—that cut free the service module by guillotining all connecting lines and cleanly slicing through the skin. Then I reversed the LM thrusters and backed us away at half a fps. The explosion of the pyros screwed the service module around and set it spinning. We got a look at the damage and both Cowboy and I hurriedly photographed it: one entire side blown out, lines dangling free, crumpled hull catching the sun.

Now we switched over to our reentry batteries. Houston calculated we had enough reserve to power up. With the wall and window heaters on, things began to get warmer. I was completely fagged. So was Cowboy. Deke Slayton himself came on the private channel to suggest we pop some Dexedrine and two hours before splashdown we did. We were roaring in now like a cannonball, smoothly and visibly picking up speed. In the last quarter-turn around the big blue earth, the last ten minutes of coast before reentry, we'd accelerated from twenty-one to twenty-four thousand mph. As the earth got bigger, as it began to fill the windows of the command module, we recovered our sense of relative motion. I mean: we *felt* we were coming home. At last.

We still had to jettison the LM. Before we did that we turned it into a Demsey Dumpster, loading it from floor to ceiling with plastic bags of our trash, including two days' worth of urine we'd been unable to vent into space because the urine dump valve was frozen. Floor-to-ceiling trash—it hung wherever we put it, more or less—including our suits. We'd opted to risk the hatch seals. If they failed we'd lose our air, we'd be dead men because there wouldn't be time left to put on our suits—and no suits then to put on—but the suits were just as bulky and impossible to work in now as they had been when we decided not to wear them two days ago.

We went through the hatch check on schedule and the hatch was okay.

We also had to make sure the hatch that led to the LM was solid. We finished our move into the command module, closed off the hatches, vented the tunnel down to half pressure and watched the numbers. They looked good. The LM was holding our attitude on automatic and those numbers didn't look so good: it was maneuvering us close to gimbal lock. Houston was watching and asked us to jettison the LM as soon as possible. We didn't mess around. When the word came up that everything was go Cowboy fired the pyros. The air pressure in the tunnel between the two spacecraft pushed us apart, sending the LM in one direction and the command module in another. It was an improvised system, but it worked. We were back to where we ought to have been at that point in the timeline, we were all three alive, we had our two boxes of moon rocks and enough amperage on the batteries to see us down. The command module flew like a fighter now and we were raring to go. Credit the Dexedrine with some of that.

So we make our last giddy turn around the rushing fantastic globe of the earth, brushing the fringes of its atmosphere, and begin the ride. The base of the command module faces forward; we face backward and upside down. A light on the panel above my head goes on to signal half a G of deceleration. Wisps of glowing gas begin to blow past the windows. Off to the right I can see the Pacific Ocean—we're coming in over the Indian. We fire our thrusters to roll, a little roll to change our angle of attack, and suddenly outside and below my windows are mountain summits fresh with snow—the crisp, clean mountains of New Zealand.

The view burns away in light, not the pale glow of ionized gases I saw at first, pinks and lavenders and blues, but white light flooding the cabin, light almost blinding in high whiteness, and we know we're at the center of a fireball that trails its meteor's tail back behind us hundreds of miles, and since our backs are cool we know we've got a heat shield.

With the light comes the heavy burden of deceleration, weight that since we left the earth a week ago we haven't had to bear. It builds rapidly as we rush down the reentry corridor into denser air, from that initial teasing half a G to three, four, five, finally to six and a half G's, making each of us weigh more than a thousand pounds so that we can't lift our arms, so that our cheeks drag back, drag open our mouths, so that we can only breathe by panting lightly high in our chests, and poor Charlie feels the weight most cruelly hauling down his crusted skull, and involuntarily he groans.

Then quickly the weight lifts, the light dims. We're back on the radio, we can see the white scattered clouds below and the blue Pacific coming up to meet us, we can breathe. At twenty-four thousand feet we feel a jerk as our two drogue parachutes deploy and we see them above us luffing at the ends of their long lines. They're reefed; the reefs work off and they fill. Pyros cut the drogues away and three pilot chutes pop up dragging the big main chutes behind them, a great business of color out the forward windows. The main chutes come out reefed and the reefs work off and then the three chutes flare, filling the sky so that all we can see above us is their lines and their red-and-white striped canopies like balloon spinnakers running with the wind.

We splash down into a sunlit sea, staying base down in mode one, I'm glad to say, and soon the frogmen are pounding on the hatch, we're smelling the fantastic warm smell of the sea, the hatch is open and we're helping Charlie with the life jacket the frogmen have thrown in and putting on our own; and exiting the hatch the first thing I do, believe me, the first thing I do is scoop up a handful of seawater and splash my face. Taste. Taste the brothy salt of thick sea we came from, the salt of the earth, glad to be back, glad to be alive.

So I did go away, lying on the bed in the Hyatt, didn't I. For a little while. And brought back hope. If disasters are analogous, brought back hope.

"Al wants to help," Cowboy said. "The trouble is, his partner's in Riyadh. He's hard to reach. Al can't commit that much money without him."

I sat up. "Maybe he can commit part of it. Half of it."

Cowboy nodded. "That's what we talked about—"

The phone started ringing. I crossed to the desk and answered it.

"Reeve?" Paige, her voice urgent. "It's set. It's fixed. I have it for you."

I sat. "Who?"

"I can't say. It's a favor. You'll see. You're to talk to Richard Pettibone."

I knew the name. "Isn't he—"

Paige interrupted. "Yes. Carter's aide. You're to go to the White House."

"When?" Cowboy was watching, raising an eyebrow.

"When? Tonight. Right now. As soon as you can get over there."

"Great. I'm going."

"Get going."

"I'm going. Fantastic. How'd you swing it?"

"Never mind. Go."

And I hung up, and told Cowboy, and he said he'd call Al, and off to the White House I went.

Thirteen

Chris in darkness was coming up on Saturday night. On some level he sensed it. Late Saturday afternoon he'd decided to eat. Not even kidnapping and burial could completely suppress the gnawing teenage appetite that had regularly emptied my refrigerator at the farm. He ate sparingly only because he wanted to avoid drinking the water. He ate a Hershey bar, three or four boxes of raisins, a handful of peanuts. He filled up on apples.

The food helped, but he was still cold. He shivered. The shivering would build until he was shaking almost convulsively and then completely stop. I suppose it did its temporary work of warming as it had for us coming back from the moon. The cold seeped in again through the thin pad Chris was lying on. Even with the blanket he couldn't keep warm.

Worst was the darkness. It was worse than the cold, worse than the confinement—he found the box fairly roomy, roomier than the driver's seat in his VW. But not to see his hand in front of his face: hours of darkness, hours and hours of darkness. Part of him was still counting when I'd come. It had to be soon. I was negotiating with the weirdo. A time of that, maybe a night of that, and then the weirdo would draw a map. Then I'd get help and get going. Find the place. Dig. The shovel scraping on the lid. Daylight. Or moonlight if it was night and there was a moon. Starlight. Night was almost as bright as day compared to darkness. He'd never known that before. Moses had called down a plague of darkness on the Egyptians. Somewhere Chris had read there was still a sealed jar of that original plague of darkness in a museum in Cairo. Excellent, man, but you couldn't open it to see!

> Black of night
> Black around me
> Plague of darkness
> Plague surround me

The lyrics wouldn't quit. He'd been working on them off and on for hours and they were beginning to get it together. "Buried Alive," if that didn't remind people of Janis Joplin. Not that many rockers probably read the book about her. So "Buried Alive." It was looking more and more like a rock ballad:

> Well, I was playin' Star Trek
> Squeezin' out the fuel
> Man come along
> Shows me a pig badge
> Plays me for a fool

With the chorus he'd had before:

> Beat all, beat all, beat all beat all beat all

He'd worked out another verse, maybe the second verse:

> Shoves me in his pickup
> Hauls out his gun
> Slaps on the cuffs
> Says it's a lockup
> Says it won't be fun

Some of the lines needed filling out:

> Man said Save your breath
> . . . .
> Gonna be my death

or maybe

Goin' to my death

This one near the end:

Man got caught
Dad's an astronaut

He hoped *Man got caught.*

The *black of night* thing was excellent. It ought to go in somewhere. So should the *Ain't no j. Man dint leave us none.* So should the verse he'd come up with first:

In the autumn of that year
When the man took me away
When I first knew fear
In the autumn of that year

He'd have to find a place for all of them. It was going to be absolutely the most kick-ass song anyone ever wrote. He could hear the synthesizer working it over in the background, space sounds, sirens, growls. He wanted to set the drums against the idea of a funeral, around and against one muffled drum, almost a drone like a bagpipe.

Jesus H. Christ, Chris.

You write that yourself, man?

Uh, Chris honey, can I maybe have your autograph?

Chris produced a laugh to go with the dialogue and thought the laugh sounded in the dark echo chamber of his burial box like Wolfman Jack's.

I took a taxi to the west gate of the White House, the business entrance ordinary mortals use. The lights had just turned on along Pennsylvania Avenue. The White House was blazing. I hadn't been back since Nixon shipped a bunch of us in for dinner in the early days of Watergate. I'd talked to him that evening in the Oval Office. He'd told me about his gavel collection. Maybe I was preserved for the ages on one of the tapes.

The guards knew me. They asked me how things were going, but they still checked my driver's license before they sent me up the walk. The first time I'd walked up that walk, years before when I was passing through Washington on one of my earliest weeks in the barrel, my knees had knocked. Benefit of age if you keep your wits about you: your knees stop knocking. I suppose age. Maybe celebrity too. Until palsy sets them knocking again.

Pretty receptionist inside the door. She directed me to the striped love seat against the wall beyond her desk to wait. I'd forgotten how solid the White House is: thick walls, deep carpet, sounds absorbed into silence the way they are in expensive concert halls. Solidity made manifest in sound is a fair percentage of the impression wealth makes on those of us who lack it. I hadn't been around wealth for years, not since the post-Apollo party tour. I'd forgotten how it felt. The White House offered more than the inconceivable wealth of the wealthiest nation ever assembled (wealth enough to send a mob of jet jockeys—not even scientists, just jet jockeys—careening to the moon and back on JFK's whim). It also offered inconceivable power. If you didn't watch your marbles in a place like the White House you'd start thinking you were God. They did. One by one, almost all of them did.

"Mr Wainwright?" My guide, slim and chic, dressed to the nines as in the White House they do. "I'm Becki Ratliff. Will you come with me, please?" She didn't say she was Richard Pettibone's secretary—in the White House, secretaries had secretaries.

I followed her. We walked a hall, started up a flight of stairs. "You're working late," I said.

Professional smile. "Comes with the territory." She had a gambit prepared. "We were all so *worried* about you when you had that dreadful fire."

"You remember that? You don't look old enough." Terrible, I know. I was distracted.

"Why, thank you kind sir."

Pettibone's secretary was a woman of heft and middle age. I stood outside the little fence of solid oak uprights that penned her desk, on dense, green carpet, while she called in. Then the heavy door swung open and there was Richard Pettibone, young like all of Carter's staff men except Zbig, pink-cheeked and solid.

He shook my hand—powerful grip—looked me in the eye. Friendly and distant at the same time. "Come on in," he said. "How about coffee?" It was a comparatively cool greeting for a southerner. If he'd counted me anywhere near his rank he'd have pronounced my name two or three times to show me he admired it, pounded my back, sold me a used car.

"I'd like that," I answered the coffee question. Pettibone nodded to Becki, who glided off as we went in. The office was paneled—dark oak. The gold carpet was carved in eagles. The desk was walnut and scattered with memorabilia; more memorabilia in the bookshelves. Law books in the bookshelves too—Pettibone was a lawyer, unusual for Carter's down-home staff. Most of them were frat men, weren't they?

He closed the door behind him. There was a big color photograph of Jimmy Carter on the wall, expensively framed. Pettibone chose the couch, one concession: we didn't square off across the desk. He put me at one end and settled himself at the other. I was dressed down in slacks and turtleneck and windbreaker—that's all I'd brought from home—so he stripped to vest and white shirt. Touch of jowl at the shirt collar, like so many southern professional men. You are what you eat.

"I remember well, Red—mind I call you Red?" Pettibone began, "I remember well when you men had that fire. I wasn't long out of law school." He crossed one leg over the other, ankle cocked high at the knee. "I'd joined up with the President—he was still the Governor then—and we'd been out that day beatin' the bush over one thing or another. We caught it on the car radio. After that we followed you the whole way home." Flicker of a grin. "Tell me this, though: were you ever afraid?"

"Terrified." We were going to jaw first. Fair enough.

Pettibone nodded. "Know just what you mean. Not on that scale, but just from other things." Bigger grin. "Couple of years ago my grandma saw those first pictures of Jupiter in the papers? She asked me, 'Richard, what on earth is that?' 'That's a planet, Grandma,' I told her. 'Well, what's wrong with it?' she came back, kind of nervous. 'Is it going to crash?'"

We chuckled together. He wanted us comfortable. Becki brought a silver service, he took his coffee with cream and sugar, I took mine black.

"What's your opinion on this space shuttle deal?" he asked me when Becki left.

"I've been away from NASA for quite a few years, Mr. Pettibone."

"Richard." Flick: grin.

The press called him Pet. "Richard. The scuttlebutt I get is that morale's down around the ankle level."

He sipped his coffee. "Money, you think?"

"Probably it is by now. The first team dropped off after Apollo, but that's to be expected."

"Real hard to justify the money when we're trying to balance the budget. It's kind of like when Adam first figured out that Eve was something more than just a spare hunk of rib. It was all new to him and kind of exciting and he looks down at himself and looks up at Eve and looks back down and says, 'Stand back, honey, I don't know how big this thing gets.'"

I laughed. He guffawed. "At some point it's going to get embarrassing, isn't it?" I meant the space shuttle, folks.

"I guess it could," he nodded. "Except it isn't ours. It's kind of cold leftovers." He might have winked then, but he didn't.

"Didn't we configure some military satellites for the STS that can't ride the Atlas Centaur? They'll have to go up on schedule, won't they?"

"Right. Mid-eighties."

"So the shuttle budget will have to keep pace with that."

Pettibone set down his coffee. "Congress is watching that. Jack Schmitt's watching that. He'll see the funding comes on."

Ah. And it wouldn't be charged to Carter.

"I ought to have said earlier, Red, congratulations on your book. You must be right proud." I didn't know what to do with that one, since I'd inveighed against just such grandiose energy schemes as Carter had proposed. What I did was shrug. Modestly, I hoped. Apparently it suited Pettibone. He pulled on the lobe of his right ear. "You know what I got a kick out of? That business of giving everyone in America with a big old car a brand-new Volkswagen free of charge and still saving money over building refineries for synfuel." He let go the earlobe and it flopped. "That was real clever."

"Diesel Rabbit," I said. "Something out of Detroit as soon as they get around to building it."

"You double-check those numbers?"

"I double-checked those numbers."

He swung his hands behind his head just as I folded mine at my chest, the usual body-language ballet. "I wish it was all that easy," he sighed.

"I know it's not easy. I wanted to make the point as emphatically as I could."

"Red, I understand that. You know the President's put a lot of weight behind conservation? He's stressed that first off the mark, out in front of everything else he's proposed?"

Not to seem too agreeable, I sat forward to drink my coffee. After I'd swallowed I said, "Sure."

"Solar, too," Pettibone went on. "You remember a year ago last May third? Denver? He came out for twenty-five percent solar by the year 2000?"

"He talked to Amory Lovins."

"He made a public commitment." Glint of fire in those liquid southern eyes.

"It's a start," I said.

"It's a hell of a start. You've got to think about the politics of it. If we'd of come in here to a clean slate we'd of probably gone for more even than a quarter. We had the DOE bureaucrats to fight, we had the nuclear power boys, we had those oil senators and congressmen from those oil states. Plus coal. A quarter's about twenty percent more than any of his predecessors thought they could bring off. You got to give the man credit, Red. Credit where credit's due."

And credit I was there for, in case I'd forgotten. I hadn't. I just didn't like bullying, even the sorghum southern kind. I'd taken enough that day. I was having to swallow hard to take more. I hadn't asked myself, hadn't had time to ask myself, if there was a limit to what I'd put up with to assemble the money I needed to ransom my son, if there was a limit to how much ass I'd kiss. I don't know if there was or not. I still don't know. I do know I suspended my standard rules, which I like to think are rigorous: no ass-kissing ever, all promises kept. Grabka's violence, Grabka's depravity that he thought worked narrowly, just him and me, splashed out shit like a rock thrown into a cesspool. It wasn't important, not compared to Chris's life, but it was one more thing I owed the slimy bastard.

I settled that quarrel in the time it took to finish off the last swallow of coffee and told Pettibone, very seriously, "I do give the President credit, Richard. We're a lot farther along than we were. Hell, who am I to judge?"

Then the man winked. He'd been saving it. "Don't sell yourself short, buddy. I hear at least one senator thinks you're the top of the line."

Ah again. Ted Kennedy. I wasn't surprised anymore that everyone knew. But it amazed me that it mattered. Because who the hell *was* I? Small town, Washington. They must hold regular pissing contests over on the Mall. I looked Pettibone in the eye and told him the truth: "No one's talked to me about it."

He flicked his smile. "They will, good buddy, they will." And all of a rush he sat up straight, his arms down from behind his head—business at last, I figured, though we'd been doing business all along—and plunged in. "Hey, listen, I've just let this talk wander all over hell and gone, haven't I." Manful eye contact, a blaze of sincerity. "Paige called me." He nodded. "You know that. She told me what was going on. I think it's a hell of a note, Red. I wish you'd gotten us in on the deal the minute it happened. There's something wrong when a distinguished American astronaut can't live in peace and quiet with his family, something mean and wrong." He stopped to see how I was taking it. I was taking it. "Now," he went on, "Paige tells me you've managed to raise four hundred thousand dollars privately. Is that right?"

"Yes."

"That's great. Then there's got to be a way we can help you out with the rest of it. You need another hundred thousand, isn't that right?"

"Yes."

"Are you working with a bank?"

I told him.

"Their home office? Manhattan?" He had big white hands and they were dangling between his knees. He bit his fingernails.

"Yes." Henry Kissinger bit his fingernails too. With reason.

"When's your pickup?"

"Tomorrow morning."

"Well, just fine." He spread his hands as if he were taking hold of a basketball. He looked like a basketball player, come to think of it, small-college level, a little soft, not tall enough, but lots of hustle. "You go on and do that. It'll all be there." And spreading with his hands, beatifically, a slow smile.

"You mean you're putting in the hundred thousand?"

He leaned back, slipped his hands into his pockets. "Something like that," he said.

"Fantastic. Who do I thank?"

"I'm still studying that."

"Is it a loan?"

"It surely is."

"Are there papers to sign?" What the hell was he offering?

"You'll be dealing with the bank on that, Red. We're just kind of guaranteeing things at this end."

So. That made sense. And I *was* grateful. "Then thanks," I said. "Thank the President for me if he knows about it, will you?"

"Nothing that man doesn't know about. Sure, I'll thank him. Now, Red, to get back to this other deal, not in any way linking these two things, because there's nothing being exchanged here, the government's just expressing its interest in the situation in a humanitarian way—the energy bill is having just a hell of a time picking its way through that minefield over there on Capitol Hill. There's part of it that could of come right out of your book, isn't there?"

"Absolutely." My turn to nod. "The section on solar, the section on conservation."

"You could speak for those, couldn't you?"

"I could and I will."

"The Congress would listen to you." Pettibone frowned. "I don't mean you should do anything, you understand, until your boy's safe and sound back to home. That's first of all."

"Right."

"Sure. That's first." He pulled his hands out of his pockets and stood. We'd agreed; the meeting was over. "I don't want to rush you off, Red, but you must have a bunch of things to do." Busy man.

We shook on it and he saw me out. Becki led me down to the west door. The G's lifted on the walk. Delayed reaction. A warm, spreading glow, as if I'd just tossed down a double shot of good brandy. I had the money. I had the gold. I could pay the ransom. Tiptoe through the dangerous exchange and Chris would be safe.

Riding back in the taxi I scraped away to the obvious layer: if I testified before Congress for Carter I'd be spoiled for Kennedy.

I didn't find the deeper layer until after midnight, lying awake at the Hyatt going over the day: Pettibone was Paige's mysterious boyfriend. She'd called him and appealed to him. He was so used to laying off a deal ten ways to Sunday that he left her believing he was helping me as a favor to *her*.

And that he, the guy who'd turned her out, had that kind of power, and I, the guy she'd gone back to, did not.

Cowboy cheered a war whoop and shut down the tube—we hadn't eaten and the six-pack was empty—and listened grinning to an abbreviated version of the tale. Then I called home.

"Diana?"

"Daddy?"

"It's set, sweetheart."

"Oh my *God* that's *great*. Just *great*."

"Tell Paige."

"I will. I *will*. When are you coming back?"

"We've got the bank in the morning and then getting out of Manhattan. We cross a time zone. I'd say before noon."

"I'll tell Paige. Are you *okay?*"

"Sure. Get some sleep, sweetheart. I'll see you tomorrow."

"I don't think I can. I'll try."

"Try. Take care."

"Bye-bye."

Riding the elevator to the lobby restaurant I remembered we needed a suitcase for the gold. We rushed out, grabbed a taxi, cut in the afterburners for the nearest K-Mart.

We missed it. We got there at two minutes after ten—lights still on but doors locked. Stupid. There wasn't room for a suitcase in the T-38 anyway. Cowboy would just have to cradle that three-bar pyramid of solid gold on his lap.

Karl Grabka didn't drink. Karl Grabka didn't smoke. Karl Grabka didn't believe in dancing. For all the salacious literature he hoarded in his duffel, Karl Grabka was a prude. So once he moved out of his apartment he had hard work killing time.

He spent the afternoon wandering Kansas City's better shopping districts. Enough people stared at his blue-white, bald head that he stopped early at a jeans store and bought himself a campaign hat, a nice soft number in denim. It helped. People stopped staring, though they still moved over to let him pass on the sidewalk, either because he looked dangerous or because they smelled him bearing down on them.

He bought a double-dip cone at Baskin-Robbins, two preadolescent flavors, something like banana–peanut butter and pink bubble gum. He watched the lobsters struggle in their tank at a seafood market until a clerk offered to help him. Killing time. He studied the *Rocky Horror* poster at the Bijou in Westport. Transvestites made him fucking sick, you know?

His paranoia came and went. It always did when he was out in public. He felt people watching him. Correction. He felt people catching *him* watching *them*. He liked bookstores for checking out chicks across the shelves and down the aisles, but he thought they caught him. Or he'd look down at the books so they'd see that's what he was there for and the goddamned books would be something like *Gay Men* or *The Sex Life of Plants.*

It was time to eat. He never ate in restaurants, smart-ass waiters and people staring at him. He'd hit a drive-in.

The nearest drive-in was McDonald's and you could have it. We do it all for you. They were so fucking all-American. They'd load up your quarter-pounder with their standard shit and never ask you for nothing. He didn't like onions and he liked mustard instead of ketchup. He'd heard that McDonald's used eyeballs in their beef.

One all-beef patty meant eyeballs, testicles, you name it. They could get away with it because they said "all-beef." Eyeballs and testicles were beef too if they came off a steer. They weren't pork, were they?

I don't know about Karl Grabka. What happened to him? His parents operated well within the limits of the normal. They worked hard, they stayed married, they got drunk on Saturday nights, they didn't seriously beat their kids, they didn't seriously break the law. They were packing-house workers, which I guess means they were "coarse," but nothing in the record shows them up as crazy. Grabka's brothers turned out normal enough. One's a drill sergeant in the Marines, one of them works on the line at GM, one's on welfare with a bad back.

Where do the Karl Grabkas come from? I know I'm not an objective observer in this instance. I'm willing to concede some chemical imbalance, combined somehow with adverse childhood experience, that pushes them toward monstrosity. Them: rapists, burglars who batter the victims they surprise, robbers who murder, out to the extreme of the Daceys and the Specks. But only to a degree. You'd have to show me hard evidence, evidence that what's called conscience can be switched off by a chemical imbalance oddly widespread among American males but not American females or British males. There is none.

I can think of another line of examination that no one, to my knowledge, has seriously explored. Some kinds of criminal behavior—a rapist's, for example—correspond remarkably to the hunting behavior of predators like cheetahs or wolves. The pattern is so similar that it may be more than merely analogous. Both predators and rapists size up their victims for vulnerability, test them, isolate them and so on. If you've hunted animals, as I have, if you've watched animals hunt, you know that the hunting behavior of wild animals is highly patterned, highly formal. There's a dialogue that goes on between the hunter and the hunted, a signaling back and forth, and only if the dialogue is successful does the victim stand and the predator close for the kill. I assume human beings hunted that way in the dim reaches of the past. Much of the aesthetic of modern hunting, the aesthetic that Hemingway praised and some of us still try to practice, is an attempt to simulate or to recapture that formal dialogue. I'm not sure why. I suspect the feeling for it, the satisfaction it brings, is deeply scored into our genetic programming.

But animals that have been domesticated and then allowed to go wild again—feral animals like loose dogs and cats—don't have that feeling. They've lost some of the terms of the dialogue, almost as if they've had an information dropout. They'll maim for pleasure, they'll kill and keep on killing, not to feed but simply because the feedback loops that would otherwise shut their killing down are open. They're berserk.

If people can be feral, Grabka was. That's as generous as I can be. Even saying it, I take it back. Because obviously he had some measure of control. He wasn't interested in killing Chris, or Chris's mother, or Chris's sister, or me. He wanted to toy with us. He wanted tribute from us. He wanted a drama from us. But his primary motivation was a grotesquely bloated greed. And what could be more human than that?

He ate. He drove to Loose Park and parked and watched the girls jogging. At dark, at about nine o'clock Kansas City time, when I was skidding into the K-Mart parking lot in Washington, he drove to an outdoor phone booth at a Standard station and called.

"Paige?"

"Yes?"

"How's it going, honey?"

"It's taken care of."

"It's taken care of?"

"Is this—"

"Yeah. It is. You mean Reeve's got the gold?"

"He'll have it tomorrow morning in New York. He'll be back here by afternoon."

"Well I'll be fucked. Oh, 'scuse my bad language. Okay. So he'll make the drop tomorrow night."

"Where?"

"Never you mind, Paige. Just hang loose. Hang loose as a goose. I'll let you know. You people didn't move as fast as I figured you would, but you did a good job. Tell Reeve that for me, will you, honey? Tell him he did a good job."

"Yes." Paige heard the line open.

Nice call.

Business accomplished, Grabka motored out east to the Longview Drive-in. On the giant silver screen it had Bruce Lee, cannibal cheerleaders, mummies and ghouls. Late at night, when the children went to sleep, it had creamy blond Snowy and her seven-man motorcycle gang.

Hush. Grabka's in his pickup: all's right with the world.

Fourteen

Down in the bowels of Wall Street on that gray Sunday morning—nine o'clock or so, we'd made wizard time—Chuck Hyerding's minion Marc Lowe met Cowboy and me at the doors of the bank. Lowe paid off his cab; we kept ours. Our driver didn't mind. We were in a hurry, and Lower Manhattan on Sunday morning is a tomb.

The banker was already inside. I looked through the glass—Lowe frowned at me for the impertinence, puffy and sleepy, one of those chalk-pale city people who don't wake up until midafternoon—and saw the man signaling impatiently to the poor overweight guard to unlock one of the doors. I supposed the banker was upper-echelon. Clerks don't hand out gold bars.

The guard opened the door. His boss, whose name escapes me, shook hands heartily with Lowe but suspiciously with me. He was a big, glowering man, florid-faced, with bushy eyebrows he brushed straight up like John L. Lewis, if you're old enough to remember John L. Lewis. Or Henry Luce. (I used to think the eyebrows of tycoons grew that way; what a shock to discover they brushed them, like girls padding their bras.) He was turned out nattily in his Sunday morning emergency-call-to-the-bank clothes: houndstooth tweed jacket, gray flannels, blue oxford-cloth shirt, silk ascot; and he was suspicious of me, I suppose, for the obvious reason that he considered it sheer insanity to give away half a million in gold to *anyone*, least of all to a criminal or a criminal conspiracy.

I really didn't have any quarrel with the banker. I just took out on him my anger that relief for Chris couldn't be instantaneous, that money had to be negotiated even with a life at stake.

We followed the banker from the vestibule into the lobby and waited by the pool there, its fountain shut off, not a penny on the bottom, while the guard unlocked his way past various inner gates. The gray morning filtered in dimly through the tall, old-fashioned lobby windows. The guard came back wheeling a green steel cart with a loaf-shaped canvas bag centered on it like a restaurant birthday cake.

The banker had seen better days, and the lines of his face counted his years of foreclosing mortgages and turning widows into the street, but his hard eyes softened to tenderness as he showed us, bar by bar, the gold that moth and rust doth not corrupt. Cowboy noticed the softening too, nudged me, winked. I'll give the banker his gold—it was pretty.

"If you'll come with me, Mr. Wainwright," he said, "you'll need to sign some documents."

The guard guarded the gold. Cowboy guarded the guard. Lowe penguined along behind me, bringing up the rear. We took an elevator to another floor, walked a hall to the banker's office. I assume it was his office. There were family pictures on the desk and a stuffed pheasant behind the desk on the credenza. He'd had the documents neatly typed and stacked deep in a brown leather folder.

I signed away whatever was left. My future earnings. Maybe my soul.

"Hey, Red," Cowboy radioed from the aft cockpit of the T-38, "try to fly this bird. These boogers are heavy."

"How they doing back there?" We were maybe halfway home, racing the sun.

"Doin' fine. I'm kind of patting them every now and then. Guess I could slip them down in front of the seat, but what the hell. Not every day a man gets to hold a plug of solid gold on his lap."

I thought of something to do about the weight. I wiggled the stick. In less than a second the earth rotated above us and rotated back below. You could do that in a T-38: beautiful aileron rolls.

Cowboy let me wait a beat longer than I expected. "Over your hiccups yet?" he asked me then. "Maybe you should pull some parabolas while you're at it."

The bars wouldn't have moved from his lap. He'd have felt a momentary release of weight, no more. The reference to parabolas was a dig. When we'd first started training for zero G I'd gotten sick. Most people did. Never Cowboy, of course.

We trained for zero G in a KC-135, a military version of the Boeing 707 with its interior fuselage stripped and padded. The pilot would go into a dive, pull up hard at two or three G's and then take the aircraft over the top in a parabola that gave us about twenty seconds of weightlessness suspended between floor and ceiling (in theory—in practice we tended to bang around). Since we were jammed into unventilated pressure suits, the experience could be nauseating. For me, for a time, it was. I got used to it. I think people imagine that pilots are immune to motion sickness. Not so. I know one guy who's flown nearly four thousand hours and he still gets sick in rough air. I was that much more impressed with Darwin when I learned he was seasick on the *Beagle* the entire voyage. Three years.

There was comedy in those early tests of weightlessness. The cat-drop experiment. Sophisticated cats held upside down and dropped in ordinary flight: flipping over catlike and landing on their feet. Same sophisticated cats held upside down and released in zero G: flipping frantically, screeching, snicking out their claws and sailing toward the camera: cartoon characters, sail cats.

The pigeons were funnier yet. They expected to fly, and even in zero G they flew. They flew upside down, straight up, straight down, sideways. They looked bewildered, but more than bewildered they looked embarrassed. I'd never seen a pigeon look that way before. I didn't think it was possible to embarrass a pigeon.

I wasn't bewildered or embarrassed, flying home with the ransom, but I was light-headed and not a little giddy. A few aileron rolls, with advance warning to Cowboy, cleared the fog. If flying taught you anything, it taught you that you didn't rotate the earth when you handled the controls. You only rotated your small aircraft and the pigeons it protected inside.

Grabka was beyond giddiness. His plan was running on automatic. He hardly had to lift a finger. After the late movie at the drive-in he'd parked his pickup on a country shoulder and slept in the cab, slouched against the door, until dawn. Sunday morning he'd chowed down at a greasy spoon—eggs over hard, sausage patties, hash browns, coffee and a 3 Musketeers bar. He stopped at a filling station for gas and bought a city map. He was ready to decide on a drop point.

He shifted over to his daydream mode. It was more or less the way he thought. In the daydream mode you run up a series of variant simulations. Then you choose the one you want to act out. That's what Grabka did as he quartered the city.

He leapt Sunday, Sunday night, the next week, the week after that, to the point where the gold had been converted into pesos and the pesos laundered into dollars, to the point where he had a safe half million in a U.S. account. Then the delicious question was, what would he do with the money? He'd already spent it two or three times over. Now he'd spend it two or three times again.

He decided to use one of the city parks. He didn't bother with Loose, the park where he'd watched the girls jog. It was the fancy-pants park in Kansas City and too crowded. People ran there from dawn to dark and after dark hippies hung around until way after midnight getting stoned. Getting robbed and raped, too, when the niggers snuck over from east of Troost.

There was the plantation in Guyana. Stupid asshole Jones. "I tried. I tried. I tried. Mother. Mother. Mother. Mother." Billy Graham was in the papers talking about Christians buying Jonestown for a mission, for shit's sake, to give the Guyanese a better idea of what kind of people Americans were. Show 'em we all didn't drink Kool-Aid. He could buy that, Grabka thought. The Gold Way in Goldtown.

Swope Park was too big, big enough to get lost in. And not enough ways in and out, too easy to seal off the access roads.

You could do anything in California. California had to be the craziest place there ever was. The Moonies worked out there. Jones worked out there. Scientology. Manson. Hitler would have worked out there.

(Do you feel as if you're lost in a horror comic? That's Karl Grabka on the make, going about his business.)

He found the right park in the southeastern city, beside a big, white, modern Jewish temple with an auditorium that spiraled like a giant seashell. The park was one block long north and south and half a block wide. A screen of tall trees marked the eastern edge and a cemetery took up the other half of the block eastward. East of the cemetery across a boulevard was more cemetery behind a wall.

Hitler was the one. Adolf. *Sieg Heil!* You couldn't do the same thing, Grabka told himself. Couldn't do the swastika, couldn't do the Jews. But the basic idea. The basic idea was to organize so well that not just the dropouts but everyone came around.

The park had groves of trees to the west and to the north. More or less between them was a combined baseball diamond and football field. South of the football field were two fenced tennis courts. All the streets around the park had houses.

People would believe anything if you had power.

And in the center of the park, off the football field, was a flat-roofed stucco public toilet.

People believed that Jesus was the son of God. They wore little crosses because that was the way the Romans executed criminals. If the Romans had executed criminals by hanging, people would wear little nooses. If Jesus had been hit by a car, people would wear little dented cars.

Grabka left his pickup on a side street and walked into the park. He found the coarse grass freshly mown. The trees had turned red, orange, brown, but still held their leaves. Some older men played doubles tennis on one of the courts. Three black teenagers practiced breaking guard at a basketball lay-up ring in the southwest corner of the park. Mothers pushed their babies in swings to the west. Good enough. Not that much happening. It looked like it'd be dead as a doornail at night. If someone hung around, Grabka would figure a deal to scare them off.

He needed something like a cross. What was his cross? Fuck, yes. A miniature gold brick. It wouldn't have to be real. It could be plate or just gold-colored. He'd wear a real one and a kind of charm bracelet of maybe twenty of them. Two charm bracelets. He wouldn't wear a watch. He'd have advisers around to tell him what time it was.

He checked out the public toilet. It looked like every public toilet—dirty drawings and phony phone numbers, stinking urinal, filthy sink, piss on the floor. Who'd ever see it as a drop for half a million in gold?

Gold, we've got a problem down in Mobile. The battalion there is taking shit from the pigs for unlawful assembly.

Waste 'em. Beautiful.

He walked north, looking for a good place from which to watch the toilet building. There was a Boy Scout council ring in the grove of pines on the north side, next to the temple parking lot, but the lower branches of the pines had been broken off for firewood and the area was exposed. The best cover would be the screen of trees between the cemetery and the park. He could pull into the temple parking lot early, after he called me at the farm, leave his pickup, walk down the row of trees on the cemetery side and watch me make the drop. Then he could cross the open space between the trees and the toilet building, keeping the building between him and the one busy street at the west. And back to the cemetery side with the gold, back to his pickup, out the parking lot the other way going east. Easy. There was even a maintenance road through the cemetery for a back exit if he needed one.

The best thing he could do was buy a TV station. Get on the satellites. Get the show going around the country. Doing it in person would be like a rock group running a series of concerts—even in the biggest stadium you couldn't play to more than a hundred thousand or so at a time. TV hooked in people by the millions. Hypnotized them. Wave your hand in front of your TV and you could see it was a strobe. People sat there getting strobed. You could sell anything on TV. He could sell the Gold Way. From TV he'd go to local battalions. He'd have to learn to delegate authority. Put together an inner circle of trusted aides.

Not a bad day's work, Grabka told himself, back in his pickup. He marked his map and drove off. Today he'd stay out of sight. There were the theaters in town that showed stroke movies. He'd make the rounds until telephone time.

Chris had slept, miserably. He couldn't take the song any further. The words that came so fast, the words he saw himself singing at a concert, slowed and faded to the black of his prison. He wasn't onstage. There wasn't any concert. He was in a black, cold box. His shoulders hurt. His butt hurt. He couldn't *see.*

So then the weirdo was drawing the map.

He wouldn't draw a map.

So then the weirdo was telling me on the phone how to find the place where Chris was buried. So then I'm running out of the house, getting into the Saab. Then I'm driving. How far? Maybe thirty minutes. Fifteen minutes south, fifteen minutes west. How much is thirty minutes? Thirty minutes is five cuts of "A Farewell to Kings" and a little more.

With his hands, on the side of the box, in the darkness, toward the end crying, Chris played those five cuts.

So then I was pulling off the road, getting out of the Saab. I had a shovel and a flashlight. I slipped down the shoulder, pushed through the woods. I found the mound of fresh earth. I was digging.

"Dad?" Chris called. "*Dad?* I'm here!"

If there'd been digging he'd have heard it. He didn't. "Dad? Dad? Dad? *Dad?* God*damn* it, Dad! Where the fuck are you? You're never there, *Dad?* You *know?* You're never fucking *there*, you *son of a bitch*. You weren't there in Houston and you weren't there for Mom and you weren't there for Diana and you weren't there for me and you aren't here *now, are* you. You *goddamn pissing shit, where are you? Where are you?* You're such a big *fuckass*, Dad. Big shit. *Ass*tronaut. Big shit *ass*tronaut. Nobody gives a *fuck* if you walked on the moon, you know? That's like the fucking *Dark Ages*, man. Nobody gives a fuck about your *book*, either. Wrote a big *book*. Big *ass*tronaut. Big *energy* consultant. They don't know what a *phony* you are, man, but don't think *I* don't."

Chris went on like that. Probably worse. Probably he kicked his feet, beat his fists on the lid. I hope so. He'd earned it.

He did that and he cried. He'd composed, he'd sung, he'd drummed, he'd chewed me out, he cried. What else could he do? He was locked in a horror show. He did what we all do in the horror shows we're locked in: he improvised and waited, prayed for someone to let him out.

For a while he lay still. He'd been running the fan while he drummed out "A Farewell to Kings." He'd turned it off to listen for me. Now, lying still, he heard a sound. He couldn't place it. Something like a scratching. What the hell was it? Maybe I was up there!

"Dad? God, Dad, is that you?"

"*Cawk!*"

One of the crows from the rookery, working the fresh-turned earth. But a sound, something alive. Instantly Chris felt better for it. Sunday morning cartoons: he talked to the crow.

I left the aircraft first. Cowboy passed down the canvas bag of gold and followed. Once the flight crew refueled him he was going to fly on home. We'd already discussed it. He'd helped all he could. He had work in Houston. Anyway, he had to get the T-bird back.

"Let me know," he said, standing on the tarmac squinting in the midday sun. "Don't bother while you're busy, but as soon as you've got Chris give me a call."

"I will." I was peeling off my flight suit. The truck was on its way from the fuel dump.

"If you need this bird again just holler, okay?"

"Thanks, Cowboy. I will. Thanks for everything."

"No sweat."

We didn't shake hands. Brothers don't have to shake hands. He ducked into Flight Ops and I crossed to my car. The gold sunk into the passenger seat beside me. I turned the ignition key. We'd been away a little more than twenty-four hours. Hard to believe.

Exit Cowboy, pursued by lifelong thanks. I saw him climbing to altitude as I drove east.

I drove home thinking about Chris and Diana. Why I loved them. What love of children was. There's a sense where children are parasites. They struggle to maximize their advantage, to collect the greatest possible share of the family's resources. I don't mean money. That too. I mean food, emotional support, protection even at the risk of other lives. The trade-off is that they carry on their parents' genes.

You recognize the theory. It's an acceptable theory as far as it goes. I even felt that way, felt in Chris and Diana my hope for the future, my descendants who would continue what I'd started—continue my line, maybe my line of work too, and more vaguely the values and attitudes I'd spent my life assembling. Maybe Diana would get to Mars (and return!). I was the first in my family who managed college, the first to achieve at the scale I'd achieved. So I felt like a founder. Chris and Diana weren't founders. They were developers. They might turn out to be far more original than I—I wasn't exactly original: jet jockeys are only the latest in a tradition that goes back to the astronautlike wild hairs who flew linen-winged biplanes—but they were launching from my shoulders, not from the ground.

Well. All that. I turned north onto the road that led to the farm. All that doesn't quite say it. I wasn't a corporation. They weren't the new generation of execs in training. The love I felt for them *burned.* I'd been a loner. I'd held myself apart. I protected myself with a stubborn conviction of personal superiority. It didn't go to the center of my feelings about myself and others—at center I'm generous and humane and optimistic, at least I think I am—but there it was. I felt as if Chris and Diana *grew out of me,* almost literally, like special organs that drop off in maturity to lead coordinate lives of their own. Even though I hadn't always been there for them—Chris was right about that and right to be angry about it—and even when I didn't understand where they'd gone, in adolescences once removed from mine, or what they were doing. As far as I could tell, they didn't feel much separation either. It wasn't a matter of evidence. It was a matter of what I saw in their eyes.

How did Grabka know?

But who says he knew? I was the nearest celebrity at hand. Grabka's ignorance of the closeness Chris, Diana and I felt made Chris's kidnapping that much more terrible, a species of rape.

Paige and Diana came running out to meet me. It would have made a hell of a homecoming if Chris had been there. Chris's surrogate was a bag of gold, as if Midas had touched my son with a heavy metal hand.

Midafternoon my phone rang. I took it bolt upright in the Eames, Paige on the floor opposite, Diana on the couch.

"Commander Reeve Wainwright, please." A man's voice. Paige and Diana watched.

"Speaking." I shrugged. I didn't know.

"Commander Wainwright, this is Agent John Hinderliter of the Federal Bureau of Investigation." Shit, I thought. I shook my head to Paige and Diana. "The White House contacted the director regarding the situation you're facing out there. He called us immediately. He's personally interested. Are you free to talk?"

I should have sworn Pettibone to secrecy, the bastard. Protecting his investment. "No, not really," I told the agent.

"Tell me this, Commander," he said, his voice going conspiratorial—I could almost see him cupping the phone—"are the suspects actually there with you right now?"

"No, but I expect them to call. I'm trying to keep this line free."

"I see. Is there another line where we can reach you?"

"No."

"What about this Chris Wainwright's phone at the same location?"

They were already earning their pay. "Yes. You can call me on Chris's number. Give me a second to get upstairs."

Paige stayed in the living room. Diana followed me. Chris's phone rang and I picked it up. "Yes. Hello."

"Commander Wainwright? This is Agent John Hinderliter. I understand you'd rather not talk to us. A crime's been committed, however. We have to step in."

"Listen, friend, I've been told that if the FBI becomes involved, my son will be left to die. That's good enough for me. It ought to be good enough for you." I was standing beside Chris's bed. I noticed a leather cigarette case on the bedside table and picked it up and turned it in my free hand.

"I don't know how much you know about us, Commander. We've had a bad press lately. We do a pretty good job. We'll stand back and let you handle things however you want to, but we do need to be there."

"No one's crossed any state lines so far as I know."

"That's presumptive in a kidnapping, sir."

I forgot. "The Lindbergh law." Another astronautical wild hair, so to speak. Pray the Wainwrights had better luck than the Lindberghs did.

"Yes."

"I'd be glad to keep you informed." The case leather was lizardlike. I worked it under my thumb. Diana watched me.

"We need to be there, Commander. Any telephone conversations between you and the suspects count as prime evidence."

"Who's we?"

"Two agents. Myself and Agent Harlin E. Doocy. He's here with me now."

Fantastic. Hinderliter and Doocy. "Can't you tap in at the switching center?"

"We need to be there, sir." Bulldogs. J. Edgar Hoover had looked exactly like a bulldog, or had *Pogo*'s version of that famous little man corrupted my memory?

"I've been told this house is being watched." Diana pretended to strangle herself. I nodded, the phone nodding with me.

"Are you alone?"

"No. My daughter and a friend are here."

"Can your daughter drive?"

"No."

"Can your friend drive?"

"Yes."

"Then if you'll have your friend drive in and meet us, we'll ride out hidden in your car."

"Do I have a choice?" Diana took the cigarette case from my hand.

"We need to be there, Commander Wainwright. We might as well work together on this. Agent Doocy and I have had a fair amount of experience with kidnappings. We can help. If you'll work with us, I promise you we won't get in the way."

Meaning they'd arrive in the clear unless I cooperated. I said okay and they arranged to come aboard at the Safeway in Lee's Summit.

Paige would pick up a sack of groceries and park behind the house. They'd crawl out the hatchback and slip in.

Diana opened the cigarette case: Chris's rolling papers, two little orange packets of Zig Zags with the tough French Zig Zag sailor smiling out. She made a face. She wasn't a smoker, of tobacco or of dope. Neither, at the moment, was Chris.

Paige took off. She returned about an hour later with the agents. They weren't, as I'd expected, tall and short or fat and thin. Hinderliter was about my size and age, gray hair, a businessman's face, a good pinstripe suit. Doocy looked Irish, meaning blondish-brown hair, ruddy cheeks, a little taller and heavier than his teammate. Doocy fancied flannels and a blue blazer with brass buttons. They managed the hatchback crawl without serious damage to their duds.

They each dragged in a plain gray government-issue suitcase. After introductions and directions to the contact telephone Doocy set his case on its side on the couch, snapped it open—it was foam-lined, with sockets cut into the black foam—and extracted a compact Signal Corps reel-to-reel tape recorder and the suction-cup bug necessary to attach it to the phone, which he proceeded to do. The case also held a camera and a selection of lenses. Doocy left those packed. I didn't ask Hinderliter what was in his case. Weapons, I'd guess; they weren't wearing any.

Once the recorder was attached and threaded with tape and Doocy had hung his monitoring headphones at his neck like Sparks at the sinking troopship shortwave, we all settled down in the living room and Hinderliter collected the story of the kidnapping. He said he'd like us to give depositions later. For the time being, he made notes. He read the ransom letter with care. He looked over the gold, managing not to seem awed except in the way he stroked it—at least as tenderly as I'd guess he stroked his wife. He wrote down the numbers on the bars. Diana went upstairs and found one of Chris's school pictures. And so on. I took it for an imposition, not to mention a betrayal by Richard Pettibone of a confidence. Other than that it made no difference to me so long as it didn't interfere with the negotiations to come. Our phone contact had said tonight was the night. He'd said he'd call. I was waiting for his call.

Diana had never seen an FBI agent before (she'd seen Secret Service when Spiro Agnew came around, though she might not remember). She couldn't leave these two live ones alone. "What do you have to do to get into the FBI?" she asked Hinderliter.

"College," he told her, a little distracted. "Then you need either a law degree or an accounting degree. You take a competitive examination. Interviews. Security checks. Then you have to make it through the academy. It's rigorous."

"Why?" Diana asked.

"Why what?"

"Why the FBI?"

Hinderliter took off his reading glasses. He looked at Doocy and back at Diana and decided she was serious. "I wanted to work in law enforcement. The FBI's the best there is."

Diana raised an eyebrow in my direction. I knew what she meant to ask: why law enforcement? Why become a pig? I shook my head and she subsided. Hinderliter put his reading glasses back on, studied his notes. The sun came out from behind a passing cloud and splashed through the Levolors onto the living room floor.

"I understand the law degree," Diana started again. "What's the accounting for?"

"White-collar crime," Paige said, Doocy nodding confirmation.

"Embezzling," he explained. "Also income-tax evasion." He smiled at Diana. A man with daughters of his own? "It started before your time, Miss Wainwright, but income-tax evasion was what allowed the bureau to move against organized crime."

"What's the percentage these days of white-collar to violent?" Paige asked Doocy. Hinderliter was with us again; Doocy deferred to him.

"I'd guess eighty to twenty," Hinderliter said.

"How come we never *hear* about it?" Diana confronted him.

"It doesn't play in Peoria," Paige answered.

Hinderliter nodded. "That's right. It's not dramatic. They can't use it on TV. Some of it makes the newspapers." He looked to me. "Commander Wainwright—"

"Let's make it easy," I interrupted. "I'm Red. That's Paige and that's Diana. You're John—"

"Jack."

"Harlin," Doocy said.

"Okay," I told Jack Hinderliter. "What's the question?"

"Could the kidnapper be someone known to you?"

I shook my head. "I don't know any terrorist groups."

"At this point we can assume we're dealing with one man. Red."

"Why?"

"You've only had contact with one man."

"I guess. He could be the leader. Does it matter?"

"Not at the moment. It might if there's a problem."

"I'm not planning on problems."

"No," Hinderliter agreed, to be polite.

Diana pressed on. "Which college?" she asked her captive FBI.

An ordinary Sunday afternoon on a modest Missouri farm. So awkward it might as well have been a gathering of relatives.

No one called.

Fifteen

So we waited.

Diana went off to check the livestock. While she was gone Paige and I put together dinner—ham sandwiches, a pot of coffee, apples from the bushel of Jonathans I kept on the back porch. Paige drank coffee. The rest of us ate. The FBI agents appreciated the feed and got around to asking me about the moon.

Diana called her mother for permission to stay another night. What was up? Claudia wanted to know. Nothing much, Diana said. Could she speak with Chris? Claudia asked. He's not home, Diana told her. He'll be home later . . .

I hadn't forgotten the suitcase. I dug an old one of mine, nondescript brown Samsonite, out of the upstairs storage closet. The problem was packing the bars so they wouldn't clunk around. Newspaper was a mess. I didn't have enough towels. I considered requisitioning Doocy's black foam lining, but I knew how much paperwork he'd have to suffer to justify the contribution and to order more.

Diana, not long from the horse barn, brightly suggested straw. She fetched a bale to the back porch and hauled it in a flake at a time. It worked. We packed the three bars into their nest of straw bare, so that the kidnapper could see immediately what he was getting. The bars in their nest of golden straw might have been the goose's golden eggs. Diana was compelled. She'd never seen so much money concentrated in one small place in her life. I had our three space suits for comparison at one hundred thousand each. But that was government money. This was mine.

Darkness closed in on us. I cranked shut the Levolors and turned on the lights. We did what people usually do when they're waiting, traded stories. Not very cheerfully. For four randomly assembled adults we had exceptional stories to trade. Hinderliter and Doocy told us about crimes they'd investigated—they'd both worked around the edges of John Kennedy's assassination, for example. Paige told us about the last days in Saigon when the Vietnamese in power played every card they could come up with to escape before the VC arrived. Woe unto you if you had vulnerabilities they could exploit. A journalist friend of hers, a man, almost managed to get himself killed over his love for a Vietnamese boy. I wondered how that story would sit with Jack and Harlin. Surprise, they took it in good part for the love story it was. They weren't the hardnoses I'd expected them to be.

I listened more than I talked. I did what you do when you feel motion sickness coming on: kept quiet and held still. I'd learned to deal with crises, but we hadn't run any simulations on this one. I felt again as if I was floating back from the moon in that cold spacecraft, staring out the window into darkness. Did I say before that on the way out and on the way home we couldn't see the stars because the glare of sunlight off the exterior surfaces of the spacecraft constricted our pupils as bright daylight would? We saw darkness and—

The phone rang.

Doocy slipped on his headphones. He started the tape. I picked up.

"Reeve?"

"Yes." My hand shook.

"Reeve Wainwright?"

"Speaking."

"You know who this is?"

"I think so."

"You're right. Welcome back."

"I brought the three items you asked for. I have them here."

"Paige told me. That's a lot of woman, Reeve."

"How's Chris?"

"Chris? You mean Christopher? Chris is fine. Hey, you agree with me about Paige, don't you?"

"Sure."

"Sure you do. Now, Reeve. Are you alone?"

"Paige is here."

"Yeah. Okay, listen carefully. I'm only going to tell you once. If you fuck up, man, that's it."

"I'm listening."

"Fucking *A* you're listening. Okay. There's a park in Kansas City at Sixty-eighth and Holmes. There's a big Jewish temple on the north side. In the middle of the park there's a public toilet. Reeve? You listening?"

My eyes caught Harlin's. I was. So was he. "I'm listening."

"Take the gold bars—that's what you meant by *items*, right? Gold bars?"

"Right."

"Take the gold bars in the suitcase and sit the suitcase inside the men's room of the public toilet. And then get your ass out of there and don't look back. When I've made the pickup, when I've checked out the gold and know you haven't fucked me over, I'll call you and tell you where little Christopher is. And oh, man, don't you *try anything*"—he almost screamed it—"on me or Chris is *dead.* You got that?"

"I got it."

"I figured the time. It's nine-thirty. You'll make the park at ten o'clock. That's a double-nickel drive. Don't break any speed limits, Reeve. Don't do anything to wake up the pigs. You haven't woken up the pigs, have you?"

"No."

"Good boy. I didn't think you would. Get going." The line opened.

I put down the phone. I took a deep breath to stop the shaking.

"I'd say we're dealing with an individual suspect." Doocy, trying to help.

"Any advice?" I asked, looking to him and then to Hinderliter.

"Take it slowly and deliberately," Hinderliter advised. "Don't do anything that might startle him. Where's the drop?"

"A park," Doocy told him. "Inside a rest room."

I said: "I'm going." Paige smiled encouragement.

"A park rest room," Hinderliter recited. "That's original."

"*Daddy.*" Diana ran to me, hugged me. "*Please* be careful. We love you." There were tears in her eyes.

I picked up the suitcase, straw sticking through its aluminum seams. It was heavy and automatically my left hand swung out to counterbalance its weight in my right, the way you carry buckets of water on the farm. This was all a country project except for that slick grim ghoul on the phone.

I went out through the kitchen, opened the passenger door on the right side of the Saab and set the suitcase onto the seat, closed the door, walked around the front and got in. I was beginning to split, as you do in emergencies, beginning to watch myself. I started the car. I made a tight U-turn and headed down the driveway, stopped at the road, turned north toward the interstate. The bastard was right; I'd be just about thirty minutes getting to the park. I knew where it was. It had a name. It was called Holmes Park. He must have missed the sign, or maybe he couldn't read.

Cool autumn night. I drove with the window down, the slipstream at fifty miles an hour whipping the hairs on my arm. The part of me that was watching watched that and remembered when I was a kid. I'd stuck my hand out the back window of the family Nash and cupped my palm for an airfoil and made it go. I'd always known I'd fly. I hadn't tried to fly by hoisting a zinc battery plate and jumping off a garden wall, like Robert Goddard, because when I was a child the air was thick with planes. Goddard dreamed of interplanetary travel even before Orville and Wilbur Wright claimed the sky.

The rocket business had a history. The part of me that was watching connected that history now with this grotesque thing that was happening to me and mine. The rocket business was tainted with monstrosity.

Nothing very logical. Pieces. Fragments seen more than thought. The immense white Saturn V glowing blue-white at its night launch complex, Leviathan that swallowed us small as the three hypocritical monkeys couched in the center of their peach pit: see no evil, hear no evil, speak no evil. Behind the Saturn V and its mission to the moon ("We came in peace for all mankind"), all the intermediate rockets we fiddled with lined up down the Cape of my memory: Atlas, Centaur, Corporal, Hercules, Honest John, Mercury, Nike, Polaris, Redstone, Thor. Then farther down the line the V-2 on its railroad car and the small V-1 poised at the top of its portable launcher like a burly-shouldered athlete at a ski jump.

Last in line—first in line—the flat, snow-covered pasture of a Massachusetts farm, the rocket stand of two braced iron trapezoids erected beside a wooden and sheet-steel barricade, the rocket bare apparatus: an igniter-stick nose, a small cylindrical combustion chamber, a flaring nozzle, these suspended three feet above the top of the stand in a frame of light tubing; the tubing extending down into the stand to a conical shield; below the shield cylindrical pressurized tanks of liquid oxygen and gasoline. March 16, 1926. Goddard's first successful flight, the igniter lit by an assistant with a blowtorch, a steady roar of fire, the rocket clearing the flame, accelerating curving over left, smashing into the snow, skittering insanely through the snow. A fairy or an aesthetic dancer, Esther Goddard said. A flight of one hundred eighty-four feet in two and a half seconds. The Wrights at Kitty Hawk managed only one hundred twenty.

Wasn't everything monstrous deep enough down? I was. You'd have to have seen me stumbling through the house blind drunk, sweating and moaning, in the days when I drank.

The technology was ours. Independently the Germans developed it. Hitler's rockets might as well have been Allied secret weapons. The V-2 program cost the Germans almost as much as the Manhattan Project cost us. Hitler got an intermediate-range ballistic missile that carried, at best, two thousand pounds of high explosive; we got the atomic bomb. Building V-2's with high-explosive warheads was like building gem-quality large-bore Krupp cannons and firing them only once. Bombers were far more cost-effective. Hitler didn't know the difference, and apparently the rocket boys, Wernher von Braun chief among them, didn't care. Cared only for space travel, the obsession of their lives, and Goddard's, and sometimes mine.

Slaves—French Maquis, Czechs, Poles—built the vengeance weapons in cold, foul, sunless tunnels they tore from the Harz Mountains with picks and shovels, with their bare hands, fed a cup of slop a day and beaten until they rotted and died. Von Braun and his pack should have been jailed for life. Instead they built the whited sepulcher of the Saturn V.

Germany developed the vengeance weapons, we developed the nuclear, and Americans and expatriate Germans working together after the war mated the two technologies to create weapons that might rain down the death of the world.

I saw that world from orbit, blue and fresh as sea spray flashing in the sun.

As the V-2 led to the ICBM, the V-1 led to the cruise missile. Do you know that machine? It looks like a flying torpedo. It carries a nuclear warhead, the explosive equivalent of one million tons of TNT, a third of the way around the earth, at a speed of five hundred miles per hour, flying three hundred feet above the ground, following the terrain. Inside its solid-state guidance it consults a detailed digitalized map, checking its location and correcting its course, and finds its target within one hundred feet at a range of two thousand miles.

All that ingenuity in a weapon no one means ever to use? Cover your eyes, cover your ears, cover your mouth.

What could be more monstrous than dreams of universal death? What could be more monstrous than dreams of universal exodus? Both dreams share a common plexus: the men who dreamed them, the technology that makes them potential in our lives.

The clue is the names we give the rockets. We name them for the gods.

Nothing very logical. I was split. One of me drove the car. The other floated out into the night, apocalyptic. This is the watchbird watching you.

West off the interstate onto Sixty-third Street, through Kansas City's black ghetto, south on Rockhill Road past Baptist Hospital, up one last hill on Holmes. The temple, B'nai Jehudah, loomed on my left, a graceful building spiraled like a nautilus shell. I stopped off Holmes on the south side of the park—a left turn, kill the engine, silence. The moon was setting. Streetlights along Holmes—orange sodium-vapor lights—shone only a little way into the park. Back past the center was darkness.

I got out of the car, walked around to the passenger side, lifted out the heavy suitcase. I stood long enough to be seen if someone was watching, then rounded the Saab again and crossed the narrow residential street. The park grass was wet with dew that caught the moonlight. The grass clippings smelled sweet; they were making hay. I saw a basketball practice goal and passed it, following an opening between stands of pine. The black velvet rectangle ahead was the public toilet, the only building in the park. I walked beyond it to the center of the football field, turned slowly so that my silhouette would show an observer hidden anywhere around that I carried a suitcase. I went into the building then, my heart pounding as it pounded when I landed on the moon. Tonight was another moon landing for me, with less margin for error. Pitch-black inside, the stink of urine. I set the suitcase against the wall by the door, exited to the football field, turned again with empty hands, walked to my car.

And headed for home.

Grabka had checked out the park before he called me, before nightfall. The last people to leave, a little after nine, were three workmen in white T-shirts who'd lounged on the grass at the edge of the football field drinking beer. They'd left behind a brown paper sack filled with clear-glass Miller bottles. Grabka figured them for queers.

After they were gone he'd driven on south to a U-Totem store, gassed his pickup, bought and eaten a sandwich and placed his call from the drive-up pay phone outside. He'd driven back to the park another way, along Troost, the street east of the cemetery that divided ghetto Kansas City from white. North of the park he'd turned west—I was on my way—and threaded a narrow side street to the temple parking lot. He parked in the lot. He sat waiting for the next twenty minutes in his pickup, checking his watch. Then he left his pickup and walked south on the cemetery side of the screen of trees. He felt again as if he were being watched. His hands shook as mine had shaken, both of us intent on what the other would do. He could see the toilet building through the trees silhouetted against the orange streetlights. He noticed quick shadows dart under the lights and when he understood that the darting shadows were bats catching insects a chill ran up his spine and his head twitched in an involuntary spasm.

He saw the Saab slow going south, heard it turn behind the pines, heard it stop and heard the engine shut off, the door open and shut, footsteps, another door open and shut. Then he saw my silhouette separate from the dark pines, saw me stop in the field and turn, saw me walk to the toilet building with the suitcase and leave empty-handed.

He felt then, at the same time, greedy joy that made his stomach flutter and wrenching fear. The box was a box and Chris was buried, but phone calls were only phone calls that could be broken off and denied. What was in the suitcase was more real to Karl Grabka even than Chris's life. Grabka knew what life was; to him it was common; but he had never held, never seen, much less possessed, half a million dollars in gold.

He heard the Saab start, heard my careful U-turn on the narrow side street, saw me swing north onto Holmes and pass the park on the west, under the orange lights, going back the way I came.

He was sweating. His bowels were even loose, so loose he tightened himself against accident. Should he wait to see if we were fucking him over or should he move?

A bus laboring up the hill north of the park delayed his decision. It stopped on the corner northwest across the street. He heard the doors hiss. Someone was getting off. When the bus passed he saw that the someone was a nurse. She headed west from the corner, away from the park. He waited for her to disappear down the hill.

She was gone. He ducked under the screening trees and stepped into the park. He meant to cross the football field crouched low at a run but he looked to his right and saw a silhouette fighting through the pines around the council ring and then a man came fast out of the pines. Grabka pushed backward into the cemetery, ran north to the parking lot pulling his keys from his pocket. When he looked across he saw the man wasn't following him yet—was making for the toilet building. That was Grabka's chance and he jerked open the pickup door, jumped in, jammed in the key and started the engine, threw the truck into reverse, squealed around, shifted to drive and floored it, gunning from the parking lot north onto Holmes.

A stakeout! I'd set him up! Shit mother*fuck*, that was the fucking *end of it* for Chris!

I didn't know. I was pushing on home. Feeling better. With a song in my heart.

What should he do? What should he do? *Drive*. See if they followed. Down the hill, around the curve past the hospital. The hospital grounds brightly lit and no one behind him. Then a little foreign car around the curve. But coming slow. Grabka hooked a right turn into a narrow side street. Down a dip and up a short hill onto Troost. He turned left at Troost, right at the boulevard. The foreign car didn't follow. Then he was easing up the curving boulevard among routine traffic, carloads of blacks, a ghetto cruiser with buckled chrome straps bracing the trunk.

Pitying himself. It always happened. Every time he was close to getting it together something fucked it up. It was the cocaine deal all over again. They'd screw you every time.

Not *this* time. This time no deal. This time they came through or else. This time that shithead Chris could rot. He'd run out of battery in a few days. The fan wouldn't work. The air would get stale. He'd have more and more trouble breathing. He wouldn't just go to sleep the way you go to sleep with monoxide. He'd scream and cry and beg for his daddy. Then: smother. If he made it through the week. Because buried in a box you could go fucking crazy. He'd be up to his neck in his own piss and shit. Let them try to fuck me over, Grabka thought, swelling. Let them try.

He'd reached the high stone entrance of Swope Park in the eastern city, the largest Kansas City park, three square miles of lawn and woodland. It registered somewhere as he turned south and watched in the mirror to see if he was followed. No one came his way. The other cars turned north, back toward downtown.

He was calmer.

Whoever he'd seen in the park hadn't chased him. Which didn't make a whole lot of fucking sense. They knew where the gold was, they wouldn't go after the gold. They'd want him. They'd go after him. The whole point of calling at the last minute was to make sure they couldn't set up a stakeout. There wasn't time to set up a stakeout. They'd have had to get someone there in the five minutes it took him to drive from the U-Totem to the temple parking lot. No way they could do that, not even if they'd alerted every dispatcher in the city. But even if they could have, *they wouldn't have gone for the gold.*

So what the fuck was coming down?

Grabka decided then to call. The plan wasn't running on automatic anymore. The terms hadn't changed—he still controlled Chris, Chris stashed like a king in a safe corner of the board—but now he needed something from us. Information. And more than information: reassurance. Now we had to advise him on tactics as well as minister to him emotionally. And I wasn't even home yet. And Paige didn't know what had happened. But she was the one who had to take the call.

As if Karl Grabka were a swollen, malignant fetus, a teratoma, and we were the midwives it manipulated in its desperation to be born.

Paige in the living room at the farmhouse, her legs in jeans tucked under her, leaning back against the couch, talks quietly with the agents, curious about their work. Diana upstairs in Chris's room watches TV.

The phone rings. Surprised, Paige jumps to answer it. Surprised, Doocy moves to start his tape running and slip on his headphones.

So Paige unprepared: "Hello?"

"You goddamned fucking *cunt,*" Grabka hisses. "*What the fuck are you people trying to pull?*"

Paige recoils, looks to Doocy, who flushes with helpless anger. "I don't understand," Paige says, and the first words quaver, but by the last word she's pulled herself together and her voice is firm. She's heard invective before.

"*Shit* you don't understand, cunt. Where's Wainwright? You're just a goddamned *cunt,* you know that? Put the *man* on."

Deliberately Paige warms her voice and holds it calm. "He's not back yet. What's wrong?" The things we do.

"Tell me you don't *know* what's *wrong?*"

"We tried to follow your instructions. If anything's wrong we'll fix it."

"Your boy shouldn't have sent a stakeout—"

"Stakeout?" Paige breaks in, shaking her head as if the man on the phone could see her, Doocy sympathetically shaking his head in time, Hinderliter listening frustrated, trying to piece together the conversation from Paige's side of it alone. "No," Paige carries on. "We sent *no one*. Believe me. Only Reeve. *No one* else."

Grabka's mouth tastes of brass. He's beginning to believe her. But if she's telling the truth, someone has seen the suitcase and decided to cop it on the chance it's valuable. "Then tell me this, cunt," he says to Paige, "*who was the cocksucker in the park?*"

Paige is assembling the pieces: this hood on the phone hiding in the park, I leave the suitcase, someone else shows up, the hood panics and runs. "There must have been someone else there by accident," she says.

"Sure. By accident. That's why they went for the suitcase. Bullshit. Try again."

The last piece. Inspiration. She's been drinking coffee and her own bladder keys her. "Reeve left the suitcase in the toilet building, didn't he? Couldn't it have been someone going to the toilet?"

Silence. All Paige can hear is breathing, behind the breathing the occasional quick rush of a fast-moving car.

Grabka explodes. He sees he's wrong. "*Then-that's-Chris's-fucking-tough-luck!*"

Paige is already moving to meet it. "No. Please. Listen. Reeve's due here any moment. I'll tell him. He had the gold. Three gold bars. Five hundred thousand dollar's worth. Exactly what you wanted. He'll go back and get it. He'll meet you somewhere else. You can make the exchange again. I *promise* you we've been straight with you. Will you call back? Will you call back in an hour? Please?"

And Grabka, very quietly, seeming to take the bit: "Sure, Paige. I'll call back in an hour. Tell Reeve to move it. Tell our astronaut, you know, tell him not to fuck around. Because if the gold's not there, cunt, that kid's *wasted*."

Sixteen

I wasn't dawdling. I drove straight home, thinking it was almost over, feeling relief. I was sure Chris was alive. The ghoul had his money; now we'd only have to wait for him to check it out and call. I thought of Chris. I thought of seeing Chris standing tall and skinny in his faded jeans, his braces showing across his grin. I thought of what a hell of a guy he was, of what an ordeal all this had been for him. He'd wonder why we hadn't released him sooner. I'd want to try to explain.

When I turned in at the farmhouse my lights caught Jack Hinderliter standing in the driveway waving for me to stop. He'd broken cover—I remember thinking he must have had good reason. He did. He jogged around to my side of the car. "Red," he blurted, "there's a problem. Someone showed up at the park."

"Shit," I said, anger instantly flooding my system again. That anger comes so fast you can actually feel the adrenalin dumped into the bloodstream, you know?

"The guy called," Jack said, peering at me in the reflected high-beam light. "He thought we'd set him up. Paige convinced him. She negotiated another drop. You need to get back there and retrieve that gold."

"He didn't make the pickup?" I didn't really understand. It had looked so damned easy.

"Whoever showed up spooked him. It sounds as if someone wanted to use the facility. The case is probably still sitting there. All I'd have to do is make one call and one of our people could be there in five minutes to secure it."

That was a question. I gave it about two seconds' thought. "Don't. Leave it alone. If the kidnapper's anywhere in the vicinity that would be all she wrote, Jack. I'll get back there. I'll shag ass this time. What do I do when I pick up the gold?"

Hinderliter had been leaning down on the windowsill. Now he knelt beside the door. "Get to a phone and call us. The suspect's agreed to call Paige in about an hour with a new drop point. You'll go directly there and make the drop again. Okay?"

"Okay. Tell Paige thanks." I didn't wait to hear. I turned around, my tires spitting chat, and took off up the road.

It's all information now, isn't it. You didn't want to hear about the landscaping anyway. The month was October, the night was probably still fine. I didn't see it or feel it on that second pass, second orbit. I saw the tunnel of the highway ahead of me, the cars I approached and overtook, the headlights of cars across the median coming the other way. I saw the signs that alerted me to exits and entrances. In my mind's eye I saw the park, the toilet building, the case inside the door, and beyond that I saw a mound of earth, below the mound some kind of box, inside the box my son. I saw him flexed like an Indian burial. I saw him wrapped in rotting linen, his flesh falling away. I couldn't help it. The picture looped and stuck.

I'd known before that the ghoul was hiding in the park. Now he could be anywhere. Following me. Watching me. I was being watched. It occurred to me that since the beginning, since Chris disappeared and I found that vicious letter in my mailbox, we'd had a tyrant slapping us around. This was the way tyranny felt. Anonymous people gave you orders. Your relatives were hauled away without notice or explanation in the middle of the night. You did things you didn't want to do and people watched you from hiding. Even if you complied with their directives you still depended on the caprice of their goodwill—on *their* compliance, which they might arbitrarily withhold. And chance could demolish all the careful structures you built. I'd never in my life been so constrained before, not by human beings. Accident had constrained me on the way home from the moon. Accident was bearable because it was involuntary. No one willed it. This human tyranny filled me with rage.

* * *

I turned up Holmes. Up the hill. The orange streetlights made the trees orange and black along the curbs. Halloween. From the air these new lights made whole cities look as if they were lit at night with candles. The light reflected orange off the slanted skylight at the top of the spiraled temple auditorium. After the temple the park.

Left at the south side. I stopped where I'd stopped before. Killed the engine. Peaceful night, windless. Not so windless as the moon: the flag we raised there was battened to seem to wave.

I took the flashlight from the glove compartment. I hadn't used it before. Now I could. It was a heavy three-battery aluminum flashlight. It made a weapon too.

I left the car, crossed the street. Kept the flashlight off at first to watch for movement. Nothing. The pines smelled of pine as I passed between them, the grass smelled of hay. Then the velvet rectangle of the toilet building. I slowed, stopped, listened. Nothing. Moved to the wall beside the open door.

Stepped around. Stepped inside.

Turned on the flashlight: someone lying on the floor: a kid, dirty bare feet, shredded jeans, a black T-shirt: his head cradled on his arms. He moaned at the light in his eyes, drew up his knees, coughed, retched. The smell of vomit was stronger than the smell of urine in the room and wine-colored vomit dripped from the urinal and puddled below.

That was one quick look. Then smoothly I swung the flashlight beam around the wall, the beam shortening and brightening as it approached the door.

And the suitcase.

I moved, picked it up. It was heavy. Still.

I used the flashlight to find my footing and ran the case back to the car. Set it on the passenger seat and kneeling on the curbside grass pushed open its latches and looked.

Three gold bars. Reflecting back the light.

My hands shook again as I closed the case. I forced the latches. They worked hard across the straw. I stood, brushed my knees, closed the passenger door, walked around and got in. I held the steering wheel hard. I put my head against the steering wheel and breathed deep.

There are all kinds of dangerous voyages. It was easier coming home from the moon.

I looked at the clock on the dash: 11:04. I might beat the ghoul to his call. Then he'd know the gold was in hand. I started the Saab, drove straight ahead to Troost, drove out Troost to Eighty-fifth and back west to Holmes. I called Paige from the U-Totem there. I didn't know then that I called her from the same phone Karl Grabka had used.

I told Paige I had the case.

"Thank God," she said. She'd come upstairs: I'd dialed Chris's phone. "He hasn't called. Can you stay on the line? Keep this line open?"

"You bet."

"I'll go watch the other one."

She gave the phone to Diana. "Daddy?" Diana came on.

"Hi, sweetheart. It's okay. I found the suitcase."

"Where *was* it?"

"Where I'd left it." I explained about the drunken kid.

"God, that's *gross*. If he only knew. He'll think he had a crazy dream."

"Listen, I'll talk to you later, okay?" Who felt like talking?

"Okay." She understood.

"Don't hang up."

"I won't." I heard her leave the handset on the table.

I rested mine on my shoulder and shut off the car. Time to wait, as it had been before. Tonight was a night of ugly waiting.

Paige, in the living room at the farm. She'd had to fight the agents about sending someone to pick up the suitcase, about waiting for me to get home. With half a million dollars at stake they were understandably worried. That much money awed them. It didn't awe Paige. She saw the greater risk to Chris. She debated it with them. She understood they wouldn't comfortably lose a debate to a woman. The answers to Diana's questions about colleges had been Notre Dame and Fordham. Paige turned the corner by proposing they let me decide.

My instinct matched Paige's. Which says something about her, because Chris was my son and she even had no children. The rightness of her argument may seem obvious from a distance. It didn't seem obvious to Hinderliter and Doocy, two trained professionals. They'd handled the gold, seen it, smelled the fresh straw of its nest. Its sheer weight was compelling—more than three times as heavy as iron. It worked on them as powerfully as kryptonite works on Superman. And if on them, how much more would it work on Karl Grabka? And to what effect? But he hadn't seen it yet.

The phone. Months would pass before Paige or I again comfortably answered the phone.

Paige picked up.

"Hey, Paige." Grabka, whispering. "Did your boyfriend find his suitcase?"

"Yes," Paige said, watching Doocy turn the recording volume up and then down. "He has it. He's waiting for my call. Near the park. He'll go directly to wherever you want."

"Tell him to go directly to hell." The ghoul in good spirits, recovering.

"Please," Paige said. "We want to make this exchange. He has five hundred thousand dollars in gold. It's yours. Please tell us where to leave it for you."

"Now that's pretty convincing, Paige. You sound like you care."

"I do care."

"Sure you do. What was the dealie with the guy in the park?"

"A teenager. He was drunk. He wanted to use the toilet." Diana had brought the story downstairs.

"No shit. He's fucking lucky he's alive."

"Where should Reeve deliver the gold?" Paige urged.

"You from Kansas City, Paige?"

"No."

"How the hell am I supposed to give Reeve directions if you don't know your fucking way around?"

"I'll get them straight. I'll write them down."

"You going to marry him, Paige?"

"That's not important right now," she said calmly. "What's important is that you receive this half-million dollars in gold."

He took it. In a way she tamed him. "Yeah. Tell him to leave it in the doorway at the Swope Park pool."

"Is that a swimming pool? Will he know what you mean?"

"Yeah. He grew up around here. He'll know what I mean. It's the pool the niggers took. Hey, I got to get off. We won't have a chance to talk again, Paige. Paige? You know what? I'd sure like to fuck you." He hung up laughing.

Doocy shook his head and shut off the recorder. Paige ran upstairs and called me to pick up, her voice thin in the night. I did and she gave me directions. I might have been on a scavenger hunt. Off again I went.

Swope Park, the park that Grabka had noticed when he was running from the first drop, wasn't far. I drove there in five minutes, turned in at the high stone gate. I'd known it all my life, picnicked in its shelter houses, camped in its woods, visited its zoo two or three times annually when I was a kid. The Army Reserve displayed tanks there once, the Naval Reserve flew in carrier-based aircraft I stood in line again and again to see.

I headed down the entrance road and remembered the soapbox derby I'd watched there as a Boy Scout when the winner was disqualified for cheating. For having built into the nose of his car, with his father's direction and collusion, an electromagnet that held the car to the starting gate, as the gate pulled forward, long enough to give him an advantageous start on his coast toward fame and fortune. I was simple enough to be shocked. We didn't do things that way in the Midwest.

And turned past the zoo where I had talked to the animals in their cages in imitation of Doctor Dolittle, not the tall, gaudy Doctor Dolittle of the Rex Harrison film but the original short, pudgy, plain Doctor Dolittle of Hugh Lofting's books, who voyaged to the moon on the back of a giant moth, breathing oxygen from the mask of an oversized flower.

Those memories were microdots. They came unbidden and compressed and they didn't take long to think. Longer to tell. I should have been concentrated on Chris but I was sensitized by emergency. The earth was layered thick in the park with personal history. I hadn't told Chris much of it. I'd meant to. I would.

One more memory that flashed as I drove to rendezvous. When I was eight, in Kansas City winter, I'd lost a library book. The librarian told me to bring the book or bring five dollars or not to come to school. I asked Dad for the money. He told me to find the book. I panicked and decided to run away. The librarian had inadvertently given me permission.

I stole five dollars from the closet where I knew Dad hid a nest egg of cash and pretended to leave for school. (Why didn't I give that five to the librarian?) Instead I walked to the corner drugstore through the cold, through a scattered light dusting of flurried snow, bought a package of three-ring notebook paper and a cardboard box of wooden kitchen matches. Waited outside the drugstore for the southward-bound electric trolley. Took the trolley to the right transfer point, waited in the cold wind, took the transfer trolley to Swope Park. I was good at navigation even then.

Stubbornly I marched down the road where later the soapbox derby racer would cheat, past the zoo where already I talked to the animals, past the lagoon and the native limestone walls of the swimming pool on the long curving road, and hiked offroad up the frozen hillside to the marble monument erected there, a modest palisade, to Colonel Swope. I settled in behind the monument out of the wind, sat on my thin haunches, wadded sheets of notebook paper and lit them for warmth. In the winter daylight I could hardly see the flame.

I meant to live in Swope Park. I meant to grow up there a hermit with wild-man's hair and wisdom. I would appear to the world with white hair, carrying a shepherd's crook and wrapped in the skins of animals. People from all over America would seek me out for advice.

I meant to be the wise father Dad hadn't been for me that day. By my reckoning. Chris must have felt the same way, long before now. At some point every kid must.

I got cold. I didn't know yet how to build a fire. I cried. I gave up hermetics and rode the trolleys home. In due time I found the book under my bed. I still remember it. It was Charles Lindbergh's *The Spirit of St. Louis.*

The swimming pool. The same native limestone walls surrounding it, walls eight feet high built by hand during the Depression years when public works were plentiful.

The moon was swelling in the western sky as it set. I could see the Ocean of Storms plainly on its face. I hauled out the suitcase, carried it up the steps and left it at the dark wooden doors. I walked quickly back to my car, got in, looked only ahead, drove away.

Karl Grabka watched me from the shelter house across the road. His pickup parked out of sight behind the open building beside overflowing cans of trash, he sat in the darkness at one of the heavy, bolted-down wooden tables. Before him on the table lay the cheap .22 pistol he'd bought to control Chris. This time he was calm. This time no one was going to chase him off.

He caught a glimpse of my face as I walked back to the car, enough to recognize me. He'd noticed in the other park that I was smaller than he thought I'd be from the photographs.

He watched me drive away. He followed the sound of my car out to the boulevard, heard me turn eastward heading back to the farm. After I'd turned he stood, picked up the pistol, went to the front edge of the raised shelter-house slab and looked up and down the road. Then he stepped off the slab and crossed.

He never took his eyes off the case. He found the handle and lifted. The first thrill was the weight.

He grinned.

Hooking the pistol into his belt, he lugged the suitcase across the road and around the shelter house to his pickup. He flung open the door, hoisted the suitcase up to seat level, tipped it onto the seat and slid it across to the passenger side. He pulled the pistol from his belt and climbed into the cab. Put the pistol away in the glove compartment. Started the engine. Shifted into reverse, backed up, pulled forward to the road. Looked across at the pool building, at the black darkness of the doorway. Swung left and drove off.

The suitcase on the seat beside him might have been incandescent. It glowed and it burned. He wanted to open it, to see, but the first priority was getting clear. The magnetic force of the suitcase pulled at his hand. He fought it. At the boulevard he turned left, west, because I had turned right and eastward. He'd drive back to Holmes and south to the interstate. From there he'd head south down the western border of Missouri on U.S. 71. Outside of Kansas City he'd pass the road that led to Chris.

What if it wasn't the gold?

He waited for the light at the intersection. When it turned he took off. He couldn't leave the street for a couple more blocks. The only turnouts were private driveways until then. His foot twitched on the accelerator. Thirty-five miles an hour was a crawl. It would have to be the gold. Otherwise the pigs would be crawling all over him by now. Beyond the next intersection was a lot where he could check.

The light went green as he approached. He downshifted and pulled through, pulling into the parking lot of a fish market converted from a filling station. The fish market was closed. He cut his lights, set his parking brake.

Was it gold?

He swung the suitcase around to face him. Turned the latches.

Was it gold?

The latches cleared. He lifted the lid. Fucking straw. What the hell was that?

Gold! Three numbered bars. Gold. He'd asked for gold.

He reached behind him, found the light switch, turned on the interior light long enough to check the color, turned it off.

Gold.

He closed the case. He was shaking. He managed to lock one of the two latches.

He switched on his lights, released the parking brake and left the lot, driving west. He felt like a little kid. The hot summer in Kansas City when he'd spent the morning at the dump playing with the junk. He didn't even have any toys. He played with junk. In the afternoon he began to get hungry. He followed the streetcar tracks along to near where he lived. There was a drive-in two blocks from his house. It was pale yellow. It had rounded corners set with glass bricks that you could almost see through. Behind was a loading dock. Sometimes he'd find stuff to eat in the trash back there. That day there were three five-gallon paper cartons of ice cream sitting on the loading dock in the hot sun. It was crazy. He couldn't figure it out. Why would they leave ice cream sitting in the sun? He pulled himself up onto the loading dock, over the iron band at the edge of the dock that protected the concrete from the trucks. Two of the ice-cream cartons were open. They were more than half full. One was chocolate. The other was strawberry. The one that still had a lid was stamped VANILLA.

He wondered if he should tell them. Maybe they didn't know.

The screen door beyond the loading dock led to a kitchen. He tried to see in through the screen but the sun was too bright. He smelled steam and onions and grease. He was afraid, but he pushed the screen anyway and went in.

He saw a man in a dirty white apron at a big black grill. The man looked up. "Whatdaya want, kid?" the man asked. He sounded friendly. Grabka told him about the ice cream. "The freezer broke down," the man said. "We're throwin' it out."

"Can I have it?" Grabka dared to ask.

The man said—the man said!—"Sure, why not? Just don't leave it around the parking lot. Carry it off somewhere and throw the cartons in the trash when you're through." The man winked at Grabka. "Think you can eat it all?"

He couldn't start to eat it all. He ran home for his brothers. They brought the wagon they used to haul pop bottles back to the store and loaded the three cartons and wheeled them home. They called in all the kids they knew in the neighborhood. They had a feast. The only feast he'd ever been to in his whole life and he had to set it up himself.

Think you can eat it all? Fucking old man.

Grabka had turned south a couple of miles back. Now he pulled off his hat and felt his shaved head. It felt real weird. It was starting to stubble. He'd have to shave it every day to keep it smooth. Stubble on his face too. When he grew the beard he'd have hair on his jaw instead of on his head. He'd be invisible. He'd be able to walk right past people he'd known for years, like people at the hospital, and they wouldn't know him from Adam.

The bottom line was, he was rich. You just had to tough the cocksuckers out, man. Tough the cocksuckers out. They're all fucking cowards when it gets down to the nut-cutting.

Don't get mad—get even.

Drive on over to Albuquerque. There'd still be guys around he knew. Drive on down to El Paso, Texas, hide the gold and cross the border. Maybe spray-paint it aluminum and toss it back in the toolbox. Fake them out. He had plenty of time to worry about that one. Plenty of open border down beyond El Paso, too.

Should he let Reeve have little Christopher back? Maybe he should, maybe he shouldn't. He'd think about it. Only his hairdresser knew for sure.

Outside the city Grabka drove south toward Joplin on 71. It was cool enough now to roll up the window. The moon had set. The sky was black above the bouncing beams of his headlights. Beside him sat his friend. He had a friend beside him and it was a friend he could trust.

If there'd been enough love in the world nothing would ever of had to happen. If there'd been enough love in the world everybody would of shared. They didn't let it. They knew what would happen if they did. If everyone could fuck everyone whenever they wanted to and if everyone had enough of everything then no one would want to work. No one would want to fight. No one would need anything anyone else had. There wouldn't be any power to grab off. Because that's what they did. They grabbed off power.

He'd wanted power. He'd gotten it. It sat on the seat beside him. If it'd been a snake it would of bitten him. It just sat there solid as the Rock of Gibraltar. He'd never want for anything again.

Gold was power. Gold was money. Gold was women. Women came around wherever there was money and power. They came like bugs to streetlights. It didn't matter how mean you were, how ugly you were, whether or not you treated them like shit, they came around. Gold meant doing whatever he wanted to do every minute of every day and no questions asked, no fucking jobs, nothing.

One of the things he'd do was get an American Express card.

What it bought was respect. You had to be a killer to put together the big bucks. You had to be cold, hard, crueler than the next asshole you beat out and faster on your feet. And everyone like waiters, hotel managers, call girls et cetera et cetera knew that. You better believe they knew it. And acted accordingly. Cleared the way.

It also bought time. Time was money. You had time to operate.

In the eye of his mind he could see a golden city. The golden city swarmed with people beautiful in metallic jump suits of gold and silver and copper and bronze. They crowded the streets. Some of them moved toward the center of the city, some of them moved away. The ones that moved toward the center had a look of yearning on their faces but the ones that moved away were smiling. They looked happy and relaxed. At the center of the city there was a golden dome. Under the dome was a circular golden hall. In the center of the golden hall was a golden platform. The people swarmed around the platform. He lay on the platform, naked as the day he was born. The people came to touch him. They touched him with love. They stroked him. They caressed him. The beautiful women slipped from their metallic jump suits and mounted him wet with passion. He was love. He gave them love, all his people. Gold he gave them love.

Steering with his left hand Grabka reached across the suitcase to the glove compartment. He punched the latch and the door dropped open. He felt for the pistol and found its cold plastic grip molded in a pattern of sharp diamonds. He slipped his fingers around the grip, his index finger around the trigger inside the guard and brought the pistol out into the cab. He held it across in front of him at chest level parallel with the pickup's steering wheel, pointing out the window on the driver's side. The safety was on. He rotated his thumb behind the crudely stamped hammer and down to release the safety. And staring ahead then, the light that bounced ahead on the road blurring and clearing as he blinked, blurring and clearing, he stuck the barrel of the cheap pistol into his mouth.

He knew why. He did what he was told.

The barrel tasted of oil. He fitted his tongue into the bore. He could feel the rough rifling with the tip of his tongue.

They could take the gold and shove it. It wasn't the gold. It was showing that they couldn't just keep on grinding people down. He'd take fucking shittypants little Chrissie with him. They'd never find little Chrissie shittypants unless he called them. They'd find a smashed truck and a dead man and a suitcase full of gold. They'd have search parties out everywhere. It'd be all over TV. Why did this man die? They'd no more guess than shit. How the hell would they know? What the hell would they know about it?

His nose was running. He opened his mouth and swung the pistol barrel aside. He held the steering wheel with his gun hand and wiped his nose on his arm, wiped his eyes with a knuckle. But he didn't put the pistol away. Fuck 'em. Fuck 'em all. He'd drive for a while. He'd just see.

Seventeen

Chris had slept, running the fan, and dreamed another nightmare and waked cold, clammy with sweat. The fan was rattling, a sound it hadn't made before. Reaching back over his shoulder he turned it off. Lying awake was grim but it was better in that place than sleeping. Chris's body knew its prison now. He turned easily from side to side without bumping his elbows or his knees. He could find the fan switch without fumbling. He accepted the darkness and no longer needed the light. The terror that curled at the base of his brain was terror of abandonment now, not terror of confinement. He was assigned to a one-man submarine that swam through earth instead of water, the single air duct both his snorkel and his periscope. The only living species the expedition had encountered so far had been a crow. The crow had reported daylight conditions on the surface. Otherwise it would have been roosting. By now day was probably night.

Chris conjured the air duct to a periscope and imagined turning it around. What he saw was Middle Earth. The weirdo who kidnapped him wasn't Sauron, but he was sure as hell one of Sauron's henchmen. The Dark Lord, the unblinking eye in the tower, was watching Chris. He could feel the eye searching the broken land of Mordor like a spotlight, could feel the evil like a shock of electricity sweep over him and hesitate and move on. He wasn't Frodo. He was buried as Gandalf had been buried at the bottom of a mountain but he wasn't Gandalf either. He was one of the riders of Rohan, one of the men. His work wasn't delivering the ring. It was lesser work. It had its place. His work was toughing it out. He hadn't really understood before what evil was. Now he did. Tolkien had it right. Evil was cold, evil was darkness, evil was the kind of mind that could bury another human being alive and never think about how it would feel. Or act big and let itself off by thinking being buried alive was better than being murdered.

"You can't have evil unless there's a God," Chris announced aloud.

"Sure you can."

"How, smart ass? If there isn't a God then there aren't any rules. There aren't any Ten Commandments. Jesus wasn't the son of God if there isn't a God to be son of, so the Sermon on the Mount doesn't go either. Anybody can say anything they want is good or anything is evil. They could say shooting rockers dead in cold blood was good or they could say blue was evil."

"Who's *they?*"

"People. Enough people. The majority."

"Just because they said it doesn't mean you'd have to believe it. Just because more of them believe it doesn't mean they're right. Most of them think rock is evil anyway. You don't believe that and you never will."

"Asshole. Look at the Russians."

"Why the Russians?"

"Because they don't believe in God. So they made up their own rules. The stuff they believe is a hundred eighty degrees the opposite of what we believe. Like, they believe capitalism is evil. They don't believe in freedom of the press."

"That doesn't prove anything. They're evil for their Gulags. They keep people down."

"How do you know that's evil?"

"Kiss off, I just know it."

He didn't have the answer and he didn't know where to take the argument. It was something he hadn't had to think about before because he'd been sheltered. He couldn't believe how sheltered he'd been. He thought the world was great and everything was okay. There were lots of little hassles but he'd never had to sweat the big stuff. Now he knew better.

Chris remembered the year before—was it October then too?—when the pig had caught him and Kevin Gadberry out in the school parking lot in Kevin's car. Kevin was selling, Chris was making a buy, and since Kevin was eighteen he could have been charged with a felony as an adult and sent up for one to five. When the pig suddenly pulled up behind them and spun his light—he didn't whoop his siren—Chris had grabbed the two ounces, the one he was buying and the one Kevin was carrying, and stuffed them into the top of his boot. The pig moseyed around to the driver's side of the car, a kickass Charger Kevin was fixing up, and looked in and asked them what they thought they were doing.

Kevin hated pigs. "Getting high, man," he said.

The pig didn't blink. "That's what I thought," he said. He was suntanned with a pig face like the bad guys in western flicks and his navy-blue pig shirt was pressed with extra creases running down the pockets and probably down the back the way they did in the military.

"We're just taking a break," Chris said. "It's our lunch block."

The pig grinned and pointed to Kevin. "I believe *him.*" He hit the latch and swung open Kevin's door. "Let's get out, boys."

Outside Kevin said, "You want us up against the door?"

"You armed?" the pig asked. Crazy Kevin shrugged. The pig started searching them, Kevin first and then Chris. He was looking weird at them, keeping up a little grin because he knew he had all the power on his side. When he patted down Kevin's legs, starting in the crotch, he said, "I don't want to play with your peckers, boys, I just have to check you out." He was really egotistical.

He found the ounces in Chris's boot. He tried to get Chris to admit that one of the bags was Kevin's or that Kevin had been dealing. Chris wouldn't. You didn't rat on a friend anyway, least of all when it would get him in worse trouble than you.

Where was the good and where was the evil? He'd need hours to unravel that one. The pig representing good and the reefer evil and vice versa. Chris taking the heat off Kevin because he was a juvenile. An eighteen-year-old facing jail and a sixteen-year-old getting off with a lecture. The pig's grinning and his bullshit about playing with peckers. Kevin's craziness. Hours of it.

Remembering the bust, remembering the egotism of the pig back at the station when he called me, linking the experience now with his imprisonment in this unending darkness, Chris remembered pieces of the Neil Young song that Young sang in *The Last Waltz*, filling in with his harmonica, with Joni Mitchell and the Band backing him up:

There is a town in north Ontario
. . .
In my mind I still need a place to go
All my changes were there

Blue blue windows behind the stars
Yellow moon on the rise
Big birds flying across the sky
Throwing shadows on our eyes

And the chorus, not so much sung as wailed, wailed again and again until it seemed to cry with all the hurt of the world:

Leave us
Helpless, helpless, hee*elll*pluuus
We were
Helpless, helpless, hee*elll*pluuus

Oh babe can you hear me now?
. . .
The chains are locked tight across the door
. . .
Throwing shadows on our eyes
We were
Helpless, helpless, hee*elll*pluus
Helpless, helpless, hee*elll*pluuus

It wasn't something he'd worked up with his band. It wasn't a song he'd normally even listen to, which is why he hadn't memorized all the words. But it was how he felt then: *The chains are locked tight across the door: Throwing shadows on our eyes* . . .

The box was smelly from the pan down at his feet. Chris reached over his shoulder and flipped the fan switch. The fan didn't come on. He cycled the switch, waited, cycled it quickly back and forth three or four more times. Then he wasn't sure which setting was off and which was on. He left the switch where he'd cycled it the last time. He felt prickling on his neck, the first stirring of panic. He lay still in the blackness trying to think what to do. Without the fan he'd have to breathe through the air duct. But what if it didn't work? How could he fix the fan? Was the problem the fan or the switch?

Then without warning something stung his eyes. He inhaled the acrid phenolic harshness of hot plastic and smoking varnish. His eyes teared and burned and he coughed. His lungs filled in reflex and burned with his eyes and more coughing racked him, coughing so deep he retched. Fighting his body's convulsion he stuck his hand through the hole in the partition and felt for the wires from the switch to the fan. He found them, tore them away. His hand touched the fan body and jerked backward reflexively from the hot cowling, the rough-sawn edge of the hole in the partition ripping skin from his arm and shooting pain from the knob of bone on his wrist.

He was choking. He couldn't breathe. He had to have air. Fighting his coughing, he stuck his hand through the partition hole again, reached up past the fan to the nailed-down air duct, took hold of it and began pulling it steadily toward him. He felt it giving. He didn't have time to be careful with it. He pulled as hard as he could. It tore free and he scraped his wrist again painfully on the partition hole. He didn't care. He had to breathe. His eyes were burning and his lungs. He worked the ducting through the hole, jiggling it left and right to free its wire hoops, round wired tube through square hole. It came hard and his lungs were bursting from holding his breath.

Abruptly it gave and came through. He clamped it over his nose and mouth, blew out first as hard as he could with what was left of his air to clear it, inhaled then carefully to test, inhaled deeply when he sensed that the air in the duct was fresher.

Breathing again he noticed what he hadn't noticed before: a warm, spreading wetness in his crotch. He'd wet his goddamned pants.

His eyes still burned. When he'd first felt the smoke hitting them he'd squeezed them tight shut. The box was still filled with smoke. No place for it to go. It would just hang in there. What the hell happened to the fan? He'd have to keep his eyes closed. Maybe he could do something with the fan when it cooled, tear it loose and hold it in the duct and work it by hand. Clear out the smoke that way. But for now he'd have to keep his eyes shut and breathe through the duct. And where was his dad? Where the shit was his dad?

The tears started then. Sixteen isn't even eighteen, much less forty-seven. The tears soothed his eyes, which is what tears are for. Chris lay on his back, his eyes closed, quietly crying, holding the air duct with both hands, squeezing it to an oblong to make a mask when he breathed, and sang in his head, wailing, sang what he felt.

Helpless, helpless, hee*elll*pluuus

We didn't know—didn't know that Chris was struggling for his life, didn't know that Grabka was playing at ending his. If we'd known, what could we have done? Or rather, what could we have done other than what we did? By now the FBI men had taken off their jackets and loosened their ties. They were least involved but sympathetic. Diana sprawled on the floor, propping her head on her elbow, nervously wide awake. Sometimes she sat up to talk. Paige kept the coffee coming. I took to the Eames and guarded the phone beside me. We were waiting as families wait when sons go into battle, wound tight and trying not to show it. Trying to keep each other going.

When sons go into battle—or when fathers go off on dangerous expeditions. Diana had been through a variation on this waiting before, when I went to the moon. We had better communications then, and so less anxiety even in emergency—better communications to and from the moon than with Chris buried only miles from the farm.

I wasn't tired. None of us was. If anything, we were hyperalert. We were primed for the phone to ring. After that, and after we'd recovered Chris, we'd all be absolutely exhausted.

I felt hope intensely and I felt intense fear. You'd think the two emotions would cancel each other out, but they never merged. They worked separately within me like quanta of energy, alternating, one coming up as the other faded back. I could hope because the gold had been delivered and that was what the kidnapper said he wanted in exchange for Chris. But I felt fear equally because how could I trust some son of a bitch who was so cold-bloodedly sadistic he had kidnapped my son and buried him alive?

The moon was long set. The earth had turned away the side where we waited, the side where Chris was buried. Through the earth the moon still worked on us. Its tides worked, moving on the water, moving in our blood. Women's periods cycle with the moon and so do the sanity and the murderousness of men, as if the extra weight of the moon's attraction at the nodes of the lunar month is oppression enough for some to tip the scale. It is.

In human extremity, even now, years after I went there, I still fly away to the moon. I can't help it. I haven't said, in all the telling of this story—none of the astronauts who walked on the moon has said, has dared to say—what is incontrovertibly true: that traveling to another body in the heavens beyond the earth is an experience figuratively as well as literally beyond anything the earth has left to offer, as haunting as rebirth might be, as haunting as it must have been to step ashore for the first time on the New World.

Doocy was lecturing Diana on the perils of what he called "pot." She was listening alertly, reining her anger. She didn't party. She didn't like the stuff. But she also knew the track record of the perils Doocy was reciting and she was waiting her turn.

I caught Hinderliter's eye. "Once this bastard calls, what's your move?"

He swung around to face me, recrossing his legs. "We've got a crew of four agents waiting downtown." News to me. "As soon as we know where your boy is we'll give them a call. They'll come running. They've got a complete set of county road maps for Kansas and Missouri. They can meet us along the way and help us pinpoint the area."

No local police. The legendary FBI operation, center stage. I didn't care except I didn't want them to find Chris before I did. I wanted him out of his torture chamber as soon as humanly possible, but I hoped I'd be there to help him onto his feet. He deserved that for what he'd been through, deserved more than rescue by strangers.

"*Everything* causes chromosome damage," Diana was saying to Doocy in rebuttal. Hinderliter turned to listen. "It doesn't mean that much. Aspirin causes chromosome damage. Alcohol's the *worst*, you know?"

They were off. Hinderliter glanced back at me as if to say, What kind of kids are you raising? I let it alone. In a way Diana was defending Chris. It was something for her to do.

Leaving the LM, once we landed on the moon, was like crawling through a basement window. Or maybe like being born. We had to suit up first, layer over layer starting with a thick knit diaper the engineers called a "fecal-containment garment," and then we had to crawl on our bellies out that smallish awkward hatch. We each directed the other so our PLSS's wouldn't get banged or stuck. From the porch beyond the hatch we descended the ladder. It was still a jump from the end of the ladder to the powdery ground, but not a bad one.

The first thing I did when I stood on the moon, the fifth human being in the history of the world to get there, was take a leak. I was excited. I'd been too busy to go before I left home. I was wearing a urine dump system, a condom with a tube that led to a bag in the leg of my suit, and I used it.

Then I just looked around. Standing up took some getting used to. In the moon's lighter gravity you don't have the same clear sense of the vertical. You can tip farther forward or backward without realizing you're leaning. It's a strange sensation and it's a little unnerving. I worked on adjusting. I scanned the crater around us. I could see distinctly all the way to the crater walls, the far walls.

There was none of the fading and bluing with distance that you get through the atmosphere on earth. I took the first of hundreds of photographs. While Cowboy was preparing to back out the hatch, I deployed the television away from the LM.

My suit served me well. It had a liquid cooling system that kept me completely comfortable except the last day, when the sun was higher (the lunar day lasts two weeks—we landed early in lunar morning). I could bend my head inside my helmet, take the end of a plastic tube into my mouth and collect a squirt of drinking water. I could turn the other cheek and bite off bites from a food stick. I sported a chronograph up above my elbow on my right arm, a camera strapped conveniently to my chest like any tourist, a checklist Velcroed to my cuff, a pen and a penlight stashed in a sort of cigarette pocket at my shoulder. Oxygen and reserve oxygen in my PLSS, on my back, plus a radio that put me in touch with the LM that put me in touch with the earth. All the amenities, really, an entire earthlike environment transported on tennis shoes.

Walking was fairly easy—like trampolining, as I've said. The powder we kicked up flew ahead and behind in lazy arcs.I watched the TV transmission after I got home. It looked like slow motion up there, but it wasn't. Just one-sixth G. On our last EVA I hefted a big chunk of basalt and threw it completely out of sight.

The lighter gravity was a boon. It was also a toy. Cowboy and I both concentrated on our work. We were busy every minute of all three EVAs. But somewhere underneath that responsibility I was taking healthy delight in the totally different sensation of lunar gravity. Everyone who swims has some sense of what weightlessness feels like. Lesser gravity is absolutely new. We enjoyed it most when we took off our suits inside the LM (and left them standing sentinel along the wall). We slept better than in zero G. No dreams of falling. Our hammocks hung so light they felt like water beds. Out on EVA we had the strength of six and packed gear, PLSS's, rockboxes with the superhuman grace of comic-book heroes, which, in a way, we were. In space and on the moon I understood something of what the dolphins feel who live out their happy lives in the low-gravity world of the ocean.

None of these experiences justifies the incomprehensible billions of dollars you and I and all of us spent to send me to the moon. That either justifies itself in your mind or it doesn't. If it does, you'll understand the personal awe I felt: Cowboy and I, like the other few men before and after us, climbed down from the LM and walked on the moon with exactly the same responsibility and to the same purpose as the early explorers of the New World (and at approximately the same degree of risk—if anything, ours was somewhat less than theirs). Now that I think of it, I'm surprised we didn't name a LM after one of Columbus's ships.

I don't mean that going to the moon corresponds across the board to the discovery of America. In some ways they're comparable. Most of all historically: the one led, directly I think, to the other. But reaching out to the moon pledged us to reach on out into the larger universe. It will stand as a challenge to administrations to come, governments to come, generations to come. The challenge may be worthwhile or it may not. That judgment will change with changing circumstance. But the challenge stands, and it will stand, and others will strive in time to surpass it.

All of us who went to the moon were faulted for our verbal inadequacies, especially during EVAs. Even forgetting that we were busy with science and engineering details, how could we have found words for the newness of the moon? Its lighter gravity let us glide and multiplied our strength. The vacuum of its atmosphere was finer than the finest laboratory vacuum made on earth—the entire gaseous envelope of the moon could be stored frozen inside one average moving van, compared to the earth's billions of tons—which gave us unparalleled seeing. Except that the light from the unearthly, corona-haloed sun was blindingly bright (or would have been if we had been rash enough to raise our gold-plated visors) and the shadows were so dark that I had to stop to allow my eyes to adjust whenever I stepped into one, the shadow of the LM for example. The moon's waterless, lifeless landscape was pure and chemically unaltered. It preserved a precise record of its physical history that extended back more than four billion years.

All that, and overhead the blue, cloud-swirled earth and the untwinkling, undeviating stars.

I had to dig a ditch. I'd practiced on earth. My shovel, really a scoop, was no more than three inches wide. The only way I could work properly in the lighter gravity was to shove the thing back between my legs like a dog digging for a bone. Cowboy said something to that effect.

I counteracted the ignominy of that effort with a demonstration I called the Galileo Show. I'd brought along a feather from the tail of the Air Force Academy's mascot falcon. I dropped it side by side with a moon rock and millions of schoolchildren saw the two objects reach the ground together. Maybe that proved something. It was fun.

Best of all were the traverses, the simple walking tours we made, after we finished digging ditches and deploying packages of experiments, to look for rocks. Physically and visually they were fantastic. We found small craters splashed with sprays of delicately colored glass where incoming meteorites had melted the rock by the force of their impact. We found bubbly chunks of cooled-out lava that looked like dark, hardened sponges. The walls of Copernicus rose up around us like the walls of an earthly caldera. We had landed close enough to one curve of wall to walk over near it, almost under it, on our last and longest traverse. We collected samples there of the mixture of broken, fused rock called breccia. And stood and gawked like country visitors. We were, and that was worthwhile too.

Near the end of our final EVA I finished up outside while Cowboy climbed aboard the LM that would take us home. Together, using a system of pulleys and lines, we loaded the two gleaming rockboxes. My work done, I looked around as I had in the beginning, the last that trip to go. Our waffled footprints packed the powder solidly at the base of the LM where I was standing and trailed out in single and double lines from there in every direction across the crater. The experiment packages we had deployed shone in the sunlight, now uncomfortably warm. The flag that flew from its stand hammered into the moon was a splash of color against the gray but meretricious in that landscape still safely beyond nationalism. I was leaving a place I had come to cherish as mountain climbers cherish the one peak that challenges them to their limits and most nearly claims their lives. A quest was ended that I had pursued through seven single-minded years. The leaving would be final as the leaving that is death, because I would never walk there again, never come back.

Not many of our lives divide so absolutely. A voyage to the moon divided mine. A kidnapping now divided Chris's. I fell with him through that chasm, waiting out the night, and wished he had my memories or I were in his place.

At nearly two in the morning, when we were grim with despair, the ringing phone jerked us alert. Doocy took up position at his recorder and I answered.

"Reeve Wainwright."

"Just a moment, sir," the operator said, and I heard coins going in one by one—it meant the kidnapper was running, reason for the long delay, reason for hope—and saw Doocy efficiently making a count of them on his notepad, a measure of sorts of the kidnapper's range. And then the voice I'd been waiting for. Who could ever have convinced me I'd be glad to hear it?

"You done good, Reeve." I didn't know his name yet, but it was unmistakably Grabka. He'd decided to put his pistol away and live. And, thank God, to open the way to Chris.

"You found the suitcase," I said stupidly.

"Fuck yes. You think I'd be calling you if I didn't? Now listen up. I'm going to give you little Christopher's location *once*. Then it's all yours. You ready?"

"Yes." I had scratch pad and ballpoint. Doocy would also write it down. Plus the tape.

"Okay." Straightforwardly he gave me directions. And abruptly, when he was finished, he hung up.

Our last conversation, Karl Grabka and I. Technical data, as on the moon. That banal. But I still didn't know—neither did Grabka—if Chris was alive.

Eighteen

Paige, Diana and I ran for the Saab. I'd passed Hinderliter the keys to the farm pickup. He and Doocy had to connect with their crew. I didn't need their maps. They could find their own way.

The chill woke us up. We could see our breaths blowing out warm in the October air. Not for the first time I thought of how Chris had been dressed when he left for school on Friday morning, more than sixty-six hours ago. If he was buried by eight o'clock Friday night, which was probable if you allowed the kidnapper time to deliver the ransom letter, he'd been underground more than fifty hours. I was intensely alert, without outward anger, but at the thought of Chris's long, punishing ordeal I felt the thick gathering of my rage.

I started the Saab and almost simultaneously dropped it into gear, throwing Diana against the back seat. She didn't mind. Her eyes flashed. It took away some of the tension. Paige beside me looked calmer. She was completely a pro; her calm steadied me.

The directions pointed us south about fifteen miles and westward. South of Kansas City, US 71 and Bypass 71 parallel each other through a stretch of countryside before the two highways merge south of Harrisonville, Missouri. Highway 150 runs east and west between the US routes past the Air Force base where Cowboy met me with the T-38, Richards-Gebaur. South of 150, then, the three highways define a triangle. It was within that triangle, some fifteen miles long and ten miles wide, that we had to thread a network of county and section roads to find Chris.

I was amazed how close we were. Chris was hidden no more than twenty miles from the farm. It was obvious why. The kidnapper had watched the farm. He got used to driving in the area and knew, or found out, that farmland reached in closer to Kansas City from the south than from any of the other three directions, where the suburbs and the exurbs—the slurbs, energy people call them—run on for miles. The closer to town, the less distance he had to transport Chris once he subdued him.

I drove. I didn't give a good goddamn for speed limits. If we caught a police escort, so much the better. I picked up Bypass 71 almost right outside my front door—it was the road I'd used to connect with the interstate—and raced south toward 150. The kidnapper's directions ran us into the triangle off 71 from the exit nearest the Air Force base, over west, the way he would have come out from Kansas City, but I knew from past experience that we could make the crossover off Bypass 71 too, and I stayed on it to save the drive all the way around the base of the triangle. The bypass highway was only two lanes, but no one was out at that hour of the night and I wound the Saab up to eighty between intersections, braking down smoothly for side roads when the view was obscured.

Diana leaned forward between the front seats. "Will we get there first?"

"You mean before the FBI?"

"Yeah."

"Probably. They had to hook up with the others. They were coming out from downtown." I hadn't seen Hinderliter and Doocy behind us. We got a head start and the Saab with its front-wheel drive could corner better than the pickup. They might have gone some other way.

"I hope we do. I want Chris to see us first. I want him to know we were *there* for him."

Paige glanced back at Diana and smiled. My sentiments too. Ahead was the intersection I was looking for, on the right a country filling station with low, rusty Fifties pumps under the eave of an overhang. Away from the pumps the station yard was dirt. Rather than slow at the corner I cut across, the rear end breaking away in the dirt as I swung around west and then taking hold on the highway pavement.

"Wow, Daddy, you learned that at Cocoa Beach, right?" Diana called from the corner of the backseat where she'd swayed.

"Edwards." I said. "Before you were born." On the desert at

Edwards Air Force Base in California where we test-piloted we raced whatever we had—mostly broken-down Fords. Cocoa Beach was Corvettes, leased at a dollar a year from astronaut-struck dealers who pulled the right strings at GM. Like professional athletes, but covertly—because we were government employees—we endorsed products. So some of the guys also drove Thunderbirds, or their wives did. Saab is Swedish. They make jet fighters. They engineer their car the same way, which is why I liked it.

Paige had been navigating, watching out and trying to read my scrawled notes by the light of the dash. "There's a sign for Raymore," she said now, spotting the small city-limits rectangle I could easily have missed. She held up the scratch pad where I could see it beside the steering wheel. "It says 'water tower.'"

"It's really a standpipe," I said. "Like an overgrown hot-water tank."

She was curious. "Have you been here before?"

"I've driven out this way looking at cattle."

"I hope it's not too far off the road. If it's beyond our lights we could miss it."

"I remember roughly where it is." We were racing through Raymore, which didn't take long.

On the other side of town, across the railroad tracks and two pastures beyond a pocket-sized development of expensive houses, we saw the tall, narrow silhouette of the water tower dark against the starry sky. The turnoff came next, an unmarked road except for a sign at the southwest corner pointing the way to a sod farm. I spun left, south, and we were back on track with the directions on the pad.

"Seven miles south to a dirt road," Paige said. "Check your odometer."

"Twenty-eight seven zero five and three-tenths."

"So we want seven twelve and about two-tenths."

"I'll watch it," Diana said over my shoulder.

I nodded. The road was rough. Washboard. Like most county roads in Missouri it was oiled dirt. They still disked them in summer, sprayed crude oil on the dirt and let the cars and trucks pack them down. I was glad for the Saab. Another car I'd have had to throttle back.

We beat it out. Black mounds of sleeping cattle in the fields around us and sometimes dense, rolling stands of dwarf milo that would be rich rust by daylight, ready for the combine.

"Is that seven miles?" Paige asked. "Here's a road but I don't see one ahead."

"That's not seven miles," Diana said. "That's only six point six."

I was about to go by. "Is there a road?" I asked them. I shot past and kept on.

"That's seven miles, Daddy."

Nothing. Fenced pasture. I hit the brakes, felt the Saab start to skid, let up, pumped, took the car down slowly. Turned around. We raced back and I made the turn.

Before I turned I noticed headlights coming south behind us, still a few miles off. They were moving as fast as we were—maybe nobody, maybe the Raymore patrol, maybe the FBI.

"Now two miles east," Paige said. She looked to Diana. "What's the odometer reading?"

"Count the section roads," I told them.

"What's that?" Diana asked.

I thought she knew. Sometimes I forget that my children are city children. I'm sorry they are. "A section's a square mile, sweetheart. Here's one." Dirt lane abutted dirt road. Crossing the eroded intersection we bounced.

"Then it's the next one."

The car behind us was coming up on the turn but I still couldn't see if it was a patrol car or unmarked. We hung a left, turning back north, at the second section lane. The ground sloped upward to a rounded hill.

"You wrote 'woods,'" Paige said.

"There's supposed to be a woods on the east side of the road up the next hill." The following car was closing behind us, eating our dust. The clouds of dust we rolled out caught its headlights and glowed. We bounced our way down the north slope of the first hill and started up the second, a long, easy grade.

I saw the trees as darkness first, an absence of stars along the rise of the hill like the absence of stars blocked by the moon. I floored the Saab then. It leapt forward, more than a match for the loose roadbed even though I was fighting washboard and steering in and out of ruts. "What's the rest of it?" I asked Paige. Diana leaned forward again.

"It just says 'clearing.'"

"He said to work in through the trees. He didn't say how far." We were already there—at the near edge of the grove of trees, which ran up the hill eastward and over—and I pumped the brakes to keep from skidding and slowed and pulled off onto the narrow shoulder, cut the ignition and jumped out. Paige went out the other side with the flashlight, scrambling down the shoulder and across the dry ditch, Diana behind her. I jumped across the ditch and Paige handed me the flashlight.

The car that had followed us skidded to a stop in the middle of the road. I looked around long enough to see the doors flung open, to see Hinderliter and Doocy coming out. They'd transferred from the pickup. I hoped they remembered where they'd left it. Totally irrelevant worry at that point in time, but that's what I worried.

I didn't wait for them. I took off. I could hear Hinderliter shouting deployments as I went.

Paige and Diana spread out behind me, working off my light. The woods was a typical cutover Missouri stand of cedar and blackjack oak, dense with undergrowth. I doubted if we'd have to search back very far from the road. By daylight we'd probably have been able to follow the broken trail of the box the kidnapper had dragged in. It was too dark for that now.

I pushed through, the vines drying to winter and the fallen dead leaves crackling under my feet. The same noise from Paige and Diana located them for me. Lights cut through the trees farther right and left. Several. Four. The other two agents, Hinderliter told me later, had stayed downtown to start up the search for the kidnapper now that they knew for sure he was running.

I was working uphill. Away from the road there were larger trees interspersed with the scrub, elms by the look of them, some of them dead—probably of Dutch elm disease—their gnarled, open hands of major branches grasping for the sky. So far I'd seen no clearing of any kind. My heart was pounding, not from exertion but from tension. Infuriating that we had to hunt by night. By day the light would lead us directly in to any clearing, brightening as we went. In the moonless darkness we could pass only a few feet away and walk right by.

"Chris!" Diana shouted.

I jerked to look. "*Where?*"

"I didn't *see* anything, Daddy!" she called over. "I'm just *calling* him."

"Good! But give him time to answer you!"

Then ahead of me, off to the left, outside the beam of my light, I saw something move. I swung the light in that direction and it ducked behind a tree. I stopped and held the tree steadily in the light. Nothing.

"Reeve?" Paige called. "What is it?"

"I don't know! Maybe nothing!" I pushed on, still fixing the tree in my light, but with nothing forthcoming I swung the beam ahead.

And then again motion. I swung the light quickly back and it was gone. But I thought I knew, and now I directed the light ahead and watched out of the corner of my eye.

It might have been Diana, but Diana was crashing through the brush behind me on my left. It might have been Diana when she was a child, maybe nothing, maybe long straight schoolgirl hair. I knew who it was. "Go on," I said quietly, and glimpsed the figure crossing ahead through the trees and kept the light away and followed.

Diana broke the spell. "Chris!" she shouted again. There erupted above us squawking and flapping. Diana screeched in surprise.

"They're birds!" Paige called to calm her.

I'd turned back. I turned ahead now and the figure was gone. But to my left, farther up the hill, I saw darkness that might be a clearing. I moved out, pushing aside the lashing branches and tearing my legs free of the undergrowth that wanted to seize them as legs are seized in nightmares and then I broke into the clearing, sweeping it with my light.

The mound. Loose earth and burial. The white pipe curling from the ground like a drowned, curling worm. I ran to it, dropped on my knees, took the pipe end in both hands and called, "Chris? *Chris?*"

And heard, thank God, heard Chris's voice alive and hollow through the pipe. "Dad?" Breaking even as it began, breaking down to weeping, coughing too. "Dad? Get me out of here, Dad! It's full of smoke! Can you dig me out?"

I almost panicked. "Smoke? Have you got fire?" What the hell could I do?

"Not now," Chris called, choking on his tears. "I did before. I'm okay now."

Paige gripped my shoulder, standing beside me. I was empty-handed. Stupidly I'd forgotten to bring a shovel. Maybe the FBI. Diana fell on the mound of loose dirt and began digging with her bare hands. The lights that had flashed through the trees came in to center on us and four FBI men, Hinderliter leading, surrounded the mound.

They no more remembered shovels than I did.

"We'll get them," Hinderliter announced sternly to hide his chagrin.

"Let's get tire irons," I said. "They'll do for a start." Hinderliter sent his two junior agents back to the cars, one to scout shovels at the nearest farm, one to collect the tire irons. I spoke into the air duct. "Chris? Can you hear me?"

"I've got my face in the pipe, Dad," Chris said in a quiet, strained voice, as if he'd pulled himself together again long enough at least to wait out the excavation. "I can hear you perfectly."

"We're starting to dig you out. It'll take a while. We've got a real pile of dirt up here. What's your situation?"

"There's a fan in this compartment at the head of the box, you know? It overheated. It put out a lot of smoke. I ripped out the wires but the smoke's been stuck down here."

I was digging with my hands as I listened. So were Diana, Doocy, Hinderliter. The dirt was loose and we were flattening it but we were obviously going to need shovels to make any real progress below ground. "How's your air?" I asked Chris. My God it was good to hear his voice.

"It's okay. I pulled the duct into my side of the box. I'm holding it right over my face. My lungs feel kind of funny. Like they tickle. My eyes are the worst. They're itchy and if I rub them they burn. I had to keep them closed for hours."

"Don't rub them," I said automatically. And then thought: good, mother. Buried for two days and you tell him not to rub his eyes.

One of the junior FBI agents came crashing back through the trees. He had tire irons from both cars and the scooplike bases off the jacks. Not exactly ideal digging tools but we took them and got to work. He'd also brought up Doocy's suitcase with the camera gear. I put Diana on the speaking tube.

"*Chris?*" she called down. "Hey, this is Diana. God, how *are* you?"

"Not too great, man. It's really been a drag."

"We got here as soon as we could. We had to collect the *ransom.*"

"You did?" Chris still thought the kidnapping was political. "Did those weirdos get on TV?"

"Why would they get on TV?"

"That's why they kidnapped me." He launched into a fit of coughing.

"Tell him not to talk," I said to Diana.

"Daddy says not to talk," she relayed through the pipe.

"I won't," Chris managed between coughs.

"No," Diana said then, "he didn't want to get on TV. He must have told you that to mix you up. There was just *one* guy and he wanted half a million dollars in *gold.* Daddy and Cowboy went off to get it in a T-38 Cowboy borrowed from NASA. He had to go to New York and he had to go to Washington. To the White House. And now we're *broke* but Daddy thinks we'll get it all back when the FBI catches the kidnapper. God, you should have seen those gold bars, Chris. They were *beautiful.*"

Paige looked up wryly from across the mound. Diana was an expert commentator. She'd had plenty of practice in marathon phone calls to her girl friends. Her average time was just under five hours.

The mound was level when the fourth FBI agent brought the

shovels. He'd commandeered them at a farmhouse two sections over—two grain scoops, a long-handled shovel and a spade. We ranged ourselves around the outside of the excavation so we wouldn't get in each other's way and went to work with a will. I took the long-handled shovel. The dig was on my nickel, so to speak. I thought the part of the box with the fan in it might be hinged separately, with a separate lid, so I started in around the air duct.

We dug hard and fast. Paige watched—it was all at that moment she could do. Doocy photographed us for posterity. Diana chattered away at Chris.

Down below us he waited, holding shut his eyes, trying to breathe slowly and evenly without inhaling smoke. With rescue so near, with safety so near, he started shivering. It was the worst shivering yet. It jerked his arms and legs. He wondered if he was having convulsions but he figured he wasn't because convulsions knocked you out. So it was just the excitement. He didn't think he could stand it. He tried to listen to Diana but all he could hear was the sound of the shovels crunching through the soil, coming nearer. It played back in his head like a reverse of the shoveling that had fallen first on the lid of the box and then become fainter and fainter as the grave filled. Time had run forward then and he'd been forced into hell and now time was running backward and he was getting out.

I went straight down around the duct and in ten minutes my shovel hit the lid of the box.

"Dad?" Chris called, plaintively.

"I'm just down at the top," I told him, speaking up without using the pipe. "Does the upper part open separately?"

"Huh-uh."

But I'd already seen that it didn't and I was afraid to tear out the duct—the fill was too loose to risk it. I started cutting away at the body of the fill. The men were down about halfway. "Chris?" I called to my son. "You want some light?"

"It's okay." His voice came more muffled through the box than through the pipe Diana held off to one side now, out of my way. "Just get me out." He sounded querulous, like a sick child. I'd been digging fast. I dug faster still.

We were nearly there when a distant faint wailing became a siren winding closer and then screaming up the road. Cars skidded to a stop directly west of us, a spotlight swept through the trees. We heard doors slam and a dispatcher's voice reached us from the police car and then swearing men crashed through the woods. Into the clearing stumbled a bleary-looking patrolman and behind him, talking it up, excited for their exclusive, came a TV newsman and his battery-belted cameraman lugging a film camera. I learned later that the farmer who loaned the FBI the shovels had called the local police, just to be on the safe side—he feared for his steers—and the local police, bless their hearts, had tipped their favorite TV news team.

The TV crew's timing was perfect. The cameraman got his light bar set up just as we were scraping the last of the dirt from the lid of the ugly goddamned box Chris was buried in.

Lights, camera, and we climbed every which way out of the hole. I flopped down and pulled on the lid as Chris pushed from inside. The lid swung back, dirt sliding off, smoke billowed out in one full-length swirl like the smoke at the climax of a magic trick, disappearing elephants, and Chris was scrambling shakily to his feet, throwing his arm over his eyes to block the lights, I was up and helping him up to the ground and swearing at the cameraman—Paige simply stepped over to the guy and hit the switch and cut the lights, which started *him* swearing—Diana was there hugging Chris with me, helping Chris with me, Doocy was clicking off flashes to record the reunion and blinding us all. Pandemonium.

Things settled down. Chris cried on my shoulder, his wiry arms around me. I hadn't held him like that in years. He was shaking. Shivering. "*God,*" he kept repeating. "*God,* Dad. *God. God.*" It was a hiccup of terror held in check through all those dark hours.

I took off my jacket and wrapped it around Chris's shoulders. By now his eyes had adjusted to the light. His face was sooty with smoke, the soot tracked with the meanders of his tears and smeared where he had knuckled his eyes. I asked him if they still burned. Not bad, he said. He looked good considering what he'd been through. I figured we could run him straight home without stopping at the hospital.

Hinderliter joined us. "I know it's an imposition," he said after I introduced him to Chris, "but we need to find out a couple of things."

"What?" I wanted to move it along.

"A description of the kidnapper," Hinderliter said to Chris.

Chris nodded wearily. "A big guy. Big nose. He had his hair in a ponytail. It was weird because he was kind of balding in front."

Hinderliter made notes. "What was he wearing?"

"I don't remember." Chris shrugged. "But he really stunk."

"He stunk?" Hinderliter said, looking up from his notebook. "More than—more than a day's worth?"

"Yeah. Really foul."

"What about the vehicle?" Hinderliter had gone back to his notebook.

"It was a pickup."

"Make? Model? Year?"

Chris shook his head. "I don't remember."

Hinderliter looked up again. "Try. It would help."

I slipped my arm around Chris's waist to support him. He accepted it and leaned into me. For a time he was silent while behind us Doocy flashed his camera strobe, making a record of the grave and its contents. "I'm sorry," Chris said then. "There was too much going on. A pickup. Maybe it was a big American job."

It wasn't. Chris remembered it bigger than it was.

Then the TV people wanted an interview. I didn't see how I could easily get around them. People submit to interviews now when they return—from out of the body, from death, from the moon. Paige had briefed the newsman—I recognized his face but didn't remember his name—so that we wouldn't be long. He'd voice-over the identifications later.

"My son was kidnapped," I told him, the bar of lights glaring in my eyes. "Now he's free. We're glad to have him back." That was all I had to say.

"Is it true the ransom was five hundred thousand dollars in gold, Commander Wainwright?"

"We paid a ransom." They'd get the story, but I couldn't help thinking: what if some other bastard decides to try it? And I don't know the answer to that one even now.

A few more questions and the man turned to Chris. I saw in the glare that Chris's lips were cracked. And his poor bloodshot eyes. I'd let him answer one or two; then we'd go. I looked back over my shoulder while he was answering and saw that grotesque box, the junk inside, the bedpan. "What was it like in there, Chris?" the newsman brightly asked.

"It was hell, man," Chris said, bowing and shaking his head. "Just hell."

"You were buried for more than two days. How did you spend all that time?" The foam-covered microphone swinging over.

Chris looked into the camera, blinked, seemed to realize for the first time what it was, and then slowly on that sooty face spread a big grin. "Singing."

"Singing?" The newsman didn't know how to field it.

"Yeah. I've got a rock band. Andromeda. I wrote a song. If there's a recording company out there that wants it, man, it's available."

That was enough even for the newsman. I led Chris away. Paige and Diana worked ahead of us, holding back branches. The policeman came along and the cameraman saw us off with his lights. Hinderliter called to get some rest, that he'd be in touch.

Paige sat in back with Chris, Diana in front with me. We got a police escort. We burned up the road, the siren wailing in the night. I knew Chris would recover when I heard him pitching the newsman his song. Rock 'n' roll will never die. It's true what they say.

The first thing I did when I got home was call Cowboy.

Nineteen

The story made front pages, news magazines and all three networks. Wherever he was running, the kidnapper would have to fence his gold with caution. He'd be smart to bury it. I fielded the interviews from the farm. Paige stayed on the next week instead of flying to Chicago as she'd planned. We spent most of our mornings in bed.

I gave Chris a week's vacation from school. I wanted him to sleep—I figured he needed it—but because he'd had to take his confinement lying down or because he was hot to perfect his song, perfect his band and generally get on with living, he was up with the buffalo and the dawn. He shifted his drum set to the barn, took over the big tack room. His band moved in its considerable gear. Some nights they worked until midnight even with school. It looked like a way Chris had found to postpone his reaction to the kidnapping. I let it ride. He'd have time, and work should be healing.

Paige stayed partly to add to the *Playboy* interview—we weren't nearly finished, especially with the kidnapping to cover, though I didn't much care to talk about it—but more to decide what she and I meant to do. We knew the ordeal of the weekend had brought us closer than before. We didn't know if the intimacy of emergency was something that might endure.

One of those mornings I asked Paige about Richard Pettibone. Not all that tactfully: "Was he the guy?" I was sitting up with my pillow folded double behind me against the wall. No headboard on the bed. I couldn't afford it at divorce time and I certainly couldn't afford it now.

Paige slept nude, as I did. I liked her shoulders small and smooth above the chocolate-brown sheets. "Is it necessary for you to know?" she asked me in return, quietly and seriously.

Which told me. "I know already."

"You sound disappointed."

I meant to keep it serious but I couldn't help flashing this big, shit-eating grin. So I went ahead and played it jet-jockey style, worked my eyebrows, winked, leered. "Not at all, little lady."

Paige looked away, maybe exasperated, mostly amused. She shook her head. "Never fails," she said, as much to herself as to me. And looking around: "What is it? Washington?"

"Other than people passing through, ever met anyone really first-rate in Washington?"

"I used to think I had. For a while I thought I had with Richard."

I told her what he arranged for me when I visited him at the White House. I hadn't told her before, not the terms. But why hold back?

"The shit," Paige said flatly who almost never swore.

"Par for the course."

"I never quite believe it."

"I don't either, but I'm a country boy."

"You can repudiate it," she said, meaning Pettibone's terms.

"Something." I didn't want to think about them. I was thinking about the people who are first-rate. "They're in the sciences now." Paige hadn't lost the thread. She knew what I meant. "That's where the best ones go. Watson, Feynman, Gell-Mann, Hawking. I could make a list."

"I don't know if that's fair. Government never was a science. It's everything that's left when people aren't working at their specialities, which means it's everything that's primitive, everything that's disordered."

"Insane."

"Insane. It's had its first-rate minds. It still does."

"I take it we're not talking about Richard Pettibone."

"The shit."

I slid my hand toward Paige under the covers. I said: "This is a heat-seeking hand seeking your crotch."

"Oh Christ," she mocked, "years of this, yes?" But she suffered the hand, and as I turned over to kiss her, lingering at her mouth, it rested springily on that zone of antigravity where her thighs met.

"Yes," I said quietly then, my hand now at her waist and holding her. "Years. That's what I want. Do you?"

Her eyes were enormous. "I don't know."

"What don't you know?"

"It's not like love."

"Meaning like Pettibone?"

"Yes."

"That was love?"

"That's what I told myself it was."

"Then I hope this isn't."

She brought her head to my shoulder and talked along my chest. "I can say it's better. Most of the time it is. Something worked between us before, Reeve, you know?"

"I know. And now I don't drink anymore."

"Yes. So it's back and it might be permanent. Except I have to be free to come and go."

"In terms of men?" To hell with that.

She shook her head, her hair grazing my chest and my arm where I held her. "In terms of work. It came to me during the weekend. I suppose it's connected. If it is, the connection isn't obvious."

"What?"

"Hunger. A book. It's the next major world crisis and so far as I know, no one is writing about it except statisticians and government agencies. No one who's willing to find her way inside it and feel it and come back to say. I think I can do that." She looked up at me and moved a little aside so that she could see my eyes and my mouth—she watched one, she watched the other. "But it's going to be terribly painful, Reeve. I'll have to go away. I'll have to immerse myself in it. I need a place to come back to besides an apartment in Manhattan."

It wasn't exactly a blank check, was it. I studied her face, trying to decide.

"Now *you* don't know," she said, interpreting my silence.

"I know it's your work and you should do it. I don't know if I want to live half the time in Houston and half the time at the Cape. So to speak."

She blinked, and she was warm, and properly she stood her ground. "It's not a question of where anyone lives. It's a question of you and me."

Don't believe them when they tell you it's not a question of where anyone lives. It is. But Paige and I could hack it if any two people could. I'd seen her before and I'd seen barrages of other women since.

I'd seen her through the weekend. So then solemnly, as solemn as I get: "Let's try it."

She smiled. "As in 'what's to lose'?"

"As in 'what's to lose.'"

"Fair enough," she said.

No man's a hero to his ex-wife. And vice versa. Claudia gave me holy hell. She was furious she'd been left out, furious that other people knew of her son's peril and rescue before she did, furious she hadn't been trusted. She mobilized all her considerable histrionics. I suppose her feelings were real enough. I'd never quite believed in them because they could be turned on and off at will, and they were: when the press had come knocking she'd been calm, concerned, cool, collected. She never let on. She was something else on the phone—which was how we communicated, had communicated since the divorce. We avoided seeing each other. I know: infantile. Infantile it was. We preferred it. Who needed the grief?

A couple of days into the week I thought it had blown over. The histrionics left me feeling justified, right? that I'd excluded Claudia from the festivities. And then she called. Late afternoon—at least I wasn't in bed with Paige. So what if I had been, but long marriages seem to extend a proprietary interest years down the road.

"Red?"

"I've heard it, Claudia."

"No, wait. Please. I'm not going to shout at you anymore. I'm still angry. I know it doesn't do any good."

I listened. I'd learned with Claudia not to commit. Sweet reason was usually the next stage after the screaming, a continuation of war by other means.

"Are you there?"

"I'm here," I said.

"I've been trying to think through what I'm angry *about*. I think I see." She paused. When she started again there was tension in that rich contralto voice. "It's that I was prevented from functioning as a parent. From being a source of strength for Chris or for Diana. Do you understand what I mean?"

"Not really." I was sitting in the Eames. I stared out past the plants to the farm, the violent reds and yellows of American fall.

"*As if they weren't mine.*" Said all at once and urgently.

It sent a chill up my back. Because it was true—the accusation was true. I didn't much think of Chris and Diana as Claudia's anymore. All those married years we'd struggled along by a kind of precarious negotiation. I hadn't had time for that bullshit. But by not having time I'd shut her out entirely. The kidnapping bound Chris and Diana and me now in a way Claudia could never share. It was something I might try to make up some other way.

The counterargument was, I did what I had to do. Part of the compulsion, the determinism if you will, of what happened had to be my own pattern of moves, and I've said those were loner. I made the moves I make. They work well most of the time. They worked well here for everyone but Claudia. Can you be ashamed of behaving as you invariably behave? Should you be?

I've since thought of an analogy: commercial aircraft crashes. You always find a lot more male survivors standing dazed on the field watching the fuselage char than women and children. That's ugly, but it's true, and I'm not sure it admits of moral judgment. Or am I excusing myself for leaving Claudia behind? Aren't disasters cute?

I don't know if I can describe what it was like out in the barn. I don't know that much about the destructive-testing equipment that goes with a heavy-metal, edge-of-hyperspace rock band. Chris's gang—they were five all together, four who played and one who came along to watch and soak it in and work as a roadie—played synthesizer, electric and amplified acoustic guitars and (Chris himself) drums. Chris sang. They all sang. They had the synthesizer like a disembodied piano keyboard on a stand, and that fine set of Sonors, and brute hardened speakers for the wired instruments that looked as if they could withstand a preemptive first strike. They took the grid of sound that Chris had heard behind the fragments of his song, "Buried Alive," and pumped it up with molten liquid sodium to something bizarre and dangerous. Chris had written more verses at the center of the song, so that its structure was basically a ballad now, but he stuck in the odds and ends too, attached them jaggedly to the basic framework like uncut crystals growing off a parent stem. The song was low, brutal, frightening and hallucinogenic all at once, and totally effective, and, surprisingly, very moving. I don't usually even hear that stuff. With "Buried Alive" I heard most of all the muffled drum. None of us who lived through the funerals of the sixties could ever again quite trust ourselves with muffled drums.

One of those weekdays, after school, when Chris was lounging in the cool October barn dripping sweat earned from two hours of solid practice, the buffalo contented at the fence, Claudia brought Diana out to the farm to see him. Brought out poor convalescent Diana and let her off. Diana had crossed the woods through poison ivy that Paige and I had graciously been spared. Where the vines touched her, despite subsequent shots and salves, they raised ugly yellow-purple welts. The rest—hands, arms, neck, terribly on her face, her eyes swollen nearly shut at first but opening now—was livid inflammation.

"How's it going?" Chris asked her when she came in, his standard hippie-dippy greeting even when he was merely crossing through a room. He was sitting on his drummer's stool that he'd lined with brown woolly sheepskin cut from the Antartex coat he'd worn when he was a kid, a nice historical continuity.

"Real cool, *man*," Diana returned, doing her friendly-sarcastic number. She settled on the floor, leaned back carefully against a bale of straw. "Where's the band?"

"I let 'em off tonight. They were getting kinda burned out."

"Oh wow, *you* let them off. You in charge now?"

"Sure." Chris was hanging his head, his long arms dangling between his thighs. Parade rest. The abrasions on his wrist and arm were healing.

"Since when?"

"Since always."

"You weren't in *charge* before. You guys were just jamming."

"Shit, Diana, what do you know about it? You come over here to hassle me or what?"

Diana liked to make Chris mad, her modest exercise of power and her practice at war-gaming, but she remembered she'd forgotten the recent ordeal of the kidnapping and she signaled her ships dead in the water. So, gently: "No. To see how you were."

"I'm okay." He looked at her. "Hell of a lot better than you. What is it, leprosy?"

"You know what it is and you know the noble cause. Did you see my nails?" She showed him. They'd been long and polished before. Digging Chris out had broken them and she'd filed them down. They were almost as short as Chris's. He bit his to the quick.

"Yeah." He smiled at her, flashing his braces. "The song's really getting good, man. I think it's gonna go. It just really kicks ass." Flailing those Spiderman arms: "*Damn* it's good."

"We're *real mod*est," Diana said nasally. She did imitations. "When's it going to be done?"

"Another couple of weeks."

"You think you'll sell it?"

"We're not going to sell it. We're going to record it."

Diana, in jeans, hooked her right ankle on her left knee, macho-style. "Is Daddy going to pay for the session?"

"Nope."

"Who is?"

"Nobody, yet."

"Then how do you know you'll get to record it?"

Chris glared at her. "I just *know*, okay?"

"Okay, okay." Diana referred Chris's irritation to the weekend. "Listen," she said, looking away, "I wanted to tell you."

"Tell me what?" Chris stretched, his arms above his head, and shook his head slowly to settle his long hair.

"I don't think I'm going to move out here."

"Why not?"

"I don't know. Mommy needs some company."

Chris lowered his arms, his elbows on his knees. "I thought you'd already decided. What changed your mind?"

"I didn't decide."

"You told me you did."

"No I didn't. You just misunderstood me."

"Did you tell Dad?"

"Kind of."

"How'd he take it?" Picking up his sticks one by one Chris slid his hands down their length, handle to tip, feeling for cracks. He found cause for suspicion, retrieved the roll of electrical tape he kept on the floor under his stool and began taping.

"He said it was okay with him."

Chris looked suspicious. "What'd you tell him?"

"I sort of told him I can't decide."

"That's what I thought."

Diana sat straight, ready to lock and load. "Well, I *can't*."

"What's the big hang-up?"

"Nothing."

"There's something. What is it?"

"You always think you *know* me."

Nodding his head vigorously: "I do."

"No you don't. You knew me *years* ago."

"Wanna bet?"

"Yeah."

"Okay," Chris said. He put down the tape and the stick and faced her squarely. "The reason you changed your mind about moving over here—which by the way is just great with me, there isn't enough room for you anyway and I'd just as soon not have to spend all my time driving you around—is that you're afraid you'll get kidnapped." He smirked, and watched, and saw in her eyes that he was right.

"God, Chris, that's just *bullshit*, you know?" Diana at her most brittle, dodging and feinting, and for a moment she missed that Chris's eyes were filling, remembering, that he had to look abruptly away.

We can bow out here. You know how it goes. They love each other.

I said we got calls. *Time* interrupted our lovemaking Thursday morning, fairly early, eight-thirty or nine. I wasn't going to answer but we were at the heavy petting stage and I figured I'd get it out of the way. I rolled over onto my back and said my name and reporter-researcher Margaret Hannis-Regalado announced herself.

She asked me for facts. The famous guaranteed-accurate facts of *Time* magazine. When they wrote up the Apollo 12B mission they managed to screw up the facts about half the time. Whenever their stories touch on anything I know anything about, they always read to me like stories translated literally from an unknown tongue by someone who doesn't even know where to find the rest rooms.

"About fifteen miles," I said.

Paige was listening.

"No, I don't think so. It looked like raw plywood. I didn't really get a good look at it. Why don't you call the FBI?"

Paige wasn't only listening. Paige was fooling *around.* "Cut it out, Paige." I covered the mouthpiece for that. And uncovered it for Margaret Hannis-Regalado. "Be that as it may, darlin', *they've* got it in custody, I don't. You'll have to get the measurements from them."

There was more, a little more. About the ransom.

"I don't know. We haven't heard. Hell yes I'd like it back. So would my creditors."

I accepted grudging thanks and hung up. I'd hardly dropped the handset when the phone began ringing again, and I seriously considered cycling the damned thing and then leaving it off the hook.

I'm glad I didn't. "Reeve Wainwright."

"Reeve? This is Jack Hinderliter. FBI. We've got our man."

"You do?" I was vague. It didn't register because I'd just been talking about it with *Time.*

"You'll be pleased to hear we recovered all three of the gold bars."

Then I whooped. Paige understood, grinned, sat up.

"They were still in the original suitcase."

"Fantastic, Jack. Did you get the guy?" It still hadn't registered completely. Now it did and I was angry. "Who the hell is he?"

"His name's Karl Loring Grabka. DD from the Air Force for drug smuggling. Served eighteen months at Leavenworth."

"Never heard of the bastard. Why'd he pick on me?"

"What's his name?" Paige asked.

"Grabka," I told her.

"We don't know," Hinderliter said. "He won't talk to us. Probably no particular reason. Just that you're well known."

Grab-ka? Paige mouthed. She rolled her eyes toward the ceiling. I nodded.

"How far'd he get?" I asked Jack. "Where'd you pick him up?"

"El Paso."

"No shit. Obviously going into Mexico." Paige watched me calmly. She looked serene. I felt it too: tension flooding away. Half a million dollars is half a million dollars. It was all I had and more.

"He was working on it. He's a strange fellow, Reeve. He was making the rounds of the Mexican jewelry shops, trying to strike up a friendship with the jewelers."

Paige slipped over next to me, her head on my shoulder. I felt her breast warm against my side. That's a good feeling. "Trying to find someone to melt down the gold?"

"Looks that way. It made them suspicious. We had two different calls to our Albuquerque office."

"Crazy Anglo asking about gold, huh?"

"That. But I said he's a strange fellow. Chris was right. He smells."

"Smells how?"

"Stinks. Never takes a bath."

"Nice guy."

"Second, he went around to the jewelry stores wearing a gold lamé cape."

"A gold lamé *cape?*"

"Right."

"What for?"

"I have no idea. The agent who made the arrest said it looked like something he'd basted up himself."

"Amazing. What's third?"

"Third? No, that's all. We're arranging for extradition back to Missouri. How's your boy?"

Paige lay back on my side of the bed to wait. "He's holding up," I told Hinderliter. "I don't think it's actually hit him yet."

"Delayed reaction. That's fairly standard. You might want to think about letting him see some kind of counselor. Might do him some good. Well, I asked because when we arraign Grabka we'd like Chris to make the identification."

"No problem. Just give us a call. When do you think it'll be?"

"Take us a week or so. Next Wednesday or Thursday. Friday at the latest, I hope."

"We'll plan on it." I almost forgot: "When do I see the gold?"

"Well. That's a little difficult. We'll need to impound it as evidence."

"Hey, Jack, wait a minute. For how long?"

"Until the trial. Two months at the outside."

I was ready to argue, but I thought, one, it was a loan, I still had my savings and my income, and, two, they needed it to convict Mr. Karl Grabka. I really wanted to nail that son of a bitch. "Okay," I said. "No sweat. Just don't *lose* it, will you?"

Hinderliter laughed. It was the first time I'd heard him laugh. He had a nice warm laugh, like a scoutmaster. "We'll take good care of it, Red."

And that was that. Nothing but happy endings.

Not really. People don't brutalize people without consequences. Everyone was still in shock.

I gave Paige the details. She was relieved, as I was, and fascinated, as I truly wasn't. I'm not a student of the criminal mind, nor care to be. Anyway, talking about it calmed me down.

Outside was crisp sunny morning. I pulled on a pair of jeans and went down to the barn to tell Chris the good news. Didn't dawdle. Returned to the bedroom again. Paige and I found our way back to lovemaking, reversed on each other like the symbol of the zodiacal Crab. I got the best of that, it seemed to me: petals at my tongue like roses, firm Venusian buns to cup, an animal visitor gentle and wet that nuzzled—and then a ride for my rocket, Elder in command, seventeen times as high as the moon.

Twenty

What's left here?

Karl Grabka was extradited from Texas to Kansas City, tried under Missouri law, convicted of kidnapping and half a dozen related offenses and sentenced to life in prison, which means he'll be eligible for parole in eight years. People from New York and Los Angeles who usually only fly over the Middle West blew into town even before Grabka's trial to negotiate for the book and film rights to his story. It begins to look as if he might earn as much as he attempted to extort by kidnapping my son.

This book may forestall that absurdity. Thanks for buying a copy.

Chris wasn't all right. Working on his song kept him manic and distracted until the trial, but reliving his burial for the jury and the crowds—the media played the story as a second Lindbergh kidnapping despite the different outcomes—triggered his postponed reaction. He suffered from nightmares, insomnia, crying jags, depression indistinguishable from grief. So many terrible lessons were compressed into those three days: the determinism of extremity, the impotence of parental magic, the gratuitous malevolence of his fellow man; worst of all, the premature demonstration, like a simulation display, of his own certain eventual death, an iron truth young men normally only suffer to learn in time of war. He didn't see then, as those of us around him saw, what exceptional competence he'd shown.

Counseling tided him over, but his music pulled him through. Andromeda recorded "Buried Alive" for Mercury Records before the trial; the trial's publicity put the song on the charts and the band in the running; the song went gold and Andromeda is talking with promoters about its first concert tour, Chris's dream—warming up for Rush. School's a pale second in that competition. I keep Chris at it. College will probably have to be postponed. I tell Chris the music business is like pro sports, likely to be over and done with by the time he's thirty or thirty-five. He'll need something after that to see him through. He listens, but he's his own man. He left his childhood in the grave Karl Grabka dug, as abruptly as young warriors leave theirs beside some cold-running tribal river in the bush. I'd like to have spared him that abrupt brutality. He doesn't agree: he says it made him tough.

Beat all, beat all, beat all beat all beat all

I returned Ernie Defleurs's money. I couldn't recover the actual Watergate bills he'd hoarded so nostalgically; those will circulate through the system for a while yet like beef contaminated with contraband DES. I put in an appearance on the *Prodigal Sons Show*, but I didn't give God the credit for saving Chris's life. I gave part of the credit to Ernie and he passed it on, passed part of it on, to God.

I repaid the bank's brief loan, with interest, but chose not to testify for the administration to the virtue of its misguided, misshapen energy bill. On the other hand, I didn't go to work for Senator Kennedy either. He found more competent help. Pettibone retaliated for my refusal to testify (and for winning Paige whom he'd rejected?) by muscling the DOE into canceling EAI's contract. That hurt, but we'll live.

Paige has begun research for her book on hunger. She's gone a month at a time. She comes home to the farm for her sanity. Right now she's officially in Thailand, though in fact she's making illegal forays into Cambodia. We'll live too.

I haven't said all I meant to say about the space program. The book in your head is never the book you end up with on paper. Among other things, I left out one quality of the experience that shouldn't give space top priority but that deserves to be weighed in, a quality it shared with much else that is worthwhile in science: its beauty. Not a quality that politicians and bureaucrats can talk about, if they even notice, but I'm a former astronaut, now retired, and I can.

The Cape was barren before we came along—dirty sand, scrub pine and palmetto, swamp, a hot, humid wind blowing off the ocean carrying inland the stench of rotting vegetation. Onto that landscape we grafted a millennial enterprise: high red gantries, enormous buildings, jet-jockey adventurers, scientists and engineers by the thousands, the American equivalent of royalty (meaning the Kennedys and their superstar crowd), the great white rockets standing floodlit in the night, billions and billions of dollars. Not that different from those earlier days, was it? From Walter Raleigh? From Columbus? The same rash commitment of national treasure, the same daring and exceptional men, the same sweet wildness at the bold leaving of one shore and the mysterious landfall upon another.

Despite their complex technology, something elemental about the rockets mated them with the elemental place where they were launched. Land met ocean; the sky was wide above; the white monumental machine was less machine than a space-fitted equivalent to the clipper ship. Kennedy caught a sense of it when he talked about charting the oceans of space and sailing them. He was a sailor and he knew the grace of close-hauled ships.

So there on the frayed eastern shore of the continent the great rockets beat against their moorings at our command, spewed red and yellow fire and then rose, steadied, found bearings, drove through the sky out into another element wider and more challenging even than the wide oceans. If you don't see the beauty in that, I feel sorry for you.

On the other hand, I think we were right to pause. There's unfinished business down here on the ground, business we ought to attend to before we start floating away into space like pollen. If it's a question of saving the baby or saving the work of art, I'm for saving the baby. Aren't you?

Ernie Defleurs and Richard Pettibone didn't really owe me loyalty. I felt Jeremy Utter and Charles Hyerding, my editor and publisher, did. So I chose not to turn back the money they advanced me. I went ahead with the big book Hyerding wanted about the space program, the book that would name names and tell all.

Paige helped me with the research.

Hyerding, you son of a bitch, here's your *book.*

Kansas City, Missouri
August 1979-August 1980

LEE COUNTY LIBRARY SYSTEM
DISCARD
3 3262 00045 6589

DISCARD
LEE COUNTY LIBRARY
107 HAWKINS AVE.
SANFORD, N. C. 27330